FAE OR FOE

THE CRACKLOCK SAGA: BOOK 1

C. A. DEEGAN

For information, contact www.thecracklocksaga.com

ISBN: 978-1-7399081-0-2

This book is dedicated to Helen, for giving me the time I needed and all the encouragement in the world. Love ya darlin'! And to Harry and Alice; good guys who know not to disturb me when I'm tapping away.

FAE OR FOE

THE CRACKLOCK SAGA: BOOK 1

C. A. DEEGAN

"The iron tongue of midnight hath told twelve; lovers to bed; 'tis almost fairy time."

-William Shakespeare

CHAPTER 1

Six-year-old Jannie Smith believed in fairies. "I've seen some," she had told her grandmother one wintery Sunday afternoon as the rain battered against the windows. Shrek, Pinocchio, Father Christmas, and many other fantastic people had been parading around the garden, Jannie had said, her eyes wide with excitement. She had seen them all, but they hadn't seen her, so she knew absolutely that they were real. Granny had nodded and smiled along, agreeing that Jannie had seen such things. Granny had caught her daughter's gaze and had given her a smile and a slight shrug. 'Childhood is so fleeting; enjoy it while you can', her eyes had said.

Jannie had been cooped up inside for so long during the dreary winter and spring months that the sunny third Saturday of May meant just one thing – that a garden party was in the offing. Mummy was working, but it was okay to play in the garden, so she had dragged her best blanket down from her bedroom and spread it out on the bottom lawn in the shady part near the trees. "Weeping willows" was what her daddy called them, but she was not sure why, as they didn't seem sad to her at all, just droopy. They did make great hiding places, though;

underneath the branches, there was a cool green cave smelling of green and soil and shielded from the sun. It was a little damp under there, which is why it wasn't a good place for tea parties, but maybe later the guests might like to indulge in a game of hide and seek? Then they could all hide under there, away from the seeker, and pretend they were in another world. Anyhow, that was for later; now was for setting up the first and best tea party of the year.

Upstairs in her room, Jannie gathered up her tea set and the magic teapot. The cups were made of red plastic, the plates a rich blue. The teapot itself was rainbow coloured, which added nicely to its magic effects. It wasn't magical, of course, just pretend, but Jannie quite liked to imagine that any drink she wanted could come flowing from its curved spout. Putting the tea set into her plastic box, she now had an important decision to make. Who would be the Princess of the Lake today, and who would be her guests to the best garden party of the year?

Lined up in a row on top of her toy box were her three dolls; two blonde ones, Sally and Rita, and a dark-haired one, Emily, who was the Princess of the Lake more times than not. Next to the dolls sat Elefumf, Jannie's stuffed elephant, who was a greedy pig at tea parties, stuffing cakes and biscuits into his mouth as quickly as his grasping trunk could scoop them up. Slumped next to him sat Benjamin, a stuffed bear who used to belong to Jannie's mummy, who was a little threadbare now; his stuffing long since squashed as he peeped back at Jannie out mismatched eyes. Then there was Puss, an elegant cat, jet-black with long whiskers and gleaming green eyes that would glow in the dark if you held him up to the light for long enough. Jannie's usual tea party guests sat there, looking back, waiting for her to decide who would come to the party.

As Jannie scanned her potential guests, slightly back from the others, there sat somebody new at the end of the row. A boy doll, wearing a bright coloured suit of yellow and blue patches.

2

On its feet were wooden shoes, sandal-like, with red and yellow shoelaces, striped like a candy cane. The little head had long brown hair covering his ears, and his face was long with rosy cheeks. Jannie couldn't see the doll's eyes; it sat with its chin down and its eyelids were closed.

Ooh, thought Jannie, *Mummy's bought me a surprise doll. A Prince for the Princess.* Reaching for the doll at the end of the row, she jumped with surprise when the boy doll suddenly opened his eyes, looking up at her, and smiling. It was an endearing smile, quite beautiful, with shiny little white teeth that enhanced the bright blue eyes that twinkled up at the little girl. Jannie took a step back in surprise at this development; none of her dolls had previously looked at her in real life before. She stared at the boy doll, a little scared of its friendly smile.

The boy doll jumped to its feet with a neat little hop, the wooden shoes making a *click-clack* noise on the top of the toy box. It continued to smile as it raised its right hand and wriggled all four fingers and thumb at the little girl, waving hello at her in a merry way. Stood upright, the boy doll was about as tall as Jannie's knee, and he gazed up at the little girl with a cheeky twinkle in those blue eyes. Jannie stood with her mouth open, still not believing what she saw; one of the dolls had come to life! The doll gave her both thumbs up and performed a dainty twirl on top of the toy box. As he did so, he knocked into Elefunk's trunk, unbalancing himself mid-spin to sit down with a plop on the top of the toy box. Jannie giggled at the doll's clumsiness, so like her own, and he laughed silently back, holding his stomach as he jiggled with mirth. Climbing to his feet again, he gazed up at Jannie, hands on his hips, and continued to smile his lovely smile.

"Hello," said Jannie to the doll shyly. Close up, the boy doll did not look like any of her other dolls; the shiny hint of plastic was not present on his face. Jannie poked out a finger and pressed it towards the boy doll's face. He didn't flinch at all but stood, beaming up at Jannie, watching her intently. Lightly pressing on the dolls' cheek, Jannie felt warmth and soft skin. With a gasp, she jerked her finger back.

"You're real," she said. "You're a real person?" The little boy nodded up and down quickly. "I'm Jannie. What's your name?" The little boy shook his head, the smile dropping from his face. "Don't you have a name?" said Jannie. The boy nodded, smiling again. "What is it then?" said Jannie.

The boy shook his head again and, raising one hand, covered his mouth. He looked like something had caught him by surprise as he looked at Jannie, his lips and teeth covered up and pointing at his face with his other hand. Jannie's brow creased with puzzlement. Then, a smile spread across her face. "You can't talk," she said, understanding what the little boy was trying to do.

The boy threw both hands into the air and nodded frantically. "Well," said Jannie. "Do you have a name but just can't tell me?" The boy nodded again, raised his right hand and made a shape like a bird's beak, and started pecking at the air with it. "What do you mean?" asked Jannie. "I don't understand."

The boy held up his hand in a 'wait' gesture while he looked at the ceiling, obviously thinking. Then he looked at Jannie and mimed opening a book. He took out an imaginary something from his pocket and then started to scribble in the invisible book. Looking at Jannie while he did it, he mimed writing some more, then slammed the book shut.

"You want to write something?" asked Jannie, a little puzzled. The boy nodded his head violently, again miming the pecking noise in the air. "Ah!" said Jannie. "You want to write down your name!" The little boy clapped his hand to his forehead before looking at Jannie and giving her the thumbs up again. Jannie rummaged on her small desk and found a felt tip and some paper. "Here," she said.

The little boy smiled and took the pen, which looked

absurdly huge in his little hand. He tried to hold it like Jannie had been shown at school, but it was too thick for his fingers. Grasping it in his fist instead, he pulled the paper towards him and scrawled in small letters

popkiN

"Popkin?" said Jannie. "Your name's Popkin?" The little boy nodded frantically and pointed to himself. "I think that's a lovely name." Popkin smiled again, giving her the thumbs up.

"What are you doing here?" asked Jannie. Popkin bent his head back down to the paper and scribbled away again. Moving back, he let Jannie read what he had written.

caMe 2 pLaY

"Really?" said Jannie. "You came to play with me?" Popkin nodded his head and gave her another smile.

"That's great," said Jannie. "I am going to have a garden party. You can be the guest of honour! The princess of the lake will be so pleased to meet you!"

Popkin frowned and bent his head back to the paper.

noT gardeN. here

"What?" asked Jannie. "Not in the garden?"

Popkin shook his head and pointed to the carpet. He pulled the box of tea things towards him and took out a plate and cup.

"No," said Jannie. "We can't have a garden party in my

bedroom. It's a lovely day, and I've already put the picnic blanket out. Come outside; mummy has left us some food to eat. Are you hungry?"

Popkin shook his head and folded his arms. "Well," said Jannie. "I'm not going to sit in this bedroom when it's so lovely. Come with me outside." Popkin shook his head again and, pulling the pen and paper towards him, underlined what he had already written.

noT gardeN. here

Turning the paper over, he set to writing again and then showed Jannie.

PLease. noT Safe

"Of course, it's safe," said Jannie. "The gate's locked, and nobody is there. Come and see with me."

Popkin shook his head violently at this and sat back, his arms folded. Thinking again, he reached over, grabbed the magic teapot out of the box, and put it behind his back, frowning up at the girl.

"You're being silly," said Jannie. "Give me that back." Popkin shook his head again and scooted back on his bottom towards the wall. Jannie stormed over to him, reached over Popkin's head, and plucked the teapot from his hands. Throwing it into the box, she grabbed the whole set and set off towards her door.

"I'm taking this down and then coming back for the guests," she snapped. "You should stop being so silly and come and join us." Popkin stood up and, without seeming to move at all, was suddenly in front of Jannie, blocking the door. He shook his head again, violently.

Jannie was getting cross. She barged past Popkin, who tried to tug at her skirt as she went, but she shook him loose and ran down the landing. She stopped at the top of the stairs and looked back, but there was no sign of the boy. *'He can stay there and sulk,'* thought Jannie. *'He really is a big silly.'*

TEN MINUTES LATER, Jannie had the tea party fully set up on the blanket. The guests were all present, and the food, a plate of biscuits, some sandwiches, and a bottle of juice for the teapot, stood ready.

"Why, Princess, it is so kind of you to join us," gushed Jannie, as she busied herself putting food onto the various plates. "What's that you say? I'm welcome?" Emily stared back blankly at Jannie, the doll's plastic face reflecting the glow of sunshine filtering through the top branches of the willow trees. Jannie turned to offer Rita the plate of biscuits, and out of the corner of her eye, she caught a quick flash of something as it buzzed past her. It then zoomed past again on the other side, but Jannie wasn't quick enough to follow it, a blur in the air.

'What was that? It was too big for a bee and too fast for a butterfly,' Jannie thought as she got to her feet, head turning as she looked for the fast thing. Her eyes caught movement again, this time near the flowerbeds, and she shuffled over there, the biscuits still in her hand. Jannie looked for the shape again, but there was nothing there; the nodding flower heads looked empty. She poked at the flowers, trying to disturb whatever was hiding, but nothing dashed out. She turned back to the tea party and gasped, the plate of biscuits thudding to the soft grass.

Hovering there, right in front of her eyes, was a fairy. A real fairy, like in Peter Pan! A lady in a little dress, flickering wings on her back as it hovered in front of her face. The fairy was beautiful; rosy red lips, curly blonde hair, and beautiful blue eyes. The blue colour swam about in those tiny eyes like smoke as Jannie stared, her mouth open.

Recovering her wits, Jannie gulped, "Hello?" The fairy swooped around her head so fast that she could barely see her and then returned to hover in front of Jannie's face.

"Are you real?"

"*Yes, of course. Fairies are always real.*" The reply came, a tiny tinkling voice that sang in Jannie's ears.

"What are you doing here?"

"*My friend and I came to play.*"

"Your friend? Do you mean Popkin?"

The fairy gave another swoop and then hovered again.

"*My friend is shy. He's hiding from you. Come and find him with me.*"

"He's hiding?"

"*Yes, over there.*" The fairy pointed at the fronds of the weeping willow.

Shading her eyes, Jannie saw something blue was moving about in the cave that the tree branches made. It had pulled back out of sight when Jannie looked over that way.

"Is your friend hiding in the cave?" asked Jannie.

The fairy swooped down and seized one of Jannie's hands. "*Come with me; he's in there and would like to play. Will you come and see him?*" The fairy tugged Jannie in the direction of the tree, causing her to stumble. The fairy was strong, and Jannie was unable to resist.

She allowed herself to be led over to the willow tree. As she moved towards it, a little face appeared in a gap, familiar, although the view of it was fleeting, as it pulled back almost straight away when it saw Jannie coming towards it.

"Popkin?" called Jannie. Nothing came back, but she could

see traces of blue moving back away from the edges of the branches. "Popkin. Is that you?" Again nothing, but silence.

But Popkin couldn't talk, so he couldn't answer her, could he? He really was being very silly; Jannie had a short memory and forgave quickly, the charm of most six-year-olds, and would be very happy if Popkin could join the tea party.

"Popkin," Jannie called. "Would you like to come and have a biscuit with us?"

"I think he would. Let's go in," the fairy tinkled.

There was no reply, although the blue shape moved further back into the dim green light of the tree cave, the fronds of the willow tree blocking a clear view of the little boy.

Jannie tried again. "I'm sorry I got cross. Please come out." The blue shape moved but did not come any closer to the edge of the branches.

Jannie parted the fronds and pushed through into the cool green cave, the fairy zipping in as she did so. Standing around the back of the tree's trunk that stood in the centre of the hollow, partially obscured, was the little figure, blue and red patchwork suit visible.

"Come on, Popkin," Jannie said. "Come out."

The figure moved out from behind the tree trunk so Jannie could see him better. Although very similar in looks, he wasn't Popkin. He didn't look at her like Popkin had done, and his suit was different; Jannie noticed that the patches of colour were a lot smaller, and they were red, not yellow. He looked Jannie up and down, and then his lips upturned. It wasn't a pleasant smile; his teeth were white and even, but there was something about how his mouth curled. His eyes were what scared her the most; they were strange. Like the fairy's, they had a tinge of what looked like blue smoke in them that rolled around as he stared at her. His face was not at all welcoming like Popkin's had been. He smiled, a leering look, which did not reach those strange eyes, and Jannie gave a gasp of fright.

9

"Who are you?" she whispered, starting to shuffle backwards.

The nasty-looking little boy put a finger on his lips in a *shushing* gesture and took a step towards her. Jannie, her heart beating hard in her chest, shuffled further back towards the willow's hanging fronds and the sunshine-lit garden beyond.

"You stay away from me," Jannie whispered, her words choking in her throat. Something wasn't right about this nasty little boy. Fear raced into her chest, making her breathing difficult. "You stay right there, please."

The nasty little boy slid a hand into an invisible pocket and pulled out a little purple ball of fluff. Holding it in the flat of his hand, he raised it towards his mouth and, pursing his lips as if he was going to blow her a kiss, puffed the fluff in Jannie's direction.

Twirling in the air, the fluff circled a couple of turns, dancing like a dust mote in the breeze. Then little stubby gossamer wings sprouted from the centre, and it uncurled. It looked like a tiny bee, with grasping legs and blurred wings beating rapidly. It hovered for a moment, floating in the cool air of the cave, and then streaked towards Jannie, a purple blur too fast to follow. It hit her on the exposed skin of her neck, where it tickled for a moment. And then it stung. Jannie screamed as a sharp pain shot through her neck, burning but cold, fingers of icy fire squirming in her throat. She grasped for the purple bee, and her fingers closed around it, a furry sticky thing that she barely registered. Jannie felt resistance as she pulled it away from her neck, the stinger buried in her throat, making it difficult to remove. As it popped free, she threw it on the floor, where it lay there twitching.

"Got you good," said a voice, low and silky. "How do you do, girl? We have business, and it's easier if you can understand me, as I need as much as you can spare. The most you can."

"What?" croaked Jannie, her voice a whisper. Her mouth felt

dry, and her throat was hurting now. She also felt dizzy and sick but kept moving back towards the sunlight, her limbs leaden.

The nasty little boy cocked his head to one side. "I need your grackles, and they come better if you're scared."

Jannie did not understand what he had said, but she was certainly scared. She watched as he reached into his pocket again and pulled out something that looked like the inside of a toilet paper roll. It was a hollow tube, made of some dark, almost black material, and thin all around. It looked greasy and oily, and Jannie felt her stomach clench again.

"Now come here," he said. "There's no point you trying to leave; the venom is working, and you won't get away. Make it easy on yourself."

Jannie's legs and arms stiffened as if starting to turn to wood, not doing what she asked them. She slumped down to the ground on her back, the cold dampness of the earth of the cave welcome against her burning skin. Willing her leaden limbs, Jannie managed to roll over, the wispy fronds of the willow tree brushing her nose. With the last of her strength, she pushed forwards, bursting through the curtain of branches and into the sunlight. The sun felt good on her face, but she realised that she couldn't move anymore. The bee's poison had finished its job. She opened her mouth to scream for her mummy, but only a hoarse "Ackkk" whisper came out.

Next to her prone body, the tree's fronds parted, and out strolled the nasty little creature, a smug, self-satisfied smile on his face. Moving to Jannie's head, he squatted down on his haunches next to her face. Putting two fingers into her nostrils, he turned her head towards him so that their faces were only inches apart. Behind him, the sunlight burned her eyes.

The fairy was hovering now, no longer beautiful as it stared down at Jannie, a horrible smile on her face.

"Go and make sure that we aren't interrupted. There's a house brownie in there, and I don't want no trouble with it.

Make sure it stays put," the bigger creature commanded. The fairy nodded and then streaked away towards the house.

Turning to Jannie, the creature squatted down and gently purred, "Now, my pretty. You're going to give me those grackles. It is going to hurt, but I don't care. Try and scream if you want, but it won't do you no good."

With that, he placed the end of the oily dark tube onto the centre of Jannie's forehead. At first, she felt only the edge of the tube, slightly sharp, pressing hard into her forehead. Then it felt like the vacuum cleaner did when she held it next to her hand, sucking and fixing it into position. She could feel a tingling on her forehead, a tickling sensation as if ants were scurrying all over her head. The imaginary ants then started to bite; little pinpricks of pain that rapidly began to blend and burn, like pressing your hand against the oven door by accident. Jannie stared into the nasty little boy's face, taking in the pleasure that her tormentor was getting from her suffering. The burning sensation got worst; Jannie tried to grit her teeth, but her mouth wouldn't close; oh, the pain! She trembled despite her muscles not replying to her, fighting the burning with all she had. And then suddenly, it stopped, the burning, dowsed by cold water. The coldness flooded her, and now it ached like a cramp. The tingling was going, but as it did, so did her warmth. It came out of her and into the tube, her breathing getting slower as the iciness poured into her bones. She struggled to remember what had happened; all she could see was the unkind creature's face staring back. As she stared up at him, everything around her seemed to get brighter; the light was almost blinding, blocking out the nasty little boy's leering expression. As the light expanded to take over her entire field of view, she saw a flash of red and yellow blur past close to her face, and suddenly the sensation of the tube pressing against her head was gone. Jannie closed her eyes, and everything went dark as she slipped away from the cold into welcome oblivion.

POPKIN STOOD over the little girl lying half in and half out of the weeping willow cave, tears pouring down his face. He tossed away the stick he had used to drive off the other Faery and dropped down to lift Jannie's head into his lap. His small tears fell onto the upturned face. Placing his ear to her mouth, he listened to the too-shallow breaths that the girl pulled into her lungs. Her face had become sallow and grey, wrinkled, and her hair seemed to be thin and lifeless.

Popkin carefully extracted himself from under Jannie, gently placing her head down onto the ground. Wiping his tear-stained face on his sleeve, he looked pitifully at the little girl again. With a slight shake of his head, he stepped sideways and faded from view.

AMY SAVED the spreadsheet she was working on and pushed herself away from the desk. She'd been working solidly on the project for three hours, and it was a relief to be finished finally. Having the time to get it done had been welcome; Jannie was entertaining herself with her 'party guests' and had been a good girl, not pestering for things. '*Well, that is two good girls who've earned an ice cream tea today,*' thought Amy, rising from her chair and heading for the door.

Downstairs in the kitchen, Amy clicked on the kettle and shouted, "*Jannie!*" No answer. Moving to the kitchen door, Amy called "Jannie" again. Still no answer. That was unusual; her daughter didn't have headphones or a tablet to block out any noise, and Amy could see the blanket at the bottom of the garden with the toys on it from where she stood. "*Jannie?*" she yelled again, a flutter of fear in her stomach.

Stepping into the garden, Amy walked down the path to the

13

bottom garden to where the blanket was. Getting to the halfway point on the garden path, she could see something jutting out from under the weeping willow tree. *"Jannie?"* Amy screamed, breaking into a run towards the motionless patch of hair she could see underneath the tree.

Dropping next to her face-down daughter, Amy moved Jannie's head and gasped with shock. Her beautiful daughter looked like an elderly woman; grey crinkled skin and red-rimmed eyes firmly closed. She was breathing, a slow wheezing noise, and each puff of air smelt sour and harsh, like gone-off milk. "Jannie baby, wake up," gulped Amy, rubbing her daughter's back. "Jannie, please." Her daughter did not move and lay silent apart from the tortured breaths. "Oh, Jannie," said Amy, tears starting. Hands trembling, she fumbled for the phone in her pocket, swiped it open, and dialled three digits.

"Emergency, which service, please?" said the operator. "Ambulance," croaked Amy. "It's my daughter. Please, I need help."

CHAPTER 2

"C'mon, c'mon, c'mon, c'mon," chanted Jack Crackley, legs pumping the pedals of his bike as he strived towards the top of the hill, the bag of newspapers bouncing on the back of his hips as he rode. Standing up on the pedals, he pumped his legs as hard as he could, the familiar burn of the last part of Brierly Hill settling deep into his thighs. The September sun was starting to strengthen now as early morning stretched its way into the day to come, and it bathed the back of his neck with welcome warmth. Blood pounding in his head, Jack worked the pedals as hard as he could as the brow of the hill moved towards him at a snail's pace.

The last part of Jack's morning newspaper route was always the worst. Starting at the bottom of the estate, it twisted its way around the various streets and crescents where the house-holders received their morning tabloid newspaper fix courtesy of Jack. The route wended its way out of the estate to the bigger houses, where he dropped off the broadsheets. The final part of the round ended at the biggest houses, perched along the leg-killer of Brierly Hill, which presided over the little town of Bloxton. The homes here were older than the main housing estate that they watched over, looking over the newer houses like arrogant overseers. They were the last few on Jack's route; thankfully, because by this point, his newspaper bag was near empty, meaning that the hill was manageable. On the first day of his round, Jack had had an excellent idea of doing the 'Hill' first, so he could freewheel back down towards home and school to deliver the rest. Having to push his bike up the hill, the bag resting on the seat, soaked in sweat and panting for a drink, had put paid to that notion. Two years later, the morning paper route was well plotted out for ease and speed, and the improved fitness from the daily deliveries meant that the hill wasn't so bad anymore. True, he had lost a few customers; the nationals going online meant that people could get their morning reading material without waiting for newspaper deliveries. But there were still old-school readers who wanted a hard copy but were too lazy to go down to the shop and hence needed Jack's services.

Jack held down a couple of jobs, the morning paper round being the first of the day. Later he would pick up his evening paper route and, on some evenings, finish off with a 'Kitchen Porter' shift at the Bull, a local pub near his house. It was a grand name for washing up, but the money was good, thanks to the fake ID that Jimmy from school made Jack, which said he was 18 and eligible for minimum wage. In reality, the landlord was fully aware of Jack's age, but he had a soft spot for the boy who always worked hard and without complaint.

It was difficult sometimes to fit work in around school and homework, but at fifteen, Jack would be leaving education next year, meaning it would be easier to find work and bring home more money. They could use it; Jack's dad died when he was four, and his mum worked all the hours she could at the shop, as well as cleaning part-time out of hours. The money Jack made paid for them to eat; Mum's wages everything else. They were not well off, and luxuries were rare, but they did okay. Jack worried about his mum sometimes; she was always so tired and could be short-tempered, and he did what he could to help her. "How much?" was her general response nowadays, and Jack longed to take more of the pressure off her. He planned to leave school and start work as soon as he could; he would find something.

Anyhow, that was for later. For now, the six houses on Brierly Hill each wanted their broadsheet delivery to enjoy with breakfast. Glancing at his watch, Jack saw that he was late again; number five has told him, clearly and with no uncertain terms, that he expected his paper by '0730 hours sharp'. He had actually said it like that, 'Oh-seven-thirty hours,' as if he was some sort of army major commanding the troops, rather than a chubby middle manager in an ill-fitting shirt. The time now was closer to eight, but if Jack was quiet and quick, he could get the newspaper through the letterbox and be away before Sergeant Chubs knew he had been. He had to speed up anyway; school started at eight-thirty, and he had to go back to the shop to grab his bag of books before he could make his way there. He darted up the drive of number five, lifted the letter box as quietly as he could and slid the paper in, making sure it didn't thump onto the floor and alert the occupant. Sprinting back down the drive, he heard the door go and a shout of "OI!", but before Chubs could catch him, he was on his bike and away.

The last house on Brierly Hill was an apartment block, formed by an enterprising individual converting the large building into separate units. Twillington House sat in some lovely gardens; the driveway down to the house was the longest on Jack's route and bikeable if you were so inclined. However, the best thing about Twillington House was that the post boxes for the apartments sat at the end of the drive. There were seven individual boxes in total, neatly labelled with each resident's names and flat numbers. The biggest of them all carried the legend 'Mr M Binks' and did not have a number, just a name;

this was the owner who also lived at the house. Mr Binks was a kindly old chap; he always left a thank you card with a five-pound note for Jack at Easter and Christmas. Sometimes when Jack arrived, the old man was pottering about at the end of the drive, where he would take the paper with a polite "thank you" and some comment about the weather or similar. Jack was happy to spend the time of day with Mr Binks; the gentleman never complained about the deliveries, which was good, because some days, mainly weekends, Jack could be very late. Mr Binks was just a pleasant old man, part of the scenery on a routine paper delivery round.

Jack pulled up to the post boxes outside of Twillington House, fishing the last newspaper out of his bag to complete today's deliveries. Jack rarely noticed the papers; delivering the wretched things was enough, and he rarely had time to read them, given his lackadaisical approach to timekeeping. He was starting to fold the paper when the headline caught his eye:

"Child Aging Illness reaching Epidemic Proportions."

Jack was vaguely aware of what the headline meant; it has been on the TV news a few times, and while he was usually preoccupied with fiddling with his phone in the evening, stuff sometimes filtered into his brain. He also saw it on his social media feed from time to time, the usual memes and sarcastic comments, as well as the snowflakes who pleaded for everyone else to please stop it. It seemed to be affecting children of school age and below; kids appeared to age rapidly almost overnight and slip into a coma, to be discovered by shocked loved ones later on when they failed to put in an appearance. It was a mystery; there did not seem to be any reason for it that the doctors could deduce, nor any known cure. This summer, the disease, if that is what it was, had come to the notice of the media as cases increased rapidly as the longer days progressed.

The paper's article seemed to imply that more and more children were suffering from the 'Boofs' as some online troll had named it based on 'burned out old farts.' Skimming it, Jack shrugged; nobody he knew had it.

He was just shoving the folded-up newspaper into a slot when the figure of Mr Binks stepped out from behind the brick-built pillar that housed the post boxes. "Good morning, young Jack," he said with a slight accent that Jack had never entirely placed, a smile on his face and walking stick in hand.

"Morning, Mr Binks," Jack replied, pulling the paper out of the slot and handing it to the old man.

"A lovely day for it, eh, young Jack? Make the most of it; autumn is just around the corner."

"Certainly intend to, Sir," Jack replied.

"Now," said Mr Binks, "I'm glad I caught you."

'Oh, bugger,' thought Jack, 'Here we go. Complaint time.'

"I've been wondering if I could ask you for a small favour. I'd be happy to pay, of course," said Mr Binks.

"Ookkkayyy," said Jack slowly; it was unusual, but there was money involved. "What can I do for you, Sir?"

"Well," said Mr Binks. "I've got a small table that I need to move from a lower to an upper floor. It is rather heavy, and I am afraid that I can't manage it myself on the stairs, you see," as he held up his walking stick. "I was wondering if you would be kind enough to move it for me? You should manage it on your own quite well, being fit and able, and there is no one else I can ask. The other residents are all elderly like myself, and I do not get many visitors. Indeed, you are one of the few people I see around here regularly. And that isn't that regular, as you know."

"Sure," said Jack, relieved at not having another complainant to try to avoid on the round. "I'd be happy to help. However, I am already running late for school, and…."

"No problems, young Jack," Mr Binks interrupted. "The table

will wait; it's been in the same spot for over twenty years. Whenever you can, it would be most appreciated."

"Look," said Jack, "I can't do it now, but I'd be happy to pop round later after my evening paper round. It wouldn't be too late, and Mum won't mind if I'm a few minutes extra before tea; she's used to it."

"Splendid," said Mr Binks, clasping his hands together. "So, I will see you later then, young Jack. Please come up to the house and ring at the door. I'll be expecting you after four then."

"Sure, no worries. Happy to help."

"Excellent, excellent," said Mr Binks. "Now away with you to school; it must be getting near that time?"

Jack glanced at his watch and muttered a mild oath under his breath. "Yes, Mr Binks; I'd better go." Turning the front wheel of his bike towards the hill, he waved at Mr Binks and kicked off. A few pumps of the pedals got him going, and he sailed off down the hill.

Mr Binks watched him go, waving a little goodbye of his own. As Jack retreated, the smile fell off his face, and a coy grin replaced it. "Yes, yes," he muttered, seemingly to himself. "I know." He cocked his head to one side as if listening to someone whose comments were not audible and then replied, "I said yes. It will be risky, but we must contribute, or else I risk his wrath. Moreover, I can hardly go marching around the town now, like a child catcher, can I? Your master has seen to that." Listening again, he said, "Carefully, of course, and it will be done. Will you assist me? Good. Then let us make ready." Turning on his heel, he placed the walking stick over his shoulder like a decrepit Dick Whittington and marched quickly up the drive towards the house.

~

JACK ARRIVED AT SCHOOL, panting for breath; the last sprint through the morning rush hour streets after grabbing his schoolbag had been frantic. Bloxton Academy, by virtue of its name, strained to be considered upmarket and progressive. In reality, it was anything but. Changing its name from Bloxton Senior School when it became a sponsored academy didn't hide the early 1980's build concrete blocks that formed the bulk of the school buildings; the odd single storey pre-fabricated blocks scattered about for good measure. As a previously underper-forming school, Bloxton was now run by an academy chain, which employed the staff. Nothing else had changed much other than the fact that less money seemed to be available for anything of substance. Academy chains ran schools as a busi-ness, it seemed.

As he cycled through the school gates, Headmaster 'Taffy' Howell, on duty as always, bawled after him, *"Crackley, slow down, boy!"*, his lilting Welsh accent clear in the reprimand. Taffy was okay as a Headmaster; he wasn't afraid to stand up for his staff and put up with little nonsense from the student body. Jack was on the right side of him at the moment and intended to stay that way; Taffy's dressing downs consisted of having the man scream at you, spraying you with spittle, while he criticized you for whatever was the problem. *"Sorry, Sir!"* Jack shouted over his shoulder, freewheeling towards the bicycle store and weaving between the other kids that milled about. He still had a couple of minutes before the registration bell and wanted to get his bike locked up and be in his form room before he was late. Again. However, as always, when you are running late, nothing ever goes to plan.

Jack was putting the padlock onto his bike when out of the corner of his eye, he caught a flash of someone running at full pelt, a blur of grey uniform and red school tie. The figure went sprinting past, schoolbag banging on his legs and backside as they ran, head down and arms pumping. *'Running to beat the devil* !' Jack's grandad would have said if he had still been around. Grandad had had many old sayings for all kinds of situations. However, it was unlikely that he would have had anything polite to describe the subsequent two figures that came thundering along in hot pursuit. Across the yard, other kids gawped at the figures before turning away, not wanting to get involved and risk the wrath of the twins. Jack glanced around, but Taffy was nowhere to be seen; when you actually needed a teacher to be about, they never were. But the figures were dashing in that general direction, and it was none of his business, after all. Jack shrugged and ducked back to his bike, not knowing that fate was about to catch him with its ensnaring hands.

TYLER AND MASON LAFEY were well known in and around the school when they weren't on suspension, that is. The twins were huge by high school standards, both of them well over six feet tall and, at only sixteen years of age, starting to pack on muscle as well. If they had bothered to take part in any of the school's sporting endeavours, there was a chance that the school could fill the dusty, empty cabinet by the reception door. The LaFey's were not identical twins, but their apparent hatred of anyone outside of their immediate social circle was similar. With their shaved heads and beetled eyebrows, they looked like wise Neanderthals, both having a massive underbite beneath pug noses and dark eyes. Mason sported a scar on his left eyebrow from a pre-school fight, and Tyler was the fatter of the two. Tyler did any necessary talking, his ratty little post-pubescent moustache twitching as he did so. Tyler was proud of that moustache; he thought it made him look a cut above and gangster-like.

The LaFey's had a reputation around the local area as being a real 'problem' family. They lived in Morningside, the estate that butted up to the bottom of Brierly Hill. The houses there were tiny and packed together in rows; terraced houses built in the 1950s and seemingly not maintained since. The council placed all of the 'trouble' families in this area, preferring to corral them all together into an area where they could sort out their issues internally through the usual ways – shouting abuse at each other on the street, fistfights, and the casual vandalism of homes and property. As a result, what you ended up with was a melting pot of real tough nuts, each vying with the others to see who would be the top dog. It was not a nice place to go if the residents didn't know you; the gangs of feral children roaming the streets were usually enough to see off any casual visitors before they got into real bother with the grownups themselves. Fortunately, Jack's paper route did not go through Morningside. The shop owner had learned a long time ago that the residents there never settled accounts, and the hassle of chasing debts just wasn't worth it – it was just easier not to deliver there, and cries of prejudice be damned.

The LaFey's lived in a converted mid-terrace house in the centre of Morningside. It had initially been two houses, but as his family grew, Kevin LaFey, the family's patriarch, had decided that rather than seek a bigger house from the council, it would be simpler to knock through next door. A six-month campaign against their elderly neighbour followed, consisting of loud music, vandalism, intimidation, and general rudeness. The result was that the gentlemen left his home of some thirty years to move in with his daughter. Said daughter's husband had been on the receiving end of a particularly nasty attack from Kev LaFey when he'd tried to help his father-in-law out. The police were powerless in Morningside, so the decision to move the father-in-law rather than risk anything further was taken. The council tried to rehome several families in the vacant property following the original resident's departure, but all only lasted a few weeks. Eventually, the council had given up, leaving the house empty. Within a week, the heavily tattooed Kev and a few of his friends had taken two crates of strong lager and a selection of sledgehammers and crowbars into Kev's front room and converted his small home into a much larger affair. The resulting rubble was piled up in the garden and remained there still after ten years. The wreckage was one of many things that Kayleigh LaFey, Kev's wife and partner in spite, mithered him about on a routine basis.

Kayleigh topped the scales at around twenty-three stones, resulting from a diet of takeaways and never having lost the weight she put on through a series of babies that bought the total of her brood to nine kids. Tyler and Mason were numbers seven and eight, respectively (Tyler was born a full fifteen minutes before Mason). Her youngest, Jade, was making a name for herself at the local junior school, not in a good way, while numbers two through six all resided at Her Majesties pleasure in a northern prison. Number one had done well for himself; he worked in Manchester with a local gang there. Kev was constantly tapping him up for cash, and that was going to come to a head at some point. Kayleigh was known throughout the area for her screeching and washing her dirty linen in public, scolding, and criticising her family members at all times. Not that they paid any attention to her anymore, a smouldering cigarette jutting from the corner of her mouth, and her formerly lovely blonde hair pulled back in a greasy ponytail. Besides, while she subjected her family to a continuing tirade of moaning and abuse, she was always first to jump to their defence. The police, the headmaster's office, or the local court -- it made no difference; Kayleigh was vocal and always knew her 'rights.'

Anyhow, with the benefit of such a supportive family behind them, it was easy to see why Tyler and Mason had turned out how they had. The twins were inseparable and, from an early age, had learnt that they could do what they liked if they both did it together. They weren't particularly bright; nobody would ever liken them to other criminal sets of twins, but they did possess a certain amount of cunning that meant that they had been able to avoid getting into serious trouble with the police. They were on the police watch list; a nasty burglary two years ago had resulted in the elderly residents being severely beaten by the robbers, but nobody had ever been able to pin it on the twins. Their father had taught them well.

Early years at school had helped the twins understand that you could push people around when you are bigger than them. You could take stuff from them. And, if they dared to stand up to you, you could beat them down. They had been a scourge of all the years throughout lower school, detrimental to other children's educations. Parents demanded that a series of consecutive headteachers do something about it but met little success; suspensions did not work, and the twins were smart enough to not do anything in school time that would result in expulsion. Parents of particularly bullied children had tried to speak with the twin's parents, but following slanging matches in the street with Kayleigh LaFey while Kev stood behind her, his arms folded and a look of menace on his face, it was usually left alone. One parent that had tried to take it further was woken at two in the morning by the sound of his car alarm; it catching fire seeming of its own accord. As a result, the twins got away with their actions mostly, and as they moved through high school and got bigger, it became easier for them to extort, bully, and beat their fellow students with impunity.

So, it was probably no surprise that the twins attracted attention from others, creatures that thrived on anguish and were happy to revel in such antics. Unseen creatures that tagged along with the twins, enjoying the mayhem that the two started. Graz was currently enjoying their company; the red boggart had latched onto them and was going nowhere.

~

JACK never really had much bother with the LaFey twins through school; he was not a target for them because he never had any money they could take. His trainers weren't the latest or most fashionable brand, and his mobile phone was old, as was his bike. He did not radiate wealth and was someone who was just there, not popular nor disliked, part of the school scene but flying beneath the twin's radar. Sure, he'd been pushed about by the twins on more than one occasion and in the first year at school had his face pushed into his lunch by Mason for no reason other than for the twin's sick satisfaction. He had just laughed along with everyone else on that occasion, and the twins, sensing no real sport from Jack, had pretty much left him alone from then on.

However, this was not the case for the twin's latest target, Jimmy Owen, a fellow year ten and a nodding acquaintance of Jack's. Jimmy was, well...Jimmy. *"A strong character"* was how one teacher had described Jimmy on his school report, that same teacher calling Jimmy a *"loud-mouthed know it all little sod"* one morning in the school staff room where the teachers hid from the kids during break time. Jimmy was one of those types who was outspoken and would not let things go if he felt he had a case to argue, which, in Jimmy's case, was quite often. He had once reduced a supply teacher, new to the trade with a grand total of two months actual teaching under her belt, to genuine sobs when she had stated that a mile was less than a kilometre. She was sure of herself; she was the teacher, and these kids would listen to her. Not Jimmy. He asked her for proof, politely at first, and then less so as the supply took the attitude of *'do as I say.'* It ended with Jimmy rousting the whole class, who, to be fair, took little encouragement, to chant "Useless, useless, useless...," standing on their desks and pelting the supply teacher with screwed up paper. Later that day, that same teacher took herself off the supply list and called her old tutor to discuss the availability of perhaps further training in behaviour management. It also earned Jimmy one week's worth of lunchtime detentions, which was not a problem to him as he spent the time on his phone secretly reading up on whatever subject was of interest to him that particular week.

Jimmy's main problem was that he did not know when to shut up. It was like the filter between his thoughts and his brain was broken, and whatever he thought just came flooding on out. Sometimes it was hilarious, like when he was cutting into a teacher or in some sort of row with a fellow student. Mostly it was just annoying to people; Jimmy liked the sound of his own voice and didn't know when it was best just not to say anything at all. It got him into all kinds of trouble – teachers, fellow kids who would punch him, fellow kids' parents (who would have liked to punch him), shop keepers, everybody really. But most of all, the LaFey twins.

The LaFey twins didn't like Jimmy; he was kind of popular due to his outbursts, and he was relatively well off with his dad having his own business. He also had a decent side-line going in school, knocking up fake IDs for people, handy if you wanted to get your hands on some booze for a weekend party or hanging around the streets. As a result, being financially viable, he was often a target for the twins when they needed to shake some-body down for some cash. Jimmy was usually more of a target than most, both in school and out of it, if he was daft enough to wander where the twins hung out. Tyler had broken his nose once following some altercation, and Jimmy had been to the hospital twice, once with a dislocated shoulder as Mason liked to twist arms and have people beg him, and once with suspected broken ribs when both twins had pinned him down and knelt on him. As it stood, both times he'd been lucky to escape serious injury, but he just didn't learn. Mouthing off at the twins was never a good idea, and nearly all the kids at Bloxton Academy were well aware of this. But not Jimmy. He just wasn't wired that way.

The morning for Jimmy had started with his regular routine. His mother shouted him out of bed with the usual threats of cutting off the Wi-Fi, finally rousting him into action. He had made good time getting ready and eating breakfast, meaning that he was actually in time to accept the lift from his dad when it was offered. His dad dropped him off at school for once with everything with him that he'd need for the school day. Waving his dad off, Jimmy had fished his phone out of his pocket and scrolled straight to social media for his daily catch up on current affairs. Skipping over the news feed, he became engrossed in the screen, not looking where he was going as he headed down the path towards the schoolyard, where the kids were forced to wait in all weathers for the school day to start.

Mason and Tyler had climbed through the back hedge of the school. This was the quickest way to get into school premises from Morningside, the alleyway in that part of the estate adjourning the school. It also meant that they avoided which-ever staff member was on the gates and, as they were often late, any associated trouble. The hedgerow gap had been used by countless Morningside school-goers over the years and was well established. The school did not have the money to fence it off, so it was left as it was, the hedge having given up stretching branches across the gap many years ago. Strolling down the path towards the schoolyard, Mason noticed the lone figure ahead, engrossed in his phone. Other students were milling about in the distance, but nowhere near the distracted boy; a perfect target. He nudged Tyler and grunted, gesturing with his head. Tyler nodded back, and the twins sped up in Jimmy's direction.

Jimmy was engrossed in reading an incredibly vivid news article on the ageing disease when a large meaty hand plucked the phone from his hand. "Hey, what..." said Jimmy, his voice dying in his throat as he recognised Tyler LaFey in front of him. A quick glance over his shoulder confirmed the worst; Mason was behind him, cutting off any potential retreat in that direction.

Tyler gave a small, insincere smile and said, "Good morning Owen. Nice phone." Tyler's voice was smooth, not guttural, as his appearance implied. Almost courteous in its tone.

"Aah, come on, give it back, Tyler. Please," said Jimmy.

"Of course, of course," said Tyler, slipping the phone into his pocket. "I'd be happy to let you have this rather nice phone. It'll cost you ten pounds."

"C'mon Tyler. I haven't got ten pounds. Just give it back."

"In that case, the cost will be twenty pounds. Tomorrow. Cash on delivery."

"Please, Tyler, I need the phone. I'll give you the money tomorrow, but I need it today."

"Now then, what guarantee have we got that you'll pay up?" said Tyler, warming to the begging. Mason stood behind him, blank-faced. "Seems to me that you could well deny our arrangement exists."

"I promise I'll give it to you tomorrow. Look, you'll see me here at school anyway, or I'll come and find you. If you find me first, then all the better, eh? I'll have the money, I swear."

"And then you'll have a phone," replied Tyler with a sneer. "We'll see you tomorrow."

With that, he turned and walked away. Mason followed and deliberately barged Jimmy as he walked past him, his broad shoulder bashing Jimmy hard enough to send tingles down his arm.

It was at this point that Jimmy knew that he would not see his phone again. It would lock so that they couldn't do anything with it, but he was reasonably sure that it'd be behind the counter of the town pawnshop by the end of the day. Jimmy was angry with himself for not being more assertive but more so with the twins for being such nasty swines. And, in true Jimmy fashion, before he knew what he was doing, his mouth started in.

The twins had gotten about fifteen or so paces away when Jimmy called out: "I'll give you fifty pounds' cash tomorrow if you let me have the phone back now." The twins stopped; this was more than they would get punting it on to a third party with no charger or ownership record. Besides, they could take the money and thieve the phone back if they wanted. "On one condition, though," continued Jimmy.

"I'm listening," said Tyler turning his head to focus on Jimmy; conditions did not mean anything to him, but cash did.

"With the money, you buy Mason there some deodorant; he really needs it. Jesus, you boys had the water cut off at home or something? And when you're mooching around the toiletries aisle, why not pick yourself out a nice little Ladyshave razor? There appears to be a caterpillar doing something to your top lip, and while I guess that you're no stranger to insects, fleas mainly, having their way with your bloated idiotic face, it could benefit from a trim. And if you accidentally cut anything off during the exercise, you'd only improve your looks, you stupid stinking ape."

Jimmy's mouth slowly stopped, half an eye on his escape route back the way he had come, the rest of his attention on the twins. His brain was screaming at him, one part saying 'nice, mate, nice,' the other howling 'go, go, go, get out of here.' Tyler's face had started to turn puce at the end of Jimmy's first sentence and was now a mask of rage.

"What did you say, you little...."

Jimmy cut him off. "And get yourself something to unclog your ears as well, you piece of...."

He stopped as Mason charged at him. Turning smartly, Jimmy took to his heels; the twins lumbering stomps all too clear to him as they surged after him. He was in for a severe beating this time, no mistake.

FROM THE RELATIVE safety of the bike shed, Jack watched as Jimmy Owen dashed by the door, a look of fear on his face, but also a hint of apparent glee in the smile plastered to it as well. He was heading in the direction of the school gates, it seemed, and the apparent safety that Taffy Howell would provide, assuming he was still milling about. If he made it. Jimmy was faster than the twins, but the twins had a much longer stride, and whatever Jimmy had done, they were hell-bent on catching him. Jack watched as Mason, outpacing his brother by a few steps, thundered past, a look of murderous intent on his face, closely followed by Tyler. As all parties left Jack's view, obscured by the shed door, there came a sudden howl, and Tyler's voice shouting a victorious, "Yes!"

JIMMY HAD BEEN sprinting as if his life depended on it. He was past the school's corner, dodging the open door to the bike shed, and was on the home straight towards the school entrance, where there were plenty of others hanging about. Risking a glance over his shoulder, he gave a start as he saw how close Mason LaFey was behind him, his purple face flushed and sweaty, one meaty paw outstretched to grab that back of Jimmy's jacket. The start was all it needed; Jimmy's left foot caught the back of his right in his panic, and he fell forward in an ungraceful dive onto the path. Banging his jaw onto the asphalt as he went head-first, he saw stars, and his mouth filled with blood as pain from his bitten tongue spiked through his jaw. Seconds later, Mason LaFey clamped a hand down on the back of Jimmy's neck, pinning him to the floor in his prone position.

"Well then," panted Tyler, slowing to a stop beside them. "Clumsy, clumsy, Owen. In there. Don't want no witnesses." He gestured with his head back at the bike shed. Mason nodded an understanding, a big grin spreading across his face. He released his grip, and Jimmy, squirming on the floor as he tried to get up, said, "Mush, pleeashh," before spitting out more blood to clear his mouth. "Plleeash Tylersh, I'm shorry."

Jack watched from the bike shed as Mason hauled Jimmy to his feet, whilst Tyler raised a menacing finger at the nearest kids, his face dark. The other witnesses to the chase all found something else to occupy their attention very quickly, and Tyler sneered at Jimmy, who stared at him in horror. With a firm grip on the back of his jacket, all three started to march back towards the bike shed. 'Damn,' thought Jack, '*Just what I needed.*' Scuttling towards the back, Jack crouched down in the darkest part of the shed, putting the racks of bikes between himself and the door. If he was quiet, they might not see him. Entering the threshold, Mason shoved Jimmy, his mouth still streaming with blood, hard from behind. Jimmy stumbled forwards and fell to his knees. Mason entered the shed, closely followed by Tyler, who pulled the door shut behind him. Only the frosted plastic skylights now gave any light in the shed, but in the gloom, Jack could still see what was going to happen. He watched as Tyler placed one foot in the centre of Jimmy's back and pushed him firmly so that he was face down on the floor, his lips curled in a sinister smile.

"Now then," said Tyler, as he grinned down at Jimmy. "One thing I cannot, and I mean absolutely cannot stand, is a smart mouth. Particularly when you are trying to do the owner of said smart mouth a favour."

Jimmy turned his head to look up sideways. "Pleashe Tyler,

I'm shorry. I should never have shaid those thingsh. I'm really, really shorry. Look, I'll give you the moneysh."

"SSShhhhh," said Tyler, one finger going to his lips. "We don't want your money. We want everyone to understand what happens when people smart mouth us. And you're going to help us do that."

"How?" said Jimmy, his face now dark with panic, the blood still running from the corner of his mouth. He struggled under Tyler's foot that securely pinned him in place.

"You're going to be a shining example to everyone else as to what happens when people don't do what we ask." Tyler ground his heel slowly in the small of Jimmy's back, and Jimmy whimpered in pain. He squirmed again but wasn't going anywhere. Tyler beckoned to Mason, who was standing at the door, grinning from ear to ear. "Mason, pop Jimmy's arm out for me, mate, would yer?" Mason nodded, a look of glee on his face as he lumbered forward to Tyler's side.

Now, Jack did not think of himself as brave, but he did know right from wrong, and he wasn't going to hide while someone he knew was about to be hurt. Taking a deep breath, he stood up from behind the bike racks and said, in a quavering voice. "Leave him alone."

Tyler started as the figure appeared at the back of the shed. "Who's there?" he called. Jack moved from his hiding place so that he was in full view, stepping into the gloomy light cast by the skylights.

"Crackley, that you?" said Tyler, shifting his weight forwards for a better view, the leg that pinned Jimmy pressing down and causing a gasp of pain.

"Yes. Leave him alone, Tyler. He's bleeding. Whatever he'd done to you, you can take it up another time."

"You telling me what I can and can't do, Crackley?" said Tyler, his face again starting to darken. Mason began to drift in Jack's direction now, his face also thunderous.

"No," said Jack warily. "I'd never do that, Tyler. I'm just saying that he's hurt and, from what I can see, very sorry for whatever he's done. You're going to be in serious trouble if you hurt him anymore."

"Unlikely. It'd be his word against ours."

"No, it'd be his and mine," replied Jack.

Tyler twitched slightly. "But you're not going to see anything, Crackley. Cos what you are going to do is be a good little boy and trot on out of here. Now." Tyler gestured towards the door. "Do one, or else you'll be having an *accident* too."

Jack took a deep breath. "I'm not leaving. Now, leave him alone before I shout the place down and...."

He was cut off mid-sentence by Mason's strong right hand grabbing him by the throat, squeezing it shut. He looked up into the leering Neanderthal-like face as Mason's other hand grabbed him by the front of his jumper. Mason pushed him back a few steps, his grip strong.

"Nice one, Mase," said Tyler. "Now then. I'm going to take care of business with young Jimmy here, and you're going to watch, nice and quiet like. Moreover, if you breathe a word of this to anyone, you'll be getting the same. Ten times over." Tyler glanced down at Jimmy, smiling again, and, lacing his fingers together, lazily cracked his knuckles.

Jack was also starting to panic now; he couldn't draw breath thanks to Mason's hand clamping around his neck, and his fear of watching Jimmy getting a beating was spiking in his brain; his fight or flight instincts kicking in as adrenaline dumped into his system. He clutched at Mason's hand with both hands but could not move it; the thug was just too strong for him. He watched Tyler grab Jimmy's arm, his knee now on the small of Jimmy's back.

Watching Tyler stoop down caused a memory to flair in Jack's oxygen-starved brain. The stooping down movement made by Tyler reminded him strangely again of Grandad, whose arthritis had meant he had moved about with a stoop of his own, slightly hunched. In this memory, he was sitting with Grandad in the back garden of the old man's terraced home on the little bench there. He was sipping a can of cola, Grandad slurping a cup of tea, and Grandad had said, "Well then, Jack..."

∾

"...WITH your Dad not being around anymore, I guess it falls to me to share with you a few life stories. If you'd like to hear them, of course?" Jack loved Grandad's stories; the old man could tell a great tale, particularly after having had a nip or two of his favourite tipple. The stories usually revolved around the adventures he and his friends had, both in his youth and later with his mates from the steelworks, where he had worked all his life.

"Okay, Grandad," said Jack, "Are they exciting stories?" and then giggled as the old man had ruffled his hair. "They're always exciting, Jackie boy," he admonished. They had been pulling rhubarb in the tiny garden; the old man had a bumper crop each year, and Jack's mum made a mean crumble. The two had retired to the bench now for 'a bit of respite,' as Grandad called it, rubbing his back and wincing.

With the drinks served, the old man studied the boy. He took a gulp of tea, smacked his lips appreciatively and said, "Well then, Jack, I'm no expert, but I did pick up a tip or two along the way. Most dads have a few pearls of wisdom to depart, although most boys don't listen until they're older and wiser."

"I'm listening, Grandad,"

"Okay, then. I'm going to tell you a few secrets that'll help you get on in life. Are you ready for wisdom?" Grandad spread his arms wide.

"Yes, Grandad. I'm ready for the wisdom," Jack giggled.

"When I was younger, much younger than today – that's an

old song, Jack, by the way, but I digress. Anyhow, I had to go for a job interview. Not for the steelworks, it was at the big shop in town. All gone now, but back then, it was huge. Anyway, when I got up on the day in question, I put on my suit and got out the tie my dad had left for me. It was then that I realised I had never tied a tie; I didn't know how, hadn't a clue! I dashed downstairs, but my mum and dad, your great granny and grandad, had already left for work. I was stuck, and I wanted that job; good first impressions and all that. I ran for the bus anyway and got on; I did not want to be late. Anyhow, when the conductor came 'round to sell me my ticket, I said, 'Excuse me, sir. I've got this job interview I'm going to and have no idea how to tie this tie'. 'No problems, ' said the conductor. 'Lie yourself down across that empty seat there, and I'll sort it out for you.' Once I was lying down, he tied my tie for me; it looked great, a proper knot and everything. When he had finished, I thanked him but was a bit curious about why I had to lie down. When I asked him, he said, 'Well, in my previous job, I learned how to tie ties on other people when they were lying down.' 'What was your previous job?' I asked. He replied, 'I used to be an undertaker.' A true story that, Jack, about sixty years ago it was. And the moral of the story is?"

"I don't know, Grandad. Learn to tie a tie?"

"Good try, lad, but no. The moral of the story is *always try to help others.* People like helpful people. Never let people take advantage of you, though. Not ever. There's being kind, and there's being put upon."

"Okay, Grandad. Be helpful. Can I have some crisps, and, err, can I get you anything?"

Grandad laughed. "Maybe later when we've finished talking, Jack, but nice try at being helpful there. Don't want to spoil your tea, though."

"I won't, Grandad."

"Right. My second secret of life is choosing to be

happy. When I was a young man, I was given some advice that stuck with me, and I think it is the main reason I've enjoyed my life. The piece of advice I got was, 'You can be right, or you can be happy.' I'm not telling you to not stand up for the things you believe in; you should always do that. No, I am talking about the little things we row about; that just doesn't matter. For me, something's got to be pretty vital for me to fight over being right about it. If you learn to let it go, you'll find that just knowing you're right is often enough."

"Mmm," said Jack thoughtfully. "So, I shouldn't fight with people?"

"No, not exactly. Fight for the things you believe strongly in. But it's okay to let things go occasionally. Providing folks aren't taking advantage, of course."

"Okay. So fight if I think I need to?"

"Exactly. Be happy and choose your battles. Now, time is getting on, and your mum will be here in a bit to pick you up. But I think we've got time for a couple more rules of life if you like?"

"Yes, please, Grandad. These are great!"

Grandad ruffled Jack's hair. "You're a good lad, Jack, listening to an old man waffling on. Listen, can you bundle up that rhubarb; I don't like leaving it lying there once it's been pulled."

Jack bounded to his feet straight away and retrieved the fruit they'd picked. Grandpa nodded and pointed at the little shed. "There's some newspaper in there; wrap them in that."

When Jack had finished, he plopped back down next to the old man, who put an arm around him.

"You're a good lad, Jack. I'm glad you find my stories interesting, even if you don't really understand them. But I promise you; they will help you later in life if you remember any of them."

"I will, Grandad, I promise!"

Grandad laughed. "Okay, then. One more important thing to remember is that you are who you believe you are. Your thoughts are powerful things – they determine what you think of yourself, and the actions you take are based on who you think you are. How you choose to think makes you who you are inside and defines your actions. And the best part? You can change your mind and be something new; do something new. What you have done is not as important as what you do next; people live in the now. Sure, they remember, but if you have to put something right, really put it right. Never be afraid to try something new. So...." Grandad poked Jack in a ticklish spot, soliciting another giggle. "...always," - *poke* - "think," – *poke* - "good," - *poke* – "of yourself."

Jack had squirmed off the bench by now, shrieking with laughter. Grandad smiled down at him and then put out his hand to pull him up. Jack plopped down onto the bench again.

"I've got a life rule for you, Grandad," said Jack, panting as his laughter subsided.

"What's that then? No tickling?"

"Noooo, Grandad," said Jack, giggling again. "A real rule."

"Go on then."

"You should never hit anyone between the legs."

Grandad frowned a little. "Now then, where did you hear that?"

"My teacher said it. Some boys were fighting in the playground at school, and one had to go to the hospital!"

"Well, if you're teacher said it, I guess that's a good rule. But I'd add to that rule if I may?"

"Of course, Grandad."

"Never hit anyone between the legs unless you absolutely have to."

Jack mulled this over. "So, when do you know that you absolutely have to, Grandad?"

"Only you'll know that at the time, Jack. Nevertheless, I

would think it is when you have no other choice. That'd be my advice."

～

JACK LOOKED up at Mason's face as the thug watched his brother mess Jimmy up. His attention wasn't on Jack; he was gleefully watching the humiliation of the smaller boy. Therefore, he was caught completely unaware, as Jack, with a heave of effort, planted his right knee as hard as he could in Mason's groin. Which was pretty hard; cycling every day with heavy paper bags had built Jack's legs up just fine, and he had plenty of underlying muscle there. That, combined with the anger he felt for what was happening, meant that he loaded the blow with as much power as he could manage, pushing up from the floor with everything he had. Mason lifted slightly off the floor before releasing his grip on Jack, both hands flying instead to his groin as he howled out a scream of total agony. He wilted slowly, his face an angry purple, tears running down his cheeks. He then rolled slowly onto his side, curling his legs up like a newborn, still cradling his crotch.

Tyler had jumped at Mason's yowl and, turning to see his brother collapsing onto the floor, released his hold on Jimmy. "Crackley, you little git. What you done?"

"He was choking me. Enough's enough now, Tyler. Pack it in and get lost." Jack balled his fists, his anger now running wild in him. How dare they?

Tyler got up slowly from Jimmy's prone form. He advanced towards Jack with heavy footsteps but stopped at the sight of his twin lying shuddering on the dusty floor of the bike shed.

"Mase," he said, "You okay, bruv?" Mason just gasped something incoherent, wriggling away on the floor. Tyler looked back at Jack. "You're dead."

Stepping over his brother, he raised his fists and stalked

towards Jack. Jack backed up a step, the fear now starting to creep in. There was no way that he would be able to beat Tyler LaFey; he was too big. Still, he raised his own fists to try to counter Tyler's punches; he wasn't going down without a fight, not today. He was squaring up when a battle cry came from nowhere. With it, Tyler suddenly shot forward, as if propelled by some higher force, stomach leading and arms flailing.

Jimmy had been watching the exchange, momentarily forgotten by Tyler. He had seen what Jack had done, what was about to happen and had gotten a good dose of anger on himself. Getting silently to his feet, Jimmy fixed his eyes on the middle of Tyler's back and dropped his right shoulder down. Screaming a war cry at the top of his lungs, he launched himself forward, tensing as he went, and shoulder barged Tyler from behind as hard as he could. Tyler barrelled forwards at high speed, ploughing straight into Jack at full force. Given the rules of momentum, Jack stood no chance, shooting backwards himself, his feet lifted off the floor. Without the time to put his hands down to arrest his fall, his head collided with the low brick wall that formed the foundation of the bike shed, a resounding crack echoing out.

Jack slumped to the floor, and as he raised his aching head, he saw bright blue speckles swirling all around everyone, like a firefly show. And then, within the dancing lights, a small red gremlin-like figure with big eyes suddenly appeared, sitting astride Tyler's shoulders. The creature was bouncing up and down, its sharp teeth visible over its leering grin, with what looked like tiny wings beating furiously. It suddenly stiffened as Jack's glance fixed on it. Jack saw the creature point at him, its smile gone and a look of concern on its little face as it gnashed its overly large jaw. Jack raised one arm slowly from the floor and pointed back at it. He watched the creature start to climb down off Tyler before darkness filled his eyes, and he passed out.

CHAPTER 3

*J*ack came around slowly, his vision clearing to see
the figure of Taffy standing over him, tapping his
face gently. "Crackley," he said softly. "Crackley."
Jack shook his aching head to clear his wits and said, "Sir?"

"You okay, Crackley?"

"Head hurts, Sir," said Jack. Jack looked past Taffy to see
Jimmy anxiously peering around him. Behind Jimmy, next to
the door, were the LaFey's, shoulders firmly gripped by 'Beasty'
Best, the PE teacher. Both twins were glowering in Jack's direction, Mason pale and still clutching his crotch area and Tyler
with murder in his eyes. "I'll be fine, Sir," said Jack, his eyes on
the twins.

GRAZ HAD BEEN HAVING a wonderful time that morning with the
twins; he thrived on the misery of others. The thuggish twins
were some of his favourite lifers to hang out with, as they were
endlessly looking to prey on smaller, weaker victims, something
Graz liked a lot. Graz hitched a shoulder ride with Tyler

normally; Tyler was in charge, and it was easy for Graz to whisper sweet subliminal ideas into Tyler's ears to maximise his enjoyment. It had been Graz's idea to twist Jimmy's arm; other than that, he had stayed mainly silent today, revelling in the twin's own inventiveness.

Used to being unseen, it had therefore been a shock to Graz when one of the lifers had looked straight at him; lifers weren't supposed to be able to see the Fae folk unless they revealed themselves to them. Revealing yourself was not allowed, not unless you had express permission to do so, or there were dire circumstances. A Fae like Graz would never have permission to show himself to lifers, not that he had any desire to do so. Punishments for doing so were harsh, the rule being 'stay hidden'. He had heard the Unseelie Court's rumours about older lifers who could supposedly see his kind without invitation, but he was not privy to such discussions, just snippets he had picked up sneaking around the edges. In his long experience, lifers could not see the Fae.

Graz had watched things unfold from on top of Tyler's shoulders, and when the older lifers, alerted by a good Samaritan, had arrived following the screaming attack on Tyler, he had hopped down. The smaller lifer was still slumped against the wall, but he was waking up now. Graz hopped between the older lifer's legs and stood staring at the boy as he opened his eyes. The boy looked straight through Graz with no sign of recognition, staring at the figures in the doorway. Graz snapped his fingers in front of the young lifer's face and got no reaction. He poked for his eyes, and again nothing; no flinch or anything. Satisfied that it was probably a coincidence brought on by the trauma of being knocked out, Graz hopped back over to the doorway to where the twins were. It looked like the fun was over for today; the twins did not care about being punished, so it wasn't worth staying to see if they would cry. Nah, Graz would head on over to one of the many pubs instead; it was always easy to get lifers to fight when they'd had a drink or two. Patting Tyler fondly on the knee, Graz stepped to the left and faded from view.

∾

"C'MON, Crackley, get to the school nurse. I want an official opinion on that bang to the head. If you need to go to the hospital, we'll have to call your mother," Taffy said, pulling Jack to his feet and dusting him off.

"I'll be fine, Sir," said Jack. "Please don't call my mother; she's working, and it's difficult for her."

"Well, we'll let the nurse be the judge of that, boy. I am not having anyone say that I am not following the procedures if the worst should happen. Nurse. Now. Owen here will escort you." Taffy turned to Jimmy. "And while you're getting sorted, I'll take Mr and Mr LaFey here for a chat in my office. Again."

"March," said Beastly Best, shoving the twins out of the bike shed. Tyler cast one last glare at Jack before the hulking PE teacher removed him from sight.

"Go on," said Taffy, a little more gently this time. "Get yourself checked over properly." With that, he turned and left, no doubt mulling over yet another conversation with the LaFey twins and their wretched mother.

"Jack," said Jimmy. "Thanks."

"No worries. Wasn't about to stand there and let him break your arm, was I?"

"I'm just glad you were there. They were going to do me properly this time."

"What did you do to them to get them so mad?"

"Just the usual; home truths with a bit of spite thrown in. They took my phone; still got it."

"You should go to the office and get it back while they're with Taffy."

43

"I will do once I've got you to the nurse. And Jack," Jimmy looked down at his shoes, shuffling uncomfortably, "I owe you one for this. Anything you need, let me know."

"Nah, it's fine," said Jack, a little embarrassed. "Anyone would have done the same."

"That I doubt," said Jimmy with a laugh, pushing Jack towards the open door of the bike shed. "Let's go and get you looked over. We're going to be late for registration."

THE SCHOOL NURSE checked Jack over thoroughly, having received a call from the headmaster before the boys' arrival, and hence proceeded on the basis that it could be followed up instead of her usual lazy approach. She asked Jack repeated questions and ran her fingers over his head. Apart from a smallish lump on the back of his head where he had hit the wall, the nurse gave him a clean bill of health. "Although Jack..." she looked at her sheet, "...Crackley, if you start feeling dizzy or sick, or the headache comes back, you need to go straight to accident and emergency. I cannot see an actual concussion, and some people don't experience or report symptoms until hours or days after the injury. So anything happens, you feel strange or anything, you go. Okay?"

"No problems, Miss. If I start to feel ill over the next few days, I promise to get it checked out again. So, you don't need to call my mum?"

"No, I think it'll be okay for now. You can get on. You've missed registration but are still in time for assembly. Tell them at the school office on your way, please."

"Thanks, Miss." Jack got up and gathered his belongings before leaving the medical office. Closing the door behind him, he was pleased to see Jimmy walking down the corridor, glued as usual to his phone.

"Got it back then?" he said.

Jimmy looked up and smiled. "Yep. No problems; I went in and said that I thought Tyler might have picked up my phone by accident. Taffy knew what I was driving at and made him turn out his pockets. It's fine; they didn't even get a chance to try and open it by the looks of it. The pair of them, though, if looks could kill...."

Jack laughed. "What's going to happen to them?"

"Don't know," said Jimmy. "But on my way out, I overheard Taffy saying something about exclusion for a bit."

"That'd be great," said Jack. "Give us some breathing space and let things calm down a bit."

"Agreed," said Jimmy, waving his phone. "Now, I'm not planning on going to assembly, too dull. Want to come and sit in the form room and look at some of the new games I've got?"

"Sounds like a plan," said Jack. Jimmy patted him on the shoulder, and the two boys walked together in the direction of the form room.

Despite the somewhat exciting start, the rest of the day was pretty average. Jack went through the usual lessons, incognito in the middle of the class. The only real difference was the fact that he was now enjoying a blossoming friendship with Jimmy. Following the morning's phone games viewing, Jimmy had laughed, not unkindly, at Jack's older model phone. He had offered Jack one of his old phones, not the latest model, but certainly newer than Jack's antique. He had waved away Jack's offer of payment, to Jack's secret relief, and had offered to bring it into school the next day. The boys had eaten lunch together and had sat together in the afternoon classes, quietly winding each other up.

Walking out of school at the end of the day, Jimmy said to Jack, "What are you doing later?"

"Just my paper round, then off home. Not got the dishes on tonight at the Bull."

"Fancy coming round mine after then? We can fire up the console and get us some shooting action on. I'll chuck some pizza in the oven, and we can sort that phone out."

"That sounds good to me," said Jack. "I'll text my mum and let her know."

He took out his phone and glanced at the time —3:32 pm. Something jogged in his memory.

"Ah, wait a sec," said Jack. "I promised to go and help the old feller up on the hill to move some stuff. Not sure how long that will take, but I have to go after my round."

"No worries, mate," said Jimmy. "Let's do it tomorrow instead. You can clear it with your ma, and we can go after your round. I may even give you a hand with it."

"I'm not paying you," laughed Jack. "Slave labour as it is."

"Jack," said Jimmy, mock seriously. "It would be my pleasure."

"Cheers, pal. See you tomorrow morning then."

"No worries. Don't work too hard." Jimmy waved Jack away and walked off towards the school gates, swinging his bag as he went.

Jack headed into the bike sheds, the scene of so much drama earlier, and unlocked his bike. The familiar setting flared something in his mind about the goblin type character he had seen astride Tyler earlier. Shaking his head in bemusement, he thought, *'must be losing it.'* He wheeled his bike out, jumped aboard, and set off for the shop and that evening's round.

JACK FINALLY CYCLED into the driveway of Twillington House at ten to five. He would have been earlier, but the papers were late, putting him behind. He'd texted Mum to tell her what he was up to; she'd not replied, but that wasn't unusual if she was working. Jack wasn't too worried about the reception he'd get from Mr

Binks; he was doing the old chap a favour after all, and it was not too far 'after four,' as requested.

Jack weaved his way down the drive, through some immaculate gardens to where the big house stood in the corner of the plot. It had a small carpark attached to it with a couple of cars present in nicely labelled slots; the spots owner neatly printed on a sign next to the space. The vehicles were dusty, as if they hadn't been driven for a while, but they were all reasonably new according to the registration numbers. Jack glanced briefly at them and freewheeled around to the huge porch that led to Twillington House's entrance.

The porch leading to the front door was enormous. It had its own roof, held up by carved supporting columns, an intricately tiled floor and wooden benching down both sides, immaculately polished to a high sheen. At the end, the front door glowed; burnished dark wood with brass rivets, a huge lion's head knocker positioned proudly in the centre. A sign at the entrance to the porch, in engraved bronze, read "Twillington House. No salesmen, hawkers, or religion welcome." Jack lifted his bike over the step into the porch and rested it gently against one of the benches, being careful not to mark the wood.

Walking to the front door, he reached for the knocker before noticing an old-fashioned bell-pull hanging down from the side of the door. He gave it a gentle pull and was rewarded with a jangling chime from somewhere in the depths of the house. Standing waiting, he started to fiddle with the lion knocker, pulling it up and letting it drop slowly onto the knocking plate. *Clunk. Clunk. Clunk.* Rhythmic. Hypnotising. *Clunk. Clunk.*

The door was suddenly wrenched open, and the figure of Mr Binks stood there, his face furious.

"Okay, okay, I heard you the first bloody time, you flaming idiot," he screeched, spittle spraying from his mouth. He had not focused on Jack, seeming instead to look straight through him.

His hair was awry, and he looked deranged, lips curled in a furious snarl.

"Oh, Mr Binks, I'm sorry," said Jack, taking a step backwards. "I didn't realise it was so loud inside; I was just waiting and...."

Mr Binks focused on Jack, and the furious expression on his face seemed to drain off, quickly replaced by the affable look that Jack was more familiar with.

"Ah, young Jack," the old man said with a smile, "My apologies. I was napping, and the bell awoke me. I am always cranky when I just wake up."

Jack inwardly sighed with relief. The outburst has shocked him a little, to be honest, being totally out of character, but he understood.

"I am sorry, though. I didn't mean to make lots of noise; I was just fiddling with the knocker while I was waiting."

"No harm was done, young Jack. Now then, why don't you come in, and I can show you the table I would like your assistance with?"

"Sure, Mr Binks, no problems. Will my bike be okay just there – not in the way of the other residents, is it?"

"It'll be fine there, Jack. Come along; we don't want you to be late now, do we?"

Jack wondered what he was going to be late for but put it down to the eccentric ways of Mr Binks. With a slight shrug, he followed Mr Binks into the gloomy reception area of Twillington House.

Once inside, Jack looked around the foyer, his mouth agape. It was like nothing he had ever seen before; it was like walking into a museum but without the ropes and glass cases. Lining the walls were large-scale portraits of people from days gone by; oil paintings by their look, not that Jack was an expert. He had seen them on TV but never close up like this. Although these did not look as old, too clean and detailed, there were also man-size marble statues. Various vases and urns sat atop tables and display units, some with flowers poking out of them. A staircase, ornately carved, curved up to the first floor and was richly carpeted in a maroon and gold pattern. The whole place had a decidedly musty smell, sweet and sickly. 'Old people smell,' thought Jack with a secret smile to himself.

"Ah, my little collection," said Mr Binks, mistaking Jack's smile for one of pleasure and interest. "I like to collect beautiful things, Jack, and have been fortunate enough to obtain many things over my lifetime. What do you think?"

"I don't know, Mr Binks. I've never seen anything like this outside of a museum."

"Well, there are treasures here, Jack. I may show them to you later, once our business is concluded. I believe that everyone should have an appreciation of beauty. The residents here enjoy my artworks very much; we debate them often in the common areas."

"That would be nice, Mr Binks," said Jack politely. "And talking of why I'm here, which table is it that you want me to move?"

"Ah, the intemperate youth. Always so hasty. Come then, Jack, let us address our business and put talk of pleasure to later times."

Mr Binks headed through a side door, beckoning Jack over his shoulder with one crooked finger. Jack followed him into a large corridor shod in dark wood panels. Set about halfway down was a door, a large number five in shiny brass fixed to it. As Mr Binks walked past it, he stuck out his hand and dragged his nails across the door; the scratching sounds small but decisively odd like the action itself. As Jack walked past the door, he heard a muffled thumping followed by a crashing sound.

"Damn that cat," Mr Binks snarled, whirling around. "Number five is the residence of Miss Earnshaw. She has a cat, something that I was not aware of when she took out her lease. I hate the wretched creature, but as the lease had been agreed and did not specify any animals exactly, I have had to comply and allow her to keep the creature. It is confined to her rooms." His face took on a crafty look. "I made a special exception in her case."

Jack didn't think that it had sounded much like a cat if he was honest with himself, but he gave a nervous smile and shrugged. None of his business. Mr Binks gestured onwards.

"Right this way, Jack. Just at the bottom of the old servant stairs through here."

Mr Binks pulled open the door at the end of the corridor and flicked the brass toggle light switch. The area lit up with the dull light of a low wattage bulb. There were no windows to let in natural light, making the area dim and gloomy. Mr Binks stepped to one side and pointed.

"That one, please, if you would, young Jack. Straight to the top of the stairs, please."

The object of Mr Bink's request was a small side table, tall, with a shiny black top the size of a large dinner plate. Not a table in Jack's mind, more something to stand a vase on; nobody was ever going to eat a meal off something this size. Jack moved over to the table and tapped the top lightly with his knuckles. The shiny black surface was stone, presumably marble or granite, grains of a lighter coloured stone flecking the black surface. Flexing his knees, Jack moved to lift the table with both hands. To his surprise, despite the stone top, the table was remarkably light, so light that he could balance it with one hand.

"Not as heavy as it looks, Mr Binks," said Jack. "Be easy to shift this for you."

"Thank you, Jack. While I appreciate that it's not so heavy, I do worry about my footing on the stairs with this stick."

"Not a problem," said Jack, lifting the table with both hands and heading towards the bottom of the stairs.

❀

FIVE MINUTES later and the job was done. At Mr Bink's direction, Jack had positioned the table underneath a window on the upper floor; the early evening sunlight glinting off the stone surface, causing the minerals to glitter.

"My thanks, young Jack," said Mr Binks. "Now, if you'll come with me, I have your payment downstairs as well as a drink for all your hard work."

"It's fine, Mr Binks; it wasn't a big job. No payment necessary." Jack smiled at Mr Binks.

"Oh, but I insist."

"It's really not necessary," said Jack.

Mr Bink's demeanour changed again, his pleasant smile disappearing. "We agreed on payment, Jack. You will receive this payment. Now, come with me." He turned and walked down a side corridor, stopping once to look back at Jack.

Jack sighed. '*Okay,*' he thought to himself. '*If he is so insistent, he can pay me. But then, I'm out of here; this place is odd.*' Shrugging again, Jack smiled at Mr Binks and said, "Okay, but really, a drink will be payment enough." He followed Mr Binks along the corridor, which emerged at the head of the elaborate main staircase.

Mr Binks glided down the stairs, not once leaning on his stick. Jack followed. At the bottom, Mr Binks took a right turn and marched over to a different door. "Young Jack, my wallet containing your payment is in the kitchen through here. Which I believe is fortunate for both of us, as the drink I promised you is here as well. Please follow." Mr Binks pushed through the door and into the room beyond, the door swinging shut behind him.

Jack pushed the door himself to find that the room beyond was indeed a kitchen and a brightly lit one at that; the early evening sun was streaming through the large bay window that took up one wall. Smaller windows were open above the bay window, a light breeze cooling the air. The area was spotlessly clean like the rest of the house, with stainless steel worktops and warm wood cabinets throughout. An old-fashioned oven dominated the top end of the kitchen, copper pans hanging above it. A small door, presumably the entry to a pantry, stood in the far corner.

"Wow, Mr Binks," marvelled Jack. "This place is huge. Do the residents use this kitchen? It's bigger than the school kitchens."

Mr Binks gave a wry smile and said, "Oh, no, Jack. This is for my private use only; the residents have their kitchen facilities within each apartment. I am afraid that the kitchen does not receive the use that it would benefit from nowadays. However, it is quite suitable for my limited needs. Now, please be seated."

Mr Binks gestured over to the central island in the kitchen, where two tall glasses were already set out. Two stools stood on opposite sides of the unit. Sliding onto the one facing Mr Binks, Jack watched him remove a tall jug of juice from the massive steel refrigerator on the back wall. Hobbling over to the island with his stick's aid, Mr Binks placed the juice down onto the surface and then, to Jack's surprise, followed it up by placing three separate ten-pound notes next to the jug.

"Your payment, young Jack."

"Oh, no, that's too much, Mr Binks. It was really very easy and not a problem. I can't accept that."

"You can, and you will, Jack. Humour an old man, please."

"I'll just take one; that'll be fine."

"No, Jack, please take all three."

"No, really I...."

Mr Binks bought his hand down on the surface top with an almighty bang. "You will take all of the payment Jack," he said forcefully. "As we agreed." He glared at Jack.

"Okay, if you insist," said Jack nervously, scooping the notes off the countertop and stuffing them into a trouser pocket. "It is too generous, though."

Mr Binks' face returned to its previous pleasant state. "Not at all, Jack, not at all. Now, please join me in a drink, and then be away with you."

Mr Binks poured from the jug into the two separate glasses and, pushing one over, gestured at Jack to drink. Jack picked up the glass of orange liquid and sniffed. It smelt good, a blend of mangoes and oranges, and the scent reminded Jack that he was actually very thirsty. Raising the glass to his lips, he took a large swallow; it tasted as good as the smell had promised. Jack drained half the glass in one go and gave a satisfied exhalation.

Mr Binks was watching Jack from the other stool, a look of suppressed glee on his face. His glass stood untouched before him, beaded with moisture. "Taste good, young Jack?" he asked.

"Yeth," said Jack, surprising himself at the lisping nature of his voice. He looked over at Mr Binks, who was grinning, and not in a pleasant way. "What ith it?"

"A simple glamour, young Jack," said Mr Binks. "Have another drink."

Jack looked down at the glass, but the liquid was no longer orange. It was a darkish purple and blue and seemed to swirl without agitation. Jack sniffed it again and smelt a strong copper smell, like pennies and tuppences saved in a jar. "No thankth, Mr Binkth," slurred Jack. "I'd better gow." He made to get to his feet, but his legs quivered like jelly and refused to obey his brain. Looking over at Mr Binks, he could see two versions of the old man, partially overlapping, shifting slightly.

"I think not, Jack," said Mr Binks, his face now darkening. "We have plans for you. Please, stay awhile."

Jack shook his head, and the images of Mr Binks solidified into one single image. He forced himself to focus on the old man while willing his legs to work again, a fluttering of panic starting in his stomach. Mr Binks stood from his stool, the cane falling unnoticed to the floor. Moving briskly over to the door at the other end of the kitchen, he pulled it open and clipped it onto a hook in the wall, propping it open. He gave a shrill whistle and then moved back over to the counter and Jack.

"Now, Jack. You are fortunate, indeed. You have been chosen to assist us in our works, which, shall we say, are not as progressed as the overseer would like. The harvest is slower than was anticipated for us here at Twillington, so we are looking for other ways to increase our yield. Those damn Fae are starting to avoid the place, you see, and gathering from them is not as profitable as was originally foretold. I am way behind." From the open door behind, a creaking sound came, distant but getting closer.

Jack blinked several times and shook his head again. The feeling was returning to his legs now, and the blurred edges of his vision were receding. He focused back on the old man and said, "What are you talking about?"

Mr Binks started slightly at the apparent awareness Jack was showing. He pushed his face close to Jack's and stared into his eyes; Jack's grogginess meant that he didn't flinch back, which seemed to satisfy the old man.

"We don't share the plan with lifers, Jack Crackley; it is none of your concern. We are hopeful that the older lifers just out of childhood can assist us where the Fae cannot. You will help us determine that. That is all you need to know."

Jack stared at Mr Binks in disbelief that the old man knew his full name and jumped slightly as the old man's face seemed to warp into something more monstrous. The face staring back at him was skull-like, almost ghostly but with large lips and a prominent fang jutting upwards from the lower jaw. A broad, flat nose with flared nostrils topped the lips, and wide staring eyes, reddened, stared back with a look of madness. Jack cringed backwards slightly, and the vision shifted back to Mr Binks' old man's face. Mr Binks noticed the cringe and loomed over Jack again.

"What is it, boy? What did you see?"

Jack understood that something was not right here; the old man had drugged him for no reason, and he was hallucinating. He had to get away from here as quickly as possible. Flexing his legs, Jack felt more feeling in them and decided to try again to see if they would support him. Grasping the edge of the island, he pushed himself upwards and onto his feet. His legs seemed to be working now as he stood upright, without too much swaying. Mr Binks recoiled from out of Jacks' face, a look of bewilderment painted onto his features.

"*Sit down*," he screeched, again banging his fist onto the work surface. He glanced towards the open door again and back to Jack.

Jack took a tentative step, and on determining that he could walk, put another shaky foot down in the direction of the door. "I'm sorry, Mr Binks, but I have to go. My mother will be worried." He took another step towards the door but was then distracted again by the creaking noise as it got closer and louder. Looking over at the open door in the corner, he was surprised to see a wooden handcart manoeuvre into the room, moving by itself. Jack shook his head and looked again. No, it wasn't moving; two small people were pushing it. The people looked short and squat, dressed in patchwork leather coveralls, with pug faces and little red hats. 'Goblins,' Jack thought, '*They look like goblins. What the hell?*' Their eyes were odd, though, as if blue smoke was swimming in them. They looked up at Jack from the corner of the room where they had entered and gave a small start to see Jack staring back at them. Jack blinked his eyes a few times, looked up, and the little people had gone.

'*Okay, that's it. Time to go,*' he thought and made for the safety of the foyer and the front door.

"*Stop!*" screamed Mr Binks, hobbling around the counter to Jack's side. Jack put on as much speed as he could and managed to avoid the old man's grasping hand that grabbed for the back of his jacket. A few stumbling steps got him clear of the old man with a clear run at the door.

"Damn your eyes – stop him, you idiots!" screeched Mr Binks, sweeping his hand in Jack's direction. Jack glanced over his shoulder to see the old man still coming but hampered by the stool that Jack had recently vacated. Jack got moving, his steps becoming more normal now, as the effects of whatever the crazy old man had given him wore off. A crash from behind him made him take another glance over his shoulder to see Mr Binks lying on the floor, his legs tangled in the stool. His face had a look of pure thunder as he stared up at Jack, and with a sudden flutter, as if someone had passed a hand in front of Jack's eyes, he could see the evil monster face again planted over the old man's; dark eyes staring at him with unadulterated malice.

Close behind the fallen old man were the two goblin things again, climbing over the sprawled figure, their eyes on Jack and surly expressions on their faces. The flutter came again, and they disappeared, the monster turning back to Mr Binks, who was snarling and kicking as he sought to escape the stool. Jack did not waste any time and dashed for the door; the wobbly feeling in his legs was almost gone.

Clearing the kitchen door, Jack burst into the lobby and yanked the door shut behind him, cutting Mr Binks off in mid-curse. Favouring his right leg slightly, he limped towards the front door as fast as he could, praying that it would be unlocked or at least able to be opened from this side. If it wasn't, Jack decided that he'd head for the stairs and try for the residents' apartments; one of those must surely have a key? Mr Binks wasn't so fast on the stairs based on previous experience, and there was a good chance that Jack would be able to outrun him, maybe even find a window that he could get out of if the residents didn't come through for him.

Jack reached the front door and tried the handle. It turned

okay, but despite pulling on it, it would not open. Glancing up and down, Jack could see no visible bolts or other locking mechanisms, apart from a small security chain that linked across the doorjamb. *'Damn,'* he thought, *'Stairs it is then.'* As he turned to the stairs and let go of the door, it moved slightly. Jack shook his head; he had been pulling the door to get out when, oddly, for a front door, it opened outwards. He was reaching for the chain to disconnect it when the kitchen door flung open with a bang.

Jack spun around to see Mr Binks standing there, utter outrage on his face. He dashed into the room towards Jack, seemingly unhindered even though he no longer had his cane with him. The flutter across Jack's vision came again, and he saw the monster face, as well as the two goblins, who were ahead of Mr Binks and racing in his direction, little arms pumping fast at a full sprint. The flutter again, and Mr Binks alone was coming fast.

Fumbling behind him, Jack managed to get the chain out of the catch with a quick flick of his wrist. He grabbed the handle and pushed the door open, the early evening sunshine flooding the lobby; his bike at the end of the porch exactly where he had left it. Jack stepped over the threshold to freedom at a brief jog and managed to get three steps before something barrelled into the back of his knees, flinging him forward with arms outstretched as if he was trying to fly. He crashed to the floor face first; the air knocked from his lungs with a jolt as he hit the hard tile of the porch. His head landed on an outstretched arm, giving it another bang to go with the one from earlier. The flutter came again, and Jack looked over his shoulder to see that the two goblin things had tackled him and were clinging hard to his legs, arms wrapped firmly around each limb, preventing him from bending his knees. Gasping for breath, Jack rolled over hard, twisting his whole body to land on his back, flipping his two captors over at the same time so that they lay beneath his legs. Arching backwards to lift his backside off the floor, Jack raised both legs into the air like he was trying to flip to his feet and then slammed both down as hard as he could manage. There was a pair of shrieking gasps as the weight of his legs smashed both of the things into the tiles, the one on the right letting go and giving out a low moan as it lay prone, holding the small of its back with both hands.

Jack scooted backwards on his bottom away from the prone creature, pistoning with his now freed right leg to get some space. Looking at the one holding his left leg, shaking its head to clear it, he pulled back and kicked it as hard as he could on the shoulder. The creature gave a loud shriek and let go, rolling around on the floor as it clutched the top of its arm and sobbed with pain. The one holding its back was now hauling itself to its feet, a terrible expression on its face as it glared at Jack. As Jack stared at it in fear, a figure appeared in the open doorway, and there stood Mr Binks, a look of absolute fury on his face.

With his attention focused on the old man, Jack did not see the first creature as it bared sharp little teeth and came for him at a loping run, grasping hands with crooked nails outstretched and aiming for his face. It leapt over Jack's outstretched feet, giving a strangled battle cry as it flew through the air. The noise snapped Jack's attention back to the immediate threat, and he shot out his arm, grabbing the little creature in mid-flight by the collar of its coverall. Continuing its momentum, he swung his arm backwards and slung it over his head as hard as he could. The thing screamed in terror as it streaked through the air, arms and legs flailing, before disappearing over the end of the porch near Jack's bike.

"What...?" spat Mr Binks, staring in disbelief at Jack. "You can see...."

Jack missed the rest as his attention focused on the second creature that was coming at him now in a crouch, its hand clutching its shoulder, vicious teeth bared in its snarling mouth.

It scuttled past Jack's legs, reaching out with its short arms towards Jack's face. Jack shoved back again with both legs, putting some distance between himself and the creature and closer to his bike. He pushed again, coming level with the bike, and was reaching out a hand to pull himself up when a pair of small arms circled his throat, grabbing him from behind and yanking him back down towards the floor again. The first creature howled in triumph, and the second creature launched from its crouch to land on Jacks' chest, where it started to pummel Jack's face with its nobbly fists. Jack turned his head to one side to avoid the blows, but they rained down on his cheek and chin, not overpowering but certainly not pleasant. Jack thrashed about, his hands trying to dislodge the arms wrapped around his neck and, at the same time, trying to fend off the second creature's furious attack on his tender face.

While Jack struggled, he became conscious of the shadow falling over him, heralding Mr Binks' arrival into the fray. The old man squatted down over Jack, pinning his thighs down with his weight and leaning a hand onto Jack's chest, pressing him down onto the cold stone tiles.

"Enough," he commanded the second creature, who immediately ceased its attack on Jack and instead used both hands to turn Jack's head, so it was facing up towards Mr Binks as he loomed over Jack.

"You little fool," snarled the old man. "This would have gone much better for you inside, but no matter. We can do this here just as well; nobody will see."

Jack thrashed again, pushing with his heels to try to get some leverage. "Let me go, you crazy old..."

"Ssshhhh, ssshhhhh, young Jack. This will not take a moment, and then we can move back inside. We need to discuss you, I believe. But first a little business; you have entirely too much pep in you."

"Look, just let me go; I won't tell anyone...."

"*Silence,*" screamed Mr Binks directly into Jack's face, flecks of spittle landing, the spray warm and unpleasant. The creatures clutching Jack giggled nervously.

"Yes, we need to have a discussion, and I dare say that it won't be enjoyable. For you, at least. I want you to start thinking about explaining yourself to me. An explanation about how strickler venom, which lifers cannot resist, did not affect you over much. And how you can see my companions here." Mr Binks swallowed and then suddenly screamed again into Jack's face, "*Who sent you, boy?*"

"I don't know what you're talking about," croaked Jack, creature one's arms restricting his throat. "You're insane."

"Oh, no, no, no, no, no, young Jack. I am far from that. Not insane, but certainly mad at the circumstances. Hold him," he suddenly barked at the creatures. The grip on Jack tightened even more; the strength of the little creatures far beyond what their size belied.

"And now," whispered Mr Binks, his face close to Jack's, breath smelling sour, "Let's get you a little more compliant before we go back in. Removing a few grackles should make you more amenable, I should think." He shuffled further up Jack's torso, fumbling in his pocket. With a smile, he pulled out a black tube about the size of a toilet roll inner. It was oily and greasy looking, dark brown bordering on black. Placing a further restraining hand onto Jack's chest, he leaned over and pressed the end of the tube to Jack's forehead.

Jack tried to struggle and shake his head to dislodge the tube, but the creatures held him firm. Mr Binks grinned down at Jack as he pressed the tube down firmly. At first, Jack felt a little suck on his head as the tube settled down. Then nothing, just the unpleasant digging into the skin of the edge of the tube. He continued to struggle to free himself. Mr Binks' face took on a look of puzzlement at the apparent lack of effect on Jack. He removed the tube and looked into it, shaking it slightly. He then placed it back onto Jack's head again, grinding it painfully back into place. This time, Jack felt nothing other than the painful pressure caused by the tube and Mr Binks' weight bearing down on him.

Jack let the pressure build, the old man putting two hands onto the tube to press it down harder, the look of puzzlement still on his face. As the old man pushed down, with a sharp twist of his neck, Jack unbalanced the old man, causing Mr Binks to topple forward. At the same time, he reached out with his right arm, groping for the bike, for something, anything, that he could use to free himself. The two creatures wriggled and tried to tighten their grasp on Jack as his questing hand touched the pedal, then the frame, and finally the bike pump. Jack yanked it free from its clip and jabbed it towards the creature on his chest like a bayonet. The creature raised its hands to defend itself, leaving Jack's head unheld. Jack jabbed the bike pump as hard as he could at the creature's face, at the same time lifting his head. Catching the first creature a glancing blow to the face, it squealed in pain, and it clutched at its head. While it was distracted, Jack fired his head back onto the second creature clutching him from behind. Pain shot through Jack from the bump on the back of his head, but the satisfying crunch from the creature's face more than made up for it. It croaked out a scream, letting go of Jack's throat as it clutched at its mangled nose.

Jack wasted no time. Sitting up, he pulled the heavy D-Lock from the frame of his bike. It was a good one, a birthday present, very heavy and designed to ensure that nobody would be able to steal his bike. He swung it like a sword, the curved part a broad blade, and connected with creature one's already wounded shoulder. The D-Lock's weight knocked the creature into the air, where it flew a short distance before connecting with the porch railing. It collided head-first, slumping down to the ground, its eyes closed. The flutter again, and the creature winked out of Jack's vision.

Mr Binks had managed in this time to get his hands underneath himself, one still clutching the black tube. "How dare..." he began before the D-Lock finished its second arc through the air into his ribs with a satisfying thud. "OOohhhhhfffff," Mr Binks exhaled a colossal gasp of pain as the air was driven from his lungs by Jack's improvised weapon. Jack hit him again in the same place for good measure, prompting the elderly lunatic to curl into a foetal position, whimpering as he did so.

Jack pulled himself to his feet and looped the D-Lock through his arm and onto his shoulder; he just wanted to get away now and didn't want to waste time stashing it back into its holder. He looked around for the second creature, but there was no sign; it had vanished. Jack shook his head to clear it.

"*I'm going to the police,*" he yelled to Mr Binks. "*You tried to drug me and assaulted me with god knows what. Moreover, I have the bruises to prove it. You bloody maniac!*"

Mr Binks uncurled and looked up at Jack. He smiled, and with that came the flutter again, the monstrous face appearing. Jack recoiled in horror at the face; the look of insane rage on it was enough to scare the most hardened person. Jack grabbed his bike.

"There will be others I can use, Jack Crackley," snarled Mr Binks. "But I cannot permit you to interfere. I will put you in the garden with the other useless ones; you can feed *him* if you won't help *us*. I will have use of you yet." With that, he vaulted to his feet as if someone had yanked him up, a puppet on its strings.

Jack recoiled and then got going at a run, pushing his bike down the drive. As he got some speed up, he vaulted one leg over and started pumping the pedals. Chancing a look back over his shoulder, he was shocked to see the monstrous form running at speed, its hands outstretched and about a metre behind, closing. Jack stood up on his pedals and pumped them for his life, the bike picking up speed as the slope of the drive increased and gave him a slight lead.

As the driveway ended, Jack was thankful to see that the gates were still open. The road outside was not usually busy, but he would have to time this just right to get out and clear. He chanced another glance over his shoulder to see the monstrous figure of Mr Binks falling back as Jack outpaced him. Jack let out a sigh of relief and headed for the gate at a good clip. Squeezing his brakes as he approached the threshold, he turned the handlebars to the right and shot out of the gate like a bullet and onto the pavement.

Unfortunately, a few yards down the hill was a young woman, talking loudly into a phone as she shoved a pushchair in front of her. Jack registered her a split second after exiting the driveway and jerked his handlebars over to the left. Leaping off the pavement at speed into the road, he narrowly missed the young mum. Turning to the road, he heard the blare of a horn as a car headed directly towards him. He tried to turn right again and almost made it, but his luck deserted him this time. The car hit his back wheel at close to thirty miles an hour, flipping both the bike and rider into the air. Jack saw the figure of Mr Binks standing at the gates, a look of glee on his deranged face as he watched the boy twist through the air; the goblin stood next to him, gesturing rapid hand motions in his direction. The ground came up to meet him, and with a tremendous crash that shook him to the core, everything went black.

Mr Binks stared at the twisted bicycle as its rear-wheel clicked to a stop. He nodded to the shocked young mother, turned on his heel and closed the gates behind him.

CHAPTER 4

*D*rifting. Drifting. Lights overhead; square lights -- too
bright, too bright, they burn. Dark again; the dark was
calm; the dark was comforting. Stay in the dark.

*A memory. A face looking down at him. A man's face, a father's
face, kind and smiling. Softness enveloping him. The father's face
replaced. Another face, a kind face. An odd face. Long ears and long
nose but comforting. Smiling down at him. Little hands are grasping
for the face, the face laughing. The face gone. Darkness. Comfort.*

Skip.

*A garden. A ball. The father again, kicking the ball to him. Others,
small others, laughing and floating the ball to him. Dancing sparkles
in the air and the ball with its own life. All of them floating, laughing,
blue sparkles. Fluttering wings and butterflies.*

Skip.

*The lovely, odd face again looking at him, smiling, holding cakes.
Taking the cakes, the face's owner was too fat; they all laughed. The
odd face looking sad and then smiling. Tracing golden patterns in the
air that glittered like sunshine. Holding his hand.*

Skip.

Sitting up in bed. Dark. The monster in the room at the end of the bed. Teeth and black hands. Screaming. The nice odd one hitting the monster with a stubby thick stick. The father is throwing the monster out, the monster sad. The monster leaving, father holding him close as he sobbed.

Darkness. Comforting.

The garden. Running up the garden, the nice odd one's fat hand pulling him, fast. Behind him crackles and flashes; fireworks. The nice odd one's face scared. The father gesturing them to run, to run. Faster. Run faster. Darkness.

The father, the mother. Loud talking, the mother crying. The nice odd one is holding him close. Doors banging. Tears. Fade.

Bright lights above. Sounds. Beeping sounds repetitive. Beep. Beep. Beep. A presence, a touch on his hand. Harsh smells, chemical smells. Darkness.

JACK LET OUT a huge gasp and sat up in one quick motion. Everything was black, dark; he couldn't see. Blind. He grabbed his face and felt cloth; his eyes were covered, and he could feel plastic tubes on his face.

"Jack?" A familiar voice. "Jack, thank god you're awake. We've all been so worried."

"Mum, is that you?" croaked Jack. "I can't see. Why can't I see?"

"Easy, baby, easy. It's just a bandage." Jack felt a hand clutch his own.

"A bandage?"

"Yes, Jack. Your whole head is covered. You were in an accident."

"An accident?"

"Oh god, you don't remember? The doctors said there might be some damage, but, oh my god. My poor baby. I'll ring for the nurses, for the doctor." Jack could hear his mum's panicked breathing, hard and fast as she fumbled for something, her hand squeezing his tight.

"Mum, it's okay. I remember. I got hit by a car at the top of Brierly Hill. After…" But it was gone, the thoughts leading up to the accident.

The voice came again. "Thank goodness, you do remember. Now, do you remember what day it is?"

"It's Monday, mum."

"No. No, it's not; it's Friday. Oh my god, my baby has brain damage! Nurse. Nurse. *Nuuuurrrsssseee!*"

"Mum, calm down, I can remember…."

Jack was interrupted by the scraping sound of a door opening, and a light flowery smell filled his nostrils.

"Nurse, Nurse, he's awake, but he can't remember what day it is." Jack's mum squeezed his hand again, painfully

A female voice confidently spoke. "Now, now. Let us not be too hasty. Hello, Jack. My name is Denise; it's nice to have you back with us in the land of the living."

"Hi, Denise. I'm okay, honestly. My head and ribs ache, but I don't feel so bad."

"Well, we'll be the judge of that in due course. When you were brought in, your X-rays showed significant swelling and contusions, so we need to be sure. The doctor will be along in a few moments. While we're waiting, do you feel up to a few questions; kind of get a head start on things?"

"Sure," said Jack. "But could I have a drink first? My throat feels like it's on fire."

"Of course," said Denise. Jack heard the sound of water being poured and then felt the welcome coldness of a glass being pressed into his hand.

"There's a straw there for you," said Denise. "Try and sip to start with; if you gulp it down, it will just come straight back up."

Jack sipped the water slowly as instructed, the coldness

soothing his throat. With a gurgle, the glass was soon empty, and he held it out so that an unseen hand could remove it.

"No more for now," said Denise. "Let that settle. You can have another glass once we've finished talking."

Jack sat back in the bed and relaxed. He gave both thumbs up to his unseen audience.

"Okay then, Jack. I just want to test you to see if there is any noticeable cognitive damage. We will CT scan you later and probably conduct an MRI as well. However, for now, a couple of questions should give us a good idea. Ready?"

"Sure," said Jack. "Fire away."

"Okay. What day do you think it is?"

"Monday," said Jack. "But Mum said it's Friday."

"Well, as you've been asleep for close to four days now, I guess we can excuse that one. It is Friday, but you had your accident on Monday."

"Really?" said Jack. "I've been asleep for four days?"

"Yes," said Denise. "Induced coma; you received a nasty bang to the head, as well as some other lumps and bumps. Standard practice for brain injuries for people in the condition you are in. It appears that your bike cushioned your fall; you can call that lucky, or it would have been a lot worse."

"My bike?"

Jack's mum interjected, "Don't you worry about that now; we can get you a new bike. The main thing is to get you mended."

"But what about my papers and the Bull?"

"I've spoken to both Mr Singh at the shop and John at the Bull. They both wish you well and told me to tell you not to worry. Your jobs are safe and ready for you when you are."

"Well," said Denise interrupting, "I think that your cognitive abilities seem to be fine, based on that little conversation. Let's see how your brain is working. Which foot am I squeezing?"

Jack felt a gentle pressure on his right foot through the sheets.

"Right,"

"Good. Now, how many times did I tap your foot?"

Jack felt three light taps

"Three."

"Excellent. Now, hold out your right hand." Jack did as he was told.

"We can't test your vision just yet because of the bandages, but can you tell me how many fingers I am holding up?"

Jack clutched at the air until he found a hand. Fumbling, he counted two fingers outstretched.

"Two."

"Okay, all seems to be working on the sense of touch as well; no damage that I can ascertain."

They were again interrupted by the door opening, and another presence came into the room.

"Hello, Jack. I'm Dr Osmir. Nice to see you awake at last; how are you feeling?"

"Not too bad, Doctor; a little achy."

"That's to be expected, Jack. Any dizziness or feeling sick?"

"No, doctor."

"Jack's passed the initial cognition tests, Dr Osmir," said Denise.

"Good lad. We need to check you over with some of the equipment, but you didn't crack your noggin open too much. If the swelling on your brain has gone down, we can get that bandage off and have a look at your peepers, make sure everything's okay. However, you did have quite a knock, so I would like to keep you in for a bit longer; make sure there is nothing sinister. Assuming the tests come back okay, we can then look at getting you out of here."

"So soon, Doctor?" said Jack's mum.

"Sure, Mrs Crackley," said Dr Osmir. "He'll be better off

recuperating at home if the signs are all good. We won't throw him out until we're sure he's up to it, though." Jack heard humour in his voice as he patted Jack's leg through the sheet.

Jack laughed a little at the joke, which started him off coughing. The doctor patted him again.

"Don't worry, Jack; we had to ventilate you for a couple of days. Any soreness in your throat will soon wear off."

"Okay, thanks," said Jack.

"Now, get some more rest. Denise here will organise some further screening tests for you, if that's okay, Denise?"

"No problems," said Denise. "I'll go and make a start right now."

"Mrs Crackley, you are welcome to stay as long as you like, but I would like Jack to get some more rest," advised Dr Osmir. "He may have been asleep for days, but it's not proper sleep. I am satisfied he is as well as he can be, so a nap won't hurt him. Anyhow, our miracles of modern technology will let us know if there are any other problems." He gestured to the various bits of kit around Jack's bed.

"I'll stay for a bit longer," said Jack's mum. "I'm just so pleased he's back with us. And please, call me Sammy."

"No problems at all, Sammy."

Denise and Dr Osmir made their farewells and left the room. Jack felt his mum take his hand and squeeze it.

"We'll get you right, my lovely. I promise you."

THE REST of the day passed quickly for Jack. Not being able to see made it a little surreal, as he was wheeled around the hospital for various tests under the watchful eye of his mother. Everyone was very reassuring and incredibly kind as he couldn't see them. Back in his room, he was served a meal that his mum helped him to eat. He was surprised at his appetite and wolfed down everything he could, his mum guiding his hand and spoon.

"Whoa, Jack, slow down!" she exclaimed at one point. "Is hospital food that good?"

"Delicious mum, all the better that I can't see it. Everything's a surprise!"

"I think you're going to be fine," laughed Sammy, the relief evident in her voice.

"I don't feel too bad, mum."

"What happened Jack? Why were you up at that end of town?"

"I was helping the old man who lives there; he asked me to come and help him move a table. We did that, and then…."

"What, Jack?"

"I don't know; it's all a blur. I don't remember that part or leaving. Or getting hit by that car. Is the driver alright?"

"We don't know; he didn't stop. A lady called it in; she saw the whole thing. There was no old man, though; he must have let you out and shut the gates. The police questioned him, and he was very shocked. He sends his best wishes to you for a speedy recovery."

That didn't feel right to Jack, but he didn't question it; he was too tired and wrung out. He sat chatting with his mum as day turned into evening, and he started to nod. Around him, the sounds of the hospital had become steadily more subdued as people settled for the night.

"Jack, I'm going to go now," said Sammy. "I'll be back first thing, though."

"What time is it, Mum?"

"Nine o'clock."

"Okay," said Jack blearily. "I'll see you tomorrow."

He felt a gentle pressure on the top of his head as his mum kissed him.

"See you in the morning, lovely boy," Sammy whispered.

Jack smiled sleepily as she left.

JACK AWOKE to the sounds of muttering and scraping, a barely concealed conversation. He came awake suddenly, no yawning or gentle drifting back to consciousness. It was odd; one moment he was asleep, the next wide awake, his heart beating quickly. He fumbled around, a little confused by the complete darkness, before remembering that the bandages still covered his eyes.

Jack strained his ears to listen for whatever had woken him and was rewarded with the sounds of muttering again; the words muted but definitely a conversation. His surroundings were surprisingly quiet, but without a watch, the time escaped him. There was no traffic noise from outside of the general hospital noise he had grown used to, so Jack assumed that it must still be nighttime.

Listening again, the voices became more lucid. Two different people, talking to each other in quiet tones; they sounded high pitched and excitable. Moreover, they were in the room with him. Sitting up, Jack ventured a "Hello?"

The voices stopped instantly.

"Hello, who is that, please?" Jack repeated.

The voices whispered to each other, chattering but low.

"*Hello!*" demanded Jack. "I can hear you talking."

"You can hear us?" an enquiring high-pitched voice suddenly said, clearly.

"Yes. Who is it, please?"

"He can hear us!" the second voice exclaimed. "You there? Who are you?"

Jack thought that this was decisively odd. "I asked first," he said.

"How can he hear us?" said the first voice. "We haven't revealed."

"I have no idea," said the second voice. Jack felt pressure on his legs as if someone was leaning on him.

"Can you see us?" came the second voice, much closer this time.

"No, of course I can't," said Jack. "Look at my eyes."

There came a titter. "Of course, my apologies. But could you see us?"

Jack was more than a little puzzled now. "Of course, there's nothing wrong with my eyesight. Well, there was nothing wrong with it, but now I don't know...." He trailed off.

"Yes, yes, but could you *really* see us?" the second voice asked, sounding a little troubled.

"If there's nothing wrong with my eyes, then yes, I guess so. I don't wear glasses or anything."

"But how?" came the first voice. "If he can hear us, then he can probably see us. And that's not allowed."

"Look," said Jack, "I don't really understand what you are saying here. I can hear you talking, and you are in my room. Who are you and what are you doing here?"

"Oh, just passing through," said the second voice airily. "But this is very interesting. We've never had a lifer talk to us before without our permission!"

"Yes," said the first voice. "It is forbidden."

"What?" said Jack. "What's a lifer? I've heard that before, but...anyway, why can't you talk to me? Is this some silly hospital rule or something? Because I can talk to whoever I choose, and everyone here is really nice, so why would I not be allowed to talk to you?"

"You talk away, little lifer. As to your question, to help the lifers is why we come here. To ease them and their pain where we can," said the second voice.

Jack felt sure it was some of the night staff playing silly games with him.

"So, you're nurses then? Livening up the night shift a bit by having some fun with the blind boy?"

"Of course not," snapped the second voice. "We're here to assist someone who deserves our help. Not you, of course, although you are unusual."

"Maybe we should come back later?" said the first voice. "See if he can hear us then?"

"Maybe, maybe..." said the second voice thoughtfully. "Okay, we shall see. Farewell for now."

There was a snap, and with that, the voices just stopped. Jack strained to hear them leave, but there was no scrape of the door. His inner senses told him that they were gone and no longer in the room with him.

Jack felt a shiver down his spine. The whole conversation had been very odd when he thought about it, and the fact that it just stopped with no conclusion made Jack a little uncomfortable. Still, if they were coming back later, then he would try to get some more answers.

Jack tossed and turned for the next twenty minutes or so before settling back into a welcome doze as sleep once again embraced him.

JACK AWOKE AGAIN MUCH LATER, this time by the sound of someone bustling about near his bed. His awakening this time was not so sudden, more a drifting back up towards consciousness. "Hello?" he muttered fuzzily.

"Good morning," a cheerful female voice came back. "I'm sorry, did I wake you? I was just checking these machines were behaving themselves; they've got a mind of their own if you don't watch them."

"No, all good," said Jack. "What time is it?"

"Six-thirty in the wonderful morning," came the voice. "How are you feeling? Fancy some breakfast?"

"I'd like a drink if that's possible?"

"Sure, no problems." The sound of water pouring again, and then the glass was pushed into his hand.

"How did you sleep?" the female voice asked.

"Okay, apart from those nurses who woke me up in the early hours."

"Oh, that's not on," said the female voice. "Who was it?"

"I don't know," said Jack," A couple of male nurses, messing about and being cryptic."

"Are you sure?" the female voice asked, sounding puzzled. "Male nurses?"

"Yes; two of them, in here talking. I didn't make out what they were saying at first, but I did speak to them. Didn't get their names; they said that it was forbidden for them to talk to me."

"You must have been dreaming," said the voice, giving a little laugh.

"No, I definitely spoke to them."

"Jack, mate, there are no male nurses on the rota until Monday. Just us girls. Moreover, this is a sealed unit, so there are no casual visitors, especially not at night. I've been at the nurse's station for most of the night apart from my rounds, and no-ones been in, not even the porters. Been dead quiet all night."

"But they were here...."

"Jack, you've had a bang to the head and all kinds of medicine since they bought you in. Last night was the first proper sleep you've had. I'd be surprised if you didn't dream about something weird."

"I suppose, but it all seemed so real."

"Those high strength meds can really mess with you. Still,

looking at these notes, you won't be needing them much longer. Dr Osmir seems to think that you are pretty much good to go. All looking good, matey!"

"Good. It is nice here, but I would like to go home. I'm sure that others could make better use of this bed. I just want to get these bandages off; check my eyes are okay."

"Later today, looking at this. If you're clear, and yesterday's results seem to show that you are, then you're off the hook and homeward bound."

"That'd be great."

"Right then. I'll go and sort you out some breakfast, get you ready for when everyone's in and ready to start poking at you."

"Thanks...sorry, I didn't get your name."

"It's Cass, mate. Cass Gee."

"Well, thanks, Cass, that'd be great. I'm starving again."

"No worries. Now, do you need me to help you into the bathroom before I go?"

"Yes, if you don't mind."

"C'mon then, buddy. Let's get you sorted."

JACK SAT IN A COMFORTABLE CHAIR, his hand clutched in a ferocious grip by his mum. They were awaiting Dr Osmir to put in an appearance with hopefully good news about being able to leave. Jack was conscious of some whispering going on, but his mum didn't seem to be too bothered about it, instead keeping up a diatribe about some ladies at her work who were apparently organising something or other. It was quite a relief to Jack when he heard the door go, and someone entered the room.

"Hello, Jack," came the familiar voice of Dr Osmir. "How are you today?"

"I feel fine, Doctor, although I can't wait to get this bandage off."

"Well, the good news is that it can come off. Your scans have come back clear, and there doesn't appear to be any lasting damage. You must have a thick head."

"He gets that from me," said Jack's mum with a chuckle.

"Ha," Dr Osmir laughed. "Okay then, Jack. Shall we have a look at those eyes of yours then?"

"Yes, please. This bandage is quite itchy."

Jack felt deft hands moving over his head, and then the pressure of the bandages started to lessen as Dr Osmir unwound it. Jack could sense light as they were slowly removed from his head until, with a final twist, the last of them came loose.

Jack blinked a few times to clear the gum from his eyes, and while he could perceive a certain lightness back in his vision, he couldn't see.

"How is it?" asked Dr Osmir

"Erm, I can't see."

"Blink a few times; see if that clears it?"

Jack blinked and rubbed his eyes with the back of his hand. No difference.

"This is very odd," said Dr Osmir. "There's no reason why your vision shouldn't have come back. There is no residual damage present in the scans; if anything, it's like the accident didn't happen based on what we can see from yesterday's investigations. We better have a closer look."

Jack felt a gentle hand tip his head back, and the light got brighter, moving from one eye to the other.

"What can you see?" asked Dr Osmir.

"It is lighter than it was. When you were checking me then, the light got brighter in each eye."

"Yes, that would be the light on my ophthalmoscope. It's odd; there seems to be no real problem with the eyes that I can see; they're clear, and the pupils are contracting."

"Oh my God, my baby's blind," gasped Jacks' mum, crushing his hand again.

"I don't think so, Mrs Crackley," said Dr Osmir. "The fact that Jack can tell the difference between light intensity would indicate that he's got some vision. I think that it should all come back in time."

Jack was relieved, some of his tension draining away. "How long, Doctor?"

"Can't say for sure. I think that what we will do is give you some medicated eye drops to put in and send you home. We can make an appointment for you to come back in in a couple of days if things have not improved. But I'm confident that they will have, and you'll be back to normal in a week or so, and your family doctor can take over."

"Oh," Jack heard his mum say. "A week or so?"

"Don't worry, Mum, I'll be fine on my own," said Jack.

"I'm afraid I don't understand, Mrs Crackley?" said Dr Osmir.

"Please call me Sammy; everyone does. And, well, things are a little 'hand to mouth.' If I have to take a week off work, it will make things very difficult. I will, of course, put Jack first, that goes without saying, but I don't know how we'll cope."

"Are there any friends or relatives that can help you out with Jack? Be around while you're out at work?"

"Not really," said Sammy. "My few friends all work themselves, and we have no close relatives. And I have no one really; my parents aren't with us anymore, and I have no brothers or sisters."

"What about Jack's dad, if you don't mind me asking?"

"He died when Jack was four, and he had no relations either. Apart from…"

Sammy tailed off, thoughtfully.

"Great Aunt Elsie?" said Jack. He'd only met the old lady a couple of times, but she never forgot a birthday or Christmas, sending a crisp five-pound note each time with the card.

"I don't know if we should ask," Sammy replied. "I've not

seen her properly for at least five years, and it's a little rude to ask out of the blue. We do speak on the phone, but..."

"Nothing ventured," said Dr Osmir. "We can't really keep Jack in, to be honest, although I'm happy to try and swing it if it will help?"

Sammy was deep in thought. "I suppose I could try her, given the circumstances," she finally said. "She is always asking after Jack, and if I explain, she may be able to find some time to help us. She is retired."

"Do you want to try her now?" said Dr Osmir, gesturing to the phone on his desk. "If she isn't available, then we can look at perhaps putting Jack on one of the wards as an option. Although I do feel that he would be better off out of here and in his own environment."

Sammy pulled out her mobile. "It's fine; I've got some credit," she said. "Will you excuse me?"

With that, she left the room, and Jack could hear her muted tones from the corridor.

"You're doing remarkably well for someone who was asleep for four days," said Dr Osmir.

"I feel fine, apart from the eyesight," said Jack.

"I've never seen anything like it in twenty years of practice. I'd expect you to be here for at least another week."

"Just lucky, I guess; must have landed right. And like you said, I have a thick head!"

Dr Osmir laughed. "Just promise me that if you have any symptoms, and I mean any, you go straight to a doctor. Back here if they can't see you."

"Sure," said Jack.

They were interrupted by the sound of the door opening, and Jack's mum came in.

"She said yes," she said excitedly. "She's going to get the train down this afternoon and be with us this evening. Sooner, if she can. Bless Elsie."

"That's great," said Dr Osmir. "Okay then, let's start the discharge procedures. It can take a little while, but we should have finished everything up and you back home in time for your Auntie Elsie's arrival."

~

DURING JACK'S time in the hospital, Mr Binks received a visitor at Twillington House. The visitor in question was not anticipated nor very welcome. The visitor came with questions.

"The success of your so-called experiment?"

"I am afraid that we did not get the chance to try it," said Mr Binks.

"Why? You assured us that you could obtain a suitable lifer of age to work on."

"I did, I did, but there were complications."

"Complications?"

"Yes. I procured the teenage boy, as was agreed. I got him here on false pretences, nobody knew he was coming, and we were all set to work."

"And?"

Mr Binks trembled. "And the strickler venom didn't work."

"*What?*" screamed the visitor. "Impossible! Lifers succumb to strickler venom. They have no protection against it."

"It's true, it's true," cowered Mr Binks. "Lograal and Gnux saw everything."

"Getting Redcaps to lie for you is unlikely to spare you her wrath," the visitor said, his voice low and full of malice.

"It's true. And something else…."

"What else, you idiot?"

"The boy could see Lograal and Gnux. And I think he could see me. Not this cursed flesh, but me. Myself; how I should be."

"You go too far with your falsehoods," said the visitor. "Lifers cannot see Fae folk without the reveal."

"But he could, he could. I swear it. Please, let your damned servants confirm it," snivelled Mr Binks. *"Lograal, Gnux, come here,"* he bellowed.

The two Redcaps came out from behind the door that they had been listening behind. Both shivered with fear; the visitor's reputation preceded him. The visitor stared at them.

"Devil!" he snarled, pointing at Gnux. "Your face. What happened?"

"Please m'lud, the boy. He beat me," trembled Gnux.

"And me, m'lud," stuttered Lograal. "Look."

He pulled his shirt up to show massive bruising across his chest and ribs.

The visitor stared at Mr Binks. "When did you reveal yourselves?"

"We did not."

"I do not believe you. Lifers cannot see the devils without the reveal; it is natural law. I will tell you what happened here." The visitor's voice was dangerously low. "You decided to terrify him. Helps to extract more grackles. To do this, you revealed to him, to scare, to bewilder."

"I swear we didn't; I swear it," grovelled Mr Binks, the Redcaps cowering behind him.

"Lies. Falsehoods and lies," said the visitor silkily. "I knew that you were not to be trusted on this matter. Your harvests are incomplete, and you surround yourself with these old lifers who are poor in what we require. I will report to my mother; see how she deems fit to reward you for this incompetence."

"Plleeeasssse, Dr Cracklock, please," shrieked Mr Binks and the Redcaps in chorus.

"Enough." Dr Cracklock turned from them and headed towards the pantry door.

Mr Binks had begun to sob. "But he couldn't see us all the time," he wailed.

Dr Cracklock stopped. "What did you say?"

"He couldn't see us all the time. It was strange. Like he could, then he'd blink and shake his head, and we'd get him, and then he could see us again and…" blubbered Gnux.

Dr Cracklock was silent for a moment. And then, to himself: "Surely not…it cannot be, not now?"

He reeled back to face the cowering trio.

"The boy. How did you find him?"

"He delivers newspapers to the house."

"And he presumably hasn't been back since you allowed him to escape?"

"No," snivelled Mr Binks. "He was hit by a car outside. If it didn't kill him, I'd be surprised. I had Gnux glamour him and the witness both to forget everything. He was taken away by ambulance."

"The boy's name?" demanded Dr Cracklock.

"Crackley. Jack Crackley."

"Crackley, Crackley… Coincidence? Maybe not. I will investigate further. As will you. Find him but do not approach him. I need to see this boy who apparently can see devils without invitation."

The stranger walked to the pantry door and pulled out a quill. Turning back, he stared at the trio.

"And Binks. You had better be correct on this matter, or your others will pay the price. I await your findings. And be quick."

JACK MANAGED to leave the hospital in relatively good order, in only three hours. Clutching Sammy's arm, he'd been led into a taxi, which had dropped them off at home. Once they got in, Jack took a walk through the house, first of all holding Sammy and then by himself. Anything potentially damageable to either itself or Jack had been moved out of the way, meaning that Jack had a clear run around the ground floor. Fortunately, the house was not large, a small mid-terraced, so there wasn't much to navigate. They were both confident that Jack could get himself around while his eyesight improved, including the stairs to the two bedrooms and bathroom.

As he settled into an armchair, feeling more than a little worn out, the doorbell chimed. Jack got to his feet, but Sammy called from upstairs, "I'll get it." Jack sat back down, wondering who it could be; it was too early for Great Aunt Elsie.

"Alright, mate?" said a voice.

"It's Jimmy, Jack," said Sammy.

"Alright, mate. Mum, how do you know Jimmy?"

"Jimmy's been a regular visitor here over the last few days; he couldn't come to the hospital but has been very concerned; 'round here every night after news. Why haven't you brought Jimmy over before Jack?"

"We didn't really know each other until last week, Mum."

"Yes, and then Jack was kind enough to let me whip him badly on Command and Conquer at lunch, and I was hoping to give him the chance to salvage a little bit of pride that evening. But he decided that kissing the pavement was preferable to my company, so..."

Jack laughed. "It was me who whipped you, as I recall."

"Seriously, mate," said Jimmy. "How are you doing? Your mum told me you'd been in a coma for days."

"Yeah, I was. I took a bit of a bang to the head, and the doctors put me in an induced coma to make sure I was okay. I feel fine now, apart from the fact that I can only see a blur of light."

"Seriously? You're blind?"

"For now, although the doctor reckoned it's temporary, a week at most."

"Whoa, that's mental," said Jimmy. "Take it you're not going into school then?"

"Not until I can see again. Can you imagine me blundering

'round in that place? And my writing's bad enough when I can see."

Jimmy laughed. "You've got that right, mate; can't copy off you even if you weren't looking."

"Jimmy," Sammy called, "Do you want to stay for tea?"

"I can't, Mrs Crackley, but thanks. I've got to get home; I just wanted to check on old Jacksie boy here on my way. But how about tomorrow night if Jack fancies some company?"

"My great Aunt Elsie's coming down to look after me while Mum's at work. But that'd be great if you can come over."

"Sure," said Jimmy. "Do you need anything bringing?"

"No, I'm good. But can you stick the T.V on if you're going? I can't seem to locate the remote."

Jimmy rooted around down the side of the sofa before brandishing the controller. He clicked the T.V on and then pushed it firmly into Jack's hand. Moving Jack's thumb onto the channel button, he nodded in satisfaction.

"There you go, bud; pick whatever sounds best," he said with a laugh.

"Funny," said Jack, smiling back. "Go on, clear off. See you tomorrow."

"Yep, you will. I'll bring you some grapes."

"Don't let the door hit you on the way out."

Jack heard the front door open and a, *'Bye, Mrs Crackley,'* followed by a slam. Shortly afterwards, he heard his mum click the lock on; she always kept the door locked and had done so as long as Jack could remember.

Jack focused his attention on the sound of the T.V. He could see approximately where it was as there was a lighter patch in his vision, but no amount of straining his eyes revealed any more than a light blur. With a sigh, he settled back to what appeared to be a news programme.

To recap on our top story, scientists are no closer to finding the cause of the chronic ageing sickness afflicting young children. Whilst the United Kingdom remains the epicentre, cases are now being reported worldwide. Scientists from the Public Health's Centre of Infectious Disease Surveillance and Control are liaising closely with personnel from the US Center for Disease Control and Prevention and scientists in China and Japan. The Head of the UK Disease Control, Dr Norman Blackwell, gave us the following in an earlier interview:

"We are at a loss as to the cause of the symptoms that the affected are displaying. There seems to be no root cause of the effects; the children just appear to have aged at an accelerated rate and have fallen into a deep sleep from which we cannot wake them. They do not respond to any of the usual stimulants we utilise to try to wake them. Quite simply, nothing works."

"Is it contagious, Dr Blackwell?"

"We don't think so. There are no indicators from the many tests conducted that it is contagious, and staff investigating the children have now dispensed with hazardous material protocols with no ill effects. We have yet to determine the cause, and until we can discover that, it's challenging to prepare any reactive response."

"So, it affects only children?"

"From what we can determine; certainly all of the reported cases so far involve only children, and then only children seemingly below twelve years of age. There are no cases above that age that we are aware of."

"What can the public do to protect their families?"

"Again, we don't know. The illness just seems to strike at random, with no pattern that we can discern. Affected children have been with other children on the same day, in school or nurseries, and succumbed overnight, but with no ill effects on their peers. All we can advise is to keep a close eye on your family members, and if you are concerned, please call the dedicated NHS helpline number for further advice. And if a family member is affected, then please call the specialist incident number; this is available via the NHS and on the website."

"Is there a cause for panic? We understand that the number of cases seems to be accelerating worldwide."

"I cannot comment on that, I'm afraid; my team is focused on finding a way to help those poor children already affected and stop this. I would advise people to remain calm and understand that we are doing everything we can to stop this epidemic."

"Dr Blackwell, thank you."

"It's just awful, isn't it?" Jack heard Sammy say, interrupting the programme.

"Is it that bad?"

"Yes, it seems to be. Phil from work, his lad has caught it. Phil's not been back in, but his brother says that the boy is all old and grey and won't wake up."

"Wonder what's causing it?"

"They don't know. It's all over Facebook. Some reckon it's some sort of terrorist attack, but it's everywhere apparently, so if it is, everyone's affected."

Jack thought suddenly again about Mr Binks, although his recollection was hazy, like seeing it through a mist. No, it couldn't be; Jack was too old, according to the news expert. *Just a crazy old man and a couple of dwarves,* he thought randomly. That was odd…

He was interrupted from his thoughts by a waft of lavender hitting his nose. Almost instantly, a voice shouted, *"Cooooeeeeeeee. It's just me. I've let myself in."*

Great Aunt Elsie had arrived.

CHAPTER 5

Great Aunt Elsie erupted into the room like a whirlwind of strong flowery perfume and noise. Jack heard a crash as she dropped whatever it was she was carrying, and then a whoosh of exhaled air as she seized Sammy in what he assumed was a bear hug.

"Hello, hello, hello, my dears. Jack, Jack, you got so big! Sammy, you are looking so well; tell me, what is your secret? I swear you need to tell me. I use a mashed-up avocado with some sap from my aloe vera plant; does me a world of good; being a poor old age pensioner I can't afford none of those fancy creams you youngsters all use. Ooh, I love what you have done with the place; it's been too long since I was here last. Why don't you invite me more often? And where did you get that paint; was it expensive? I just love the colour of it; that would go lovely in my little kitchen. I do all my own decorating, you know, I still do even at my age. I know, I know, I don't look old at all, but..."

Elsie tailed off, and Jack could sense her scrutinising him.

"My goodness! And what exactly has happened to you, young man?" she said, kind concern in her voice.

Sammy managed to extract herself from Elsie's vice-like grip and stood back, smoothing down her blouse.

"Hi Elsie, you've made good time," she said. "How was your journey?"

"Simply wonderful, my dear, no hitches at all."

"Hi, Auntie Elsie," said Jack, bracing himself.

The old lady practically launched herself onto the sofa next to Jack and flung her arms around him. Jack could feel the bones of his spine creaking.

"Ooooh, you poor, poor thing. Car accident, your mum said? I didn't know you were old enough to drive. They grow up so fast nowadays, eh, Sammy? How is the car? Was it a write-off? Your mum said that you had been in a coma. Oh..."

Elsie released her death grip and patted Jack gently on the knee.

"Just awful, awful, I didn't hurt you, did I? I don't know my own strength," she said. "I'm here now; we'll soon have you as right as rain, right as rain, I say, you mark my words."

"I wasn't driving Auntie Elsie. I was on my bike."

"Oh, my goodness! Drivers today just don't care, do they? 'Think Bike' my backside. Too busy by far on the roads today. I don't drive anymore, too dangerous for us elderly. No respect for other drivers and cyclists. And that's just my generation!" Elsie punched Jack's mum lightly on the leg and guffawed at her own joke.

"Would you like a cup of tea, Elsie?" said Jack's mum

"That would be lovely, dear. I'm parched; travelling always makes me spit feathers. Can I help you with that?"

"No, no, it's fine," said Jack's mum, looking for a way to escape. "I'll make us a pot."

Jack heard his mum leave the room, and then a few seconds later, an almighty scream.

"Don't worry, dear," whispered Elsie directly in Jack's ear. "I think your mum has just found her other house guest."

"*Elsie!*" bawled Sammy, storming back into the room with a clanking noise. "What the hell is this?"

"Oh him," said Elsie innocently. "That's just Fermy. He's come to stay too. I couldn't leave him at home; I wasn't sure how long I'd be away for, Jack's health coming first and all that."

"Is that what I think it is?" said Sammy.

"Probably. He's a ferret."

"Does he bite?"

"Only if he doesn't like you."

"He's trying to bite me through the cage."

"There's your answer then."

Jack started giggling; he couldn't help it. It was like being stuck in some strange pantomime.

"Oh, he wouldn't hurt a fly, really; he's lovely. Here, let me get him out."

"I'm making tea. Keep that thing away from me," warned Sammy.

Jack sat listening to the sounds of metal scraping and then flinched as something small, warm, and furry plopped itself into his lap.

"Ooh, he likes you," said Elsie. "Give him a fuss."

Jack gave the bundle a stroke, and it purred like a cat. He then scratched it, and he felt it squirm as it rolled over to receive more fuss. He could sense Aunt Elsie looking down at him.

"He'll settle well here, I think."

"He's lovely," said Jack.

They were interrupted by the sound of chinking mugs as Sammy reappeared in the room. "Tea's up."

The next minute or two was taken up with slurping and keeping Fermy off the table where the biscuits were.

"Elsie," said Sammy, "Was the front door unlocked when you got here?"

"Yes, dear; I just let myself in."

"Funny, I swore that I locked in when Jimmy went. Did you lock it behind you when you came in?"

"I don't recall, dear. More than likely, although I had all my bags and Fermy's cage to manage."

"Well, it's locked now. Let's finish this tea up, and then we can get you properly settled into my room; I'll take the sofa for now. Then I'll sort some food out for us."

"Dinner's on me tonight, dearies!" said Elsie. "I just love pizza. Can we get that here?"

"Oh, yes. All the modern conveniences available here, Auntie Elsie."

ELSIE SETTLED in with her usual banter and bluster, taking Sammy's room where she insisted on housing Fermy's cage, much to Sammy's disgust. They had enjoyed their evening together, with Elsie making many promises about all the entertaining things they would be doing while she was 'in charge,' as she put it. Jack couldn't see them doing half of those things, given the state of his eyesight, but it was fun to join in with the planning. Eventually, yawning, Elsie had taken herself off to bed, and Jack had followed shortly after, feeling his way up without any assistance; Sammy watching him anxiously from the foot of the stairs.

Jack was coming out of the bathroom when he heard the voices coming from his mum's room. Two distinctive voices were talking in low muttered tones. Feeling his way along the wall, Jack pressed his ear to the door, curious to know whom Auntie Elsie was talking to.

"There's more to that blindness than a simple road accident. The boy is fine other than that," he heard Auntie Elsie say, her voice serious and most 'un-Elsie' like.

A deep male voice, strangely rich and comforting, replied, "I agree. Do you think that the glamour is responsible? I could still feel it, but it was faint, not strong like before. And I swear he has another glamour on him as well, a dark one."

"I don't know," said Elsie. "Tomorrow, we need to examine him. Carefully though, he must not suspect anything. I don't know what to do if it is fading; there is no way that we two can bolster it alone, and we can't call for outside help other than Timothy, can we? If the secret gets out..."

"Agreed," said the voice. "It may be for the best, though, if it does fade. The boy cannot deny what he is."

"His father said no," snapped Elsie. "This was all done to keep them safe, and we have to respect his wishes. We agreed to that. David insisted before he went."

"But that was on the assumption that David would be back; it was a short-term measure only. He isn't."

"He may yet. Time in whatever realm he went to may be different to here, as you well know."

"Elsie, it has been eleven years. Even figuring for any differences, he should have returned years ago; David knows about time shifts and how to counter them. Not one of the court scouts can locate him nor hear a word of him. Which is all well and good, considering, but it doesn't help us."

"Don't you think I don't know that? I miss him every day, and it is worse somehow, knowing his little family thinks differently. And just look at their circumstances, living hand to mouth in this tiny house."

"It may be time for the boy to learn then. If the glamour is truly fading, then it could be a blessing in disguise. He could help."

"I just don't know." Elsie now, softly. "I don't want to put Jack through all this if we can help it. He is happy now, normal, despite their hardships. If we go down that route, he will change forever. And his mother, bless her...."

Jack had no idea who Elsie was talking to; it didn't sound

like a speakerphone; it was like the person was in the room with her. He pressed his ear harder against the door to hear better, and the door, misaligned like so many in older houses, creaked open slightly.

"Who's there?" demanded Elsie.

"It's just me, Aunt Elsie. I heard you talking to someone, that's all."

"Oh, Jack dearie, it's just an old lady's ramblings. Sometimes I just get the most sensible conversation out of myself, hearing myself out loud. The habit of living alone!"

"But I heard a man's voice. That's what made me stop."

There was silence from Elsie. Then she said, "A man's voice? You heard a man's voice? In my room? Oh, dearie, whatever are you suggesting? A man in my room? At my age!" She started giggling behind the door.

Jack pushed the door open fully so that Elsie could see him. "I heard a man's voice Aunt Elsie; I just wanted to check that you were okay."

"But there's no-one here, Jack, see? Oh, you can't, can you? Well, you are quite welcome to come in and have a feel about if you like; the room's not that big. There's no one here but me and Fermy."

"No, it's fine. I must have been mistaken."

"Well then, what did this man sound like? Was he hunky?"

Jack thought for a moment. "His voice was rich, and it sounded comforting, silly as that sounds. Not deep, but full. Like that actor, Morgan Freeman."

"Well, if I had Morgan Freeman in my room, I wouldn't be keeping it a secret. I'd be shouting it from the rooftops," Elsie chuckled.

"Well...okay," said Jack, hesitantly.

"Go to bed, Jack," said Elsie kindly. "We'll have a look at those eyes tomorrow. I may have a few home recipes up my sleeve that can help. Does your mother have any gin in the house; we might need it for 'medicinal purposes' whilst I'm sorting you out?"

"I don't know, Auntie. However, we can ask her in the morning. Good night."

"Good night, Jack. I'll let you get yourself to bed; do you good to fumble about and remember where everything is."

Jack, his hand guiding him along the wall, walked the short distance to his bedroom. As he was closing the door, he heard Elsie whisper. "Well, that answers that then. The glamour is definitely on its way out."

JACK AWOKE the following morning to the clash of metal on metal; it sounded like someone was emptying the pan cupboard downstairs or possibly waging a mini-war with the crockery. He could sense a dim light through his vision, indicating morning, as it was brighter when he turned his head in the direction of his bedroom window. He lay there, warm and comfortable in bed, listening to the growing noises downstairs as they reached a crescendo, then stopped altogether. Shortly afterwards, the delicious smell of bacon wafted its way up the stairs. Jack sat up and reached out to his bedside table to steady himself as he pulled himself up. In doing so, he dislodged a lukewarm mug of something that fell onto the floor, splashing the bottom of his pyjamas and his bare feet. Sighing, he felt about on the floor with his feet for his slippers and put his foot on something warm and hairy, which screeched before sinking its claws into his soft foot.

"Oooww!" yelled Jack, lashing out with his foot but not connecting. A second later, something jumped into his lap and rubbed itself on the bottom of his ribs with a purr. Jack clutched at the bundle and said, "Fermy?" A high-pitched chattering confirmed that the ferret had indeed found its way into his room.

"I can't fuss you now; I'm getting up."

The ferret responded by hauling himself up Jack's pyjamas to sit on his shoulder. Jack felt whiskers tickle his ear and a few warm breaths on his cheek.

"Well, I guess you're along for the ride then," said Jack, getting up. Forgoing his slippers that had done a vanishing act in the night, he started for the bedroom door, both arms out in front to feel his way ahead. He felt a light tap on the right side of his head as he was walking and veered right, straight into the open doorway.

"Are you directing me, Fermy?" he asked the ferret and was greeted by a squeaking chatter. "Well, okay then, you clever little thing!"

Jack made it downstairs without a single bump, responding to the ferret's taps on his head as he went, becoming more and more surprised as he did so. He thought it was odd that the pet could guide him in this manner, but it really helped. The creature seemed to be directing him correctly, avoiding his mum's knick-knack table on the landing and stopping him at the top of the stairs. As he approached the bottom of the stairs, the ferret put both paws on Jack's eyes, and Jack stopped.

"Well, well, well, looks who's finally up and about," came Elsie's voice. "Come on in here, Jackie boy, and have yourself a bacon sandwich. Your mum's already away to work." It did smell good, and Jack stepped off the stairs in anticipation, making his way to the kitchen with one hand running along the wall. As he entered the room, the ferret scrambled down and disappeared.

"There you are, you scamp!" said Elsie. "Been waking poor Jack up, have you?" The ferret chattered back, almost as if he were talking.

"I think you woke me up, Aunt Elsie. Were you playing the cymbals down here?"

"You cheeky boy! Of course not, just finding my way about the kitchen cupboards. Did you sleep well?"

"Yes, thanks."

"And I can see that you are finding your way around okay now. Especially on those stairs."

"It was weird, Auntie Elsie; Fermy sat on my shoulder, and it seemed like he was guiding me downstairs."

"That's because he's a clever lickle boy, aren't you, my sweet?" More chattering, this time, a little angrier sounding.

"Okay, Jack, after you eat, I want to take a look at your eyes, if I may? Are they any better today?"

"If you want, Aunt Elsie. And no, still pretty much the same. I can see light and dark, but only really as shadows."

"Well, dear, Fermy here and I have an idea about what the problem could be."

"I'm pretty sure it's the accident, Aunt Elsie; I could see fine before it. And how would Fermy know?"

"Just an old lady's musing; he's one of the family. You could see fine, could you, before the accident?"

"Erm, yes?" said Jack.

"And what exactly could you see? Anything unusual at all?" Aunt Elsie's voice was quiet, serious-sounding.

"I'm not sure what you mean, Aunt Elsie?"

"I mean, what happened before the accident, Jack? Your mum said you are more than careful on that bike of yours. I appreciate accidents can happen to anyone, but what were you doing up at that house? Did the old people there frighten you?" Elsie's voice was lower, almost hypnotic.

"I can remember banging my head at school; I was knocked out, but I was okay. I saw...well, nothing. And I had to go to help Mr Binks later on; he asked me in the morning, which was why I was up at...."

Memories of what happened at Twillington House suddenly came flooding back to Jack clearly at that point. "Mr Binks and his dwarves," he said to himself and shook his head, "Attacked me."

"Dwarves attacked you?" said Elsie with a sharp intake of breath.

"Yes," said Jack dully, his head full of strange memories, unreal. Dancing lights. "No. I don't know; I can't remember."

"Think, Jack. It's very important. What happened to you? What did you see?"

"I don't know. The accident has left things muddled. I think I know, and then it goes away. Like dreaming."

"Elsie," came the rich, comforting male voice. "Take it off the boy. It's time enough now; it's clear that the glamour isn't working as it should."

Jack started. "Who is that?" he said, shaking himself from his stupor.

"Okay, okay, I agree; it's too far gone. I will get my things. Jack, just wait there for me, my dear; I won't be a second."

Jack heard Elsie leave the room, followed by footsteps on the stairs. The stranger spoke again.

"Jack, listen to me. We will help you, but what comes afterwards will be a little difficult for you to understand. At first."

"Who are you?"

"An old family friend, Jack. I knew your father for a long time, and I promised him that I would keep an eye on you. Which I have, from afar; I was not allowed to interfere, but I have watched you grow up. But with your accident, things have changed and cannot go on now as they once did."

"What do you mean?"

"All in good time, Jack. Let us help you first; it will answer some of your questions before they can be asked."

Jack heard Elsie come back into the room.

"Okay, I'm ready. Jack, love, sit back in the chair for me. I think I can fix your eyes," said Elsie, her hand pressing on Jack's shoulder. To the unseen stranger: "I hope that we do not regret this."

"Who is that man?" demanded Jack.

"As he said, an old friend of mine and your father's. You can see him in a minute if you'll let me help you."

"I feel strange," said Jack, memories swirling in his head. "Like I know something but don't know it."

"I know, I know. But we can help with that, I promise."

Jack slumped back in his chair, feeling weak. He felt Elsie's hands on his head, cupping him gently.

"Okay, my love. Close your eyes."

Jack did as she asked. He felt Elsie's hands move off his head, and then a feeling like his skin was stretching. It felt like a plaster as you pulled it off your graze, stretchy and a little tight. It continued to tighten until he felt something tear. It wasn't painful; it was like pulling off the skin after a sunburn when it was ready to go. Jack felt it completely tear, unravelling from his whole body, and then the memories stopped swirling abruptly.

"Open your eyes, Jack."

Jack did, and the light flooded in, causing him to squint. He blinked a few times and marvelled at that colours as he took in the sights of the kitchen again. Everything seemed intense, and the sun shining in through the windows dappled rays across the kitchen worktops.

"*I can see!*" he shouted, hands coming up to his face to rub his eyes. "*I can see, Auntie Elsie!*"

He looked to his side at the old lady, who stood there with a slight smile on her face, her hands gleaming with a shining silvery thing that was slowly fading away, like water draining. Jack turned back towards the window, and he gasped as he saw a dapper little man, elegantly dressed, standing in front of him on the tabletop. Jack's jaw dropped. About twelve inches tall, he had pale skin underneath his smart green suit. He doffed his red hat to Jack with a smile and said in the rich, comforting voice that Jack had heard before, "I take it from the look on your face that you can see me, Jack?"

Jack fainted clean away.

∾

JACK CAME AROUND to feel a breeze on his face. He opened his eyes to see Aunt Elsie flapping a tea towel in his direction, fanning him. Of the little man, there was no sign.

"Ooh, Jack, you gave us quite a fright then. We expected it to be a shock, but oh my grockles." Elsie dropped the tea towel and clapped her hands to her cheeks.

"How long was I out for?" Jack glanced around, looking for the little man. Only Fermy sat on the table.

"Only a couple of minutes. I am sorry; I should have prepared you better. Are you alright?"

"I'm fine, Auntie Elsie, just feeling a little weird. What was that thing?"

"That thing," came the rich voice, "Has a name. And that is Fermerillion. But you may call me Fermy, Jack."

Jack jerked back in his chair, staring at the ferret, who gave a little wave with one of his front paws. Fermy crossed the table to where Jack was sitting and sat on his haunches, looking up at the boy.

"I am so sorry I startled you, Jack," the ferret said. "I guess it was a little frightening to see me as I should be, rather than in this rather itchy but more familiar form?"

"Wha...what are you?" Jack croaked.

"You really don't remember anything, do you? Well, Jack, I am a Feeorin. I guess you would say that I am a kind of Faery if you want a better description. Us Fae folk don't really like to be generalised in such a manner if I am honest with you, but 'Faery' will do for now if it will help."

Jack glanced at Elsie, who smiled and shrugged her shoulders.

"Fermy is one of the Fae folk, Jack. Briefly, the Fae are from the Faery Realm and generally come here to our realm to help. Or to hinder. Fermy here has been a friend of our family for many years; you used to love to play with him and the others when you were younger."

"What?" said Jack, sitting forwards. "I used to play with him?"

"Yes, Jack," said Fermy. "Myself, amongst others. I was a regular visitor to your home when you were younger and your father, too, when he was small."

"But how can I see you? I don't believe in Faeries; they don't exist apart from in kids' books and films."

"Well, I think that you may well change your mind on that, Jack. I can assure you that we very much do exist. Listen, may I assume my proper form? This ferret glamour is quite uncomfortable, and it is rather warm to be wearing it on a day like this. Plus, it encourages Elsie to make silly comments like 'lickle boy,' which I really don't enjoy."

Jack nodded his approval, still a little shocked at the highly unusual turn of events. With a slight waving of the air, like a heat shimmer, the little man stood again in front of Jack.

"That's better; thank you, Jack. Now, as to how you can see me, well, that is a story that deserves telling properly. Your family is unique, you know, and the circumstances of how it came to be that you can see my kind is an extremely rare happening. Elsie?"

"Jack, I think it's best if we perhaps go to my house; it'll be easier to explain if I can show you one or two things," replied Elsie

"But it's miles away, Auntie, and you don't drive. Mum will

be worried if she gets home and we're gone. And talking of which, we should let her know that I can see again."

"Jack, don't worry. We can be at my house in just under two minutes. It's one of the, shall we say, benefits of being what we are."

"I'm sorry, I have no idea what you mean," said Jack, still staring at Fermy, who was looking back with a broad smile on his face.

"Well, Elsie, I guess that now Jack is back with us, we can start him off with a lesson in realm travel. What do you think?"

"I think that it's as good a place as any to start him off remembering his history. Let me get my bag."

"But what about Mum?" said Jack. "She'll be worried if she gets home and we're not here."

"Oh, dear, don't worry. We'll be back in good time; I'll even get the tea ready for when she comes in," said Elsie with a smile. "Now stop fussing and come with me."

Elsie marched out into the hall, and Jack followed her, bemused. Fermy followed up the rear, having hopped down smartly from the kitchen table. Elsie stopped in front of the lounge door and pulled it closed before rummaging in her bag. From it, she pulled out a black marker pen and proceeded to draw on the door, a strange symbol composed of loops and lines.

"Whoa, Auntie Elsie, what are you doing? Mum will go mad!" said Jack, staring in disbelief.

"Just watch," said Fermy.

The symbol Elsie had drawn on the door started to glitter with gold motes, shimmering in the semi-darkness of the hall-way. Elsie suddenly slapped the symbol with the flat of her hand, and it drained off the door as if someone was pouring glitter.

"Come on then, team, step lively. Jack, take careful note of what I did there," said Elsie, pushing open the door and walking into the living room.

Jack followed her and gasped with amazement. It appeared that his entire living room was on fire with blue flames. They danced on the furniture, streaked up and down the curtains and twisted across the carpet, but gave off no heat, nor seemed to be damaging anything that Jack could see.

"What...what is this?" said Jack, his voice shaky and then jumped as Fermy slammed the lounge door shut behind him, sealing them in the room.

WHILE THIS WAS GOING ON, nobody had noticed the small figure crouched on the kitchen windowsill. It wasn't surprising, really; Dix was only six inches tall and went pretty much unnoticed, even when he was visible. At that particular moment, he was the colour of the red tile that made up the windowsill and had blended in quite well. He'd been tasked to spy on the boy and had been loitering around the area since Jack arrived home from the hospital the previous day. He had watched with interest when the old female lifer had turned up and had been shocked when it turned out that the caged creature was actually that damn Fermerillion; if that meddler had seen him there, there would have been a lot of trouble. Fortunately, he had remained unnoticed and watched with interest as the old lifer had restored Jack's sight. And he had almost fallen off the windowsill when it became apparent that both the boy and the old lady could see Fermerillion without any kind of reveal. As he watched developments with increasing excitement, the old woman had opened a realm door, and the group has slipped through.

'Oh, yes. This information will pay handsomely,' thought the imp, rubbing his hands together.

⁓

IN THE LIGHT of dancing blue flames, Elsie smiled. "Please don't be concerned, Jack. This isn't really your living room anymore. Think of it as kind of a waiting room for when we are in between where we were and where we want to go. Now, please again take careful note of what I do."

Stepping between Jack and Fermy, Elsie raised the pen again and drew another symbol on the door they had just come through. It was similar but slightly different from the previous one; again, loops and lines.

The symbol again started to glitter gold in the flickering blue light, and again Elsie slapped it to make it drain away like sand through an hourglass. Elsie then opened the door and stepped through it. Jack followed her and looked around in awe. He had just walked into what appeared to be a small, cluttered kitchen; clean, but with stuff everywhere. Plants lined the windowsill, pans hung down from the ceiling, and an old-style gas oven stood in the corner, giving off a delicious odour of baking. Jack glanced back behind him to see a small wooden door that they had just come through. Reaching past Fermy, he pulled it open to see a small pantry, the shelves lined with tins and packets. Fermy got out of the way, taking off his hat to hang it on a small hook set about a foot off the floor next to the pantry door.

"Erm, what just happened?" said Jack. "Did we just come out of the pantry?"

"Yes, dear," said Elsie with another smile. "Never a problem coming and going via a pantry. The neighbours don't see, so can't gossip; much better than the front door!"

"But how?" said Jack, in wonder.

"Realm travel," said Fermy. "It's how we can get about quickly, and I am led to believe by my 'lifer' friends that it's much better than public transport."

"Lifer?" queried Jack. "Like in prison?"

"No, no," laughed Elsie. "'Lifer' is how the Fae folk refer to those that dwell in this realm. It's because we lead such short lives. In their eyes, anyway. It's a bit of an insulting way to refer to us, to be honest, but it's what they say. Probably some sort of joke in its own way."

"How long do Faeries live then?"

"A long time in how you measure it, Jack," said Fermy. "We don't go by months and years as you do. We simply are and, at some point, cease to be."

"I'm not sure what you mean?" said Jack.

"Well," said Fermy, "I always liked that chap Conan Doyle's take on us in that book of his, the *Coming of the Fairies*. I can quote it word for word, as it really is rather eloquent. It goes like this. *'Any estimate of the length of life is misleading because the comparison with ourselves cannot be made. There is no real birth nor death, as we understand the terms — simply a gradual emergence from, and a return to, a subtler state of being. This process takes some time, probably years in certain varieties. However, there is nothing definite in all this except the fact of the gradual emergence and return.'* Taking myself as an example, I've been familiar with your family's young for around twelve generations. And I don't feel old."

Jack did some quick calculations in his head. "So you're about three hundred years old? Wow."

Fermy laughed. "I don't know Jack, but I was here a long time before I met your family. So I can't say for sure I'm afraid."

Jack looked at the little Feeorin with his mouth agape. Fermy squirmed a little in embarrassment before shrugging. He was about to respond when Jack heard another voice, female this time, call out from upstairs. "Elsie, is that you's, my dears?"

"Yes, Dorcas, just popped back for a short while. And I've bought someone to see you."

There was a thundering noise on the stairs, and then the door at one side of the kitchen flew open with a crash. Standing there was an extremely odd figure. It was almost square like in appearance, as it was as wide as it was tall, with a bulky body filling the doorway. As Jack looked closer, he could see a chubby head perched on top of the bulky body, with long ears and a long nose. It had curly black hair that sprouted out of it at all kinds of angles, giving the figure a look as if it had been playing with static electricity. Its head was about as tall as Jack's waist, and it stood there quivering in its flowery misshaped dress. Jack realised that the figure was actually not square, just very fat. It stood staring at Jack, its lips wobbling and a tear running down its face.

"Oh my goodness, oh my goodness," the figure said, wringing its hands. "You got so's big! My dear sweet boy got all bigs and talls and strong! Oh my, oh my….."

And with that, the figure launched itself across the kitchen in a blur of flowery dress and barrelled into Jack like a rugby player, its arms wrapping around the top of his thighs. Jack staggered and slipped backwards, his backside hitting the flagstones of the kitchen floor, Fermy stepping neatly out of the way as the boy lost his balance.

The newcomer threw its arms around Jack's shoulders and pulled him in close to its bosom, showering slobbery kisses down onto Jack's head and face with the speed of a woodpecker. Jack was too shocked to put up a defence and instead sat there while the figure assaulted his face with kisses. Pulling back, it took Jack's head in both hands with a surprisingly gentle touch and said,

"It's definitely you's. My Jacksie. Oh, how I's missed you's. And now I's missed you growing ups as well, my dear, sweet boy. I wasn't allowed to come and sees you, even if I's stayed hidden. But how I's wish I hadn't listened. Not a day has gone by's when I hasn't wondered about you's. Elsie shows me the pictors, of course, but it's not the same. I's never missed a Cracklock grow ups ever until now. Oh my goodness…." And with that, the figure burst in blubbering sobs, burying its head against Jack's shoulder.

Jack sat there on the floor with the sobbing figure's arms wrapped firmly around his neck, and suddenly a memory of cakes appeared. In it, this little person was offering a tray of cakes to him; he could see his hand outstretched to take one. The figure was beaming down at him; it was taller than him then, and a man stood in the background, his face familiar. Then it was gone.

"I know you!" exclaimed Jack. "You used to give me cakes when I was small,"

The figure pulled itself away to look at Jack with beautiful brown eyes nestled in its chubby face.

"Yes, yes, he remembers me! Oh, spackle my grackles; he's remembers poors Dorcas." With that, the face buried again into Jack's shoulder, and the sobbing continued.

"Come on now, Dorcas," said Elsie gently. "Be careful with Jack. He's not been well lately, and…"

Elsie did not get a chance to finish. Dorcas leapt back off Jack like a flea before fixing Elsie with a stare.

"Not's been well? I know you went to take care of him and wouldn't lets poor Dorcas comes as well, but what has happenings to him? I knews that this would happen if Dorcas weren't there to take's care of things. Why hasn't he been's well?" Dorcas clenched her fists and glared around at the group.

"I had an accident, Dorcas. I got hit by a car."

Dorcas turned back to Jack and started running her hands all over him. "Oh my, oh my, Dorcas wills make it all better, I swear's. I has many things that can helps. I will mend's you, my poor, sweet, dear boy."

"I'm fine, Dorcas, really," said Jack, pushing her hands off him. "All better now but finding this all a bit strange."

Dorcas froze. "Of course, the glamour! You should not be able to see's us; it is not safes. David was very insistent." She whirled to face Elsie. "What did you do's? Why did you's remove the glamour?"

"Dorcas, we had no choice. After his accident, the glamour was damaged. Jack could hear Fae folk, and I daresay he would have been able to see them if he wasn't blinded by what happened."

"*Blinded? Blinded?*" screamed Dorcas, tears gushing from her eyes. "Oh, Jack!"

"I'm fine now, Dorcas, really," said Jack quickly, as the squat figure turned to him again. "Elsie and Fermy did something to me, and I can see again really well now."

"Dorcas, listen," said Fermy, his voice calm. "We believed that Jack's blindness was the last defensive part of the glamour he had on him. If he could not actually see Fae folk, then there would be no reason for him to start questioning what he was seeing. We believe that the blindness was an unintended consequence of the glamour, a last-ditch thing that nobody realised would happen. The specifics of such a strong glamour were always bound to be difficult, and rather than leave him blind, we decided to remove the glamour to see if it would help. It did."

"But it's not safe's for him," wailed Dorcas. "He was safe befores."

"Yes, we know," said Elsie. "But we had no real choice. So now, we have to help Jack to look after himself. He needs to know what he is."

Dorcas stopped crying and, still sniffing, said, "Can we puts the glamour back on, makes it how it was?"

"No," said Fermy. "He's too old for that to work properly now the original is broken. We need to show him what he is and what it means. Then, he can hopefully help us make things right."

Dorcas considered this, her head cocked to one side, thinking deeply. Finally, she said, "Okay, Dorcas will help's. Of course, I will help's. What can I's do?"

"Firstly," said Elsie, "Can you go and get my book for me? I think that is somewhere to start. And then, if I'm not mistaken, are those cakes I can smell in the oven? Perhaps some of those and a pot of tea? A nice sit-down and a chat, that's what we need now."

"Okay," sniffled Dorcas. "Dorcas will get what we need."

CHAPTER 6

Ten minutes later saw the little group sat comfortably in Elsie's small lounge. Dorcas busied herself serving everyone, making sure that Jack was first and got the largest freshly baked bun and the biggest cup filled with sweet tea. Jack noticed that she kept one eye on him at all times, as if ready to spring into action on his behalf. He found it surprisingly endearing.

Putting down her cup, Elsie picked up what appeared to be a bulging scrapbook. Odds and ends were sticking out of the closed pages at all angles, and the scuffed red cover was tied shut with a piece of string. The book looked old and well handled, and as she cradled it in her lap, she looked over at Jack.

"Okay, then, young man. Before we start, I want to make one thing clear to you from the off. What we are about to talk about is a secret. It is not for discussion with other people, including your friends and your mother. For now, your mum does not need to know anything about this; her glamour is still in place and working. It would be best for all of us if things appear to be normal at home. Which, I can assure you, they won't be now that you're 'back in the fold' as they say."

"I don't think anyone would believe me anyway, Auntie Elsie," said Jack. "Mum is likely to want to get me sectioned if I start talking about seeing faeries. But does she know about all this?"

"She used to, but not now. I promise you I will explain, but essentially, your dad wanted to ensure that you were both protected before he went away."

"Went away? My dad died when I was four, Auntie Elsie."

Elsie hesitated a little, looking at Fermy and Dorcas. They both nodded as an unseen agreement passed between them. She looked back at Jack and gave a sad smile. "No, he went away when you were four," she said gently.

"I'm sorry, Aunty, but I don't understand. What do you mean, 'went away'?"

The old lady leaned over and took Jack's hand. "Everything is not as it seems, Jack. There was some trouble way back when; trouble that you needed to be kept safe from whilst your dad tried to put a stop to it. As part of that, we needed to hide you and your mum; it was his idea, but we helped. It wasn't supposed to be for so long, though, and we thought it would be better if you thought he was no longer with us. If we'd known, we would never have done that. I'm so sorry. We're all so sorry."

The implications of this set Jack's eyes shining. "It doesn't matter; it could change everything! Does that mean my dad is still alive? Then where is he?" he said, sitting up straight in his chair, a rush of excitement fizzing down his spine.

Elsie patted his hand again. Fermy took a finger of Jacks other hand in his tiny palm. "That's just it, Jack; we don't know if he is still alive; we hope so, but it has been eleven years. That's a long time to be away for, especially for someone like David, for you and Sammy meant more than life itself to him."

Jack was excited now as he processed this. His dad could still be alive! Lost somewhere, but... his dad could still be alive! He looked around at the others, his eyes bright.

"We have to find him. How can I help?"

The others looked sadly at each other again, and then Dorcas spoke.

"We's tried, Jack-Jack, we really has. But we's cannot find him; we has searched everywhere."

"But there must be something…somewhere you haven't looked. What about in Faeryland?"

The others chuckled at this. "The polite term is Faery, Jack," said Fermy, "And, yes, we've scoured the seven sub-realms Nothing."

"Seven sub-realms?"

"We're getting ahead of ourselves here, I think," Fermy replied, "Jack, can we explain? It may help you make sense of things if we do. I understand that this news is a lot to take in, but can we help you understand things. And then, we can think about how we can start looking again?"

Jack slumped back in his chair, but he still bristled with excitement. "Okay, if you think that's best. It's just a lot to take in, that's all."

"We do understand, Jack. Really we do. But you need to know everything, so you can see that it's not so simple. Your dad isn't playing hide and seek with us; he is missing."

Jack nodded his understanding, but the pleasant feeling stayed with him.

Elsie took a swallow of tea. "Right, where was I. Oh, yes! Jack, I meant what I said. No talking to friends or anyone about this. It will bring you unwanted attention, believe me, and not just from medical professionals. The best thing is to say nothing, even when you see something odd. You will have to learn how to hide your surprise, and quickly at that."

Elsie made room and placed the red scrapbook on the coffee table. Pulling the string undone, she said to Jack, "This is the history of the Cracklock family; our side anyhow. This book passes down from generation to generation; all being well, it will come to you one day. It's been updated and replaced a few times over the years, but the content is all here. Each generation adds to the book before it passes it along."

"Who are the Cracklock family, Auntie Elsie?" asked Jack, "And what have they go to do with my dad?"

"Why we are, Jack," said Elsie, with a big smile.

"No, I'm a Crackley. As dad's aunt, you're a Crackley too, aren't you?"

Elsie laughed at Jack's puzzled face. "Oh boy, that was some glamour! No, Jack, your real name is Cracklock. Jack Cracklock. Moreover, to keep you safe eleven years ago, a powerful glamour was placed on yourself and your mother. Your dad chose Crackley as a surrogate name when he was leaving. He wanted something close to your proper name but wouldn't turn up in any searches if someone was looking for you. The name of Crackley is masked from Faery glamours. We will come to why later once we have filled in some of the gaps for you. But your real name, the name you were born with, is Jack Cracklock. Your father is David Cracklock, and my full name is Elsie Elizabeth Cracklock. I didn't have any glamours out on me, as I didn't need to hide."

Jack looked puzzled at this. "I don't understand, Auntie Elsie. Why did we need to have a new name? Moreover, what is this glamour that you keep talking about? I'm not glamorous."

The small group all laughed aloud at this statement apart from Jack. They stopped when they saw Jack's bemused face.

"I will try and explain a little, Jack," said Fermy. "Glamour is the word we use for Faery magic. All Faeries can use the glamour to some extent or other, but how that ability is used is up to the individual. It is what we use to hide Faery and ourselves from lifers and for the protection of everyone we care about. Glamours bend to the will of the individual, and we can use them in many different applications. For example…"

Fermy snapped his fingers, and the stack of buns on the

table glowed yellow before whirling into the air. They streaked around the room in a perfect line before forming a spinning halo around Jack's head. They whirled faster and faster before zipping back onto the plate, where they stacked themselves into a perfect pyramid.

"Wow," said Jack, his eyes bulging out of his head. "Do that again!"

"Maybe later I'll show you how to do that for yourself," replied Fermy. "If you've got it in you. For now, it is enough to say that glamour is our magic. We use it for all kinds of things. Bewitching people like the legends would have you believe, protecting ourselves, and yes, that sometimes means fighting as well. We use stunning glamours and stinging ones as well for that. One of the most useful kinds is the shield glamour."

Fermy made a series of rapid gestures and then beckoned to Jack, his hand out. "Shake my hand, young man."

Jack stuck out his hand, but it struck something invisible as he reached for the petite Fae. He felt around it, placing his hands flat on the smooth surface. Tiny ripples echoed out from his palms.

"That's a shield glamour. Useful in a pinch."

"There are lots of other kinds as well, Jack," said Elsie, "The travel room we just came through is one of them."

"And I can cast these spells; I mean glamours?"

"Maybe, maybe," replied Fermy, "We'd need to see."

Jack was slightly stunned by this revelation. '*This is too much. I'm Jack Cracklock, who can see Faeries? And do magic?*' he thought. He pinched himself on the leg and winced a little. "Still awake," he muttered.

Dorcas noticed the look on Jack's face and patted him gently on the knee.

"Don't worry, Jack. It will all make sense," said Elsie kindly. "It seems a lot right now, but it will all become clear, I promise."

Jack nodded, the look of confusion still on his face.

"Okay then," said Elsie. "Let's talk about the Cracklock family. Before we do, Jack, what do you know about Faeries?"

Jack thought for a moment. "Not a lot, Auntie Elsie, other than the usual kid's stuff. Mum read me the stories when I was younger, and I know about Peter Pan and Tinkerbell, and Rumpelstiltskin and others from films and stuff."

"Okay...sorry to tell you, Jack, but none of that stuff is true. Just the imaginings of some very gifted people who, I am quite sure, had never met a real faery. As far as I know, the only person who ever met one and wrote about it in public was the Reverend Robert Kirk, a Scottish clergyman. He wrote a book in 1691 called 'The Secret Commonwealth of Elves, Fauns and Fairies' and, my goodness, did he make the Seelie Court angry! Despite that, most of it was nonsense anyway; his book tells you how to contact Faeries and how to avoid them. As this is at the discretion of the Fae themselves, such instructions are essentially useless. But the book makes a lot of people feel better about life's great mysteries, so there was no real harm done."

"So people can't contact Faeries?" said Jack.

"Ordinary people can't, Jack. They can go to places where Faeries are supposed to come through from 'Fairyland' to summon them, but it never works. Some Fae like to watch such things; they find it an enjoyable day out, particularly when people leave gifts for them, which they will gladly take. But people cannot see faeries unless that particular member of the Fae decides to reveal themselves to them. Which, to be honest, never happens."

Fermy interjected, "Very young children can see the Fae folk, Jack, as they still have a sense of wonder at the world, but they are the only real exceptions. But generally, by the time they start walking and talking, a sense of their own reality has crept into their lives, and they lose the ability."

"So, why can the Cracklocks see faeries then? I don't understand."

"Because the Cracklock family is far from ordinary, Jack," said Elsie, opening the book up. "Come and take a look at this family history."

Jack moved next to Elsie and looked at the page she was showing. The page's spread was covered in a complicated family tree, with additional bits of paper stuck in to allow further branches to be drawn. Elsie folded the pages out and smoothed them down. Jack looked at the diagram, fascinated, seeing that the family tree seemed to go back a long way into medieval times if the dates were anything to go by. Individual names had rings drawn around them as they moved through history, different colours denoting something that was not obvious. The final ring circled a certain "Ichabod Cracklock" in the year 1612. Jack could see his mum and dad's names right down near the bottom of the diagram, with a little offshoot giving his own name. His was the lowest name on the diagram.

"Let's make it a little easier to look at, shall we?" said Elsie with a smile. She performed a rapid series of gestures, and the book began to glow. From the pages of the book, a single shoot sprouted, and then a few more. As Jack watched, branches and leaves exploded from the pages, shooting up to form a fully grown but extremely small tree. Golden buds formed along the miniature branches before bursting into tiny little apples. Gold writing adorned each apple, and several of them had coloured rings slowly rotating around the fruits that hung there, swinging in an invisible breeze. Jack stared at it in wonder, pushing at the branches. They were solid and warm beneath his fingers. He traced his hand over the coloured rings.

"What are these for, Auntie Elsie?" he asked.

"Ah, those denote the people in our family from whom we think our 'special' nature comes from. To further understand, I'll allow Fermy to explain the Faery realm in a little more detail. If you would be so kind, Fermy?"

"Well, I will try and summarise, of course, but our history is complicated. To put it simply, Jack, the Faery realm exists alongside this one, and Faeries can come and go between the two as they wish. Lifers, or humans, if you prefer, generally cannot unless a Fae takes them over to Faery. However, certain humans, those blessed with some Fae abilities, can travel between this realm and the Faery Realms. And to other realms, as well, if they are so inclined and have access to the necessary secrets to enable them to do so."

"Other realms?" said Jack in amazement. "We can go to other realms that aren't, well... here, if we want? Is that where my dad went?"

"Later, Jack. One thing at a time," said Elsie.

"Thank you, Elsie," said Fermy. "Anyhow, as I was saying, Faeries can come and go as they wish. Therefore, we see a wide variety of different kinds of Faeries coming here for all kinds of reasons. We like it here, you see; lifers amuse us. Some people are kind, some are cruel, just like the Fae folk. And like attracts like."

"So there are good and bad fairies?" asked Jack.

"Well, yes and no," replied Fermy. "Like people, Fae can be either or both at the same time. Certain types are supposed to be 'good' and some 'bad,' but it is just a reputation that certain folk have come by over the centuries. Take Dorcas here." Dorcas puffed herself up proudly.

"Dorcas is a Brownie, or 'nim,'" continued Fermy. "Brownies are considered to be one of the most helpful faeries; they help out in the home and look after the family in return for a little food."

"I's been helping the Cracklock family for many years," said Dorcas proudly. "I's cooking and cleaning and helping's to look after children like you, Jack."

"Brownies are considered to be 'good,' as are Elves, Pixies, Kobolds, and Feeorin like myself. There are many more, and we have different names, depending on where in the world we are, but generally, we are considered by lifer populations to be 'good' based on legends and so forth," smiled Fermy. "Likewise, there are types that are considered to be 'bad' fairies – boggarts, goblins, imps, and so on. But I know goblins who are incredibly lovely and Elves who are downright awful."

"And our perception is all skewed by the books and films and stuff," interjected Elsie. "I mean, look at mermaids. All nicey-nice in the kids' books and stuff. No pictures of them drowning and eating people, though, is there, which is what they pretty much do?"

Fermy shot Elsie a glare and continued. "Only some do, Elsie, as you well know. Anyway, so it depends on the Fae itself, rather than any typecasting that goes on. Which brings me onto the Courts."

"The courts?" asked Jack.

"Yes," said Fermy. "All Fae are a member of one of the two courts, the Seelie and Unseelie. In simple terms, these are the good and bad or 'evil' gatherings of the Fae folk; it is like being on a team, and like any team, you can switch sides if you like, but your teammates might not like it. It's quite complex to understand, but the Seelie court could be described as containing those Fae interested in lifers and who want to help them. However, if they are crossed, they can seek revenge for any wrongs or slights against themselves, and even a Seelie fairy, like an Elf, could be 'bad' if they are looking for revenge. Of course, the Seelie court is generally not known to harm people without reason, though, and will warn people before doing something terrible. However, the Unseelie court is the direct opposite of the Seelie court. The Unseelie court is always unfavourable towards lifers and like nothing better than to hurt people and cause illness and, on rare occasions, death. It is comprised of those Fae who have evil natures. However, just as

115

the Seelie court can cause harm if they feel they have to, sometimes Unseelie faeries can act kindly towards lifers. Therefore, there is good and evil in both, just like here in the lifer's realm. But my advice is to stay away from members of the Unseelie court."

"Riiiighhhtt..." said Jack, drawing it out. "So there are good guys and bad guys, and they are on certain teams."

"I think that that analogy will fit," said Fermy primly. "Anyhow, we will need to present you to the Seelie court in due course; there is a requirement that any lifers with Fae abilities are presented and registered. I don't believe that you were registered before; it's normal to present a person when they are old enough to understand the rules. As you were only four when the glamour was placed upon you, then you would never have been presented. We will seek if this is the truth, though."

"So I get to go to the Faery realm?" said Jack. "When? I can't wait to see it!"

"Yes, you do," said Elsie. "Perhaps tomorrow, though, once you have a better idea of what you are getting into. I don't think we will have time today before your mum gets home."

"Okay. I guess I can wait. I still want to know why I can see Faeries."

"I am getting to it, I promise, Jack," said Fermy. "But you do need to have some more background so you can understand."

"I'm sorry to keep interrupting, Fermy," said Jack. "I will try to save any questions for when you've finished. It's just all so... I don't know how to describe it!"

"It's fine, Jack. I appreciate that this is all new to you; it is great to see you excited about it and not fearful. Anyhow, where was I...?"

"The Courts, Fermy," said Elsie.

"Ah, yes. Well, we've talked about that and a little about the Fae folk, so I guess that we need to look now at the alignments."

"Alignments?" said Jack.

"At the end, please, Jack," said Elsie. Jack nodded and mimed zipping up his mouth.

"Well, Jack, the Faery realm is composed of various sub-realms, which the Fae folk are aligned with. When you first visit our realm, you will arrive at what the Irish call 'Tir Na Nog' or the 'Land of the Young.' We also know it as the realm of sun, moon, and stars, as like here, our realm has both light and darkness. All Fae can visit and reside here in this part of our realm – all are welcome – and is it the location of the meeting places for the courts themselves. It's the central part of Faery that people refer to when they talk about 'Fairyland' and so on."

Jack sat, trying to take this all in.

"Now, all Fae are aligned to one of the seven sects. These are composed of the main three sects in the key realm: sun, moon, and stars. There are then four sub-realms that you can travel to from within the Faery Realm; they are not accessible from other locations; you have to be within Tir Na Nog itself to travel to them. These realms are fire, earth, air, and water, or the elemental realms. Fae from these realms have specific attributes; for example, the trees' custodians come from the Earth sub-realm. Generally, only Fae aligned to these specific realms can reside there, although others may visit with an appropriate invitation. And those alignments, Jack, are the key to the Cracklock's abilities."

Jack looked around the little party with a puzzled look on his face. Elsie laughed.

"Look at the family tree again, Jack. What do you see, with regards to the coloured rings?" She gestured to the glowing tree that spouted from the book.

Jack studied the tree carefully, turning the book this way and that, rotating the branches and tracing his finger along the different branches, tapping each circled name as he did so. He could see that the rings were different colours, but they seemed to be random and disorderly; there was no pattern in the generations that he could see, and they bounced around over different names and strands of the tree. It made no sense.

"Any ideas?" asked Elsie.

"No, not really. There doesn't seem to be any sense in it."

"Count the rings, Jack."

Jack did, and then realisation dawned. There were seven distant family members on the diagram, whose names were each ringed with a different coloured circle.

"There are seven rings, Auntie Elsie. Like the seven different alignments associated with Faeries."

"Bingo!" laughed Elsie. "Keep that in mind."

"Excellent deduction," said Fermy with a smile, and then, "Jack, do you know what a Changeling is?"

"A what?" replied Jack.

"A Changeling," repeated Fermy.

"I have no idea," said Jack, looking at Elsie for a hint, who winked back at him.

"Well, Jack, according to legends, a changeling is a fairy child left in a human child's place when the human child is taken away by the Fae. The legends say that changeling children were evil and did many misdeeds as they were growing up. Now, given our earlier discussions, it was probably the case that some changelings were bad. However, some good changelings were given as a replacement to parents when their child was dying at a young age. The parents often didn't know that a switch had been made, and the child was raised and had a normal life. Such children often went on to great things; it was their Fae nature that made that possible. In your family tree, there have been five switches and five changelings over the years. However, the unusual thing is that the Fae made each one from a different alignment – air, water, earth, moon, and stars. The last changeling was Ichabod, who was an earth changeling. It was his marriage that founded the current Cracklock line."

"Wow," said Jack open-mouthed.

"But that's not all," said Fermy pointing at two separate circles. "There are also two Faelings in your family tree, Elspeth and Constance."

"Failings?" asked Jack, "What did they fail at?".

Fermy gave a little chuckle. "Faelings, with an 'e,' not an 'i,'" he said. "Faelings are the result of humans and Fae falling in love, and such unions almost always produce girls; we don't know why. If the child is born in the fairylands, they turn into a Fae almost immediately. If born in the lifer world, she may never know about her faery nature. Elspeth and later Constance resulted from some handsome Fire and Sun Faeries respectively falling for lifer females, supposedly of exceptional beauty."

"So," said Elsie, "When we trace the family line back, you can see that, except for Ichabod, all of the other six people with Faery influence over the years ended up, by various marriages and generations, producing Clarice. Ichabod's wife. And their first child, Jeremiah Cracklock, could see Faeries without them ever revealing themselves to him!"

"Seriously?" said Jack in amazement.

"Yes, it's all documented in the book here. It was Ichabod who first started to write down these things; look here." Elsie gestured again, and the tree sank back into the pages again. She flipped to near the book's start, where ornate, old-fashioned writing was printed neatly on thick time-yellowed paper. "He was cautious to make sure that Jeremiah's abilities were kept secret from other lifers, though; in those times, you could be burned as a witch for something like this."

"So, the reason we can see Faeries is the fact that over the years, members of our family have come from things that happened, and they each had a different Faery alignment?"

"Yes, you've got it, Jack!" said Fermy with a broad smile. "The

Cracklocks are pretty much unique in their circumstances, which allowed the correct mixture of Fae and Lifer to come together at a single point. And every generation of Cracklock since Jeremiah has had the gift to see the Faery realm, as well as the use of certain Fae abilities such as the realm doors and Fae glamours."

"I just can't believe it," said Jack. "I am part Faery! Can I use glamours then?"

"We shall see," said Fermy. "Some Cracklocks over the years haven't been able to, although they had no problems with the realm doors, once they'd been shown how."

"Are there many other Cracklocks? Surely Ichabod and Clarice had more children?" said Jack, thrilled at the prospect of relations that he had never met.

Fermy's and Elsie's faces both fell at the same time. "Yes," said Elsie. "There are some other family members. We don't associate with them, though. They have a *different* outlook on things; I think it's fair to say."

"What do you mean?" asked Jack again, puzzled.

"Look, Jack, you'll hopefully never meet them. They do not share our values and are not the type of people you should associate with. I have not seen them for years and would strongly suggest you don't go looking for them."

"Why not?" asked Jack stubbornly.

"Because they are the reason why your father hid you away," said Elsie. "Enough, for now, I don't want to talk about them."

"Bad's people," said Dorcas with a little shudder. "Not good Cracklocks. Jack should nots seek them out."

"Dorcas," said Fermy sharply. "That's enough; no need to discuss this matter any further now. We will talk about it when we discuss Jack's father. I would suggest that we do that tomorrow when we present Jack at court. There is someone I would like you to meet, Jack, in the Faery Realm. A scholar friend of mine who knew your father well and helped him study. I hope that he will help with your ongoing education in matters Faery, and it is only polite that we introduce you. He is another old family friend of the Cracklocks."

"But why can't we talk about it now? I want to know about my dad," said Jack, feeling a little letdown.

"Because the story of your dad and the other Cracklocks is intertwined, and I would prefer to discuss this with our friend in the Faery realm. He will be able to tell you more than I can, as he had extensive discussions with David before he left," replied Fermy.

"But we will talk about it tomorrow?" said Jack.

"Yes, I promise."

"Well, look at the time," said Elsie. "We better be getting back to yours, Jack, and put the tea on; your mum will be home in an hour or so. Dorcas, do you want to come and help?"

"I's love to come to see's Sammy again, like old times," said Dorcas, clapping her hands together in glee.

"But she won't be able to see you, Dorcas," said Jack. "Not while she has the glamour on her, if that's right?"

"It matters not," said Dorcas. "Just be's nice for Dorcas to cook's for all the Cracklock family again."

"Well then," said Elsie. "Jack, I'd like you to try and open the realm door for us. No time like the present to learn how to do this." She handed Jack a piece of paper with a diagram on it and a piece of chalk. Gesturing at the pantry door, she said, "Get to it then, lad; let's see if you've got it in you. Hold the place where you want to go in your mind's eye when you slap the glyph."

FORTY MINUTES later saw all of them back at Jack's house with the flickering of blue flames dying out behind them. It had taken Jack about fifteen attempts to get the realm door to appear, but he did it in the end. The others hadn't helped, just encouraged him to get the 'open' glyph correct, which had been relatively easy, but the 'unlock' second glyph had caused him some real difficulties, as they were all crammed in the pantry, with not much room for him to move his arm to draw. Elsie has also kept nudging him, muttering something about 'doing it under pressure' and laughing each time he had slapped the glyph to no effect. Nevertheless, he'd gotten it eventually and, to his amazement, had tumbled through his lounge door into his own hallway.

"How does it work, though?" said Jack, once they were all safely back. "I mean, what happens if the door at the other end is locked, or someone is looking?"

"The realm door works like a kind of glamour, Jack," said Elsie. "Once you've opened the door into the 'waiting room,' nobody can see you in that area; it's outside of all the realms. Then, when you try the 'unlock' glyph to come through, the glamour will not let you appear anywhere where someone could see you. Sometimes it just holds you where you are, or more often, it finds another door to come through in the location you want. It makes no difference if the door is locked either; you can still come through it. However, it will be locked once you're back through. Same as if you want to 'open' a locked door; the 'open' glyph allows you to do so, but you can only go to the 'waiting' room. You won't be robbing any banks!"

"But you must remember both the 'open' and the 'unlock' glyphs," said Fermy. "The 'open' one is not so critical, as you will stay where you are if you get it wrong, but once you're in the 'waiting' room, you need to unlock the way out; otherwise, you will be trapped there. And having the unlock glyph to a different realm will do you no good; the glamour works in pairs only, and each waiting room is unique at that point in time. Please DO NOT play with this until you are confident that you know both an 'open' and 'unlock' pairing off by heart. Time doesn't stand still in the 'waiting' room for lifers, even Crack-locks, and the chances of being found are slim if you get stuck."

"Okay," said Jack. "That ruins my plans for the evening then. Just joking!" he said, holding up both hands as the others glared at him.

"Jack," said Dorcas, "Where's is the kitchen, my sweets? I think's that it is time for Dorcas to shows you some magics that don't involve glamours."

"She's a mean cook," said Elsie. "This way, my dear."

SAMMY PLACED the key in the lock to the front door and then paused. She could hear laughter in the house, peals of it from Jack, and what could only be Elsie's cackles. She smiled; it had been a long day, but it sounded like Jack was feeling much better, which lifted her spirits. She pushed open the door, and the smell of something delicious hit her full in the face, her mouth watering instantly. She was just stepping in when a voice behind her said, "Good afternoon Mrs Crackley." Glancing over her shoulder, she saw Jimmy walking up the pavement to the house, his bag over his shoulder.

"Hi, Jimmy. How are you?"

"Good, thanks, Mrs Crackley. Am I okay to see Jack tonight?"

"Sure, no problems. You can probably stay for tea as well if you like, assuming that there is enough. It smells like Elsie's been busy."

"That'd be great, thanks!" said Jimmy. Sammy stood to the side and waved Jimmy in through the door, him dumping his bag on the floor as he went.

The kitchen door opened, and Elsie stuck her head out.

"Ah-ha; welcome home, Sammy. Good day at work? Expect not, never is when you have to work, eh? Still, home now; not got to go to any other work, have you? And who is this delightful young man? You haven't got yourself a fancy man, have you?" Elsie launched herself into another never-ending stream of discussion, Jimmy going bright red at the thought of him being a 'fancy man'.

"All good, thanks, Elsie," said Sammy. "Busy, though, and glad to be home. Something smells good; will there be enough for an extra guest? This is Jimmy, Jack's friend."

"Of course, yes, and... we've got a little surprise for you. Jack?"

Jack came out from behind Elsie, hands out in front of him, fumbling for the wall. Sammy stepped forward to help him when Jack dropped his hands and burst into giggles.

"Sorry, Elsie, but I can't keep it up. Mum, I can see!"

"Whh...at? How?" said Sammy.

"When I got up this morning, it was all fine. It looks like Dr Osmir was right; being at home was the best cure!"

"That's fantastic!" exclaimed Sammy with a huge smile, pulling Jack into a hug. How did that happen? Thank goodness, that's all I can say."

This has been discussed earlier, and Jack didn't hesitate. "It was when I got up this morning, mum. I just opened my eyes, and I was back to normal. Dr Osmir was right."

Sammy wiped away an errant tear. "I'm so happy, Jack; I have been fretting all day about it. I'm so pleased."

"Nice one, mate!" exclaimed Jimmy, clapping Jack on the shoulder. "That's great. Although maybe not so great if you have to be back at school!"

"I think that Jack should stay off for a few more days, just to be sure," said Elsie quickly. "Don't want any relapses, plus I don't want to cut my holiday here short, and I'd be bored here all on my own." She tipped Jack a wink.

"Yes, you're probably right," Sammy replied, ruffling her

son's hair. "He can stay off for now. Now, what is that I can smell?"

"That's the second surprise. We've cooked tea for you," said Jack.

He pushed open the kitchen door, and Jack's mum gasped. The kitchen table was laid with a gleaming white cloth, including napkins. Moreover, it was groaning with the volume of food laid out upon it. There were two different pies, steam slowly coming off them in lazy waves. There were vegetables, a large bowl of salad, what appeared to be a freshly baked loaf, an elaborate looking cake, and many smaller plates containing various delicious-looking accompaniments.

"Elsie, you shouldn't have! It's too much."

Jack glanced at Dorcas, who stood in the corner of the kitchen, a huge smile on her face. He mouthed, "Thank you," to her with his back to everyone, and she nodded, a huge beaming smile on her face.

"Well, let's eat then. Will you join us, Jimmy?" said Elsie, pulling the cork from a bottle.

"Try and stop me!" said Jimmy, pulling out a chair.

"Wait," said Sammy, glancing around anxiously. "Where's that bloody ferret?"

THE BIG HOUSE stood by itself on the edge of a town many miles away from the festivities currently underway at the Crackley / Cracklock house, appearing to continue to fall into ruin as it had done for decades. Even 'Old Jed,' the town's most senior resident who received his hundredth birthday letter from the Queen the month before, could not remember a time when the big house wasn't in a ruinous state. The town folk kept well away from it and the overgrown driveway; local folklore speaking of hauntings and evil acts in its past, making it not somewhere encouraging to visit.

Of course, the local teenagers made dares of going up to the house. Nobody had ever actually made it; there was an atmosphere the 'lucky' person encountered as they climbed over the gates and walked down the dark drive. With its over-grown bushes overhanging to form a bleak tunnel, it was enough to destroy any alcohol-induced bravery and send them scuttling back to the road that led past the house's entrance. The gates were never open, and nobody was ever seen entering or leaving the property, not even to collect from the postbox by the gates. The rumour mill had it around town that a mad old woman lived there, possibly a witch, but as nobody associated with the house ever come into town, the stories were never confirmed. If they could see the house in its unglamoured form, then they may well have tried to learn more, but as it was, they all kept well away.

Anastasia Cracklock was neither mad nor old, but she did consider herself a Lady and one of means. She sat in the window seat of the drawing-room at this particular moment, watching her son, Benedict, playing in the garden with some-thing, a frown creasing her face. There was something not entirely correct with the boy, well, man; Benedict was twenty-two years of age, and he took far too much pleasure in the Lord's work with which the family was both blessed and cursed.

Anastasia knocked on the window to attract Benedict's attention and gestured to come back to the house. Benedict strolled up the garden, the thing he was playing with clutched in his hand. Anastasia sighed and pulled the cord to open the sash window as Benedict arrived.

"What have you got there, Benedict?" she asked pleasantly.

"Nothing, Mama," came the response, both hands tucked firmly behind his back.

"Please show me what you've got behind your back, Benedict."

"Nothing, Mama," came the repeated response.

"Benedict, show me what is in your hands this instant!" Anastasia screamed suddenly into the man-boy's face.

Benedict winced and took a step back. He reluctantly bought his hands around to the front to show his mother what he had clutched in his big fist. Struggling, there was a small flower faery, tiny and fair, with one gossamer wing beating frantically. The other wing was missing, and a small bleeding tear was visible in its back where it should have been. Benedict shook the hand containing the faery as it bit into the side of his finger, its tiny teeth ineffectual against the large digits trapping it, and a little blood splattered onto his fingers.

Anastasia sighed again. "Benedict, we have discussed this many times. We do not toy with them. We remove them from existence. Now, did you pull off this faerie's wing?"

"Yes, Mother."

"Why?"

"Because I like it, Mother. I enjoy it, and they deserve to suffer; you have always said so. If we have to kill them, then why can't we have some fun? Daddy always did."

"Your father was right about a great many things, Benedict, but torturing Fae folk unnecessarily only leads to problems. We've discussed this."

"Only if they escape, Mother. And they never do now."

"That is beside the point, Benedict. If they can get in here, then the chances are that they will eventually find some way out. The glamour is good but not unfathomable. Now, get rid of it. Our guest will be here shortly."

Benedict smiled an unpleasant smile and, lifting the flower faery to his face, started to squeeze. The faeries face contorted in pain as it pounded its tiny fists against the grip, its remaining wing beating rapidly. Benedict squeezed harder, and the faery

127

issued a high-pitched scream that made the windows start to vibrate.

"Oh, for goodness sake," said Anastasia. "Give it to me."

Benedict reluctantly handed over the little faery to his mother, where it slumped weakly on her outstretched hand, panting. Pulling a large pin from her belt, Anastasia plunged it into the faery's chest. The faery hitched a little and then curled up, becoming motionless. A second or two later, it evaporated in bright sparkles, leaving a little powder that Anastasia brushed off her hand through the open window.

"There," she said. "Neat and to the point, with another of those foul little devils sent to meet its maker. Now, come inside, and neaten yourself up. And tell Nigel that we will take tea in the library when your Great Uncle arrives."

"Yes, Mama."

ANASTASIA ROSE to meet her guest as Nigel showed him into the room. The guest was dressed impeccably, as always, in costly clothing, and his eyes hidden behind the smoked glass of his spectacles. A heavy blue-jewelled pendant hung from his neck, glistening in the lamplight.

"Uncle," crooned Anastasia. "How marvellous it is to see you again."

"Anastasia," said Dr Cracklock. "Likewise. I trust that you are well?"

"Of course, of course, dear Uncle. The family here is indeed well, as I hope is your mother? Our work proceeds as always; I anticipate that is why you are here?"

Dr Cracklock didn't acknowledge the question and sat down without being asked, pulling the tea tray towards himself. Anastasia raised an eyebrow at the lack of formality but said nothing. She lowered herself into the chair opposite and watched as her

Uncle served himself first before pouring a second cup that he pushed across the table towards her. Dispensing with the small talk, he fixed Anastasia with a steely look and said, "How many this time?"

Anastasia picked up and rang a little handbell. The door creaked open at its pealing ring, and Benedict entered, pulling a small cart into the room. A rich red velvet cloth was draped over its box-like structure to conceal the contents; however, it failed to cover the sobbing sounds coming from the hidden depths.

Dr Cracklock rose and pulled the cloth from the cart in a swift motion. Staring into the cage that had just been uncovered, he counted the occupants quickly.

"Twelve, I see. A good count. Brownies are hard workers, as is the Gnome. Those I will take. I do not want the Slyph or the Pixies; they break too easily. Nor the childer either; they are too young for the works and distracting to their parents."

Inside the cage, the sobbing intensified, with the elder Fae pulling their childer towards them.

"Please, sir..." ventured one nymph.

"*Silence,*" snapped Dr Cracklock. "Benedict, take them out and ready them. And keep them quiet as well; their damned chatter makes me sick. I will take the grackles from those that are not needed before I leave; any that are left are yours to do with as you will."

"It would be my pleasure, Great Uncle," said Benedict with a sly smile. He shoved the cage, causing many of the captured little Fae folk to tumble off their feet. Laughing to himself, he left the room, pulling the cage behind him.

"The situation has not changed, Uncle?" said Anastasia. "The arrangement still stands?"

"Yes, yes, of course," said Dr Cracklock with an impatient wave. "When they have outlived their usefulness, they will be extinguished by yourselves."

"Thank you," said Anastasia. "They are an insult to the Lord with their unnatural ways. Heaven and Earth do not include their filthy realm, and we cannot permit them to exist."

"When we have completed our works, you will have no further problems," said Dr Cracklock. "The realm and its demons will no longer be of any concern for us."

"Hence why I am happy to continue with the arrangement, despite your silence about the 'works' as you put it. We will not destroy them when we capture them. However, I am curious that you came yourself on this occasion to collect the filth we had captured. We are used to, shall we say, less salubrious guests."

"Well, I come at Mother's request. She is pleased with your contribution to our cause and has very recently come by some news that may be of interest to you. If I may?"

Reaching under his coat, he pulled out a small, struggling figure bound in glowing golden rope. The imp struggled ineffectually at his bonds, a look of fear in its dark eyes. Dr Cracklock tossed it unceremoniously onto the table, where the imp groaned in pain. Anastasia recoiled.

"Uncle, really? You bring this filthy thing into my home?"

Dr Cracklock ignored her protests. "This is Dix. Until recently, it was of use to Mother and me; however, it came by some knowledge that it saw fit to ask payment for. Normally, such knowledge is freely given to us, and gladly. Of course, it has seen the error of its ways very quickly, but Mother has tired of the creature. However, the news may also be of interest to you; I believe that you have a special interest in a certain subject and that you will want to, shall we say, 'look into it'? But I would say one thing. If the boy is there, then we must have him; Mother has a particular interest in him. The rest, do as you will. Now, I must depart. Where is that son of yours?"

Intrigued by the somewhat mysterious nature of her Uncle's statement, Anastasia saw Dr Cracklock to the library door, where she again rang the little handbell. They passed muted pleasantries until Nigel appeared to take Dr Cracklock into the care of Benedict.

Upon her return to the table, Dix looked at Anastasia, his big eyes fearful and clouded with tears. Anastasia loomed over the little imp, her mouth set in a sinister sneer. "Speak," she commanded. "And if it is of interest, I shall consider releasing you."

So Dix did. In his squeaky voice and between sobs, he told his story of finding Jack Cracklock at the request of Mr Binks. Of an old woman restoring the boy's sight 'Must be Elsie' thought Anastasia to herself, 'my devil loving aunt'. Of Fermerillion's presence. Of the opening of a realm door and them leaving altogether. When he had finished, he quietly answered her few questions, not looking directly at Anastasia while he did so.

"So," said Anastasia thoughtfully, drumming her fingers on the table, "The missing family is found, along with Elsie, who has eluded me for too long. Still no sign of David, though, the Fae loving fool. And Sammy. Poor dumb Sammy, who I assume is as simple as ever. Well, I believe that a family reunion may be overdue. See if we can bring some Cracklocks back into the fold. And if Great Aunt Agatha wants the boy, then so be it."

Picking up the handbell again, she rang it for the third time. The ever-present figure of Nigel appeared at the door, his pale and glum face enquiring.

"Nigel, we shall require the car tomorrow. Please have the garage make it ready."

"Of course, my Lady."

"And clear away these things. I have some works I need to do before we leave."

As Nigel moved into the room, a small voice said, "My Lady?"

Looking down at the table, Anastasia focused again on Dix, whom she had entirely forgotten.

"My Lady, was my news of interest to you?" said Dix in a subdued voice.

"Why, yes," said Anastasia, a broad smile appearing on her face.

"You said that you might release me if my news was of interest?" said Dix, his low voice full of hope.

"Yes, I did. And I am a Lady of my word," said Anastasia giving the little imp a sweet smile.

Moving over to the table, she pulled another sharp pin from her belt. "I will be thrilled to release you, you filthy little devil."

CHAPTER 7

*J*ack was awake bright and early the following morning; in truth, he'd not slept well at all. Images of family trees, glamours and the misty face of his father had whirled around in his mind and denying him any sleep until the early hours as he tried to process everything he had learned and how it changed his view of the world. But the fact that his dad might still be alive was a thunderbolt from out of the blue, and he itched to tell his mother. He felt another ripple of excitement, but he couldn't say a word; she'd think him quite mad if he babbled about faeries and trees that grew out of books. In truth, Jack was finding it difficult not to tell his mother about all of this. Sure, he had made some new friends yesterday, but it had been difficult not to talk to them over the dinner table, particularly as he had watched Dorcas serve herself and then sit on the floor to eat. Of Fermy, there had been no sign at all. Jack hadn't felt great about the fact that his new friends couldn't join in with the conversation over the table, although Dorcas didn't seem to mind. She had watched everyone with a smile as she ate, just happy to be back in the home of the family she had spent so much time caring for over the years. Jack had tried to include her when no one else was looking, with little mouthed comments and gestures, which she had appreciated. Elsie had given Jack reassuring smiles during the meal and had helped Sammy dispose of close to two bottles of wine. She had wobbled up from the table to clear it at the end, giggling with Sammy as they set about scraping plates and filling the sink.

Jimmy had been on his usual good form during the meal, regaling the others with a series of unbelievable facts that apparently were extremely funny to the elder two as they slurped down the wine. After they had finished, he and Jack had made a sharp exit from the two giggling ladies and had headed up to Jack's bedroom.

"Got something for you, mate," said Jimmy, rummaging in his bag and pulling out a mobile phone. "It's not new, but it's in pretty good nick. Do you still want it?"

"Yes, please," said Jack, looking at his own shabby phone. "Are you sure?"

"Yes, it's fine. It's just in a drawer at home; may as well get some use out of it."

"I really appreciate this, mate; be nice to have a decent phone!"

Jimmy switched out the number and sim card from Jack's old phone and got the new one started. Jack seized it eagerly, fiddling with some of the functions and looking at the pre-installed apps.

Jimmy had sat quietly for a bit, fidgeting uncomfortably with Jack's duvet before saying. "Jack. Can I ask you something, mate?"

"Uhum," said Jack, still engrossed in the phone.

"Are you seriously alright after that accident?"

"What?" said Jack, looking up. "Of course I am. Why?"

"Well," said Jimmy awkwardly, "you seemed distracted during the dinner and were staring at the floor repeatedly and smiling. You also seemed to mouth a few words on occasion. Are you seeing things? It's cool if you are; you can get that sorted alright."

Jack cursed inwardly. He'd been a Cracklock for less than twelve hours, and already he was causing suspicions. Of course, Jimmy was pretty sharp anyway, but he'd have to try harder to hide it when he saw unusual things.

"I'm fine, mate; I don't know what you mean."

"Well, you seemed away with the fairies a bit, that's all," said Jimmy.

Jack jumped. "What did you say?"

Jimmy looked puzzled. "Away with the fairies? It's something my dad says when my brother or I am engrossed in something. Daydreaming. I was just worried, that's all; you never used to do that before the accident. Of course, we didn't know each other well, but you were pretty much focused, as I remember. Now, you seem a little, well, distracted."

"I'm just tired, mate, that's all. It took it out of me; not sure I'm completely recovered yet," said Jack, and inwardly, 'Not sure that I will ever be recovered if I'm honest.'

"Well, just to let you know, you can count on me if you need any help," said Jimmy. "I still owe you for that business with the twins. They were going to mess me up badly."

Jack waved him away. "You don't owe me anything, buddy, as I've already said. Well, actually, you do. You owe me a game on Command and Conquer," Jack gestured with the new phone. "And I am going to spank you again on this."

Jimmy laughed and pulled out his own phone. "C'mon then. Let's see what you've got. The loser goes and gets the drinks from downstairs."

∾

JACK HAD LOST the game last night, of course, and he smiled to himself at the memory as he made his way down the stairs for breakfast. He was feeling nervous for some reason; he guessed that it was because he would be going somewhere completely new and outside of his comfort zone. He had absolutely no idea what to expect in Faery; his knowledge came exclusively from the entertainment industry, and the others had already proven that what the films said wasn't right. If belief in Faeries could be considered to be true. Truth be told, Jack thought that it may still be some kind of elaborate trick or hallucination. Maybe he was still in the coma from the accident, and this was all the figment of his busted brain? It felt real, but...

All his doubts disappeared when he walked into the kitchen to see Elsie slumped backwards at the kitchen table, with what appeared to be tea bags over her eyes. Some brown liquid had run down her face, giving the illusion of rusty tears streaking through the powder on her cheeks.

"Auntie Elsie?" Jack enquired.

Elsie sat forward with a quick jerk. "Oooh, Jack, you startled me!"

"What are you doing, Auntie Elsie?"

"Trying to stop my eyes from looking so red, Jack," she said, plucking the teabags from her face. "I've such a headache, and my eyes are red. Dorcas said to use teabags, but I don't think that they have helped any. I feel awful; it must have been something I ate."

"Or drank," said Dorcas, appearing around the kitchen door where she patted Jack reassuringly on the bottom as she went past. "I says last night, Elsie, I says, you should be careful's with that grape drink, no good ever comes of it. But Elsie laughs at poor Dorcas, and her and Sammy has more. And then poor Dorcas has to clear up the mess they left, and then try to sleep in Elsie's room, where she had to have snoring and trumping and...."

"I do not do that," said Elsie primly, cutting in. "And I most certainly was not drunk."

"You's was," said Dorcas. "And I's said to use cold tea bags, not fresh ones. Face is scary now with brown lines, and eyes are still red. Something you ates, my grockles and grackles, my cooking is not bad."

Jack laughed. Elsie looked at him and said, "Does your mum have any aspirin in the house, Jack?"

"I think so. I'll go and check; take her some up too."

"No needs, no needs," said Dorcas. "Dorcas has alreadys helped poor Sammy, who had to go to her work again. Dorcas left water and pills for poor Sammy and then some breakfasts to eats before she left. Dorcas knows where pills are, Jack; you sit, and Dorcas will prepares you some breakfast. After I get's pills for Grannie Grape here." She tipped Jack a wink, who exploded with the giggles.

"Well, I'm pleased that my suffering gives you both such pleasure. Normally, I would be heading straight back to bed, but I promised Fermy that we would leave here at ten o'clock sharp for Faery. And if we don't, we may well miss each other."

"Where is Fermy, Aunt Elsie?"

"He returned to Fae yesterday to make our appointments. It's impolite to simply arrive in the Faery Realm when you are not expected; us being lifers and all that."

"Okay, understood. But why would we miss him? He would wait for us, surely?"

"Ah, yes. Well, time works differently over there in Faery; there is a time shift. Time is, well, slower in the Fae Realm. It is difficult to describe, but time just passes much slower over there. We could be there for just a few hours and then come back to find months or years had passed in our realm. Think about it like a roundabout at the park. When you are in the very middle, you are spinning, but you're okay; you aren't being pulled by gravity. However, at the outside of the roundabout, it seems like you are going very fast. This realm is like being on the outside of the roundabout, the Faery Realm in the middle. It's possible to miss an intended time spot when you go through from this side, so we could miss when Fermy is waiting for us."

"But, I thought that the Realm Doors take you to where you want to be?"

"They do. But not necessarily when you want to be, if you are moving between here and the Faery Realm. Likewise, when you come back."

"I don't want to come back here months or years later! Mum will be really worried if I'm not here when she's back from work."

"Jack, relax. It's not really a problem."

"Yes, it is, Auntie; I don't want Mum to worry or have a nationwide police hunt for me!"

"Look, Jack, we have a marker here to aim at. My house. Us Cracklocks have been visiting the Faery Realm for years and years. The secret is to have a marker to point the Realm Door at when we are going or coming back. In the Faery Realm, it is Fermy's house where we are going; we sometimes use Dorcas family home as well, although we don't like to disturb them; there are a lot of folk living there and they get, shall we say, excited if we just arrive."

"They loves company, Jack," came Dorcas' voice from behind the door.

"Yes, well, that may well be the case. It is easier to use Fermy's house to arrive in, though; it makes things a lot quicker to leave, not that it is not a pleasure to see your family, Dorcas. And Fermy and I have already agreed the time we will leave, so we will arrive when he's expecting us."

"And coming back?"

"We aim the Realm Door at my cottage, and with a few calculations, can normally arrive within an hour or so of when you want to be there. We then use a second door to come back here. Simple."

"Why don't we miss time when we travel from here to your cottage?"

"Well, because the time in this realm is constant. We can use the same Realm Doors to travel through Faery as well, as time is constant there. If you are in a realm, you can travel in that realm in real-time. It's only when we go between realms that there can be some time lag problems."

"Okay, if you're sure," said Jack, still unconvinced. "I do want to go, but I don't want to upset Mum."

"It'll be fine. Now, it's nine o'clock. We are leaving in one hour. Get some breakfast, and then we can get organised."

Jack started to get up when he noticed a large plate about the size of a bin lid wending its way towards the table. On it was bacon, eggs, sausages, tomatoes, toast, and mushrooms that Jack could identify. There was also quite a lot that he couldn't, although one item appeared to be a pile of porridge, which was definitely out of place.

"Breakfast, Jack," said Dorcas. "Must keeps my growing boy well-fed."

"That's too much, Dorcas," said Jack, his eyes popping out.

"Not at all, not at all," said Dorcas. "Eat. And would you likes tea or juice? Do you want both? Okay?"

Jack didn't say anything but stared at the mountain of food. *'If this is what being a Cracklock is all about, I could get used to it,'* he thought, picking up the knife and fork.

FORTY MINUTES LATER, and feeling decidedly better, Elsie called Jack from the kitchen, where he was staring at the half-eaten plate of food and clutching his stomach.

"Come on, Jack, please; time to go now."

"Do I need to bring anything?" asked Jack, pushing himself up from his chair with a great heave. He gave out a burp and covered his mouth, shocked, which started Dorcas laughing.

"No," said Elsie disapprovingly. "But can you please turn out your pockets before we go?"

Jack did as he was told, and Elsie poked through the jumble he'd removed.

"You can keep the gum and handkerchief, but leave the coins and the phone here if you don't mind?"

"Why?"

"Because it is considered extremely rude to take anything made of iron into the Realm of the Fae; they really don't like it. That goes for iron alloys to some extent; they don't mind bits on clothing, but anything loose is a big no-no. So, to be on the safe side, I just tend to leave anything that could potentially have iron in it here in this realm. And your phone won't work over there, so no point in taking it."

Elsie looked at Jack's puzzled face. "Are you alright, my sweet?"

"I can understand about the phone; that's no issue. But iron?"

"The Fae have kind of an aversion to it. Nobody, not us or the Fae scholars, is sure why it has such an effect on them. Some think it is because it's magnetic and it disrupts the magical nature of the Fae, others because of its heritage for making weapons and such, and that affects their sensitivities. Nevertheless, everyone knows that it isn't welcome; they will shy away from iron and don't really like things made with iron – steel and such. Iron itself will definitely hurt them, and in most circumstances, will kill them if exposed. So, if you take any into the Fae realm, you will receive short measures from the Fae, and they will seek to remove it and you. Normally by force."

"Sounds serious, Auntie," said Jack, rechecking his pockets.

"It is, really; it's like them turning up here with explosives or poison. Deadly in the wrong hands, and you don't want it around you if you have the choice."

"Okay, I'm good to go; iron-free."

"Right then. Now again, watch carefully. I am going to open the realm door to Faery; note the differences from last time."

Elsie again moved to the lounge door and pulled out her marker pen. She carefully drew another symbol on the door, different from the one from yesterday, before slapping it with the palm of her hand. The symbol glowed again, and then the falling glitter effect happened as the glyph dropped off the door.

"After you, Jack," said Elsie, picking up her bag.

Jack pushed open the door, and this time, instead of the blue flames, Jack saw dancing green flames throughout the living room. He moved into the room eagerly, and Elsie followed, shutting the door behind her as she came.

"Wait, what about Dorcas?" said Jack, looking around for the brownie.

"Dorcas is going to stay here and do some 'organising', as she puts it. I think she is going to clean the house from top to bottom; she loves doing that. And I am on a winner as well, as your mum will think that I've done it," said Elsie with a cheeky smile. "Gives a whole new meaning to the phrase 'Brownie Points', eh?"

Jack was disappointed that the nice little brownie wasn't coming, but he understood. He watched as Elsie drew the 'unlock' symbol on the back of the lounge door; it was again different from the one that he saw the day before.

"Are the symbols different for each Realm then, Auntie?" asked Jack.

"Yes, and you have to remember both of them like we discussed if you don't want to get stuck."

"I'll never remember them all if there are loads; my memory's rubbish!"

"Well, the person we are going to see today may be able to

help you with that. I'll mention it," said Elsie. "Now quiet a moment, if you please; I need to concentrate. Shifting between the realms needs a little thought on the destination."

This time when she slapped the glyph, the green flames reacted; going from lazily waving to frantic flickering; the green light dancing madly on the furniture and walls. Jack jumped at how frantic it became and looked at Elsie.

"Don't worry, Jack. It's just the time shift; we are now in the waiting room in Faery, but some of our realm is still here with us. It's perfectly normal; don't be concerned about it." Seeing Jack relax slightly, she said, "Okay then, let's go."

Elsie pushed open the lounge door into a small room with a shallow ceiling. Stooping down, she ducked into the room and beckoned Jack to follow her. Jack did, and as the door swung shut behind him, he looked around to see his first glimpse of Faeryland. Which, as it transpired, was a little disappointing. The room that they were in was tiny; there was barely enough room for both of them, and Jack was glad that Dorcas has stayed behind now for the sake of more breathing space. Jack looked at the door they had just come through and pulled it open. A bare wall lay behind it. Elsie was fumbling in her bag for something and muttering under her breath.

"Are we in a pantry again, Auntie?" asked Jack.

"No, no, not this time. We are in some sort of secret room, by the looks of it, although where that is, I have no idea. There must have been a problem with the doors at Fermy's house; it's extraordinary."

"How are we going to get out? There's no real door."

"I'm working on it," said Elsie, rummaging in her bag. "Here, hold these."

She handed Jack a bag of what appeared to be dried mushrooms, a small jar of glittering lights, lipstick, a chequebook, and a large flat stone with a hole in it before announcing a triumphant, "Aha!" From the depths of her bag, she pulled out a small wooden box, its lid closed with a brass hook and eye. Flipping the catch, Elsie removed what looked like a small, rubbery black circle. She started to pull it this way and that, its surface getting slowly larger as she did so.

"What's that?" asked Jack, staring at the shape as it increased in size under Elsie's administrations.

"Portable hole," said Elsie, concentrating.

"A what?"

"A portable hole. It's a Faery childers plaything, but I find it extremely useful. One of Dorcas' relations gave it to me; apparently, the children were using it to get up to mischief and had had it confiscated. They had thrown it on the side of a Granddad's bath while he was sitting in it. Made a lot of mess, apparently, plus the Grandparent in question was found hollering and naked, stuck half in and half out the hole with their bare bottom for all to see, covered in soapsuds. Quite inventive, really, when you think about it. Okay then, I think we're ready."

The portable hole was about the size of a large plate, and Elsie slapped it onto the wall. Where it hit, it disappeared, and a large hole through the wall instantly appeared. Jacks stood agape as Elsie pressed her face to the hole and looked. Gesturing Jack over, she placed a finger on her lips to indicate quiet, and Jack peeked into the newly formed gap. Looking through the hole, Jack could see Fermy stood in front of an open door, apparently in a deep argument with whoever was over the threshold. A purplish cloud was hovering around his feet, apparently sucking up leaves and debris that the wind was blowing in through the door. On the wall, behind the little Feeorin, a wooden face was pulling faces at whoever was at the door; a rasping tongue blowing raspberries at whoever it was. Jack couldn't see who this was, but the discussion looked agitated as Fermy was gesturing wildly, his face looking rather angry. Jack strained to hear the conversation without popping his head through the hole.

"But you aren't listening to me. I have given you an answer already." Muted murmurings in response.

"I've told you, I don't care what the Court's intelligence says. I have not seen David Cracklock's heir, I have not seen David Cracklock, and I have not, nor have any intention, either now or in the future, of seeking them out. The last time I saw David Cracklock was eleven years ago, as you well know. His family's whereabouts are unknown, and wherever they are, they can stay there. Good riddance to all the damn Cracklocks, I say."

"What's going on?" said Elsie behind Jack in a whisper. Jack flapped his hand at her.

More murmurings.

"No, I will not take that back. You know as well as I do that that family intends no good to us, regardless of the few 'good' ones that we know about. The whole family is rotten to the core, and no amount of their assistance or kowtowing to the Courts, either faction, will change my mind."

The other voice replied, raised in agitation, "Okay, okay, Fermerillion. Nonetheless, you better not be telling untruths on this matter. Court enforcement does not take kindly to being misled."

"I understand. Now, if you do not mind, I will bid you a good day."

Fermy pushed the door shut hard and then sagged against it, fanning his face with his hand. The purple cloud zoomed off out of eye-line, but Jack could see that its owner looked exhausted. Elsie, seeing her friend in distress, called through the hole: "Fermy?"

The little Feeorin jumped a little and glanced around. Elsie thrust her arm through the hole and waved.

"Over here."

"What are you doing there? And where exactly is there?" said Fermy in bemusement. He came over to the hole, and with a neat jump, landed on the rim. Dipping his head, he walked through the hole and glanced into the cubbyhole in which they were both squashed.

"Well, my grockles and grackles; I never knew that this was here," he said, shaking his head. "Where does that door lead to?"

Jack pulled open the door they had come through, but it was just a slight indentation in the wall behind it, with a wall of dried earth.

"It looks to me to be some sort of secret arrival room. I guess the realm door dropped you here as I was 'otherwise entertained' by those idiot court enforcers. The house probably put it there; it does that, you know. When I have guests, the dining room gets bigger. Never figured it out."

"Court Enforcers were here?" asked Elsie.

"Yes," said Fermy. "Both sides have them now; they 'keep an eye on things' as they put it. Those were from the Unseelie Court."

"What did they want?" asked Jack.

"In a word, you. They had information that a Cracklock could potentially be coming to Faery and, given my history with the family, wanted further information."

"But how?" said Elsie. "It was only yesterday that Jack became aware of Fae. That is fast work, even for the Courts. And there was no tracing glamour on him or anything, as they would have found him before."

"I have no idea," said Fermy. "But it will be to no good that they are actively seeking Jack so quickly. How they found out is a mystery. But with it being the Unseelie Court, if I had to guess, I would suspect the other side of your family has found out somehow."

Elsie frowned, looking puzzled. "It can't be them; not so soon. How could they know; surely they couldn't have had spies out for all this time? It would have had to be an extraordinary coincidence that a spy was there when we removed the glamour. Plus, there is no way that they would have been at the cottage when we were there; it's hidden from the Fae."

"I'm sorry," said Jack interrupting. "But why would the other side of the family be interested in me? And why would they go to the Unseelie Court to talk about it? They are the 'dark side,' aren't they?"

Fermy looked at Elsie, who raised her eyebrows. Fermy looked at his hands and said, "Jack, as we said yesterday, the other Cracklocks aren't good people. While they wouldn't go to the Unseelie Court directly, they would take steps to make things difficult for you if they could, particularly where Faery Folk are concerned. A message to the right person would cause all kinds of bother. They have another agenda."

"What agenda?" asked Jack.

Fermy sighed. "Listen, can you wait just a bit longer? The friend that I would like you to meet can explain some more about your father, and the other Cracklocks are a part of that picture."

"I guess so," said Jack. "But I would like to try and understand better; it seems very 'cloak and dagger' this whole thing."

"That's because it was and still is," said Fermy with a tone of exasperation. "Now come out of there; we're going to be late to see our friend. And he is, shall we say, somewhat eccentric when it comes to politeness and timings."

Jack looked around the small room, which still had no sign of an exit. He looked at Elsie.

"How are we going to get out? Can we make the hole bigger?"

"Nope," said Elsie. "that's as big as it will go. But aren't you a Cracklock?"

"Yes…" said Jack puzzled.

"And can't you open realm doors?"

"Yes," said Jack, understanding dawning.

"So, open a travel realm door, and get us out of here. That

door over there will be fine to come through, although admittedly, it will be on hands and knees." Elsie pointed through the hole at a small closed-door off Fermy's little hall.

"But I don't know the glyph," said Jack.

"It was the same as the one yesterday. See if you can remember it,"

"But I don't have anything to draw with."

"Really, Jack," said Elsie, pulling a pen out of her bag. "You need to start being better prepared. Never leave home without a pen." She handed it to Jack. "Now then. Let's see if you can get us out of this mess."

~

THE LARGE RED Bentley cruised along the high street of Jack's town for the third time, the occupants on the lookout for someone who may help them. In the back of the car, Anastasia was watching the crowds on the street with intense concentration. Benedict was also watching the crowds but with less interest. They had been driving this route for the last forty minutes, and he was bored with the whole thing.

"Can we stop, Mother?" he asked. "It's frightfully boring just cruising around this dull little town. I spotted a couple of devils earlier in those public gardens; we could have a little fun."

"No," said Anastasia, not looking away from the window.

"But this is ridiculous. Do you think for one minute that David's son will have a sign on him, pronouncing him so? This is like a needle in a haystack."

"I'm not looking for David's son at the moment."

"Then what are we doing here?"

"Looking for someone who knows David's son."

"Why don't we just ask that Binks character? It would be quicker."

"Because he has no idea where the boy lives. He sent a

sprite to spy out the boy's location but never learned of it because the foul little beast went directly to Great Aunt to sell his information. Besides, Binks is a wretched creature. Fae bound but sly with it. I will have no dealings with him; he is Uncle's creature."

Benedict drummed his fingers on the car door. "But doesn't Binks know what the boy looks like?"

Anastasia turned from the window and fixed him with a cold stare. "He looks like a fifteen-year-old boy. What more do we need to know? He wears jeans and trainers. Has a mobile telephone. What more of a description do you think we will get from that idiot? Nothing. No, what we need is someone that knows David's son."

"But how we will find someone?" whined Benedict.

"Use your brain, boy. What have you noticed driving around this godawful place?"

"It's busy, like any market day in these awful towns."

"And how does being busy help us?"

"I'm not sure."

"It's busy, but there are no school children in the crowds. Herewith they are all at school. And there is only one school in this area that the boy would be able to attend."

"Well, yes, but how's that going to help? We can't wait outside the school and look; people will ask questions of us."

"Yes, but we are looking for school-age children who are not at school today. They may be ill, playing truant, or 'on leave.' They are likely to know the boy and possibly where he lives. This is not a large town, quite unremarkable; David chose an excellent location to hide them. If we do not find anyone, then we can think about the school. A basic masking glamour would be all that it takes in that situation. But I don't want to wait until the end of the day."

Benedict pondered all of this; it made sense while school was in session. Leaning over the seat, he said, "Nigel, please take us into the section of the town where the houses are; this area is of no use to us." Anastasia favoured her son with a smile at this.

Nigel indicated and pulled off the main road onto a smaller street of houses that were all quiet. He took random turns left and right, cruising the streets at a slow pace, his passengers staring out of the window, seeking a target. As Anastasia had noted, Bloxton was not that big a place, and they naturally progressed through random turns into the Morningside estate.

Benedict wrinkled his nose up as he looked over the terraced houses that formed one of the estate roads. "How can people live like this, Mother? It's truly disgusting; all lumped together, living like pigs."

Anastasia was fascinated by the housing estate and not just because of the apparent lack of devils in the area. *'It must be truly desperate here if there are no Fae; those filthy creatures are every-where,'* she thought to herself. *'Interesting that there are none here.'*

The car cruised slowly down another depressing street, and it was then that Anastasia spotted two well-built boys sitting on a wall opposite a row of houses. One of them was smoking, but the thing that interested Anastasia more was that a small red demon was sitting on the shoulder of one of them.

"Nigel, please pull over here. Benedict, please go and get that imp. I'm sure it will be delighted to answer a few questions."

THE LARGE CAR pulled over to the curb next to where the LaFey twins were sitting, spending their suspension days doing very little. Looking at the expensive car, the first thing that flashed into Tyler's mind was, *'Ah great, the feds.'* The rear car door opened, and a tall young man climbed out, oddly dressed in what looked like a period costume in those programmes their ma watched.

"Hello, hello, hello," said Tyler, nudging Mason. "Short on

uniform, are they; have to raid the lost property?" He chuckled, and Mason followed his lead.

The young man gave them a broad smile and stepped over to them. He didn't say anything but instead made a lunge towards Tyler, who veered backwards on the wall. "Oi, what you think you're doing?" he said indignantly. He then looked astonished as the young man turned from them, appearing to be holding something in his hand that they couldn't see.

"Are you mental?" called Tyler. "What's wrong with you?"

Hanging around with the twins as he did, the red imp Graz had been watching the car with interest as the man had climbed out and wondered if he could goad the twins into a mugging of this person who was so out of place here. He had no real concept of the police, other than that he liked to watch them try to put a stop to troubles he had a hand in stirring up. Therefore, he was shocked when the man barged past Tyler, grabbed him in a firm grip, and turned back towards the car.

" 'Ere, what yer doing?" he screeched. "Let me go."

"Quiet," said the young man, slapping the imp hard enough on its head to stun it temporarily. The broad smile did not leave his face.

The twins watched all of this, puzzled. To them, a stranger had just walked over and was now performing some sort of elaborate play-acting. Tyler looked around to see if there was a hidden camera somewhere, but the street seemed clear.

The car door swung open further, and the man climbed back in, pulling the door shut behind him. Graz took in the elaborately dressed woman sitting in the back seat and the front's silent driver. He had a strong feeling that he was in a lot of trouble. Benedict did not release his grasp on Graz but instead tightened it as the imp squirmed.

"'Oo are yer? And 'ow can you see me?" the imp panted.

The woman fixed Graz with an icy stare. "We will ask the

questions, devil. You will answer them. And don't think you can escape; this car is Fae locked."

Graz shuddered at this; he couldn't fade out to escape if that was the case.

"You obviously don't know 'oo I am," he said, bluffing. "Yer better let me go at once."

"I do not know, nor do I care," said the woman. "You will answer what we ask, or we will extinguish you."

"I don't thi...*aaarrghhhhh!*" Graz screamed as Benedict increased his grip, squeezing the imp hard and then relaxing.

"Now," said Anastasia, "what are you doing with those boys?"

"Nuffink!" screeched the imp, and then, feeling the grasp around him tighten again, "I just foller them round. I like the things that they do."

"Which are?" said Anastasia

"Tormentin' others," said Graz with a whimper.

"And who are these boys?"

"Tyler and Mason LaFey. Everyone 'round here knows 'em."

"And their age?"

"I dunno. No, please..." as the grip tightened around him again.

"When did they leave school?" asked Anastasia.

Graz was panting now. "They haven't. Bin told to stay away from there for now. I think that they will go back; they talk about it."

Anastasia nodded at Benedict. "Secure it. Uncle can have it."

"Mama!" pleaded Benedict.

"No," said Anastasia. "Leave it be."

"What...what yer doing?" asked Graz in a panic. He was receiving a lesson in what it felt like to be a victim, and it did not feel good.

The two ignored him, and Benedict climbed out of the car, holding the imp tightly. Opening the boot, he grabbed a small cage and stuffed Graz into it.

151

"Wait. Please wait. What are..." The imp was cut off as Benedict slammed the boot shut, silencing him.

∼

THE TWINS HAD WATCHED this pantomime with interest; there was something definitely funny about all of this, and they were sure that they were being stitched up for something. Therefore, they were a little wary when the rear car window powered down, and an attractive blonde woman gestured to them.

"Gentlemen," the woman said, "I was wondering if you would be interested in assisting us?" A hand appeared, waving what looked to be a selection of banknotes.

The twins got up off the wall and approached the car; interest piqued now despite their reservations.

"What do you want?" said Tyler gruffly.

"Some simple directions. I am trying to locate some long-lost family members, who I believe are residents of this fair town. I believe that...."

"OOOIIIIIII!" came a loud voice from behind the car. Anastasia started at this and turned to look out of the opposite window.

Coming across the road was a shabby man in a dirty string vest, cheap tattoos adorning his arms and neck, and a baseball bat braced menacingly on one shoulder. Walking around the car, he stood in front of the twins and stared at Benedict in a threatening manner.

"What you want?" he said, gesturing with the handle of the bat at Anastasia while continuing to eyeball Benedict.

"Please excuse us, Sir. We are simply asking for directions," said Anastasia.

"Trying to pick up my kids are yer, in yer fancy car? Fancying a bit of rough, are you?" replied Kev LaFey with a grunt.

"No, no, nothing like..." began Benedict, but Kev shut him up by pointing the bat at him.

"Listen, Sir, we mean no harm; we are simply trying to locate a relative of ours," tried Anastasia again.

"She's got money, Dad," said Tyler. "She showed it to us. Wants some help, that's all."

"Money, eh?" said Kev, his eyes becoming sly. "Why don't you just hand over that money right now to me? Save having to have this fancy car mended; bet that would cost a pretty penny, eh?" Kev tapped the end of the bat against the car door none too lightly.

Anastasia had had enough. "Look, we want directions. Can you help us without the veiled threats or not?" she said, directing the question towards the boys.

"I ask the questions around..." began Kev and then suddenly stopped. He looked down at himself quizzically and scratched at his stomach. He then clawed at his sides, then the top of his legs. Dropping the bat, he gave a strangled cry and then started to scratch himself all over.

"What's up, Dad?" said Tyler.

"Ants. Feels like ants all over me, biting," shrieked Kev, slapping at himself even more frantically. "Aarrgghhh." He started to thrash at himself, pulling his vest up and over his head with one hand while tugging at the drawstring on his jogging bottoms. Yanking them down, he tried to kick them off over his trainers but ended up falling face down onto the pavement. He rolled around on the floor, clawing at himself.

Anastasia looked on from the car window, a smile on her face as she watched the thug roll about, slapping at nothing. She looked at Benedict and nodded. Benedict made a simple hand gesture.

Kev LaFey stopped his frantic rolls instantly and sat up, a puzzled look on his face. "They've gone," he said, bewildered. Benedict loomed over him.

"They can come back very easily if you don't shut up. We do not take threats. If you continue, I think that we can enjoy watching you with the ants again. Or perhaps you'd prefer wasps?" He opened his hand to show a large wasp, its antennae twitching, black oil eyes fixed on Kev. He closed his hand, and the wasp was gone. Staring at Kev, he put his finger on his lips in a 'ssshhhh' gesture.

"Look," said Tyler, with a glance at his cowed father. "What is going on? Is this some sort of joke that you're all in on? If so, where are the cameras? And how much money are we going to make?"

"It is not a joke," said Anastasia. "Just a basic glamour, not that I'd expect you to understand. As to how much money you are going to make, that is really dependent on if you can help us."

"What do you want?" said Tyler.

"I want to know where my family is. The name is Cracklock. A boy, about fifteen years of age, give or take. Possibly living with his parents and an older lady."

Tyler shook his head. "Don't know anyone named Cracklock; no one at school of that name."

"Very well," said Anastasia, sitting back in the car. "Get in, Benedict."

Mason leaned over and whispered into Tyler's ear.

"Wait," said Tyler. "Nobody named Cracklock, but we know a Crackley. Jack Crackley. Similar situation; only lives with just his mum, never seen no dad around. Don't know about any old lady, though; might be, but we're not exactly friends with him."

Anastasia was interested. "Okay. And where does Jack Crackley live?"

Tyler looked at Mason, who shrugged.

"Don't know. But we know someone who does. His mate, Jimmy Owen. He'd know."

"And do you think that Jimmy Owen would be likely to tell you where his friend, Jack Crackley, lives?" said Anastasia.

"Lady, I think that we can persuade him. We have some things we'd like to discuss with him ourselves," said Tyler with a sinister grin.

"Then I think that we have an arrangement. I would like to know by the end of the day, please. Here is a card with my number. And here are some expenses to assist you." Anastasia handed over the large roll of banknotes. Tyler took them, and both his and Mason's eyes bulged at the amount. They had never seen so much cash, and they were no strangers to rolls of notes.

"There will be another one if Master Jack Crackley is who I am seeking," said Anastasia.

"You've got it, lady. We'll call you as soon as we've got the address. School's out in about an hour; give us two hours to get this organised."

"Very well," said Anastasia sitting back as the window started to go back up.

Tyler and Mason set off in the direction of the school when the window came down again.

"Boys," called Anastasia, "please do not think of crossing us on this matter. Not unless you want to enjoy what your father here…" she gestured at Kev, who still sat on the ground, "… experienced. And for you, it will be for the rest of your lives."

"Understood," said Tyler. "For this amount of money, we'd sell you our mother."

Anastasia nodded, and the window went back up. Turning to Benedict, she said, "I have a feeling that this Crackley may well be who we want. I think that we can spare two hours."

"We could go back to that public area," said Benedict eagerly. "Catch a few for Uncle?"

"Extinguish a few, you mean? Very well, we need to while away the time somehow. Nigel, drive on, please."

155

CHAPTER 8

*J*ack was improving. This time it only took four attempts to get the travel glyph correct, although a few more goes were needed to get the unlock one right as well. Now, he and Elsie stood, slightly stooped, in the hallway of Fermy's small home.

"Are we going to the registration place now then? I can't wait to see what Faery looks like!" said Jack in anticipation.

Fermy looked at Elsie, and an unseen understanding passed between them, Elsie nodding.

"Jack, we aren't going to register you today," said Fermy. "With these court officials sniffing about, we need to find out why they are so keen to find you. I will have to make some subtle enquiries about what's going on."

"But what about going to see your friend?" asked Jack, a little disappointed to not be going out. "Are we going to have to travel by realm door again?"

Elsie smiled. "I think that we can do better than that, Jack; we understand how much you want to have a nose around. If you don't mind another glamour on you, then I think that we might take a little stroll to our appointment instead."

"That would be fantastic!" said Jack enthusiastically. "What do I need to do?"

"Nothing, nothing. Well, actually, just stand still for a moment without jiggling about so that Fermy can work his glamour."

Jack froze on the spot and looked at Fermy. The little Feeorin looked up at Jack and cracked his fingers together. He then performed a complicated series of hand gestures that were a blur to watch. When he was done, he smiled and nodded, and Elsie gave a little jump and clap.

"Oh, Fermy, that's the best one yet!" she said with glee. The wooden face on the wall gave a hooting laugh and then blew another raspberry in Jack's direction.

Jack looked himself up and down, puzzled. From what he could see, nothing had changed. He looked down at his slightly shabby trainers, up to his legs, and then held his hands out in front of him. Everything was still the same.

"Did it work?" asked Jack. "I don't feel any different, plus I'm not invisible or anything."

"Go and have a look in the mirror," said Elsie, gesturing down the hall.

Jack walked a few steps to the end of the small hallway, where a mirror stood fastened to the wall. He looked into it at his reflection, and his jaw dropped. Staring back at him was something out of one of the fantasy movies he liked to watch. A face, squat and ugly, with tufts of gingery hair sticking out from behind broad, protruding ears stared back at him. The nose was pug-like, and two tusk-like teeth jutted up from the lower jaw, which dribbled a small stream of saliva. The skin of this reflection had a slightly green hue. The squat head sat atop a gangly body dressed in a smock of some rough cloth. What appeared to be food stains ran the smock's length, which ended just above a pair of green knobby knees. Hard, horny feet stuck out at the bottom of each leg with long dirty toenails.

"Whoa!" said Jack. "That's brilliant. What am I supposed to be?"

"Marsh Goblin," said Fermy with a smile. "Unpleasant to look at but harmless enough. They are all over Faery doing the unpleasant jobs. I think that if I find you a sack or something to carry, then anyone looking will think that you are our servant. Avoids any awkward questions."

"But why do I look like myself to me?" asked Jack.

"Because it's a glamour, Jack. An illusion meant to fool the mind. It should work fine, providing no one tries to take it off."

"But how do I get it off?" said Jack. "I can't go around like this for the rest of my life."

"Then you'd better be a good boy," said Fermy with a chuckle. "And I'll think about taking it off later."

"Oh, leave him alone, Fermy," said Elsie with a laugh. "Jack, it'll wear off anyway; it's probably good for an hour or so."

Jack was relieved to hear it. "But what about you, Auntie? Won't people be suspicious of you?"

"Yes, I'll need something as well to avoid suspicion. And no, you're not doing it, I'll do it myself," she said firmly, looking at Fermy. With a few practised gestures, she smiled and smoothed back her hair. Her ears were now long and pointed, and her skin had a subtle glow about it.

"Elven," she said to Jack with a smile. "One of my personal favourites."

Jack turned to Fermy. "Why couldn't I be elven?"

"Because it's funny," said Fermy. "Besides, you can be whatever you like when you learn to do it yourself."

"Not fair," said Jack with a smile. "I need to learn that as soon as possible."

"All in good time, Jack," said Elsie. "Now, shall we get going? We don't want to be late."

Pushing open the front door, Fermy looked at Jack.

"Welcome, Jack, to the fabled land of Lyonesse, my small city in the Realm of Faery."

~

JACK FOLLOWED EAGERLY over the threshold of Fermy's strange house, keen to see the sights and sounds of another world, an empty basket hooked over his arm to help his disguise. He was to stay a few steps behind the others and not talk to them. Any questions they would answer when they arrived at their destination. This suited Jack; he just wanted to experience Faery for the first time.

The first thing that struck him was the cleanness of the air itself. It was incredible to breathe in and out, crisp but not cold at all. It felt invigorating, as if it was cleansing him from the inside out. He took in great panting lungfuls, standing with his mouth wide open until Elsie gave him a stern look over her shoulder and gestured onwards with her head. Shutting his mouth, he looked around at the world as he walked after the others.

He stood on what seemed to be a narrow road, hard earth compacted underneath his feet. On either side of the street were dwellings, or so Jack assumed. They were like nothing he had seen before, not built of brick or stone, but seemingly organic, akin more to tree trunks than the fabled toadstools that Faeries were supposed to live in. No two were the same; they seemed to sprout out of the ground at odd angles, with windows sprinkling the sunlight and odd-sized doors scattered randomly on the outside. They were not of uniform size either; some were tiny, no bigger than an armchair, while others further down the road towered up into the air, many hundreds of feet tall. Branches growing out of them had leaves and flowers of all shapes and hues, the flowers not the same on each branch even though they were part of the same structure.

Jack was enchanted by the richness of colour as well; everywhere he looked, what his eyes took in seemed to be, well, more 'real.' The blue of the sky was the richest he had ever seen, and the grass was of such a deep luscious green that the desire to walk barefoot in it was almost too much to bear. The houses were all a darkish brown, some mottled with green moss, others with climbing kaleidoscopic plants. Everywhere he looked, the colours blasted his senses; he could almost hear and smell how vivid they were.

There were everyday things as well; Jack saw clothes on washing lines flapping gently in the warm breeze. Admittedly the clothes were of differing sizes, some as small as dolls' clothes while others were bigger than that of a human (or lifer, Jack supposed) size. Some of the 'houses' had seats outside them, again of varying sizes. In addition, all had small gardens at the front, rich with plants of all kinds, growing tall, and flowers adding to the crispness of the air with their perfume.

There were not too many 'people' about on the street; Jack saw a group of folk in what appeared to be the distance, but they got close rapidly, and he knew then his perspective was wrong. He supposed that they were dwarves; they had bulbous noses, but other than that were similar to people back home, with ruddy pink faces peeping over the top of their shirts. None of them had bushy beards. They all stared at Jack as they marched past in their group, muttering to each other.

"Will you come on?" said Elsie, standing in front of him, her hands on her hips. "Stop staring and keep up. We need to get to the market today, not next week." She nodded to the Fae folk, the leader nodding back with raised eyebrows.

Once they had gone, Elsie whispered, "Jack, you have to stop gawping at everything. Those gnomes were getting quite angry; it's very rude to stare at them, you know."

"I'm sorry, Auntie," Jack whispered back. "But it's a lot to take in!"

"Be as that may, you're attracting attention. Like back home, people gossip. Moreover, everyone around here knows Fermy, and it's general knowledge that he does not have a servant. Hopefully, they will think that you are with me, but then they will start speculating on who I am. We don't want any enforcers dropping in; they will tear through these glamours like wet tissue paper."

"I'm sorry, Auntie. I'll just look at your back from now on. It's just all so strange here; it's taken me by surprise."

Elsie nodded sadly. "I know, and I would love to be able to show you around properly. But now isn't the time. Once we have got to the bottom of what is happening, I promise you we'll come here, and we can spend as long as you like looking at everything. Deal?"

"Deal," said Jack with a smile.

He fixed his eyes on Elsie's back and made sure that he walked a few steps behind them. Of course, he could see over Elsie's shoulder and had a partial view of what was on the horizon. He could see that the volume of houses was increasing as they walked on, the way appearing to lead into a small town of some sort, which nestled at the bottom of two hills in the distance. Also, in the distance was a significant looking building with two tall spires pointing into the sky. Fermy glanced around to check that no one was looking and then pointed at the building and nodded his head at Jack. It looked like that that was their destination, but what that meant, Jack had no idea.

WHILE JACK WAS busy looking around Faery, the opposite could be said for Jimmy Owen. He had trooped out of the gates of Bloxton Academy at the end of school, eyes down and firmly glued to his phone. There had been a lot on the social news feeds today about the 'Boofs', and he was busy reading up.

Jimmy had eagerly devoured any news on this matter as he had concerns that the thing could potentially hit his six-year-old brother, Sean. From what he could gather, only a few kids in their town were affected so far, but it did seem that the problem was growing. And the doctors were still at a loss at what was causing it or what to do about it. If Jimmy could see any way to protect Sean, then he would. He loved his little brother, who hero-worshipped him in return. They had the usual spats that siblings had, but Jimmy was fearsomely protective of Sean, and as he often said, "Nobody beats up on Sean but me."

Jimmy intended to see how Jack was getting on, as he hadn't answered a single text message all day. He'd tried ringing as well, and it had gone straight to voicemail, but as he never answered his phone either, that was okay. Jimmy was not worried about his friend; Jack has seemed fine last night, if a little 'off,' but Jimmy guessed that that was to be expected after such a severe accident. However, it would not hurt to drop in and check, plus Jack's Great Aunt Elsie was a mean cook, and hopefully, there would be some cake going begging. Jimmy licked his lips at the prospect and carried on scrolling on his phone as he walked.

Engrossed as he was with his phone, he failed to notice the LaFey twins loitering across the street. They had taken some pains to stay hidden, lolling against the corner of a wall out of direct eye line as they waited for their target to come out of the gates. Things could not have gone better for the twins, as Jimmy hadn't noticed them and had strolled straight past.

"Right, Mase," said Tyler. "Let's follow him. He's heading away from his place; he lives over on the hill. I reckon he's off to see Crackley, who must be off as he didn't come out with him. We keep our distance, right? If he gets wind of us, then he'll be off, and I don't want another chase."

Mason grunted something under his breath.

"Yep," said Tyler. "If it looks like he's headed for home, we'll just grab him somewhere secluded. He can tell us the address just as easily, I reckon, with a bit of persuasion."

Mason gave a slightly sinister smile and cracked his knuckles. The twins started to follow the engrossed Jimmy at a leisurely pace, careful to ensure they were overlooked. Despite their size, it was relatively easy to blend in with the other gangs of schoolchildren as they casually walked along.

JACK FOLLOWED Elsie and Fermy down into the town; the little Feeorin now sat on Elsie's shoulder, talking amicably. Fermy pointed out the sights in a loud voice as if acting as a tour guide to Elsie, but Jack appreciated that this was for his benefit. The town itself was pretty grand to Jack's eyes. Here, the organic tree-like structures were everywhere but formed into shapes that Jack recognised more easily – large squarish buildings with a single large door and multiple windows. In the distance, the vast building with the spires grew closer.

The road had also changed from hard-packed mud to flag-stones. And the people! There were Fae folk everywhere Jack looked. There were small, winged folk; Fairies, Jack supposed as they looked like they were straight out of a story; short people of all colours and appearances – pointed ears, broad noses, various kinds of teeth, and tusks. There were squat folk, tall folk, folk who appeared to be made of plants and trees; it was breath-taking to view, like being in some kind of movie. They all seemed happy as they went about their business, politely acknowledging each other in various languages and allowing each other the right of way. Nobody gave their party a second glance; Jack saw Fermy raise his hat to a few people who nodded back, but that was the extent of it. Jack looked around in awe at the sights and sounds as he trailed after the others, seeing how the town was very much like his own. Except for the

163

fact that there were no cars or vans, or any kind of transport at all. Not even a cart. Jack assumed some of the buildings were shops as they displayed wares on tables outside, with folk bustling about.

The town grew busier as the twin spires drew nearer, and Jack could see that the building appeared to be made of stone rather than the organic materials he was used to seeing now. The structure towered into the sky as they grew closer, windows glittering as they reflected the low orange sun that hung in the vibrant blue sky above. The spires appeared to be on each side of the structure, which was castle-like in appearance, taking the part of corner turrets. A colossal archway stood in the wall between the two towers; all traffic flow was moving through the towering walls. Jack could see carts amongst the foot passengers, stacked high with goods, pulled along by various creatures. Large white horses seemed to be prevalent as the beast of choice, although Jack was sure he could see what looked like a bear in the distance pulling a large cart full of children.

Elsie has slowed down so that she was keeping pace with Jack. Fermy hopped over onto his shoulder and whispered in his ear.

"We'll go unnoticed now, Jack, with so many folks about, so it's safe for me to talk. Up ahead, the building with the spires is the Curiosity Sanctuary. It has many functions, but today we are fortunate that it is market day. So please stay close and follow Elsie and me; do not stop under any circumstances and do not, I repeat, do not eat anything that you are offered."

"Why?" said Jack, who, despite the large breakfast earlier, could always manage a snack.

"Best case will be that after you eat it, all human food forevermore will taste bland, like dust or similar, and never be appetising again. Worst case, eating the food will trap you either temporarily or permanently. Some of these traders can be quite slippery and demand hefty fees to release you."

"Whoa!" said Jack. "How do you ever go food shopping?"

Fermy laughed. "We always reverse glamour everything before we eat it; removes anything that could be less than beneficial to us. All part of living in Faery, Jack. It is not always malicious, but we do like to play pranks on each other. Anyhow, don't accept anything that's offered; just point at us and grunt." Jack nodded his understanding.

"Now, once we get inside, we will go to the quarters of my friend. As I said earlier, the Curiosity Sanctuary has many functions. One of them is a place of learning, and many scholars live and work here. My friend, Timothy Tattingmouse, is one of those, and it is he that we are going to see. He knew your father well; he taught him, and when your father was older, they collaborated on projects as well. He knows more about your family history than anyone I know, including myself. He will be able to answer more of your questions, plus I want to see what you are like with glamours, and Timothy is best placed to teach you those."

"He's very gifted, Jack," said Elsie.

"He's going to teach me magic?" exclaimed Jack in excitement.

"No, he's going to teach you some basic glamours to start you off. Once you have the hang of those, we can look at some other things. Not before. Anyhow, it may be that you can't use them; some Cracklocks I've met over the years aren't able to. Realm doors were never a problem, but other Faery abilities were just beyond them."

"I really hope I'm not one of those!" said Jack, thrilled that he was going to be learning glamours.

"We shall see. Now come on."

The threesome walked through the crowds of the market to

the far wall of the Sanctuary, where several small doors were nestled at the floor level.

"That one, there," said Fermy, jumping off Jack's shoulder and scuttling over to a bright yellow door with a burnished knocker. He rapped smartly on the door three times and then stood back. As Jack and Elsie arrived, the door swung open, and Timothy Tattingmouse stepped into view.

JIMMY TURNED onto Jack's street, still engrossed in his phone. He knew the way pretty instinctively now, having been a daily guest at the house for the past week or so, so he didn't need to look up, apart from crossing the road. As a result, he didn't see the twins gaining on him at a sauntering speed.

Tyler noted that the street of terraced houses was surprisingly empty; nobody was on the pavements, and there were very few cars. Most people were still at work at that time, on the run-up to four o'clock, so they had a clear run at Jimmy without anyone else getting involved. If any 'have a go hero' came out of the houses, well, they'd play it by ear. They were big enough to intimidate most adults if said person was on their own, and they knew the police were stretched thin, meaning that they had plenty of time to scarper if needed. They had done it before. They were now about ten metres behind Jimmy and gaining fast.

Jimmy stopped outside Jack's house in front of the little garden that all the terraces had on the street. The space was pretty pointless, to be honest; nobody grew anything in there, but it was a handy spot to store the bins. He finished reading the last paragraph of the news feed on the Boofs and swiped the phone to leave the app. As he bought it up to his face to check his image (a bad habit of his, using it as a little mirror), he caught a moving reflection on the shiny surface of the screen.

Turning his head, his eyes widened in shock as the figure of Mason LaFey loomed over him, hands outstretched to grab him.

Jimmy stumbled back against the little gate, which fortunately wasn't on the latch, meaning it swung backwards at his touch. He tottered backwards into the little garden, the gate bouncing off the wall, and landed on his backside next to the bins. Ever the quick thinker, he lashed out with his foot, kicking the gate shut onto Mason as he made his entrance into the garden. The gate cracked hard against Mason's knees, causing the thuggish twin to wince in pain.

"Hello, Owen," said Tyler over Mason's shoulder. "How are you today? Feeling well? Not for much longer, I think; we want a word with you."

Jimmy scooted backwards on his bottom to the front door and hammered on it. "*Jack!*" he bawled at the top of his voice. "*Let me in.*" He hammered the door again with the ball of his fist, reaching behind him, never taking his eyes off the twins. "*Jack. Help me.*"

"So, this is Crackley's house, is it?" said Tyler, pushing past Mason, who was rubbing his knee, and entered the small garden. He squatted down on his haunches in front of Jimmy.

Jimmy tried to bang on the door again, but quick as lightning, Tyler seized his arm and yanked it forwards.

"Please be quiet, Owen; you'll disturb the neighbours," he said in a quiet, dangerous voice. "Looks like there's no one in, eh? How unfortunate." Tyler licked his lips and stared directly into Jimmy's face. "Now then. You've answered what we wanted to ask you, which, if I were reasonable, would be a good start for you. However, we have other business with you. The first of which is that you owe us a mobile telephone." He plucked it from Jimmy's hand and passed it to Mason.

"Next, you have caused us a few problems. Dad took his belt to us following our suspension; he was angry at the fact we got caught. So, you see, you are still in some serious debt to us. You now owe us one mobile phone, one dislocated arm, and a severe belting by my reckoning. If you behave, we won't use the buckle end."

Jimmy was terrified. "Jack," he croaked again, his fear quietening his voice. He looked with fear at Mason, who was pulling a thick leather belt from out of his jeans, the heavy eagle buckle glinting. Mason was smiling a horrible smile, his yellow teeth on full display like a broken fence panel.

"Tyler," Jimmy croaked, "I'm sorry. I really am. I didn't mean for you to get suspended. You can keep the phone."

"I know, I know," soothed Tyler, cupping Jimmy's chin. "But it makes no difference. You owe us, and it's payback time. Starting right now. Mase, if you will?" Tyler poked Jimmy a couple of times sharply in the ribs, stood up, and moved to the side, his arms folded. "Reckon I'm going to enjoy this!" he said with a smile.

Mason stepped forward, grinning like a fool, about a foot in length of leather belt hanging from his fist. He towered over Jimmy and raised his arm to administer the first blow to the cowering youth, who had raised his arms to try to protect his head. And that was when the front door behind Jimmy crashed open on its own.

DORCAS HAD HAD a lovely day since the others had headed off to Faery. She had spent the morning cleaning the house from top to bottom, getting into all the nooks and crannies. Nothing gave her more satisfaction than to see a gleaming home, dust-free and tidy, smelling nicely of flowers and baking. And baking she was indeed; in the oven was another cake, and a chicken and vegetable pie stood ready on the counter to go in when the others came back. Dorcas never had an issue with ingredients; her special glamours meant she could will into existence pretty much any kind of food she needed. She only required a closed cupboard (or fridge; that was a great invention in the lifer realm that they didn't have in Faery – everything so cold!) and the gumption to think that an item was in there. Then it was. Like all Brownies, cooking and cleaning were what she lived for, and she never glamoured ready-cooked meals; that was cheating. In Faery, folk saw it as quite a status symbol to have a Brownie keep for them.

"But not here," Dorcas sighed. "Although I thinks they likes what I does for them. Nice to have more Cracklocks to looks after again, after all this time." Dorcas took down the flour tub she had glamoured into existence, and sprinkled a dusting onto the table, her mind on the tarts she was going to make. *'Strawberry or cherry, strawberry or cherry? I does not know which Jack would likes best. So's I makes them both, then I's right!'* she thought happily.

Lost in her thoughts, she jumped violently when the loud banging at the front door started. Clutching her chest, she said out loud, "Oh, my grockles and grackles, what a noise." Although she knew that she could not answer the door to a visitor, the banging came again, along with a muffled shout that sounded like, *"Jack!"*

'Oh dear, oh dear, oh dear,' she thought, *'Who's can that be?'* Putting down the rolling pin, she jumped down from the chair she had been using to reach the table and scuttled into the lounge. Jumping onto the sofa, she twitched aside the curtain, ever so slightly, and put one eye to the gap. What she saw made her take a huge gasp.

Sitting on the floor by the door was that nice friend of Jack's, Jimmy. The boy has impressed Dorcas the night before at dinner; he was kind and polite to poor Sammy and Elsie and obviously cared about Jack. He had also raved about Dorcas's cooking, which was the easiest way to get a Brownie to like you.

Squatting next to Jimmy, with his hand on Jimmy's face, was

another boy. This one was much bigger and looked nasty. Dorcas couldn't hear what the nasty boy was saying, but it was apparent that it wasn't nice. Another big boy stood behind the first one, an idiot looking grin on his face as he stared at the two below him. Jimmy was obviously scared; he was saying something to the first boy, and by the gloating look on that boy's face, he wasn't listening. Bullying Jimmy.

Dorcas bristled a little. She hated bullies, those folk picking on others because they were bigger or because there were more of them, and all her life she had taken them on whenever she encountered such people. When the pixies had been bullying her bigger brother, it was Dorcas who had fought them. She had lost on that first occasion, but it had just made her more determined to stand up to such people. And got them she had, with the help of her father's walking cane. Those pixies left Dickens well alone after that. When bogies had hidden in the cupboards of the young Cracklock children, it had been Dorcas who had seen them off, usually with a sound walloping and a kick to their backside, to see them on their way; scaring children indeed! She'd waded into the water before to see off nymphs who were bothering the children. Moreover, once, she had had a straight-up brawl with Jenny Greenteeth at the lake when the creature had tried to take young Maisie Cracklock down into the depths with her.

Dorcas watched as the bigger boy poked Jimmy in the ribs hard a couple of times. She could see that Jimmy was close to tears, but what could she do? It wasn't allowed to reveal yourself to lifers without permission, nor do anything that would make them suspect, and hence there was nothing she could do. "I's can't stand it," she muttered to herself, eye glued to the crack in the curtains. "I's can't. Poor Jimmy. Leaves him alone."

The bigger boy suddenly stood up and stepped to the side, allowing the other to step forward. Dorcas watched this boy pull his belt from his trousers and lazily start to loop it around one meaty fist. He was grinning down at poor Jimmy, who cowered away, raising his hands to try and appease the big boy.

That did it. Dorcas saw red. Two big boys, going to beat a smaller boy with a belt? And she was supposed just to watch and accept it? A nice boy like Jimmy? The laws be damned!

"*Aaarrrgggggghhhhhhhh!*" screamed Dorcas out loud, vaulting off the sofa and sprinting for the kitchen. She held out her hand, and a rolling pin flew off the table to land in her palm, leaving a cloud of flour as she dashed to the front door. She flung it open and screamed, "*You's leave him alone!*"

THE OPENING DOOR made Mason hesitate; nobody was there, but why had it opened? He looked at Tyler.

"Who's there?" asked Tyler.

No response. Then all of a sudden, Mason howled out in pain, his hands flying to his knee and then rapidly to his groin, the belt spilling from his hands. He started to sink slowly towards the floor, his face red and tears in his eyes.

"Mase?" said Tyler, concerned now. Jimmy hadn't moved; in fact, he was staring at Mason with his mouth wide open.

"Mase?" repeated Tyler, taking a step towards his twin when suddenly a thump into his groin made him gulp for breath. Sickening pain shot into his stomach. He then felt another dull thwack onto his knee, the pain making him wince. Combined with the groin pain, he also sank slowly to the floor, his eyes on Jimmy, who looked on, apparently just as shocked as they were.

DORCAS HADN'T WAITED for the boy with the belt to take in the door opening on its own; she'd leapt over Jimmy, screaming a war cry at the top of her lungs as she did so. Dorcas was an old pro with the rolling pin; it had bested many a bully and scary thing over the years, and she knew exactly how to hit with it. It didn't matter to her how big her opponent was; it just meant more areas to hit in her eyes. She conked Mason a good one right on the side of the knee, and while his body was registering the pain of this, on an arcing upswing, drove the rolling pin right up between his legs. All males, both lifers and folk, had a weakness there usually, and it was an excellent place to hit, right at about Dorcas eye level.

Seeing the one with the belt start to crumple, she switched to the other one, who was looking at the first one with confusion in his eyes. Dorcas stepped over and gave a vicious uppercut into this one's groin area. Dorcas has twelve brothers, and knowing how to punch back was a life skill she had learned the hard way. With a wide, controlled swing, she followed this up with a crack to the knee as well with the pin. Her blood was up now, and these bullies were going to learn to leave smaller people alone. As Mason sunk to the ground, Dorcas hopped smartly back over to him and brained him with a perfect overarm swing right on top of the head. The bigger boy screamed again, hands flying to the top of his head.

TYLER WATCHED through the shock of his injuries as his brother gave another scream and clutched the top of his head with both hands as if someone had hit him there. He looked over at Jimmy, who appeared to be in shock.

"*What are you doing?*" he screamed at Jimmy.

"*Nothing!*" Jimmy screamed back.

Tyler opened his mouth to shout again when he felt a dull blow to his head. Then one to his shoulder, followed quickly by one to his arm and then the other in rapid succession. Then his shoulder again, right on the same spot, causing him to screech as the pain shot around the throbbing area. Through clenched eyes, he saw Mason crawl out of the gate on his knees, one hand clutching his crotch, the other at the top of his head.

DORCAS HEARD the other one shout at Jimmy and whirled around. The one with the belt had obviously had enough, crawling out of the gate, but the other one still looked to have some pep in him. She stepped nimbly over to the crouching figure and brought the pin down with a dull whump onto the top of his head with another screaming battle cry.

"Don't..." the pin whacked Tyler's shoulder.

"...You's..." the pin whacked his arm.

"...Bully..." the pin whacked his other arm.

"...People..." whacking back onto the original shoulder.

The bigger boy crumpled to the floor, tears rolling down his cheeks. Dorcas stood over him, panting herself; she was getting a bit old for combat nowadays, but she was pleased with the results. Jimmy looked to be unhurt, although looking at the proceedings in a state of shock.

The other boy started his crawl towards the gate. Dorcas stepped to the side to let him by, and as he crossed the threshold, she took a little run up and planted her foot squarely in the big boy's backside. The boy howled and slumped forward, his hands grazing the pavement as he stopped himself from going face first.

"There," said Dorcas, dusting her hands off, the rolling pin tucked beneath her arm. "That's a lesson froms Dorcas. You's pair better go; otherwise, you's be getting some more."

She watched the two bullies pull themselves to their feet on the little wall and then break into a shambling run down the street. Turning to Jimmy, she cast her eyes over him, checking that he wasn't hurt. He didn't seem to be.

It was then that the implications of what she had just done sank in. In complete contravention of the Faery laws, she'd just beaten up two lifers in full view of a third.

"Oh, my grockles," she said, shuddering slightly. "Oh my, oh my, I's in trouble now." She glanced around to see if any Fae folk were in the area as witnesses and could report her to the Courts. She couldn't see any, but that didn't mean they weren't there. There were rewards to be had, and the punishments severe. Long sentences in gaol were the norm; protection of the Faery realm's existence from the lifers was the number one rule.

Dorcas was no scholar of the Faery Laws but had a smattering of knowledge from her school days where the main rules had been chanted every day to drive them home. One of them was that Fae folk could reveal themselves to lifers only under exceptional circumstances. Such circumstances were few and far between and included at the end of a lifer's lifespan to provide comfort, heal exceptional individuals, and prevent loss of life or severe injury. Such circumstances meant that the reveal was acceptable, but the Fae had to reveal themselves to justify what they had done.

Dorcas's forehead wrinkled as she thought things through. Could those nasty boys have killed or seriously injured Jimmy? It was possible. The one with the belt had undoubtedly meant to hurt him a lot. Nevertheless, was it enough to justify breaking the Faery Law? This was a difficult call. If she revealed herself to Jimmy, she could possibly justify what just happened if she got into trouble, but then she would be in trouble with Elsie and Fermy. However, she couldn't just leave what had happened; Jimmy was bound to tell Jack about it so that the others would find out anyway. Dorcas glanced at Jimmy, who sat on the floor in front of the open door, shivering slightly, and felt a massive wave of sympathy for the boy.

'Okay,' she thought, 'Jimmy is a nice boys, a friend of Jack's. I can reveals to him, and then I's be okay, I thinks'.

~

JIMMY HAD WATCHED the twins flee from the scene aghast, Tyler slumping forward and only narrowly avoiding a face plant as he made his way out of the gate. He was still very shaky and didn't know what had just happened, other than that he had just avoided a serious beating again. How, he had no idea. It did not make any sense. Unless he had secret powers that he didn't know about. Perhaps they only manifested themselves in times of stress? He was just starting to get excited when he felt a gentle tug on his sleeve. The tug was pulling him in the direction of the open door.

"Who's there?" asked Jimmy, a tremor in his voice. "Is it a ghost?"

The tug came again, persistent but gentle.

"Okay, okay. You want me to come into the house?"

A couple of gentle tugs confirmed that this was the case. Jimmy got to his feet, still feeling a bit shaky, and stepped into the hallway. He turned to close the door, but before he could do so, it closed gently behind him. Jimmy stared at it in wonder and then looked down at the bottom of the door. Here the air seemed to be sparkling, like tiny bits of glitter floating in the air. They whirled around as if trapped in a small cyclone before merging into a dark shape. Colour flooded into the shape, and a figure appeared.

Jimmy took a couple of steps backwards as the figure solidified into a short, stocky dwarf-like person. A chubby head with long ears and a long nose perched on top of a fat bulky body; curly black hair sticking out at all angles. The figure came up to Jimmy's waist and was clothed in a flowery type of dress. Jimmy's jaw dropped as he stepped backwards again.

The figure warmly smiled at Jimmy. "Hello, Jimmy. I's Dorcas, and I's a friend of Jack's. It is a pleasure to meet you's properly. They didn't hurts you anywhere, did they?"

175

Jimmy snapped his mouth back shut and shook his head, totally out of character at a complete loss for words.

"Good. Now's, you have had a shock, I's thinking. Would you like somes cake? Sugar is good for shock."

Jimmy nodded, still stunned.

"Come ons then. I's making some tea as well; I's thirsty after all that exercise."

Jimmy obediently followed Dorcas into the kitchen.

CHAPTER 9

*J*ack thought that Timothy Tattingmouse looked kind of cool, albeit in an odd way. He was a little man, no taller than Jack's thighs, and completely bald. His face was heavily wrinkled, particularly around the eyes and mouth, and his blue eyes appeared enormous, magnified as they were by a large pair of thick spectacles. *'He really reminds me of someone, but who?'* Jack thought as he stood behind Fermy and Elsie at the door. Timothy was dressed like a monk, a long flowing brown gown with a wide belt tying it shut. Various odd-looking devices and tools hung from the belt, visibly sagging at the waist with the weight of them.

"Fermerillion!" said Timothy in a warm voice, holding out both hands. "I was starting to wonder if you were coming today or not!"

"Well, we had some issues with the court enforcers. Delayed us slightly," said Fermy, clutching Timothy's two outstretched hands and shaking them up and down.

"And Elsie, lovely to see you, my dear. And looking so well."

Elsie blushed and stepped forward to hug the little man, stooping down to do it. Four mice came streaking out of the

177

open door from behind Timothy and zoomed off towards the marketplace as she did so.

"Oh drat," said Timothy, pushing his glasses up onto his nose and peering after them. "I needed those. I hate grubbing about in the cellars gathering the pesky things."

Bringing his magnified eyes up, he looked Jack up and down.

"And who is this fine goblin fellow?" he asked Fermy.

"He's someone you'd like to meet," said Fermy. "Can we go inside, and we can introduce you properly?"

Timothy gave a double-take and looked again at Jack.

"Is this David's son?"

"Yes. Can we go inside; I don't want prying eyes seeing us."

"Of course, of course, please come in," said Timothy, pushing the door open and standing to one side. "I even tidied for you."

JACK COULD NOT SEE which bit Timothy had tidied due to the massive amounts of clutter that littered the hall. Piles of parchments and books were stacked everywhere you looked. There were bits and pieces of what Jack took to be machinery perched on top of the overflowing piles, some of which had fallen over, spilling papers all over the place. Timothy simply walked over them as if they weren't there. Also, the place smelt odd; quite unpleasant. Jack flinched when he caught sight of the oil-black little eyes and twitching nose of a rat peeping over one pile of books. Once he'd seen one, he noticed them everywhere, scurrying in the background. There were mice as well, jumping over the discarded piles of paper and disappearing under the furniture that Jack glimpsed as they moved down the hallway towards a well-lit room at the end.

"He could do with a pest controller," he whispered to Elsie. "Don't they have the Pied Piper here in Faery?"

"Oh, no, Jack," Elsie whispered back. "He uses the rats and mice in his work. I guess that some have escaped."

"Some?" whispered Jack incredulously. "There's hundreds of them!"

"Timothy is a Myomancer, Jack, amongst other things," whispered Elsie. "He uses them to predict the future. Well, he says he does, and I would say that there have been some amazing coincidences over the years if it isn't true."

"Like what?" Jack whispered back.

"Later, later, if we get the time. I am sure that Timothy would love to tell you all about his Myomancy, but believe me, if you get him started on the subject, we'll be here for weeks. And it is incredibly dull."

"Aha, here we are," said Timothy, ushering them into a well-lit room. Jack looked around in awe. The room itself seemed to be a combination kitchen, bedroom, and laboratory. The ceiling above towered over their heads like a cathedral, and the walls seemed to be far off in the distance. In the centre of the room, there was a large device built mainly of tubes and covered in small wheels and cages; mice and rats moved around inside it, scurrying in all directions. Various levers and lights were set into a control panel on one side, with dials and number counters scattered at random around it. The machine was making a ticking sound as numbers counted both down and up on clockwork faces.

"I can see that you've extended out," said Fermy, looking around. "Run out of space again?"

"Yes, yes," said Timothy gesturing at the machine. "A little realm manipulation to give me more room to work in. The theriomantic oscillator requires quite a lot of space to allow them to move about; gives much better readings. I'm working on a maximum capacity bleed off theory at the moment to try and minimise...."

He trailed off, again looking up at Jack.

"Well, is he really this ugly?" he asked with a grin.

Fermy walked over to Jack and grasped the air in front of him. He pulled down, and Jack felt a whisper of air around him move as the goblin glamour faded away.

"May I introduce Master Jack Cracklock?" said Fermy with a flourish.

"My goodness," said Timothy. "He got so big! Young man, I am honoured to meet you again after all this time." He stepped forward, his hand outstretched.

"We've met before?" said Jack, shaking the pro-offered hand. "I am sorry, but I'm afraid I don't remember."

"No matter, no matter," said Timothy. "And yes, we have met before. I was a regular guest at your home back in the day, as you were here. You were very small, though, so I'm not surprised that you don't remember me. Although I do recall you breaking my glasses on more than one occasion, you were always quick to grab them." Timothy chuckled to himself and was then solemn.

Turning to Fermy, Timothy said, "Why does he not have the glamour on him anymore? David was quite specific in his instructions about that."

"Jack had an accident, Timothy," said Fermy. "And as a result, it had to come off. The situation was not ideal, but it was unavoidable."

"Well, I'm surprised it lasted as long as it did," said Timothy. "The Cracklocks are nothing if not indomitable; David and I were quite sure that Jack would have shrugged it off years ago if no one removed it."

"No, only a couple of days ago," said Elsie.

"Well, that's down to the quality of the work in the glamour itself," said Timothy, sticking out his chest. "One of my finer efforts, I think."

"You put the glamour on me?" asked Jack.

"Not all by myself, no. I had help from David and Fermerillion here. Nevertheless, the enhanced masking glamour I conceived made it possible for us to hide you and your mother while David was away. Not that we expected him to be away so long." He frowned.

"Timothy," said Elsie, "We told Jack that you would be able to tell him a little more about the family and particularly David."

"Of course," said Timothy. "I will be happy to share what I know; Cracklock history is something of a hobby of mine. Although about David, I am not sure what else I can tell you." His face fell a little.

"Anything you can tell me would be great," said Jack. "Everything is all new to me, and I'm still filling in the gaps. And I'd like to know if you know whether my dad is still alive?"

Timothy gave a sad smile. "I will tell you what I can, but about your father's current status, I just don't know. I have tried my best to locate him, but the readings are so strange. That contraption there…" he pointed at the machine, "…is a theriomantic oscillator. Without going into too many details, it can be used to predict events, both current and future. Moreover, I have tried many times to get it to tell me if David is alive and well, even if we do not know where he is. The readings are, well, odd, to say the least."

"What do you mean?" asked Jack.

"Well, the readings from the machine are contradictory in that specific case, but they are always the same. The answers it gives are puzzling to me, and I am quite adept at interpreting them. The simple answer that it gives is that David is both alive and dead."

"*What?*" shouted Jack. "How can that be right? It must be broken or something."

"I assure you that it is not broken," said Timothy sharply. "But I agree that it can't be correct. It really is bizarre; it is normally quite definite about things."

"But how can he be both dead and alive? That doesn't make

181

sense." Jack was trembling a little now; another dead end and another mystery. It was too much.

"That I don't know," replied Timothy.

"I just...well, I...it just seems to me that nobody seems to know where Dad could be, or even if he's still alive. I find out yesterday that he could be, but nobody seems to have any idea about what could possibly have happened. I thought that you were all magic or glamour experts? Can't you so something, some clever way of finding him?"

Timothy grabbed both of Jack's hands in his own.

"I am sorry that this is a shock to you, Jack. Believe me; if I could have found him, I would have. He and I were great friends. Something inside me says that he's still alive, but as I'm sure the others have told you, we have no idea where."

"Well, I think he is still alive," said Jack. "I can feel it in my bones, like something is calling to me. And if he is, I intend to find him."

"As do we all, Jack," said Timothy.

"So, in order to find him, I need to know more about who I am. Perhaps there is a clue in our history? Anything that you can tell me would be very much appreciated."

"My dear boy, of course. Let's be seated, and we can have a good old discussion." Timothy wrestled an armful of books off the kitchen table to make room for them to sit around it.

"First things first, let me serve up some drinks. Talking can be thirsty work."

TIMOTHY POURED them all water from a jug into tall mugs (Jack noticed Elsie check hers first, presumably for rodent droppings) once they were all sitting at the table. He stared off into space for a while before fixing Jack with a look.

"Okay, Jack, I understand from Fermy that you already know a little bit of the history of the family?"

"Yes, I do," replied Jack. "I've seen the family tree and understand the 'why' but not much else."

Timothy nodded his understanding.

"Good. Then I can start a little way from the beginning. As you know, the first member of your family that could see the Fae, Jeremiah, was born at a time of great religious upheaval. Being able to 'see' Faeries would have been considered witchcraft then and was best kept well hidden. Jeremiah grew up learning how to mask when he saw the Fae. He used to talk to them in private, and to be fair to them, they helped him hide his abilities; my people understood the danger he would be in very well. Under their tuition, Jeremiah did learn how to use glamours, but they were only ever used for good as far as we know, and he was very discrete about it – healing someone from afar or making sure the crops were okay. What we know of Jeremiah was that he was a good man; some Fae still with us remember him as a kind and thoughtful boy and later as a grown man.

"Like many people then, Jeremiah married young and had several children. The total number was six, but only three survived; there was a lot of disease and poverty in those days, and some things are beyond even the skills of the Fae. The three that survived, Bartholomew, Nathaniel, and Philippa, could all see the Fae as their father could. Again, they were careful to hide their abilities from others for fear of accusation of witchcraft. Around this time, Fermerillion met the family and used to enjoy being with the children."

Fermy bent his head out of respect and said, "It was an extraordinary meeting that was obviously in the fates. I will tell you the story one day, Jack; it is something that I think you would enjoy. However, for this story, I would say that they were lovely children – kind, polite, and always willing to help others.

Bartholomew, in particular, was a favourite of mine, the gentlest, kindest child you could ever hope to meet. It was Bartholomew that I and a few others showed the secret of the travel realm door to. He needed to travel to see a sick friend who had written to him, but he wasn't allowed to go – too far and too dangerous a journey for a child. An old friend of mine went with him, along with his father, to make sure he did not get into any trouble. It went well, and once he was well-practised in the art, Bartholomew shared the secret of the travel glyphs with his brother and sister."

"Which old friend was it, Fermy?" said Jack, enquiringly.

Fermy's face became dark. "Josper. He is no longer with us, Jack. Listen, and you will learn why."

Timothy took a swallow of water and continued his story.

"Time moved on, Jack, and the children grew up. Nathaniel went to the New World, or America as you know it, to seek his fortune, and we never heard from him again. We are not sure about his fate; we have never been able to trace him, though we did try.

"Bartholomew and Philippa both stayed in England, the country of their birth, and Bartholomew married a lovely young lass, Alicia. The couple struggled to have children, but they eventually managed a boy, Marcus. Again, full of his father's grace, he was a friend to the Fae folk, and he loved our kind. Bartholomew kept no secrets from Alicia, and with our help, he was able to introduce her to Faery and its folk. Of course, Alicia could not see us, but she got by well enough with the help of a Hagstone. And they raised Marcus well."

"Hagstone?" asked Jack.

Elsie rummaged in her handbag before pulling out the stone with the hole in it that Jack had seen earlier.

"This is a Hagstone, Jack. Hagstones are rocks that have naturally occurring holes in them, normally caused by water. It has a variety of purposes and uses. According to legend, the Hagstone got its name because it could cure maladies attributed to spectral hags. With a little glamouring, when people who are not attuned to the Fae look through the hole, they can see and hear them. Your mother used to use them; once upon a time, she had special glasses with two of these in them."

"I can see how that would be useful," said Jack, turning the Hagstone over in his hands. It was smooth and warm to the touch.

Timothy cleared his throat.

"Anyhow, Jack, Bartholomew and Alicia were happy enough with their little family. They enjoyed the company of the Fae, and Marcus made many friends with the folk.

"Unfortunately, the same could not be said for Philippa. The girl was naturally rebellious, although a nice enough person growing up. At sixteen, she ran away from the family to seek her own fortune, and that was when everything changed.

As we know, witch fever was rife in the seventeenth century. The country was torn by civil war, and during this time, a man called Matthew Hopkins had risen to prominence and was known as the 'Witchfinder General.' He and his entourage went from town to town, seeking out witches and putting them to death or trial. Many innocent people died due to his wickedness, and it was the Puritan religious belief that drove it all."

"Puritan?" asked Jack. Timothy nodded and then continued.

"If you don't know, the Puritan movement began in England when people started to reject the teachings of the Church of England. These people believed the Bible was the definitive word of God and that the Church of England was failing to teach moral beliefs to the people. Among such beliefs was that God wanted people to live good simple lives, free from decadence and extravagance. The Puritans saw these things every day in the Church of England and believed them to be the work of the Devil, who wanted the souls of lifers for his own purposes. The Puritans believed strongly in the wrath of God and did everything they could to avoid it. This is why the witch scare was taken so seriously, and the accused punished harshly. The first women accused as witches were those who had strayed from the Puritan way of life and were considered outcasts, wicked in their fall from God's grace. Puritan laws were and still are incredibly rigid, and its practisers are expected to have a solid moral code. Anyone who goes against this code will be considered a sinner and deserving of punishment. In Puritan belief, the Devil could appear in many forms to tempt you.

"Philippa happened to be in one of the towns where a witch trial was taking place, and she had joined the crowd to witness it. And in Matthew Hopkins' retinue, there happened to be a handsome young Puritan preacher called Elphias Cavendish. The two noticed each other, and to cut the story short, Philippa fell hopelessly in love with him, and he with her. She adopted the Puritan way of life, becoming a good preacher's wife. She became obsessed with the religion itself and lived a sparse life with none of the trappings of wealth. Elphias himself became more and more radical as the witch persecutions continued, and I am sorry to say that Philippa encouraged him. The Fae Folk continued to watch her from afar but did not like what they saw, and so avoided her. It was only when she had her first son that they wanted to try and help. While the baby was small, and she was carrying her second, some of the Folk came to her to bless the baby. And that was where it all went terribly wrong.

"When the Folk came to her, she did not want anything to do with them. It was the dead of night, and she was up with the baby when they came with greetings and to meet the little one. Philippa shunned them and told them to leave. Called them 'devils' trying to tempt her away from the word of God, although she was fully aware of who and what they were; indeed, the Folk in question were her childhood friends. The Fae tried to convince her that she was wrong, and the argument grew loud and heated, in the end rousing Elphias from his slumber.

"He stormed into the child's room where Philippa was and witnessed her arguing with persons unseen. He accused Philippa, his own wife, of trafficking with the Devil and offering their child to Him. Please remember that Elphias was very much invested in witches, and it hurt him deeply to see his own wife in such a position. He yelled for the house servants to fetch the Witchfinder, and such was his anger, the Fae feared for her safety and remained to try to protect her.

"Philippa cried and begged, but her husband would not be swayed. She told him of the Fae, which, of course, Elphias dismissed as lies. In her efforts to convince him, she ran to her room and opened the small chest that she had bought with her from her childhood home. In the chest, amongst other things, was a Hagstone. Returning to the nursery, she thrust into her husband's hands and bid him look at the Fae that were still with them in the room. To stop her hysteria, he did. The Fae in question were so shocked by Philippa's actions that they did not think to leave.

"The sight of three small creatures, non-human, through the eye of the stone made Elphias shake; here were the Devil's servants, and in his own home! He stumbled backwards, fumbling for his crucifix as he did so. It was a large crucifix, Italian and made of mahogany and with a figurine of Christ on the surface. Unfortunately, the Christ was wrought of iron.

"The elder of the Fae present, a goodly soul by the name of Machia, stepped forward with his hands raised to try to stop the panicking lifer before him. Elphias saw this as an attack and lashed out with his crucifix, shouting prayers to God as he did so. The heavy iron Christ clubbed poor Machia on the head with some force, the Fae crumpling to the ground. The others cast a protective glamour, grabbed Machia, and left, fading back to Faery in disgust. Machia never recovered properly; the iron rendered him a simpleton here in Faery for the rest of his days."

Timothy paused and took a drink of water. Jack sat enraptured at the story, his eyes on Timothy alone.

"What did Elphias do next?" he asked, and Timothy smiled a sad smile.

"I wish that the state of things today was all Elphias's doing, Jack. Alas, it is not."

"Please tell me more," begged Jack.

"Okay. If you are sure. We have managed to piece together what happened afterwards with accounts from other Fae, mostly brownies which were much more common in households at the time than they are now. And a lot more nosy, it is fair to say; there was little that escaped their notice. The Fae scholars often interrogate them for information."

Elsie gave a little snort at this and nodded. "Dorcas' family are a little different to most other brownies, Jack. It's a long story, but they mind their own business for the most part."

"Agreed. Our little brownie is one in a million," said Timothy. He pushed his glasses up onto his nose and carried on.

"Elphias was in shock at what he had just seen, but that shock soon turned to righteous anger. He quizzed Philippa over what had just happened, and when Matthew Hopkins arrived and took over the interrogation, Philippa panicked. She knew very well what happened to suspected witches, and being the wife of a senior preacher would not save her. Therefore, she lied. Philippa told the Witchfinder that she believed that the 'demons' had been sent by her brother, Bartholomew, who was known to truck with the Devil himself and was a powerful warlock. Her brother had found out about the Lord's work that her husband was doing with Matthew Hopkins and had sent his minions to strike a blow against the crusade. She made it clear that none of them was safe from the Devil's servants and must have been relieved when they believed her.

"With Elphias's sworn testament as to what had happened; the slaying of a devil before driving the others off through the power of God alone, the Witchfinder knew that action was needed. In the morning, he roused his troops and set off North to confront Bartholomew. Before they left, Philippa made a further request to her husband. That the men must load their muskets with iron shot, for salt and iron is effective against witches and devils alike."

"What happened next?" said Jack, his eyes wide.

Timothy took another drink. "Bartholomew was a man of peace, Jack. His family lived in a small hamlet just outside of the place you know as Leeds, where he earned his living as a tailor and a herbalist or minor healer. Bartholomew had avoided the civil war and taking sides, seeing what a folly it all was. He was happy with his family and his Fae friends, and they kept themselves to themselves, tutoring Marcus in the family business and the ways of the Fae. Our old friend Josper was pretty much living at their cottage; he helped Bartholomew with the tailoring work, turning out good quality clothes that allowed the family to live a good life."

"Like the Elves and the Shoemaker..." Jack said to himself.

"Indeed," said Fermy. "The stories often have a foundation in reality."

"Anyway," continued Timothy, "The family were caught entirely off guard when the Witchfinder and his entourage rode into their hamlet, demanding to be taken to Bartholomew Cracklock. While loyal to one of their own, the locals had no choice but to direct them to Bartholomew's cottage. Moreover, when they arrived, it was with extreme menace and a lot of noise.

"Of course, Bartholomew was not ignorant of the works of the witch-hunters; his father had always advised him against revealing his true nature about the Fae to others. He knew what they were capable of. As it happened, on the day in question,

Josper's niece, Madrigal, was also at the house on a visit with the Cracklocks and her Uncle, and it is through her that we know of what happened that fateful day.

"When the witch-hunters arrived and banged on the door, the occupants were all thrown into a state of shock. There were many armed men, and the figure of Matthew Hopkins was very imposing by all accounts. It was the Witchfinder General himself, along with Elphias and some of the other priests and preachers who banged on the door and bade them come out for inspection. Bartholomew had looked through the covered window and had received a further shock – his own sister, Philippa, whom he had not seen for many years, appeared to be with the armed party. He needed to know that she was safe from harm; family loyalties overwhelming him at the sight of his long-lost sister.

"Josper had recovered quickly from the shock and had cast a sealing glamour on the door to prevent entry. He and Bartholomew had looked at each other in understanding; this was not a good situation. Bartholomew had turned to Alicia and told her that she and Marcus needed to get away from the witchfinder's men, and a realm door was the only option. However, Alicia did not have the skill to perform one; she was a Cracklock only by marriage, and Marcus was only six years old. He had practised the realm door glyphs a few times, but the chances of being trapped in between realms are high, as you know, if you cannot get the 'unlock' glyph correct.

"Fortunately, Madrigal offered to take them somewhere safe that she knew, an old woman healer who was sympathetic to the Fae folk and would be able to help them. Alicia begged Bartholomew to come with them, but Bartholomew, knowing they would be safe with Madrigal, wanted to stay and help his sister. Moreover, of course, his old friend Josper would stay by his side, safe in the knowledge that he could not be seen and could still help as needed.

"Therefore, Madrigal opened the realm door and took Alicia and Marcus with her. The rest of the story of what happened was told to us by Dianthe, the flower faery who tended Bartholomew's gardens. She was very old when we discovered her story, but with the help of memory glamours, we could piece enough together to know that the next part of the story is very close to what happened.

"Bartholomew had opened the door to the cottage and had walked right out, showing his hands as empty. He had several muskets and pistols levelled at him, and he was extremely conscious that he would be shot if he appeared threatening.

"My good men, I am humbled by your presence here. Pray tell, to what is the purpose of your visit?"

"Silence," snapped Matthew Hopkins. "Bartholomew Cracklock, on the authority of the Long Parliament and the good men I represent, you are hereby accused of sorcery foul and of trafficking with the Devil himself. You shall be subjected to a trial by a test of your peers and shall answer to the crimes to which you are accused."

"Please, sir, pardon my ignorance, but I know not of what you speak. I am no witch."

"That will be decided by God himself," spat back the Witchfinder General. "Seize him."

Bartholomew took a step backwards, his hands still raised. "Philippa," he called out. "It is good to see you, Sister. Are you well? Please, help me stay this madness."

Philippa pushed through the crowd; the baby balanced on her hip. She stood, looking at her brother, her lower lip trembling, and at Josper, who stood next to Bartholomew, staring back at her. She tried to speak, could not, and then cleared her throat.

"Beware, my lords, beware. His demon is with him, there, there," she screeched and pointed directly at Josper.

Elphias had retained the Hagstone and had raised it to his

eye at that point. Seeing that his wife was correct and a devil was amongst them, he screamed out and pulled out his crucifix.

"*Shoot, men, shoot. There, there,*" he screamed, pointing directly at the little old Fae.

The soldiers in the retinue dropped their muskets down to shooting position, puzzled at what they were supposed to be shooting at as the Preacher gestured at empty space, clearly agitated.

"Get in the cottage, Barty," said Josper, looking at his old friend. "I have nothing to fear here; they cannot hurt me. And I will not let them hurt you. Time for pastures new, my friend, I think." With that, he made a few gestures in the air and conjured a shielding glamour in front of him and the door to the cottage.

"Be careful," said Bartholomew, stepping back towards the cottage door.

"*The demon will bewitch us all,*" shrieked Elphias, his eye glued to the Hagstone and watching Josper's gestures.

"*Men, fire at will!*" screamed Matthew Hopkins.

"And what happened next changed everything for the Cracklocks."

Timothy stopped and paused for breath. Fermy had a slow tear rolling down his cheek. Wiping it away, he said, "I'm sorry, Jack. I have heard the story a hundred times, but it still gets to me. Poor Josper."

Timothy nodded at Fermy and patted his arm.

"If it's any consolation, the story does not get any easier for me with each telling," he said.

"What happened?" asked Jack.

"Well, the soldiers were still confused with what they were supposed to shoot at, Jack. One of them levelled his musket at Bartholomew as he retreated into the cottage, as the only real target and fired. However, of course, Bartholomew was protected by Josper's shield glamour, and the musket ball deflected off the shield with a loud crack. Of course, nobody could see that it had bounced off, but they could all see the effects, as the air in front of the cottage rippled slightly, like a pond whose surface had been disturbed. You see, the Witchfinder had listened to Philippa, and his men had all loaded with iron and lead mix balls rather than the usual lead ones. And, as you know, iron is, shall we say, not conducive to the Fae. The iron disrupted the shield charm and made it collapse on itself; the proximity to iron had broken Josper's glamour quite effectively.

"However, the charm had worked on that first shot, deflecting it away as it was supposed to. The musket ball bounced off the glamour without losing much speed; its trajectory changed. It flew through the air and hit Elphias directly in the centre of his chest. It knocked him off his feet, the solid metal ball killing him before he came to land sprawled on his back, the Hagstone flying from his hand as he hit the floor.

"*Sorcery*," screamed Matthew Hopkins as the ripples in the air died away to nothing. "*Kill the warlock.*"

"The soldiers opened fire on the cottage, where Bartholomew cowered behind the kitchen table. The heavy musket balls decimated the door and wooden shutters and punched holes in the clay brick walls. However, the table was of thick oak and took the brunt of the shots, leaving Bartholomew unharmed.

"Philippa had watched all this from behind the soldiers, but when she saw her beloved Elphias flung to the ground, she passed the baby to the nearest soldier and ran howling to her husband's side. Dropping next to him, she cradled his head in her lap, wiping the blood that issued from the corner of his mouth with her dress.

"*Please, please, please*," she cried, patting his face. "*Elphias, please. Oh no, oh no, oh, Lord, please.*" Elphias's pale white face, eyes open, spelt the truth to her that her husband was dead.

"Josper had watched the proceedings in horror; it had never

occurred to him that soldiers would use iron shot. The very presence of it made him feel the sickness creeping upon him, but he saw Philippa in so much distress at what had happened that he could not help himself. He dodged the soldiers that were now making their way into the cottage, shouting for surrender, and dashed to Philippa's side.

"Philippa," he said, laying his hand onto her arm. "Let me help. Let me see if I can help him."

"Philippa raised her tear-stained face to look at Josper. Her eyes narrowed.

"You," she spat. "You did this with your evil magic. Devil."

"Josper was taken aback by the vehemence in her face and tone.

"Philippa, I did nothing other than to try and protect your brother. I did not want this bloodshed."

"You evil little devil. You killed my husband, a good man, a servant of the Lord himself."

"She fumbled under Elphias's cloak and pulled free the flint-lock pistol her husband carried. Thumbing back the hammer, she pointed it at Josper.

"Philippa, please stop. Let me try and help him," said Josper, taking a step back.

"*You and your kind will not take my husband's soul,*" screamed Philippa. "*Back to Hell with you.*"

"And with that, she pulled the trigger, and at point-blank range, poor Josper, who had never hurt a soul in his entire life, was struck by the iron ball and extinguished forever."

Timothy stopped talking and looked at Jack, who was sitting with his mouth open, looking aghast.

"Philippa killed Josper?" he said. "That is awful. Why would she do that?"

"She was bewitched, but by the word of you lifers, rather than anything that the Fae could have glamoured. We think the poor woman was quite under the spell of that dreadful religion and had honestly thought that poor Josper was a demon sent to torment them. It was a different time Jack, remember, a time of omens and witchcraft and suspicion."

"It still doesn't excuse her," said Jack firmly, then more softly, "And what happened to Bartholomew?"

"The soldiers took him, Jack, and imprisoned him in the cellar of the local inn in the hamlet while they gathered themselves for the trial. They were all very shaken by the manner of the death of Elphias, and they looked at Philippa with newfound respect. You see, Hopkins had picked up the Hagstone and looked through it as he had seen Elphias do. He had seen Philippa kill Josper, and in his eyes, Philippa had battled a demon and had destroyed it."

"Did they put Bartholomew on trial?" asked Jack.

"No, they didn't get the chance. Bartholomew used his blood to draw the travel glyphs and create a realm door while he was imprisoned within the cellar and escaped."

"What did he do then?"

"Well, he was grief-stricken at the loss of Josper, who'd been his friend since childhood. However, he had to find Alicia and Matthew, as he knew that the Witchfinder would scour the land to find them. The only safe place for his family was either the new world or in Faery, at least until enough time had passed so that the Witchfinder and his group were long gone. Time passes differently here."

"So he found Alicia and Marcus?"

"Yes. He went to Fae, found Madrigal, and together they went and fetched them. They lived here in Fae for several years until Matthew reached his teens and then went back to your realm. In that time, some fifty years had passed; the Witchfinder was long dead, and Philippa was nearing the end of her years."

"So, all was well then for them?" Jack said with relief.

"No, not at all. This is where the origins of the current positions of the Cracklock family split start," said Timothy, looking at Elsie.

"What do you mean?" asked Jack.

"What I mean is Philippa's mind was broken by the incidents of that day. She had lost her beloved husband, who, despite what he'd accused her of, she still held dear. He was her first love, remember, and had introduced her to the religion that had taken over her life. She was alone now in the world with a small baby and another one on the way. She did not know what to do and turned to her religion for comfort in her dark days. During this time, she started to think more that the Fae were affronts to her God, them being unnatural servants of Hell itself. Something, I am sorry to say, that was encouraged by Matthew Hopkins and those of his entourage who had witnessed the events of the day and were now more certain in their mission to stamp out witchcraft in England once and for all."

"Did the Fae not try and help her?" asked Jack.

"Certainly not," said Timothy. "She had killed a Fae in cold blood for no reason. The Fae no longer went to her and avoided her whenever they could."

"So she stayed with the witch hunter retinue then?" said Jack.

Timothy sighed. "Unfortunately not. If she had, then things would not be as they are now. It seems that fate had something more for Philippa than being a simple camp follower of Matthew Hopkins. According to what we've been able to find out, a few weeks after Elphias's death, Philippa was mulling over retaking her maiden name of Cracklock and was helping Matthew Hopkins with his correspondence. On that fateful day, a rider rode into the inn where they stayed, looking for 'Mrs Philippa Cavendish.' There was news from Elphias's family that was to change her fate forever.

"You see, you may not know that there was a custom in the Middle Age among the nobility. The eldest son inherited the father's title, the second son was sent to the Church, and the third to the military. As the second son, Elphias had indeed been sent to the clergy but had converted to Puritanism. His elder brother had inherited the family estate once their father had died, and the two had maintained some correspondence over the years. There was no third brother. Philippa had never met Elphias's family; they were too involved in the witch trials at the time, and the Cavendish ancestral home was quite far south. Nevertheless, Elphias's brother was aware of the marriage and the fact that Philippa had had a son as her first-born child.

"Anyhow, it seems that Elphias's older brother had died suddenly in his sleep. He was unmarried and had no heir. This meant that the estate immediately passed to Elphias. And as Elphias was dead, the inheritance passed to his eldest son. Riders were despatched by the lawyers for the family to track down the missing son and his mother and advise them of the news. This meant that Philippa had become a wealthy woman via her son, a person of estates and means.

"This, of course, was at odds with Philippa's Puritan beliefs, and she initially rejected the rider's claims and requests to return with him to the family's estates and lawyers to complete the transfer of titles. As it happens, Matthew Hopkins had been listening in on the conversation, and he bade Philippa join him in private prayer. He had his manservant take the rider to the inn taproom for refreshment while he did so.

"In the Chapel, Matthew asked Philippa to read from *Ephesians 6:11-16*. The verse reads as follows:

> *"Put on the full armour of God so that you can take your stand against the devil's schemes. For our struggle is not against flesh and blood, but against the rulers, against the authorities, against the*

powers of this dark world and against the spiritual forces of evil in the heavenly realms.

"Matthew has asked her what she thought of the paragraph he had chosen for her, and Philippa had pondered deeply on it. With some gentle discussion, she realised that Matthew had chosen the passage to illustrate to her that they should continue to take the fight to the witches and their 'devils' that they had seen. The Witchfinder saw the inheritance as a way of allowing them further revenue and resources to do so. He advised her to return to the ancestral home of the Cavendish's and allow her son to take up his birthright. The resources could then be used to further their cause. Seeing the wisdom of the Witchfinder, Philippa readily agreed and made the journey south to claim her son's inheritance and continue the cause.

"The Cavendish's were wealthy, and Philippa wasted no time in ensuring that her son and unborn child were taken care of. She feared the Fae now; in her mind, they would always be 'devils' or 'demons,' so she started to take measures to protect her family. She invested in iron mines in Ireland and made sure that a good proportion of the metals came to the estate. She employed two blacksmiths to make various tools and weapons for use against the Fae; they thought her quite mad, but she paid them well. The mansion soon had iron bars on all windows and doors and a stock of iron weapons prepared and made ready. During this time, Matthew Hopkins died of the consumption shortly after her second child, another son, was born. Philippa's last association with witches died with him; she no longer had any interest in them and focused entirely on the Fae themselves. The Cavendish name was lost, and all children henceforth took the name of Cracklock.

"Some years later, her eldest was in the gardens of the stately home, his mother watching him from the window, when she noticed his attention on one of the flowerbeds. The little boy was quite animated, talking to person's unseen. A shiver had gone down Philippa's back, and she'd run from the house, only stopping to procure an iron dagger from one of the weapons stores that she kept all over the house. When she got to her son, he was indeed laughing with a small flower faery in the garden, who was amusing him with pretty sparks. In front of her son, and oblivious to his screams, Philippa used the dagger to ensure that the 'devil' would never come near her son again."

Timothy paused again, took another sip of water, and then continued.

"And that, Jack, is where the story nears its end. Philippa, in her madness, raised her sons to see the Fae as evil – devils and demons sent to plague lifers, that were only fit to be destroyed by decent, god-fearing folk. Moreover, they raised their children in this manner. And so on. And from that day until now, all of that side of the family are engaged in waging war against the Fae, destroying them without mercy. The name of Cracklock is feared here in Faery, and Cracklocks are not normally permitted here by order of the Seelie Courts."

"But we aren't like that," said Jack in indignation.

"No," said Fermy. "Thankfully, you are not. Elsie, David, and yourself are descended from Bartholomew's side of the family; Cracklocks that are still friends of the Fae and have always defended us from the other side of the family."

"How many of the other Cracklocks are there?" asked Jack.

"We aren't sure exactly," said Elsie. "There are many branches of the family, as you saw on the family tree, but many of them come from Philippa's side. We do know that the ones that we need to worry about are Agatha Cracklock, her son Malchiah, or 'Doctor Cracklock' as he prefers to be known, and some other loose family members such as Anastasia, her son, what's his name...."

"Benedict," said Fermy.

"Yes, Benedict, and one or two others that crop up from time to time."

"Okay," said Jack. "So I know about the 'bad' Cracklocks now. But I still don't understand what this has got to do with me and my Dad hiding us."

Timothy looked at Fermy, who nodded and cleared his throat.

"Well, Jack, it seems that your father learned something about the other side of the family that they wanted to stay hidden. It was rumours, really, and he was in the process of trying to find out more when Agatha and Malchiah got wind of the fact that he might know something. Before then, that side of the family had largely ignored you; we were too small a number to bother them, and they were happily continuing their war on the Fae as they had for centuries. However, whatever David heard, it scared him. A lot. Agatha's lot are quite scary themselves; they are extremely wealthy and have many friends in all kinds of high places. Plus, they have had hundreds of years to perfect their own manner of glamours, which they use against the Folk."

"Yes," said Timothy. "He came here one night in a terrible state. He thought he knew what they were up to, and it was imperative that it was stopped if it was true. When I pressed him on what it was, he said that he would tell me as soon as he was sure about the facts, and we would have to take it to the Courts. But he needed proof first, and to get it, he needed to go away for a while to confirm the rumours."

"Where was he going? What was it?" asked Jack in reverent tones.

"We don't know, Jack. That's the thing. All we know is that he was scared for himself and his family. You had been attacked, you see, and he begged us to help keep you safe; we, of course, would help him without question for as long as it took. That, he didn't know, but was adamant that we couldn't hide you here in

Fae; you had to stay in the lifer's realm and be hidden from both the Cracklocks and other Fae. Which is when we came up with the plan to glamour you."

"And so, dad went away to confirm these rumours and never came back?"

"Yes," said Elsie. "And I can say that he must be in some sort of trouble, as he would never have left you so long. However, we cannot find him; we have scoured both realms. Moreover, from what we know, he is not in the Realm of the Dead either."

"The Realm of the Dead?" said Jack, sitting bolt upright.

CHAPTER 10

*A*nastasia sat on the bench in the park underneath a large oak tree, the sunlight dappling her as it shone through the leaves. She was watching Benedict crash happily through the bushes in the park, whooping with delight whenever he snared a Fae. She was not unduly bothered about the looks he was getting from the other park users; from a distance, he simply appeared to be somebody fooling about, and nobody would have any idea about what he was actually doing. Which was that he'd cast a Fae lock glamour over the area in the bushes, meaning that any Fae caught within it were unable to disappear back to Faery; instead, they had to try and get clear of the glamour if they were to stand a chance. Benedict carried a small sack in his hand that was also Fae locked, into which he was stuffing his catches for his later 'amusement.' Anastasia had an idea about what happened in Benedict's 'workshop' as he called it but turned a blind eye to it usually; the Lord's work always came first, and her son had to have some outlet for his desires, despite her reservations.

Her mobile phone trilled in her small clutch bag and, pulling it free, noted that she did not recognise the number. Swiping the screen, she accepted the call.

"Hello, this is Lady Cracklock speaking."

"Missus, this is Tyler. Tyler LaFey. We spoke earlier?"

"Ah, yes, the gentlemen I commissioned to assist me. What news, please?"

"We found the house okay, but Crackley wasn't home. That place is strange."

"Whatever do you mean, dear boy? How is it strange when no one was in?"

"That's just it. Nobody was there, but then the door opened by itself, and then it got weird."

Anastasia sat up. "Weird, how?" she said sharply.

"Weird in like my brother, and I took a beating from something. We couldn't see what it was, but it did a good job, while that idiot we followed, Owen, sat and watched."

"A beating?"

"Yes, from something we couldn't see. We're covered in bruises, and my brother can barely walk. Listen, lady, what is going on?"

"Tell me exactly what happened."

Tyler gave her the whole story, from following Jimmy from school to them running from the property. He left out the frightening they had put on Jimmy and also bigged up their part, in which they did not run like cowards from the house, fearing for their lives.

"And you are sure that this boy, Jack Crackley, was not at home during these, ahem, events?" said Anastasia.

"Quite sure, missus. There was quite a lot of noise, and nobody came out."

"I see." Anastasia twirled her finger in her hair while she thought. "Master LaFey, what I need you to do is go back and keep an eye on the house. When Jack Crackley arrives back home, I need you to call me immediately. In the meantime, I will take the address for my information."

"Listen, Missus, we ain't going back there, I can tell you. Not after what just happened."

"I don't need you to go to the house. I just want you to make yourselves available to tell me when and if he arrives home. We cannot go; our car is, shall we say, conspicuous, and I do not want to surprise them until the last minute."

"I said no, Missus. You can keep the money you owe us."

"*You listen to me, you pompous little idiot,*" Anastasia suddenly screamed down the phone. "*You will do what I say, or else your miserable existence and that of your oaf of a father will be forfeit. Do you understand me? You do not want to make me ask you twice!*"

At the other end, Tyler was struck dumb by the tone of the woman he was talking to. It was as if she had flipped, and Tyler was getting a little scared now, a feeling that the twins weren't truly used to. Mason was wincing as he heard the force of the voice coming from the phone that Tyler clutched.

"Okay," he whispered. "But as soon as he's home and we've told you, we're out. Okay?"

"Of course, of course, dear boy," said Anastasia, her voice back to reasonable. "I will consider your employment discharged as soon as you give me the news that I want to hear. Now, can you please provide me with the address for future reference?"

Tyler told her the address and promised to call as soon as he saw Jack get home. The woman hung up on him as soon as he had finished.

Tyler looked at Mason. "Jeez, Mase. What have we got ourselves into with this? We have to go back, or else we're in some serious bother with this one."

Mason shuddered slightly and rubbed his head.

"You still got Owen's phone?"

"Yep," grunted Mason.

"Okay. Let's go and find a spot to sit and watch where we can't be seen. We can always say that we are looking for the owner of the phone we found if anyone asks."

Turning tail, the twins limped back towards the scene of the first severe beating they had ever received.

"WHAT DO YOU MEAN, the Realm of the Dead?" Jack asked again, taken aback.

"It's another Realm, Jack. One that we know little about. The polite term is actually the 'Realm of the Departed,'" said Timothy.

"Can we travel there?"

"Absolutely not," said Timothy and Fermy together. Fermy continued:

"Jack, listen to me. The Realm of the Departed is not some-where that the living, either lifers or Fae, are supposed to go under any circumstances. It exists as a passing place for those that are no longer with us, and it is certainly forbidden under Faery law for any Fae to go there."

"Why?" asked Jack.

"Because, from what we understand, you have to have died to go there. Moreover, if you have not passed, then you will as soon as you arrive. The realm does not allow grackles inside of it and immediately removes them."

"Grackles?" said Jack, puzzled. "You've mentioned that word before. Or was it grockles, something Dorcas said to me?"

"I think you mean both," said Timothy with a smile. "Those are the words that we Fae use to describe two very important items. Grackles are what you would probably call 'life force,' the energy that keeps you alive. Grockles are similar, but that is 'magical force' and is used to make and power all kinds of magical things, including glamours. Everybody starts out with a lot of grackles, but these slowly deplete over time. For lifers, this is within a relatively short period, but for Fae, the process takes longer – which is why we live longer. But when they are gone, Fae and lifers alike will pass on to the Realm of the Departed."

Jack took all this in. "So, if you lose all of your grackles, then you're gone? And things like an accident, etc., can remove them all at once?"

"Yes," said Timothy. "And other things can deplete them. If you have a disease, for example, that can destroy grackles and lessen the life span. You lifers are quite adept at finding ways of reducing your grackle count; it is something that the Fae have never understood – your destructive behaviours."

"Yes, well, people can be stupid," said Jack with a sad shake of his head. "And I assume that it is the same for grockles then?"

"No, they are quite different. Lifers start with some grockles, as do Fae, but as a magical race, the Fae have a lot more, and we can use them naturally. Lifers cannot. One of the things that Fermy asked me to check today was whether you already have sufficient grockles to use some glamours. Cracklocks normally do, due to their unique nature."

"Will it hurt, the checks, I mean?" asked Jack, a little alarmed.

"Not at all, no need to worry. And if you haven't got enough, then it is possible to increase the grockles you have with study and tuition."

"Like schoolwork, but with magic," said Jack with a laugh. The others joined in.

"We'll check you over when we're done talking," said Timothy.

"Okay, sure," said Jack; an idea was forming in his mind. "Timothy, you said earlier that your machine was indicating that Dad was both alive and dead. What if he was somehow in the Realm of the Departed?"

"I can understand why you think that, Jack, but it's just not possible to go there while you're alive," said Timothy. "It's like the waiting room again, but only enables those who dwell there to come back to our respective realms without grackles, if they so wish, before they carry on. Ghosts."

"Carry on where?" asked Jack.

"Nobody knows, Jack; we have little information on what happens once you've gone on, and the departed that have communicated don't seem to know either. That, or they won't tell us."

"How do you know about all of this?" asked Jack.

"Well..." said Timothy, hesitantly, "Some individuals can see and converse with Faeries, which is very rare, of course. Slightly less rare are individuals, both here in Faery and your own realm, that can see and communicate with the dead."

"Like those mediums on the television that Mum likes to watch?" asked Jack.

"I don't think so, dear," said Elsie. "The people we know are definitely able to talk to the departed. No tricks or anything, and they do not tend to like the limelight. Those people on the television are a little dubious, I think."

"You've asked these people who can see and talk to the departed about my Dad?"

"Yes, Jack, we have when we were searching. There are folk here in Faery who we have asked; we call them Whisperers. And I have a close friend as well back home who I asked. Separate sources have both been consulted and have confirmed that your Dad is not in the Realm of the Departed, nor, it appears, has ever been there. It is a real mystery," Elsie finished.

"Can we use a Realm door to go to the Realm of the Departed?" Jack asked.

"There is a travel glyph, yes. However, it is kept under lock and key in the archives of the Courts. Both Courts have deemed the glyphs too dangerous to use following this, so they hid them away."

"So, I guess that we can't go and check for ourselves then," said Jack. "Unless we don't have any grackles in us when we go."

"You'd have to be departed to be able to do that," said Timothy.

"But what if you could remove all of your grackles and then go?" said Jack.

"It's not possible," said Timothy. "Grackles are not easy to remove other than by general time passing and other immediate effects, such as accidents, illnesses, and so forth. And once they're gone, they're gone."

"But before the accident, Mr Binks had some sort of tube for removing grackles. He put it on my head when he was trying to get me back into the house."

"What?" said Fermy and Timothy together, both sitting up. "Somebody attacked you, and he had a device to remove grackles safely? You must be mistaken."

"No, I'm sure that's what he said. It may have been grockles, though, but definitely something about making me more compliant if he removed some grockles or grackles or something."

"Tell us everything that you remember," Fermy suddenly commanded, staring at Elsie as he did so. She nodded and mouthed, "David," to him.

Jack told them what he could remember about the invitation to help, the drink, the fact that the things kept slipping in and out of view (here they all nodded, further confirmation that the original glamour was fading). He talked about the fact that Mr Binks seemed to be something else other than a man and his attack on Jack with the tube and the other creatures. Jack described the tube in what detail he could remember; the strange sucking sensation, and then his struggles to be free. Apart from Elsie, the others were not familiar with the concept of a toilet roll, which made Jack privately wonder about some Fae practices, which he quickly put to one side. When he had

208

finished, both Fermy and Timothy were silent, mulling over what Jack had said. They seemed to reach some sort of mutual decision without speaking.

Looking at Jack, Fermy said, "Well, that is something. In all my years, I have never seen a device like you described that could remove either grockles or grackles; indeed, I've only ever heard mention of it once. Your father, Jack, something he over-heard. And this Mr Binks sounds like some sort of changeling or something, inhabiting a human perhaps. Very odd."

"I think that it would be prudent to see about obtaining this device," said Timothy. "I would like to be able to study it, and if it could be a key to the Realm of the Departed, then we could certainly use it to look for David there ourselves. Although I have to confess, we would have to study it in some depth to determine what it actually does."

"But how can we get it?" asked Jack. "I really don't want to have to go back to that house and ask for it. He said he'd kill me!"

"I am sure that I could sneak in there," said Fermy. "I'll just have to conceal myself as something and search for it without being seen, then make my getaway. I've done it before."

"When?" said Jack.

Fermy laughed. "I was an agent of the Seelie Court, Jack. Thankfully now retired, but in my day, I had to perform all kinds of tasks at the request of the Court. As did my counter-parts from the Unseelie Courts."

"So you're like a Faery James Bond?" said Jack.

Fermy looked puzzled. "James Pond? Is that like a water nymph?"

Elsie sniggered, as did Jack. She said, "It's a thing in the lifer realm, Fermy; we shall have to watch the movies together." Turning to Jack, she said, "Not really; I don't think that they have secret agents here in Faery. But it should work; Fermy has experience in this sort of thing."

Turning to Timothy, she said, "I tell you what. We should see if this is a good idea with that device of yours. I'm sure that Jack would like to see it work, given that he keeps staring at it."

"That would be brilliant!" said Jack, who would very much like to see what the contraption that dominated the room did.

Timothy stood up and cracked his knuckles. "Very well then," he said. "I need to take her for a spin anyway; it's been a while. Jack, would you like to formulate the question for the input, please?"

Jack thought and then said, "Ask it if Fermy going to the house to get the tube will work?"

Timothy strolled over to the control panel, stopped, and then gestured for Jack to come over.

"You can come and assist me, Jack, if you will. The theriomantic oscillator is more easily operated by two people than one. Something I have never been able to fix; one person can do it, but it's a great deal of running around."

Jack went over and looked questioningly at Timothy, who was busy twisting various knobs and flicking switches. Above him in the tubes, the scurrying rodents suddenly stopped.

"They know what's going to happen, Jack," said Timothy. "Now, if you would be so kind, go over to that wheel there, and give a couple of turns until it stops."

"What does that do?" asked Jack.

"Opens the cheese well. You will see why when you do it. On my signal, though, I need to have the question input into the machine properly."

Jack stood next to the wheel with his hands, waiting for Timothy's signal. The little Fae flipped a few more switches, clicked some clockwork cogs around, and then pointed at Jack. "Go," he said.

Jack gave the wheel a couple of turns until it locked into place. Nothing happened for a few seconds, and then it all went mad. A strong waft of rotting cheese filled the immediate area, and the rodents in the machine went crazy, scurrying every-where within the tubes. The squeaking started low and then rose in pitch as the crazed creatures scurried, searching for the source of the smell. Mice ran in wheels at a crazy pace, and the thundering sound of thousands of tiny feet filled the room as the pipework started to vibrate with the frantic efforts of the occupants. The counter dials on the machine ratcheted round and round with a wild clicking, the numbers rising at speed, and the machine started to clank. The noise was deafening.

"*Is it always this noisy?*" Jack shouted over to Timothy, his hands covering his ears.

"*Yes,*" Timothy shouted back. "*Listen. In a moment, I need you to turn the cheese wall wheel back to where it was while I reroute the rodent flow.*"

Jack had no idea what that meant, but he placed one hand on the wheel, the other covering the ear closest to the creaking machine. Timothy continued to flick various switches, moving around the machine in some strange choreography as he manipulated various levers. Above them, the pipes and tubes were vibrating, and Jack felt tiny drops of something start to land on him as things overhead started to shake at an alarming rate. He shook his head, and what looked like mice droppings fell out of his hair. Glancing over, he could see that Fermy and Elsie had gotten well clear of the machine and stood there grinning at him. He scowled at them.

"Now, Jack," called Timothy, yanking a final level, and Jack spun the wheel all the way back until it could go no further. The cheese smell disappeared almost instantly, and as if someone had flicked a switch, the mice and rats within the machine just stopped, as did the noise. In a clear tube near Jack's head, he could see that the occupants there appeared to have frozen. All the rodents sat up on their haunches, noses in the air twitching, tiny black eyes seeming unfocused. Jack could see them breathing in and out, panting as if they were exhausted.

"Quickly, Jack. This way," said Timothy, gesturing to Jack as he moved out of sight around the edge of the machine. Jack followed him, ducking under various pipes until they were in a small clear area in the centre of the machine, which spiralled above them into the roof.

"Now, Jack, when I say so, please pull that lever down there," said Timothy, flicking some more switches as he tapped a dial. Seizing another lever, he gestured at Jack. "Now," he said, yanking down the lever he was holding. Jack did likewise.

The rodents started scurrying again, but not in a frenzied manner. It was almost ordered in the way that they trotted towards the clearing that the two stood in, contained within the pipework but visible through the various meshes and glass viewing ports. The motion was uniform as they started to climb over each other into what appeared to be multiple big cages positioned halfway up the machine and surrounding the clearing.

"What are they…" began Jack before Timothy shushed him. "Quiet Jack; this next part is critical."

Jack watched as Timothy studied the dial he was tapping very carefully. The seconds ticked by, and then a small ringing bell started, like an alarm clock. Timothy yanked his lever back up and wiped his forehead.

"Okay then, let's see what the answer is," he said, pointing upwards at the cages that were filled with various mice and rats, climbing over each other. As Jack looked up, the cages started to move downwards, some quicker than others.

"It's to do with weights and measures, Jack," said Timothy airily. "Those cages are like large weighing scales. They give us the answer to the question that we inputted. This way, please."

Jack looked at the slowly descending cages, noting that some had already stopped at different points around the clearing. He followed Timothy out of the network of pipes, ducking his head as he went to another panel of instruments. Timothy studied various dials and numbers, and Jack heard him mutter under his breath, "Okay, but not? I wonder…" He then turned and waved to those sitting at the table.

"The machine says that the mission will be a success," he called simply. Jack shook his head in amazement.

"How do you know?" he asked.

"The balances show the differences between the potential fates and…" he tailed off, looking at Jack's puzzled face.

"Never mind," he said. "You just need some practice to be able to interpret the results."

"About four hundred year's practice, dear," called Elsie, a big smile on her face.

FIVE MINUTES later saw them again at the table, the machine behind them giving off a settling thrum as the rodents again hurried about their business within its bowels. Fermy looked around at the others.

"Okay, then. When we return to the lifer realm, I will go and investigate this Twillington House and see about getting in to take the tube. I'll then come back to Jack's house to check in and then take it to Elsie's to keep it safe. Then, all being well, we should be able to meet up here tomorrow to take a look at this item and determine if it does what Jack claims it can do. We can then build a further plan based on the results of that for a visit to the Realm of the Departed."

"You will have to be careful, Fermy," said Jack. "Mr Binks is not a nice character, and he has help. If you get into trouble, we won't know."

"I will be able to send a message to Elsie, Jack, if I need to," said Fermy.

"How?"

Elsie raised her right hand to show off a ring on her index

finger. It was silvery in colour and had a small dark blue stone set in it. Fermy concentrated for a moment, and the stone turned a bright red and gave off a little flash before turning back to its original blue.

"That's awesome," said Jack. "Another glamour?"

"Of course," said Fermy. "I normally use it to tell Elsie to expect a visit, but it would work quite well here, I think. Not that I expect to have to use it; I am quite adept at not being seen when I don't wish to be. I don't think it will be an issue, and besides, we already know that I will be successful; Timothy's device hasn't been wrong yet when the question is simple."

"I can take you to near where the house is, but I don't really want to be seen," said Jack.

"Not necessary," said Fermy. "I can get there myself if you can tell me roughly where it is."

"Yet another glamour?" said Jack.

"No, not this time. Fae can travel about quite well for short distances in the lifer realm. We use natural transport methods."

"It's a bit like teleporting, Jack," said Elsie. "Fae can travel short distances by harmonising with nature; I don't know exactly how it works, and to be honest, I'm not sure that they do!"

"Correct," smiled Fermy. "All Fae can do it, that's all. I'll do that rather than risk you being seen by this Mr Binks, Jack."

"I am relieved, it must be said," smiled Jack.

Timothy cracked his knuckles again. "Well then, that's decided then," he said. "I think now that we ought perhaps to have a look at Jack's glamour potential; time is starting to get away from us." As neither Elsie nor Jack had a watch with them, it was difficult for them to disagree.

Timothy went over to a small cupboard, opened it, and cursed as several mice shot out of it. He removed a small bag and brought it back to the table, where Jack looked at it in interest. Opening it, he removed what looked like a small pipe, similar to a smoking pipe, with a curved stem and bowl at one end. The bowl was made of clear crystal with what looked like white smoke curling around inside it.

"Right then, Jack. This is a glamour actuator, and it detects the glamour potential of anyone who blows into it. We are looking for the grockles trapped in here to respond to you; they will change colour based on the number of grockles you have, as they are attracted like for like. The darker the colour, the better. All you need to do is blow."

"Well, that sounds easy enough," replied Jack. "And I thought that it was going to hurt!"

Timothy held out the pipe to Jack, who took it gently. The swirling smoke immediately turned slightly darker grey from its original white colour.

"Is that good?" asked Jack.

"Yes, it's a sign that grockles are present. Blow into it as hard as you can please; let's really see what you're made of," said Timothy.

Jack took a deep breath and blew into the pipe as hard as he could, so hard that a little raspberry noise came out of the side of his mouth. The smoke in the bowl turned an immediate deep, dark red colour, almost purple in appearance. Jack passed the pipe back to Timothy and looked at him expectantly.

Timothy studied the bowl from several angles, turning the pipe over in his hands as he did so. He then looked up at Jack and smiled.

"Well, it looks like the wayward Cracklock is fine to try some glamours," he said. "Very healthy on the grockles front. I think that we can get this much darker with practice and tuition."

"Can I learn something now?" asked Jack eagerly.

Timothy looked at Elsie, who nodded. "Something fairly quick, though, please; we really have to think about heading back. It's going to be difficult enough to make sure that we arrive back in reasonable time if we leave it too much longer," she said.

"I want to learn that cake trick that Fermy did at yours, Auntie, or perhaps how to alter my appearance!" said Jack, fidgeting in his seat with excitement.

"Oh, no, no, no, that's far too advanced for a first try," said Timothy. "I think that what we will start you off with is a nice, simple remembering glamour. They are always useful, and you can use them to build on other glamours. The gestures can be quite complex, you know."

"A remembering glamour?" said Jack, unable to hide his disappointment. "That just sounds dull. What does it make you remember?"

"Well, it's a basic starter glamour that they teach young Fae children," said Timothy. "You can cast it on yourself or someone else, and it allows you to remember two things forever."

"Two things? What is the use in remembering two things?" asked Jack a little sulkily.

"Well, once you've mastered it, you can then remember something very complicated. Like the shadow glamour that was used to hide your appearance earlier, for example. It allows novices to gain knowledge of more complex glamours rapidly and improve their skills quickly."

"Okay, but is there a glamour that allows you to remember more things?" asked Jack. "That would be useful."

"Of course," said Timothy patiently. "But it is very compli-cated to learn higher remembrance glamours. Start simple and build up. Use it to remember some other items, and then once you've remembered those without any issues, cast it again and learn something else. And so on."

"Can it be used for anything?" asked Jack.

"Yes," said Timothy. "Not just glamours, but anything. For your learning in the lifer realm, for when your mother asks you to do something that you might forget, anything."

"So, what should I try and remember now?"

"Oh, that's easy," said Timothy. "Remember the actual glamour itself. In addition, remember something funny. We need to practice both on you and someone else."

At this, Elsie put up her hand. "I'll be the guinea pig, Jack, if you want; there's not a lot that can go wrong with this glamour." Jack gave her a thumbs up.

"Guinea pigs?" said Timothy. "You promised to bring me some of those for the oscillator." Elsie waved him away.

"Maybe, maybe. I just don't want to bring those poor creatures to live in that machine."

Timothy started to say something when Jack interjected.

"Okay then; what do I do?" asked Jack, a little more buoyant now.

Timothy rolled his head around on his neck. "Stand up and come over to this clear spot here. You'll need some room to practice the gestures, and we can also focus your grockles better if you can move around."

"Let's do this!" said Jack, springing from his seat. Fermy looked at Elsie and smiled.

The next hour passed quickly with some serious tutoring and a lot of huffing and puffing from Jack as he tried and failed to get the glamour to work. Timothy was insistent that he get all the aspects right, and Jack started to get frustrated and was on the verge of giving up when suddenly how to do it became fixed in his mind, crystal clear. He gasped, and his eyes widened.

"At last," said Timothy. "I think he's got it!"

Jack went through the gestures and glamour again and did it perfectly. He was extremely pleased with himself.

"Right then, Elsie, if you could step up here, please, it's time to see if Jack can cast the glamour on someone else. If you could try and resist a little as well, please?"

It went faster this time, now that Jack could perform the gestures correctly. In a matter of minutes, he had Elsie in tears of laughter, as the image of a garishly dressed dancing Prime Minister filled her mind.

"Oh, Jack, Jack, enough," she choked, dabbing at the tears. "I'll never get that out of my mind now, his stupid face, regardless of how we try and reverse the glamour." She started laughing again and started them all off.

"A good start, I think, Jack," said Timothy with some satisfaction. "We can build on this now and get you up to speed with some more useful glamours. But keep practising that one; it would be good to have it down without having to have it as part of the glamour itself."

"I'm ready for the next one," said Jack, thrilled with himself.

"Not now," said Fermy. "We need to be getting back, plus the sooner we get this tube, the better if we want to find David."

"When then?" replied Jack eagerly.

"When we've got the tube, we can come back. Timothy, would you be kind enough to tutor Jack again?"

"Of course, of course," said Timothy, waving Fermy away. "It would be my pleasure; it is rather nice to revisit some of the earlier glamours. I'll have a think about something a little more interesting for next time, Jack."

"That would be great; many thanks, Timothy," said Jack, excited now that he was learning something that made him different from others.

Elsie got to her feet and started rummaging around in her handbag. Fermy gathered up his hat and coat and looked expectantly at her.

"I know it's here somewhere," she muttered, feeling her way around in the bottom, rattling and the noise of paper scrunching accompanying her search.

"I don't know why you don't clear that bag out," said Fermy. "You can never find anything in it."

"That's what makes it so much fun," said Elsie. "Making you wait for me."

Fermy grinned to himself as Elsie pulled something from the bag with a triumphant, "Aha!" In her hand was a small ball covered in tiny little squares that twinkled in the light of Timothy's kitchen.

"Okay then," she said. "Date and time, please."

"All Fells Day, four fifteen of the clock," replied Timothy promptly without looking. Jack looked at him in wonder, and he shrugged. "I just know," he said.

Elsie spoke into the ball as Timothy had stated, and it started to hum a little.

"Jack, what time should we get home for? Bearing in mind that we need to travel from my house back to yours, and it would be good if your mother weren't there when we arrived."

"Mum gets home normally around six o'clock."

Elsie spoke into the ball again, giving the date back home and a time of four-thirty. The ball took on a different tonal hum, which Jack could feel in his teeth.

"Right then," said Elsie, marching to a door in the corner of the kitchen. "Pantry, it is."

"What is that, Auntie?" asked Jack, pointing at the ball in her hand.

"It's a pointer, Jack. Useful little device; quite magical. You can only get them here in Fae. Basically, the harmony it hums allows the waiting room to open the door at the correct time."

"Didn't we need it to come here?" asked Jack.

"No. Travelling here always puts you into the correct time in Fae, providing you focus exactly and have a specific time to aim at. It's just going back that we need to make sure that we aren't weeks or months in the future."

"I'll have to get one," said Jack.

"I will pick one up for you," replied Timothy. "Fae don't use them generally, as we can arrive in the Lifer realm as we need to. It is not time travel, more of a wish to be somewhere. We can just do it; it has been studied, and the overall conclusion was 'it just is'!"

"Okay, Jack, travel glyph time. We need to use the one for the lifer realm. Watch carefully; there will be a test on this at some point, as you will need to remember these if you want to travel about."

Elsie plucked her pen from her bag (without any issues, Jack noted) and drew another strange symbol on the door. Slapping it with the flat of her hand, the glyph glittered and fell as before. Elsie pulled it open and turned around.

"Many thanks as always, Timothy. We will hopefully see you tomorrow once Fermy has completed his little mission."

"Yes, thanks, Timothy," added Jack.

Timothy bowed low. "The pleasure was all mine, my friends. I look forward to seeing you again soon."

Fermy gave a slight bow in return, and the three moved through the open door, which indeed revealed itself to be another pantry. The green flames glowed around them, flickering as they danced along the sparse, shimmering shelves. Elsie pulled the door shut and held up the pointer. The flames immediately stopped their random dancing, and all moved together in unison.

"There," she said with some satisfaction. "Next glyph, it is." She drew on the door the unlock glyph to return to the lifer realm, slapped it, and when it fell from the door, Elsie pulled it open. The three stepped out into her small kitchen again. Glancing at the clock on the wall, which read quarter to five, Elsie gave a little clap.

"Not too bad at all," she said, with a wink at Jack, who looked puzzled.

"It's not an exact thing with the timings," Elsie said, holding up the pointer. "But it's normally pretty close. The date on the clock is the same as when we left, so we are all good. Here, catch." Elsie threw the pen to Jack and pointed at the pantry door.

"Get to it, Master Cracklock," she said with a grin.

With a sigh, Jack started to draw the travel glyph on the pantry door.

JACK HAD MUCH BETTER success this time, getting the travel glyphs correct on the second try, and the three came out through the lounge door into Jack's house with little bother. The first thing that they saw was Jimmy sitting comfortably at the kitchen table with a plate of what appeared to be buns in front of him. The threesome was, therefore, a little surprised that the door had delivered them back when there was a potential witness.

"Alright, mate?" called Jimmy, seeing Jack stood with Elsie. "Where did you come from?"

"Eeermmm…" Jack stammered, at a loss.

"How was Faery travelling?" asked Jimmy.

Jack's jaw dropped, as did Elsie's. Fermy also registered a shocked expression, but Jimmy, of course, couldn't see him.

"What…what did you say?" stammered Elsie.

"Faery travelling. That thing with the drawing on the door," said Jimmy, taking a bite from a bun. "Takes you where you want to go. Did you have a nice time in Faery?"

"But…how…oh, hang on a minute," said Fermy and yelled, *"Dorcas, you come here at once."*

The brownie's face appeared sheepishly over the top of the upstairs bannister, an embarrassed smile on her face.

"Dorcas, what the grock has been going on?" said Fermy, his hands on his hips as he fixed Dorcas with a stern expression.

Dorcas came down the stairs, wringing her hands together. "Oh, Fermy, it alrights. Some boy's try's to kill Jimmy, and I saved him, and he's was all confused and scared, so's I had to bring him in, and I had to reveal to make him feels safe, and I don't thinks anyone see'd what happened to us, but...."

"Dorcas, you know the rules," said Fermy, interrupting. "Now, what is the truth? Because you can be in a lot of trouble."

"Is that Fermy?" said Jimmy. "I can't see or hear him. But if you can hear me, it's alright; Dorcas was great."

"Of that, I don't doubt," said Fermy with a small smile. "But the laws are still the laws."

Jimmy continued to Jack, "It was the LaFey twins, Jack. They really were going to make a mess of me and cornered me in your front yard. They had a belt, and they were going to break my arm like they said before. Please don't let Dorcas be in trouble; she's been lovely to me since it happened, and they would have done me over if it wasn't for her. Please, Fermy, wherever you are, it is really fine; I won't be telling anybody. They wouldn't believe me anyway."

Dorcas smiled gratefully at Jimmy, and Jack nodded.

"It's true. The day I had my accident, they set about Jimmy in the bike sheds at school. We were both lucky not to get a hiding off them then; Tyler knocked me out anyway. They are a nasty pieces of work, although I wonder what they were doing here on this side of town. They live out in Morningside, I think?"

Dorcas again bristled at this. Bullying her Jack! She started to say something when Fermy interrupted.

"Okay, okay," he said. "I understand that this was potentially a life and death situation, so if there are any consequences, I can vouch for Dorcas in the Courts if I need to. But please don't make a habit of this, Dorcas; our realm needs to remain hidden from the lifers."

Jimmy watched Dorcas visibly relax. "Is it all okay then?" he said.

"Yes, it's fine," said Fermy and then remembered that Jimmy could not see or hear him.

"Yes," said Jack. "Fermy says it's okay."

"Tell Fermy thank you from me; Dorcas is a real hero."

"He can hear you," said Jack with a smile. "He's just there," and pointed at Fermy.

Jimmy looked around Jack. "I can't see him; it's strange talking to someone who's not there."

"Oh, this is ridiculous," said Fermy. "Hang on a moment."

He gestured a glamour into the air. Both him and Dorcas stood, their heads cocked to one side, listening.

"What are they doing?" asked Jack.

"Detection glamour," said Elsie. "If there are any Fae around, they will hear an alert; it's like the tinkling of bells. I use it sometimes if the TV detector vans are in the village; the louder the bells, the closer they are. I make a sharp exit when they get too close."

Apparently satisfied, Fermy looked over at Jimmy.

"Jack, I'm going bend the laws and reveal to Jimmy; there aren't any Fae around who could report me that we know of. Can you tell Jimmy?"

"Do you want to meet Fermy?" Jack asked.

"Absolutely!" said Jimmy. "Dorcas has told me all about him and where you've been today. Sounds totally awesome. You can tell me all about it if that's okay?"

"Sure," said Jack. "You seem to know a bit about things, so if it's okay with the others, then I'd love to."

Elsie looked at Fermy, who shrugged. "Too late now," he said. He performed a complex series of gestures in the air. As Jimmy watched them, a shadow formed in the centre of the glittering lights that appeared, slowly becoming more solid. As the lights faded, the small figure of Fermy came into view.

"Hello, Jimmy. We have, of course, met, but I was a little hairier then."

"A pleasure to meet you, Fermy. Dorcas speaks very highly of you; she's told me a lot this afternoon."

"I don't doubt it," said Fermy, looking at Dorcas, who blushed. "She's quite the talker, especially if there are tea and cake involved." They all laughed at this, including Dorcas, who had quite recovered from her embarrassment now.

"Now then," said Elsie. "Sammy will be home in a short while, so if you're going, Fermy, it may be good to get gone now before she gets back. We will wait here for you, of course. Sammy won't notice that the ferret has gone; I'll tell her it's asleep if she asks."

"And I will get's the dinner ready," said Dorcas, bustling into the kitchen.

"I won't be too long, hopefully," said Fermy. "It depends how long it takes me to get in there and find this tube, but I should be back later this evening. I will be as quick as I can. I just need to know where it is."

"I can help with that," said Jimmy, fumbling in his pockets. "Damn it, no, I can't; Mason took my phone."

"Here, use mine," said Jack, taking it off the hall table where he had emptied his pockets earlier.

Jimmy took the phone with a nod of thanks and fiddled with it. He then showed them an image from google maps of Twillington House from outside on the road.

"How did you know?" asked Jack.

"Your mum told me, and we went to pick up the bits of your bike from there while you were in the hospital."

"What an interesting device," said Fermy, looking at the big screen in front of him. "That will be fine for my purposes. I bid you farewell for now."

"Good luck," said Jack and Elsie together. Fermy bowed to them and, with a little wave, faded from view.

"Where's he gone?" asked Jimmy.

"Come up to my room," said Jack. "I'll fill you in on what's been happening. You are not going to believe it, I'm telling you!"

Elsie watched the boys go upstairs with a fond expression on her face. When they had gone, she turned to Dorcas.

"I'm a little worried about Fermy," she said. "He's gone to that house with little understanding about the place or what's in there. I know he's done this before, but normally he'd have more information."

Dorcas patted Elsie's leg reassuringly. "Fermy will be's okay," she said. "He's clever and quicks and can defends hisself well. He'll be fine."

Elsie nodded. "I just can't help it when I think that this is all going to go wrong," she sighed.

$\mathcal{T}$yler and Mason were crouched in the house's front yard a couple of doors down on the opposite side of the road to Jack's house. Fortunately, the house was unoccupied; a 'To Let' sign leaning crookedly over the wall that they were hiding behind. The twins were starting to get bored now; they had been there for half an hour and were starting to fidget.

"Shall we just bin this off?" said Tyler to Mason. Mason shrugged.

"If we do, do you reckon that lady will be able to find us?" Tyler continued.

Mason shrugged again. Tyler was still shaken from the earlier events; if the truth be told, he was scared, which was an unfamiliar sensation to him. He was sure that Mason felt the same.

"We'll give it another hour and then ring her," he decided aloud.

The situation at Jack's house had remained the same all the while they had been there. The daylight was starting to fail now, and the house looked deserted, although a light was on in the back somewhere, its dull ambience reflecting off the glass in the front door. There didn't seem to be any movement from what the twins could see, and every time they took a glance over the wall, everything remained the same. There was no sign of Jimmy Owen either.

Tyler was fiddling with Jimmy's phone to try and get it to unlock when Mason gave a grunt and nudged him. Tyler immediately peered over the wall to see what his brother had seen. At first glance, it seemed that nothing had changed, and then Tyler noticed that the light in the front door window flickered in and out as if people were moving about inside. As they watched, the hall light came on, and then the light in the room at the front flicked on.

"Looks like someone's home; must have come round the back," said Tyler to Mason. "There's no way we could have missed them. I wonder if that's Crackley? We'll have to get closer."

Mason shook his head at this statement; he had no desire for another beating. Tyler looked at him.

"Look, Mase, the only way out of this is to tell that woman when Crackley is back. We are done if we do. And I don't want to tell her something if it's not true; I have a feeling that she wouldn't like that at all."

Under duress, the two of them crept across the road to the wall surrounding Jack's front yard. Cupping his ear, Tyler listened but could not make out anything.

"We'll have to get closer," he whispered to Mason.

"Not me," grunted Mason.

Tyler shot his twin a glare and pushed open the gate as quietly as he could. Squatting on his haunches, he sidled over to the door and pushed the letterbox open slightly. Pressing his ear to it, he heard snatches of conversation as he listened

"He can hear you," he heard a male voice that he thought was Crackley. "He's just there."

A second male voice said, "I can't see him; it's strange talking to someone who's not there." That was Owen.

Tyler strained to hear more and felt a strange tingling sensation go through him, like a miniature blast of pins and needles. It lasted only half a second, but it was very odd.

'*What the...*' He thought, and then he heard Owen say, "A pleasure to meet you, Fermy. Dorcas speaks very highly of you; she's told me a lot this afternoon."

Tyler was confused. Who was Owen talking to? Fermy? The lady hadn't mentioned any bloke in the picture, and it was common knowledge that Jack was from a single-parent family. He put it to the back of his mind; he'd confirmed that Crackley was back home, so he could call the lady in good conscience now and get the hell out of this weird arrangement. He sidled back to the gate and stood up.

"Let's go; I don't want to be here when we make that call," he said to Mason, and they set off at a run, almost knocking over the woman walking up the street engrossed in her phone.

JACK AND JIMMY heard the front door go from Jack's room, followed by a querying, "Hello," from the hallway. Sticking his head over the bannister, Jack saw his mum had arrived back home and was busy removing her coat and bag.

"Hi mum," he said, coming down the stairs. "Work okay?"

"Hiya Jack. Yep, all right, thanks, typical day. Nearly got knocked over by two louts, though, just down the street; they were really going some. They only just missed me.

Jack looked up at Jimmy and mouthed, "Twins?" Jimmy shrugged his shoulders.

"I have to go out tonight to clean, though, which I can do without, but I've got a couple of hours. How are you doing?" said Sam.

"I'm good, thanks, Mum."

"Hello, Mrs Crackley," said Jimmy, appearing next to Jack.

"Hi, Jimmy. You moving in here?" said Sammy.

"I doubt we'd be able to afford to feed him," said Jack with a laugh and ducked as Jimmy faked a punch at him.

"Hello, Sammy, dear," said Elsie, coming out of the kitchen. "Dinner is almost ready. I hope it's okay that I've asked Jimmy to stay again tonight. Company for Jack that isn't an old lady." She winked at the boys, who grinned back.

"Not a problem," said Sammy.

"Now, come on in and put your feet up for a bit. I've made tea," said Elsie, gesturing into the kitchen. Sammy walked through and gasped at the sight of a classic English teapot, cups, saucers, and a plate of homemade biscuits and small cakes all laid out on a snow-white tablecloth.

"Please tell me that you're never going home!" said Sammy as she plumped down at the kitchen table. Elsie gave Dorcas a huge smile as she stood in the kitchen corner, Sammy utterly oblivious to her.

ANASTASIA HEARD the phone ringing from the depths of her bag and plucked it out. "Speak," she said.

"It's us, Missus, the LaFey's. Just ringing to tell you that Crackley is back home now like you asked. There are some other people there as well."

"Who are they?" said Anastasia pleasantly.

"Dunno. Jack's mate, who we followed before, plus some others we reckon, though we didn't hear them. Didn't hear any old lady, either."

Anastasia gave a small smile at this and thought, '*So, David has returned, has he? Good.*' She continued, "Splendid, splendid. You have done well, young man, and have my thanks."

"So we're done now?" said Tyler at the other end of the phone. "We can pick up the rest of our money, and we're done?"

"Oh, no, no, no, dear boy. I may require your services again. Consider the amount you received earlier a little retainer. I will pay you more the next time I see you."

"But you said...."

"I know what I said. I have changed my mind. You and your delightful brother please stand by on this number."

"What if we don't?" said Tyler stubbornly.

"Then you, your family, and any friends are going to be extremely miserable," said Anastasia and cut off the call. She glanced over towards where Benedict was still amusing himself in the undergrowth.

"Benedict, dear, it's time to go and eat, and then we can pay a little visit to our extended family," she called.

Benedict came blundering over, leaves in his hair, clutching the small sack he'd been collecting the Fae in.

"Did you get many, dear?" said Anastasia absently.

"Yes, seven. Well, six; one didn't quite make it. I'll take the rest home."

"That's my boy," said Anastasia and walked in the direction of the car.

ELSIE HAD MADE Sammy go and put her feet up in the lounge following her cup of tea, while she and Dorcas had busied themselves preparing the table for dinner. Dorcas had excelled herself again with a large stew, plus a variety of side dishes. The delicious aroma had wafted up the stairs and succeeded in summoning the boys without any need to call them. Their thundering feet on the stairs caused Sammy to leave the lounge as well.

"My goodness, Elsie, this looks fantastic," she said with

approval, eyeing the feast that was set out on the table. "And thanks as well for all the cleaning. You really are an excellent guest, but I don't expect you to do that."

"Oh, it was nothing," said Elsie with a grin, looking sideways at Dorcas, who scowled at her. "My pleasure."

The four seated themselves at the table and started to tuck in. The conversation was flowing like the night before, and the rattle of knives and forks on plates contributed to the general chatter and laughter. Dorcas had her own plate and was unseen by Sammy as she sat cross-legged on a small stool she'd glamoured, tucking in with the rest of them.

"Does anyone fancy some wine?" asked Sammy. "I was sure that I wouldn't want any tonight after yesterday, but one glass would pep me up well for my cleaning shift."

"I'll take a glass, dear," said Elsie, with a nod.

Sammy got up to get a bottle of wine from the fridge, with her back turned to the rest of them as she opened the door. While her back was turned, Elsie's ring suddenly gave out a bright burst of red light before turning back to its blue colour again. Jack and Elsie froze, looking at each other. Jimmy, not knowing what was happening, looked at both of them inquisitively.

"What?" he mouthed to Jack. Jack had forgotten about the ring while he was regaling him earlier with what had been going on.

Sammy turned back to the table, a little surprised at the silence.

"Why so quiet?" she said with a laugh.

"Nothing, nothing," said Elsie, recovering. "I thought I was going to burp, that's all, and the boys were looking at my face trying to stop it. Perils of old age, my dear, the terrible windy pops. It'll happen to you one day."

Jack gave a nervous laugh, and Jimmy still looked perplexed.

Dorcas had stopped eating and was looking at Elsie. The ring gave another flash.

"What was that?" asked Sammy. "It looked like a brake light, but it was pretty bright." She looked over Elsie's shoulder towards the front door in the hall.

Elsie jammed her hand under the table and covered it with the other. It flashed again but was muted by the hand covering it, and this time Sammy didn't notice.

Elsie bought her hand up and pushed the plate away.

"Phew, I'm done. Eyes bigger than my belly, I think," she said. "If you don't mind, Sammy, I'll skip that wine. I am rather full, and it is very warm in here. I might just step out back for a breath of air."

"Are you alright, Elsie? You've come over awfully pale."

"Yes, yes, of course, Sammy, dear. Sometimes when I overeat, I can get a hot flush. Again, the perils of old age, I'm afraid. I find that five minutes in the fresh air does me a world of good; it gets me back on my kilter. Would you excuse me?"

She stood and, moving delicately around Dorcas, unlocked the back door and stepped outside. Sammy looked on, concerned.

"Jack, dear," came Elsie's voice from outside. "Could you bring me my bag and a glass of water? I have some indigestion tablets and think that I could do with one."

Jack grabbed Elsie's bag from the hall and went outside, taking the glass that Sammy passed him, closely followed by Dorcas. They found Elsie round the back of the house in the garden.

Dorcas bustled up to her, chest swelled out and said, "There's nothings wrong with my cookings, Elsie Cracklock, why's would you be...."

Elsie cut her off mid-flow. "I'm fine; I just needed to talk to Jack away from Sammy. Fermy's in trouble."

"Can we be sure?" asked Jack.

"He would not have activated the ring if he was okay. Moreover, there were three flashes. That's our signal for help," said Elsie, wringing her hands together.

Jack felt fear creep up inside his stomach but pushed it away.

"Then we'll have to go and see what the problem is," he said with some resolve.

"Agreed. We need a plan, though. Your mother isn't going to just let us go; it's already getting dark," said Elsie.

"What shall we do?" asked Jack. "Mum will be leaving to go to work again in about an hour. Can we wait until then?"

"I don't know. I would rather not if the truth be told. I had a bad feeling about this whole escapade from the off, but there's no point in telling Fermy; he's rather stubborn, you know."

"Think, Auntie. We need to get out of here and get up to that house. What's the plan?"

"A plan?" came a voice as Jimmy walked around the corner of the house to join them. "What's happening?"

Jack explained quickly what the ring flash meant and how Fermy was in trouble up at Twillington House. Jimmy was quiet for a few seconds and then said, "Right then. A three-stage plan. Number one, get out of here unquestioned. That's easy. You're going to walk me home, Jack, and Elsie, you are going to come too, to get some more of that air that you said you needed."

The other two nodded; that would work.

"Number two, we get up to that house. I am assuming that you can't use any of your travelling thingies while Sammy's here, so we try from somewhere else. What do you need?"

"Just a door and enough room to go in and then come out," said Jack.

"Right. At the end of this road is the substation. It's a small brick building with a door; would that do? It's locked, though. I've walked past it a dozen times this past week or so."

"That won't matter," said Elsie. "Nor will the fact that it's dangerous inside those things. Once we're travelling, the contents of the room won't affect us."

"Okay. Number three, we have to gain access to the house. Now, this Mr Binks knows Jack, doesn't he?"

"Yes," said Jack, with a little shiver.

"But he doesn't know Elsie or me. Therefore, we go to the door and make something up; I don't know, perhaps our car has broken down, and we need to use the phone. Poor Grandma here," Jimmy indicated Elsie, "Is a bit shaken up by it all."

Elsie swatted Jimmy lightly. "Less of the Grandma, you. Nevertheless, agreed, as a ruse that could work quite well. I don't know if we'll get in, but it's worth a go. And on such short notice, it's all we've got."

"You could always say that you are visiting someone there," said Jack. "It's been converted into a load of flats."

"Do you know any names?" asked Elsie.

Jack shook his head. "No, only Mr Binks. He's the only one that has a paper delivered."

"In which case, we go with Jimmy's plan. It's too risky if we don't have a name to ask for when we get there."

Elsie turned to Dorcas. "My friend, would you stay here after perhaps fetching the medicine basket from the cottage? I want to make sure that if something has happened to Fermy, we are ready to help him if we can."

Dorcas nodded. "Dorcas can do that. I can comes too, but perhaps this is the bestest way for me's to help. And if you don't comes back in goods time, I can comes to help."

The others nodded in agreement.

"Right, let's get going," said Elsie. Dorcas gave a little wave and faded out, returning to Elsie's to pick up what she might need.

The others trooped back inside to see Sammy starting to clear the table.

"Mum, Jimmy's just had a phone call. His mum wants him

home now. If it's okay, I'm going to walk him back; I need to pick up some stuff for school."

"But it's getting dark," said Sammy, glancing out of the window.

"How about I go with the boys?" asked Elsie. "I've been cooped up here all day with Jack, and some more fresh air would be good for both of us."

Sammy thought about it and agreed. "Okay, no worries. Take your keys, though; I should probably still be here by the time you get back, as I've got an hour or so, but just to be sure. I'll make a start on this washing up, but you, young man, are on drying duty when you get back."

"No problems, Mum," said Jack and kissed the proffered cheek. "We'll see you in a bit."

Jimmy and Elsie gathered up their bags and, unlocking the front door, stepped out into the deepening dusk. The street was relatively quiet, lights in the houses were on, and the low murmur of televisions could be heard in the gloaming. With Jimmy in the lead, the three walked quickly up the street, turning left at the top. Across the road, next to a small patch of waste ground, stood the electricity substation, its tatty green door firmly closed and held in place with a large padlock.

"Come on," said Elsie, pulling her pen from her bag. "Now, keep watch; make sure no one is watching. If anyone sees us, it will just look like I'm graffitiing it anyhow."

Jimmy chuckled and whispered, "The world's oldest tagger," to Jack, who gave a nervous smile in return.

With a final look around, Elsie slapped the glyph, and it glittered before falling from the door. Jimmy's mouth dropped open at this and then dropped even further as Elsie quickly pulled open the door to show the dancing blue flames inside.

"We can't go in there," he said. "We'll be roasted alive."

"Seriously, it's fine," said Jack, pulling him by the arm. "Come on."

Elsie pulled the door shut behind Jimmy, who was glancing around the room in awe. He waved his hand through the flickering blue flames and then examined it carefully.

"This is like magic!" he exclaimed, doing it again.

"Glamour, dear," said Elsie, as she drew the unlock glyph on the inside of the door. "Now, I am aiming to get the door to open on the outside of the destination's front door. I am assuming that there won't be anyone outside, but please be aware that it may open inside the house. If it does, and we are caught, I suggest that we say that we are visiting someone there; it's the only excuse we have, albeit a poor one. Assuming that we do come through on the doorstep, Jack, you need to hide as quickly as you can. We cannot risk this Binks character seeing you. You make yourself scarce as soon as we come, though. Jimmy, you stand with me, and we go into the broken-down car routine. Okay?"

"Understood," said Jack and Jimmy in unison.

"Right then. Here we go." Elsie slapped the unlock glyph, and it trickled off the door. Jack braced himself, ready to sprint if he needed to.

"One. Two. Three," said Elsie and yanked the door open. To see the outside of the electricity substation, the terraced houses across the road with flickering lights of televisions in the windows.

"This is where we came in," said Jimmy.

"I know," said Jack.

"Oh no," said Elsie, clutching her chest. "This is much worse than I thought."

"What, Auntie?" said Jack. "Why didn't we travel?"

"It looks like the house is glamoured to prevent realm travel. Which means it is probably Fae locked as well. It's a trap. Oh, my goodness."

"What?" said Jack, not believing what he was hearing.

"It is possible to prevent realm travel into a location; it's a very powerful shielding glamour that takes a lot of grockles to maintain. Normally, the travel glyph will take you somewhere within the vicinity of where you want to be if it can't take you to it exactly. For it to return you to the point of origin, well, that is a powerful counter-glamour indeed. If this is what I think it is, it can also prevent Fae from entering or leaving at will via their natural travelling capability; it's like a giant trap, and it must have caught Fermy. That Mr Binks must have some power to put this into place; it's the type of thing usually reserved for protecting the more important buildings in Faery. This is terrible!" Elsie wrung her hands together, her face shocked as she stared at the boys in the rapidly dimming twilight.

"But we have to get Fermy out of there," said Jack. "What can we do?"

"Plan B," said Jimmy. "Jack, can I borrow your phone, please?"

"What are you going to do?" asked Jack, handing it over.

"Call a taxi," said Jimmy. "We need to get there, don't we? We can worry about what we find when we do. Number three of the plan is still in play."

"Right," said Jack.

THE CAR CARRYING Anastasia and Benedict cruised through the darkening streets towards Jack's house. Anastasia was in a pleasant mood; the evening meal that the two had enjoyed at a local hostelry had turned out to be not too bad, dining with the commoners to one side. They had received a few funny looks from the other patrons, but the two paid them no heed. A few glasses of gin had put her in an excellent mood for confronting her distant family members and to welcoming young Master Crackley back into the fold as a fully-fledged Cracklock. If necessary, by force; that side of the family had no sympathy towards the works that the family was placed on the earth to do, and Aunt Agatha could be extremely persuasive when she needed to be with wayward Cracklocks.

Shortly, they turned into the street address that the two boys had given her. Lost in thoughts of the coming confrontation, Anastasia failed to notice three people climbing into the taxicab at the end of the street. Benedict also didn't notice them, but there was nothing out of the ordinary there, and he continued to fiddle with the small knife he usually kept hidden up his sleeve.

"Number thirty-seven, please, Nigel; you can park outside if you can," said Anastasia to the silent driver, who nodded an affirmative.

The dark car cruised to a stop outside Jack's house.

THE TAXI CARRYING the three approached the top of Brierly Hill, and Jack called to the driver, "Just here, mate, please." The taxi pulled to a stop a little way down the hill from the Twillington House, and the three got out, Elsie handing the driver a ten-pound note as she did so, telling him to keep the change.

The gates to Twillington House stood closed about fifty metres further up the hill, partially in shadow of the two supporting pillars on either side of the drive. The three stared at them with a sense of dread, and Jack shuddered as he recalled the last time he was here. He automatically scouted the road for signs of his accident, but of course, there was nothing to see. He winced anyway as he remembered the car coming towards him.

"You okay?" asked Jimmy, noticing the set of Jack's face as he remembered.

"Yes. Just bad memories. C'mon, let's go."

The three walked up the road, and as they got closer, they could make out some small flashes emanating from the gate, about halfway up the painted black surface. Jack looked at Elsie, who shook her head.

"That's odd," she said. "Is it electrified?"

"I don't think so," said Jack. "They've been closed before when I've delivered here, and I've propped my bike against it while I'm getting the letterboxes open; they're in that pillar, there. It has never given me any kind of shock, and I get here fairly early in the morning."

Straining his eyes, Jimmy said, "What are you talking about? I can't see anything. Electrified?"

"Some sparks are coming off it…" said Jack. "Wait a moment. Elsie, do you still have the Hagstone?"

Elsie rummaged in her handbag and produced the smooth stone with a hole in it. She handed it to Jimmy.

"What's this?" he said.

"It's a Hagstone. Look through the hole in it at the gate and tell me what you see."

Jimmy did as instructed, squinting one eye as he did so. After ten seconds or so, he spoke up.

"You're right. There are sparks coming off it. They aren't regular or anything, but they are definitely there."

Elsie nodded to Jack. "Good thinking. There must be Faery glamours or something in place on that gate. Let's go take a closer look, but I strongly suggest that we don't touch it."

Jimmy went to hand the Hagstone back to Elsie, but she shook her head.

"Keep it for now," she said. "I don't need it, and another pair of younger eyes will be useful here."

The three approached the gate, and as they got within a few metres, the source of the sparks became clear. Hovering in front of the gate was a tiny fairy, its flittering wings a blur to see. It either hadn't noticed or didn't consider the three approaching as a threat as it made another assault on the gate. Flying as fast as it could, a blue glow surrounding it, it hit and bounced off the gate with a small thudding sound, causing the gate to emit a shower of sparks at the point of impact. The faery was sobbing loudly, given its size, and it moved back for another attempt.

"Whoa there, little one," said Elsie, kindly. "What are you doing? You're going to hurt yourself."

The fairy stopped mid-charge and hovered in the air, a fierce expression on its face. It was in front of Elsie's face in a flash, the blue glow surrounding it intensifying. Close up, it could be seen that the faery was female, but its little face was not the youthful-looking Tinkerbell type that the boys had seen popularised in the films; instead, it seemed to be more adult than that. Not old, but definitely middle-aged. The face did glisten, though, due to the tears that wet her cheeks.

"You can see me?" she said in a high-pitched quavering voice. "How?"

"Yes, we can see you," said Elsie gently. "How is a long story that we can't go into now. But please understand that we mean you no harm. Indeed, we also have an interest in that gate there."

"You want to go in there?" said the Faery

"Yes. We think our friend might be in there, and if he is, then he'll need our help."

The fairy burst into fresh tears.

"I can't get in," she wailed. "My children are in there, in that big house. But I can't get to them."

The fairy flew at the gates again and rebounded off in a small shower of sparks. It hovered in the air, shaking as the tears ran down its face and fell in tiny drops.

"Stop, stop, stop," said Elsie in a calm voice. "It looks like this whole place is Fae locked. You'll never get in like that."

"But what can I do?" sobbed the fairy. "My children went in there two hours ago; they were ahead of me as we came down this hill, and they must have seen something as they flew through these gates. The gates slammed shut behind them, and I could hear them screaming for me. The gates won't open for me, and regardless of how high I fly, I can't get over them. Breaking glamours aren't working, nor any opening glamours that I have tried. I have to get in!" she finished with a brave sob.

She backed up for another go, but Elsie gently plucked her from the air.

"Just wait a moment. Let's have a look at this gate."

She bent down with her nose almost touching the gates. Jack and Jimmy did likewise. Up close, there was nothing to distinguish the barricade from any other that Jack had seen. They appeared to be made of wood, painted in dull black paint that gave off the slight warmth of trapped sunshine. A keyhole stood about halfway up, and the hinges were also painted black. There was no clue about any kind of glamour on them from what Jack's admittedly limited knowledge could see.

"I wonder..." said Elsie. With a sudden movement, she placed her hand flat on the gates, squeezing her eyes shut as she did so.

SAMMY WAS UPSTAIRS, sorting out her cleaner's uniform. Holding it up to the light, she sighed; tonight's shift was something she could do without, but the rent wasn't going to pay itself. She was bone-tired today; after last night's wine, she yearned for an early night. 'Not going to happen,' she thought, 'So let's just get through it. With any luck, I can be home for eleven'. Sammy was not pleased with the family's circumstances, but they made do; at least she had regular work and was able to keep a roof over their heads. It wasn't what she had yearned for as a little girl with her dreams of far off places, but the shop work was routine, and she had some good friends there in the team. The evening cleaning work paid for little extras. It was easy work, if a little monotonous, and at least she got to work on the tills more now during the day, which saved her aching back. Getting old sucked.

Her thoughts turned to her departed husband. Things had been so different when David was with them; they had never been rich, but there was a lot more laughter. Not that she and Jack didn't enjoy some good times; it was just different. Having someone to share life's trials with had been all she needed, really, and she knew that she couldn't be the Dad that Jack needed, although she tried her best. Sammy just missed her husband on the occasions when she stopped to think about him. She did talk to David when she was alone, and sometimes she thought, in her own mind anyway, that he answered her. However, she thought about David less and less these days; Sammy put this down to life and moving on, but when she tried to think more about David, to conjure his face into her mind's eye, her memories were hazy about him. *'Passage of time,'* she thought to herself, *'But I wish he were still here.'*

She was shaken from her memories, or lack of them, by the trilling of the front doorbell. Sammy glanced at her watch and found it was only fifteen minutes or so since Jack and Elsie had left to walk Jimmy home. Sammy suspected that Elsie planned to take Jack to the little shop on the way back, probably for chocolate and crisps, which was fine; the boy deserved spoiling, and she didn't do it often enough. Nevertheless, there was no way that they would be back by now; it was too soon, and besides, Jack had his keys. She sighed again. Sales people, no doubt; she would just ignore them.

The doorbell trilled again, accompanied by a loud knocking. Whoever it was, it didn't sound like they were going to take no for an answer.

"Okay, okay, I'm coming," she said, dropping the cleaning tabard onto the bed. She jogged down the stairs to the door, where she could see two outlines through the glass in the rapidly darkening street outside.

"Whatever you're selling, I'm not interested," she called through the door and flipped the lock. Pulling open the door, she was surprised at the visitors standing there.

The woman on the porch was striking, with long blonde hair and high cheekbones. Her dress was odd, though; Sammy couldn't quite place why on her first glance, but something niggled at her. Behind the woman stood a handsome young man with dark curly hair and cherub lips. He was impeccably dressed in a dark suit and tie, although it was old fashioned with a button on collar and appeared slightly tatty with mud smeared on his cuffs. Sammy took all this in at first glance and said, "Can I help you?"

"I sincerely hope so, Sammy, my dear, I sincerely hope so. It's so good to see you again," said the blonde woman with a broad smile, extending her hand to shake. Sammy noticed that the smile didn't touch the woman's eyes when she did so, and the hairs on her neck prickled a little.

Ignoring the proffered hand, Sammy tightened her grip on the door. "Do I know you?" she said.

"You are Samantha Cracklock? It has been a very long time since I last saw you, and then only at a distance. The relentless march of the days and years gets us all; it changes us and our recollections. Although some of us are less, shall we say, affected by the ravages of time than others, it would seem." The woman ran a hand through her hair and preened slightly.

"No," said Sammy politely, despite the barbed comment. "I'm Samantha Crackley. And I think that you have the wrong house."

"Oh, no, Sammy, dear. I am quite sure that this is the correct house. It stinks of Fae."

"What?"

"No matter, no matter. For now," said Anastasia with a wave of her hand, "Sammy, I am so very pleased to make your acquaintance finally. My name is Anastasia Cracklock. And this is my son, Benedict. We are distant cousins of your husband, David, and believe it when I say that I have waited a long time to meet you all again, including most of all, your little boy. Jack, isn't it?"

Sammy had a mother's instincts when it came to her son, and she knew instantly that something was not right here. What that was, she had no idea, but she knew that she had to get away from these people; every fibre of her being was screaming at her.

She swallowed and said, "I'm sorry, but I have no idea what you are talking about. I have no son called Jack, and my husband passed away years ago. Whatever information you have, I am afraid that it is incorrect. I am not who you are looking for. Now, if you will excuse me, I have to get ready for work."

With that, Sammy started to push the door shut, but Anastasia placed a firm hand on it, preventing it from moving further.

"She's lying, Mother," said Benedict over his mother's shoulder in a surprisingly little boy-like voice. It was almost as if his voice had not broken, and its tone made Sammy give an involuntary little shudder.

"I know, dear," said Anastasia, pushing the door open again with surprising strength. Sammy saw red.

"Look, get the hell off of my property," she said in an angry but controlled voice. "I have no idea who you are or what you are doing here. If you don't leave, then I will call the police."

Anastasia fixed Sammy with a hurt look.

"Come now, what way is that to treat long-lost family? Where is your sense of hospitality? We have come a long way to see our distant relations, and instead of welcoming us in with open arms, you lie to us and turn us away. It really won't do, Sammy."

"Get lost, or I'm calling the police," said Sammy, finally

losing her temper. She shoved the door forcefully and almost succeeded in shutting it when she felt it stop short of the latch. The door swung back sharply towards her, causing her to stumble backwards.

Anastasia walked over the threshold uninvited, her face now wearing such a mask of anger that caused Sammy to take a few steps backwards. Benedict followed, kicking the door shut behind him.

"What the hell do you..." said Sammy but was stopped by a stinging slap across her face from Anastasia.

"I am through being nice with you, Samantha Cracklock. Now, where is David, and where is Jack?"

"How dare you?" yelled Sammy, clutching her rapidly reddening cheek. "Just who the hell do you think you...?" She stopped mid-sentence, unable to make any other sounds; her voice no longer there.

"Silence is golden," smiled Anastasia. "And I am sick of hearing your whining voice threatening *me* with law enforcement. For now, you will nod and shake your head to answer me, and answer me you will if you know what is good for you. If you don't, I will have Benedict here hurt you until you realise that you would like to have a discussion with me. He's rather good at it, you know, and *he's had a lot of practice!"*

The last words were shouted directly into Sammy's face, Anastasia's spittle forcing her to close her eyes.

Shoving Sammy into the living room, Anastasia gestured at the sofa. "Sit," she commanded.

Turning to Benedict, she said, "Go and check the rest of the house; I assume that no one else is here at the moment, as the racket this screeching wench made would have had them come at a run. And see where that damned Fae smell is coming from."

"Yes, Mama," said Benedict.

"And if you find any Fae, bring them to me. Do not, and I repeat, do not, extinguish them, and I mean it, Benedict. Any

Fae in this house, I think, will be happy to answer a few questions first."

"Again, yes, Mama," said Benedict with a sulky frown. He stalked out of the lounge in the direction of the kitchen.

Anastasia sat down in the comfortable chair opposite Sammy, who pushed herself back into the sofa as far she could, subconsciously trying to get away from the woman. Looking around the lounge, Anastasia gestured at the picture frames on the mantelpiece.

"Right then. Please confirm to me that that is your son, Jack Cracklock."

CHAPTER 12

*J*ack shut his eyes and braced himself when he saw Elsie reaching for the gate. He tensed up, waiting for something to happen, and was quite surprised when he heard Elsie chuckle. Opening his eyes, he saw Elsie stood with her hand flat against the gate, a look of relief on her face.

"What did you do?" Jack asked.

"Nothing," Elsie replied. "I had a hunch that nothing would happen."

"Why? Dangerous way to prove a hunch!"

"Well, this gate backs onto the pavement here. Now, there aren't many houses up here, but I assumed that there would be some people walking along this pavement. If they had touched this gate, either intentionally or by accident, and got an electric shock or something, then people will start complaining and draw attention to the place. So, the natural conclusion was that this gate is okay for us lifers to touch but is resistant to Fae."

"So, we can open the gate, then, and get in?" said Jack.

"I am assuming so. I think that the barrier is only blocking

Fae from entering. Which means that there will probably be something else that deters us lifers from going in there."

"When I went in that time to help Mr Binks, I didn't see anything in there. I just walked straight up to the door. Well, cycled."

"Only one way to find out," said Jimmy, pushing the handle down on the gate before the others could say anything. It moved, but the gate remained shut.

"It's locked," he said. "Anyone got a crowbar?"

"Of course not," said Elsie. "Why would I have a crowbar?"

"Well, that bag's pretty big," said Jimmy cheekily. "Who knows what you've got in there, Mary Poppins."

Elsie frowned at Jimmy. "Well, I don't have a crowbar. I'll try an unlock glamour."

The little fairy spoke. "Don't bother. I have tried every glamour I can think of to get through these doors; they don't work."

Elsie turned to the faery. "Every glamour?"

"Yes," she replied.

Elsie shook her head in exasperation. She then looked at the boys.

"Do you think that you can climb over that gate?"

"Sure," said Jimmy. "If Jack can give me a leg up, I can get over. However, we won't all be able to get over it if we do that; it's too high. I can see if there is any way to unlock it from the other side, though."

Jack had been quiet, thinking.

"I wonder if there's another way?" he said, thinking aloud, and then, "Elsie, can I borrow the portable hole, please?"

"You little genius, Jack, of course!" said Elsie, pulling her bag from her shoulder and rummaging in it. With a little exclamation, she pulled out the box containing the hole.

"How does it work?" asked Jack, taking it out of the box. It felt smooth and slippery to the touch between his fingers, its surface jet black and not reflecting the streetlights that had winked on while they had been standing there.

"You just keep pulling it until you get it to the size you want, like stretching that blue stuff you use for sticking stuff to walls," said Elsie.

Jack started to tug at the hole, turning it around in his hands as he did so. It grew in size until it had grown from the size of a coin to about that of a dinner plate.

"That's cool," said Jimmy, looking at Jack's efforts. "How big will it go? If it's a hole, we should be able to crawl through the gate if you can get it big enough."

"I don't think it will go that big," said Elsie. "That's about as far as it will stretch as a circle; you can keep going, but it will just stop when it doesn't go any bigger. It's a child's toy after all; other ones will go bigger, but not that one."

"We don't need it to go that big," said Jack. "How do I stick it to the gate?"

"Just chuck it on where you want it to go," said Elsie.

Jack looked at the gate and then slapped the hole over the keyhole. Immediately the keyhole, the handle, and a good chunk of the gate disappeared, leaving a dinner plate-sized hole where they had been. Jack pushed the right-hand gate gently, and it swung open.

"Bingo," he said. "No lock, no problem!"

The other two gave a brief round of applause. Looking at the fairy who was darting around them excitedly, Jack said, "Right, let's go. Errm, madam fairy, can you see if you can get in now?"

The little fairy darted through the gate and then flew straight back to hover in front of Jack's face.

"Thank you, oh, thank you!" she said. "And please call me Alvina. Now, I must go and find my children."

"Wait, wait," said Elsie, holding up her hand. "We should go together. Safety in numbers; we don't know what's waiting for us in there."

Looking up the drive towards the house, it certainly did look terrifying in the darkness, with the overhanging trees. There were no lights other than those in the house itself, standing forebodingly at the top of the long drive. Dark hedges following the drive along each side rustled in the slight breeze.

Alvina looked anxiously down the drive towards the house.

"We must go now," she said. "I cannot wait. The screams of my children, oh my grockles and grackles."

"Let's go then," said Elsie, stepping through the gate into the grounds. She ripped the hole off the gate and screwed it up with two hands before poking it back into the box. Jimmy looked at where the hole had been, the lock with the bolt sticking out of it, and the handle had returned. The gate was undamaged.

"I have got to get me one of those holes!" he said.

Dorcas had gotten back to Elsie's cottage without any problems, arriving in the front garden and disrupting a small group of pixies who stood plotting and looking at the house as she arrived in their midst.

"*Go ons with you,*" she yelled at them, waving her arms. Pixies were pests, digging up things in the garden and making a right mess if they got into the house. People blamed mice for the damage they caused, but of course, they couldn't see the little folk as they helped themselves to whatever they could find. Dorcas didn't tolerate them at all; who cared if they were supposed to be lucky?

Fishing around under the plant pot by the back door, she pulled out the key. She could have glamoured the door open, but that would have meant that she would then have had to glamour it locked again. Keys were so much easier to handle if you had them.

Once inside, Dorcas pulled Elsie's carpetbag out from under

the stairs and set to putting together what she thought she'd need. She threw jars and bottles of herbs from the pantry into the bag, some bandages, and some of the lifer medical stuff in the green box with the white cross on it. Hauling the bag upstairs, she went to her own small room and pulled out her possessions box from under the bed.

'*Rights then,*' she thought, pawing through the jumbled contents, '*I needs the things to help Faeries, but what about the others if they's need help as well? I guesses that I needs to take everything's here that's for healing.*'

The carpetbag clanked and clanged as Dorcas tossed in various bottles of potions and devices that she had stored for emergencies. By the time she'd finished, the bag was bulging, and she couldn't get it zipped up, despite shifting things about and wedging them in by sitting on it. Then, when she tried to lift it, she couldn't. Dorcas was strong by Brownie standards; a lifetime of domestic chores had given her impressive arm muscles – polishing repeatedly built up good muscle memory. Her large tummy belied her core strength as well. Nevertheless, in this case, the bag was just too heavy.

Dorcas was worried about the others, particularly her dear friend Fermy, and wanted to get back as soon as possible. She looked at the bulging bag, deciding on what to take or not; she couldn't travel back using Fae abilities with such an anchor. Having a half-hearted rummage through the bag, another thought suddenly struck her. She tried to drag the bag, and despite the thick carpet upstairs, she could move it easily enough.

"Rights then," she said aloud to herself. "I's not travelling; I's realm door travelling with that heavy weight." She bounced down the stairs to the larder and got the piece of chalk from the blackboard that Elsie made her shopping list on. Bounding back up the stairs to her bedroom, she drew the travel glyph on the back of the bedroom door.

She slapped it and then yanked it open to see the small landing surrounded by blue flames. She dragged the carpetbag through and kicked the door shut behind her. She then got busy with the unlock glyph, picturing the built-in wardrobe in Sammy's bedroom that she was sharing with Elsie.

As the glyph fell from the door, she pulled it open to see Sammy's bedroom ahead of her. With a sigh of relief, she pulled the carpetbag into the room and slammed the wardrobe door shut behind her. Panting a little, she turned to the bag; she may as well get set up for an emergency, as she couldn't hear the others in the house yet. However, as she started to open the bag, she heard a male voice behind her, child-like, full of menace and extremely cold, say, "Well, hello there, my foul little brownie. Going somewhere, are we?"

THE THREE FRIENDS and Alvina moved cautiously down the drive, Jimmy holding the Hagstone over one eye and keeping the other open for 'normal' vision.

"What's if there's an alarm?" he whispered to Jack.

"I don't know," replied Jack.

"What if there are motion sensors as well?" said Jimmy. "Lights could come on, and we'd be well rumbled before we even got started."

Jack turned to him. "Mate, you're not helping. I am cacking it here; the last time I was here, that maniac tried to kill me. Moreover, he nearly did, even if it was by accident. I'm worried enough, so just stop."

"Sorry, bud. Just thinking around potential problems."

"Well, think about them by all means. We just don't need to hear about them unless they're real!" Jack whispered back.

The party rounded the bend in the drive, and the hedges fell away. The house stood some fifty metres or so ahead, the downstairs lighting casting a dull glow over the surrounding immaculate lawns. Well, they looked immaculate, but on closer inspection, there were dull shadows all over the flat grass, like molehills scattered about.

Jimmy laughed. "Looks like old Binksy has a problem with moles," he said, looking through the Hagstone. Then he stopped laughing and gave a gulp.

"Jack," he said. "When I look at those molehills without the Hagstone, they're not there."

"What?" said Jack. "Impossible! Molehills just don't disappear."

Elsie looked sharply at Jimmy. "Do you mean to say that they're not there when you look through 'normal' eyes?" she said.

"Yep, they're definitely gone," said Jimmy.

"We better check," said Elsie. "Sounds like some glamour or other to me. I've never heard of this."

"Can we please hurry?" chirped Alvina. "I need to find my children, and I can't sense them here."

"I think we should check those molehills," said Elsie firmly. "There's a good chance that this is a trap. Could you just do a quick fly-by for us? Better to be informed."

"Okay, I will take a quick look; I'm not touching the ground, and I'll be fast."

Alvina swooped over to the nearest molehill, and the others jumped as she gave a shrill scream. She hovered for a moment, clutching her hands over her ears, her mouth open in shock, and then flew back to the others.

"What? What is it?" demanded Elsie.

"It's...horrible. Oh, those poor, poor folk. Oh, my grackles, my children, I must save my children." The fairy was genuinely distressed at what she had seen.

"What do you mean, 'those poor folk'?" said Elsie gently.

"See for yourself," said Alvina, shuddering, her arms

wrapped around her. "We need to go. We must go to the house."

The three walked onto the lawn but stopped when they felt a brief tremble coming up through the ground like the earth was shivering. It stopped after a few seconds, and they stood in anticipation of something terrible happening. After a minute, Elsie shrugged and beckoned them onwards. They approached the nearest 'molehill,' and Jack flicked on the torch on his phone and cast it over the mound. What he saw made him recoil in horror, the torchlight wavering in his hand. Elsie gave a little gasp, her hands flying to her open mouth, and Jimmy stumbled backwards from the sight.

The 'molehill' was nothing of the sort. It was a small mound of earth, that much was in common with a molehill, but that is where it ended. Sitting atop of the little mound of earth was the head of a medium-sized Fae. Its long ears and nose were reminiscent of Dorcas, but the greenish tint to the skin set it apart. A small root ran from out of the mound and into the nose, disappearing from view.

"My goodness," said Elsie, clutching her chest and staring at the head. "That's a mountain goblin. Oh, my goodness. The poor creature."

Jack bent down to look more closely at the head and then staggered backwards again in further shock as the head took a deep breath and settled again.

"It's still alive," he almost shouted, forgetting where he was.

"That's not possible," said Jimmy, who had turned noticeably pale, despite the poor light. "It's just a head."

Elsie had recovered a little and had plumped down on her hands and knees next to the mound.

"I'm not so sure," she said. "Help me dig around it."

The boys set too with Elsie, and after a few seconds of ferocious digging, they revealed a neck and the tops of the shoulders. The shoulders were contained in some sort of silvery metal netting.

"Oh my goodness, it's still alive and buried here in the garden," Elsie said. "What evil is this? I have never, in all my dealings with the Fae, ever seen such a thing."

"Can we get it out?" said Jack, digging a little more of the goblin out of the soil.

"I don't know," said Elsie. "Look at that root in its nose. Where does that go?" She seized the root and gently tugged on it. The goblin exhaled again, but the root stayed firmly lodged in the creature's nostril.

"I don't want to yank it out; I don't know what it is, and it could well kill the poor thing," said Elsie. "We will need to fetch more help to deal with this; who knows how many of these poor things are trapped here."

Jack stood up and shone his torch around the lawn at the mounds, trying to count them. The torchlight passed over something lying in the grass, and Jack only just caught it out of the corner of his eye. He passed the torch back and forth over the area where he thought the object was and finally located it. He gasped.

"Auntie," he said. "Is that Fermy's hat?"

DORCAS WHIRLED around at the sound of the voice to see Benedict standing there in the doorway. The young man leaned jauntily against the doorjamb, a cocksure smile on his face and his eyes boring into her.

"Who are you's, and how comes you can see me?" she said.

"I don't discuss things with filthy devils," spat the young man. "Now, step away from that bag and get on your knees. Now!"

Dorcas looked at the young man, bewildered; who was this in Jack's house? She'd only been gone fifteen minutes to Elsie's and back, and everything had gone strange. Then it dawned on her. A lifer who could see her!

"You's is a Cracklock, I's thinking?" she said.

The young man smiled, and with a deft movement, flicked his hand down. Dorcas felt a bolt of pain lance out of her shoulder, red hot and burning. Looking at it, she could see the top of a small handle sticking out of the offending area, a little pool of her blood spreading to stain her dress. She suddenly felt weakness flood her whole body.

"You like that, little brownie?" leered the young man. "That, my sweet, is the finest iron, sourced from our mines in Brazil. I do prefer it to the iron mines we have in the USA; so much purer and easier to work with."

He opened his hand to show another three throwing blades, needle-like and all a dull grey in colour. Dorcas could feel her head starting to swim.

"Does it hurt, my poppet? Can you feel that lovely iron in you?" he said with a broad smile. "Perhaps you'd like another one; a pair is better than one alone, don't you think?" He flicked his hand again expertly, and Dorcas felt another spike in the same area as the previous one. She sank to her knees.

"Two's company, but three is a crowd, isn't it?" giggled the young man in a crazy, high tone. "Do you like crowds, little brownie?"

He raised his hand again, but before he could throw, he was interrupted by a strange female voice from downstairs.

"Benedict, darling, what are you doing?"

Benedict turned to the voice, and Dorcas, her arm on fire, pulled out the two throwing pins and cast them away. She was panting now, and her face was running in sweat; she had never experienced pain like this. She groped her hand behind her for the bag and pulled it towards her.

"I'm not doing anything, Mama," the young man called down the stairs.

"Then who are you talking to up there? Have you found a devil?"

Dorcas rummaged quickly in the top of the bag and pulled out the little jar of turmeric she'd put in earlier. The herb was known to the Fae for its iron reducing properties, and it grew in both realms. Flipping the lid, Dorcas swallowed a good couple of gulps of the powder, gagging at its dry taste. She thrust the jar into her dress pocket.

"I haven't found anything, Mama."

"Don't lie to me, Benedict. If you have a Fae up there, bring it down this instant. You can have it when I'm done with it."

Benedict gave a long, exasperated sigh and turned on the little brownie. He took a couple of strides into the room and grabbed a huge handful of Dorcas's corkscrew-like hair. He yanked her to her feet.

"Upsy daisy, you little freak. Mama wants to talk to you. We can resume our little chat later."

Without ceremony, he dragged the weakened Dorcas out of the bedroom and down the stairs. Dorcas's hair felt like it was coming out at the roots, but she was feeling a little better from the iron poisoning as the turmeric worked its way into her system. Dorcas was a great many things, and stupid certainly wasn't one of them. She knew that she was in serious trouble here; this horrible young man had other iron on him – she could sense it. Moreover, if she appeared not to be suffering, then she knew full well that he would take pleasure in hurting her some more.

'I's pretend then to be really hurt. See's what I can do about this big nasty bully,' she thought.

Benedict dragged Dorcas's limp form into the living room and pushed her to the floor in front of the couch. From Sammy's perspective, she saw the brutish young man walk into the room, miming dragging something, and had then brought his arm back up, folding his arms. A charmless smile dressed his lips.

'*They are completely crazy!*' thought Sammy, '*What the hell do they want with Jack?*'

Anastasia got off the sofa and knelt on the floor, close to where Benedict had finished his mime. She thrust her face forwards into the empty air and spat out, "Name?"

She appeared to listen for a moment and then gestured at Sammy over her shoulder.

"And do you know this woman?"

Dorcas said, "I's does. But she doesn't knows me; she can't sees me."

"Is this woman Samantha Cracklock?" snarled Anastasia.

Sammy watched Anastasia suddenly slap the air, her hand stopping mid-swing. "*You will answer me, you foul little thing!*" she screamed.

Dorcas's head rocked back with the power of the slap, and despite herself, tears started to roll down her cheeks.

"Yes," she said meekly.

"That's better. Now we have a rapport," smiled Anastasia. "And is this young master Jack Cracklock?" she said, pointing at the picture on the mantelpiece.

Dorcas glanced at it and gulped but said nothing.

Anastasia frowned at her. Thrusting her hand into her belt, she pulled out a long iron pin. She hovered it in front of Dorcas's right eye.

"If you don't tell me by the count of three, I'll make sure that you will never be able to see to answer such a question again. One. Two..."

"Yes," whimpered Dorcas. "That's Jack."

Anastasia spun around to face Sammy.

"You see, your little friend here is willing to help me when you aren't."

Sammy shook her head and mouthed, "What friend?"

"I'm sorry, I can't hear you," tittered Anastasia. "What friend, did you say? Why, your filthy little faery friend, right here." She jabbed with the hand containing the pin, and Dorcas recoiled.

Anastasia then clasped her hands together in front of her mouth.

"Oh, of course, please do excuse my manners. I forgot you are a Cracklock by marriage only; how droll of me. You cannot see your little friend anymore, can you? You have neither the skills nor the heritage. But if you can't see her, how can I make an example of her to you?"

Sammy was terrified now; this woman was utterly insane, gesturing at and threatening an imaginary person.

Anastasia gestured again at Dorcas with the pin.

"You. Reveal yourself to Sammy again; there's a good little brownie. Now."

Dorcas herself was scared now, but a tiny part of her started to get mad again at these two spiteful bullies. *'Maybe two's of us are better than ones,'* she thought.

Looking up at Anastasia, she nodded her compliance and then started to make the reveal gestures.

Sammy looked on in shock as glittering lights started to dance, and a shadow formed slowly in their midst, rapidly becoming more solid.

"OH MY GOODNESS," said Elsie, springing to her feet. "Where?"

Jack shone the torchlight on the spot he had seen. Lying there was a small red hat, its feather forlornly flickering in the slight breeze. Elsie went straight over to it and picked it up, giving a slight sob as she did so.

"This is Fermy's hat. He must be here somewhere, amongst these mounds. Help me look."

She set off at a pace, dodging from mound to mound, giving

multiple gulps at the fresh horrors her search was unearthing. Jack went in the opposite direction, and Jimmy down the middle. As he looked at each mound, he saw all manner of different shapes and sizes; heads, some of them with a single root going into their nose or mouth, others almost wholly covered in roots that went into every orifice they could find. Each mound seemed to show fresh horrors as the three friends searched for Fermy.

Jimmy suddenly called in a low voice, "Here; I've got him."

"Are you sure?" replied Elsie. "You've only met him once."

"Pretty sure; he's not completely covered in those root things," he called back.

Jack and Elsie sprinted over to Jimmy and squatted down next to the mound he'd found. Shining the torch, they saw the little Feeorin's head, cocked slightly at an angle and extremely pale. His eyes were shut, and he was breathing in slow, deep breaths.

"Look," said Jimmy, pointing.

Roots were moving out of the earth and climbing slowly up the side of Fermy's neck, their pace slow, almost snail-like, but slowly twitching as they sought out his face. A single root lay against one cheek, worming its way towards his small nostrils.

"I don't think so," said Elsie fiercely and started to pull the roots away from her friend's face, snapping them in her haste. A little squeal could be heard each time she did so as if she was hurting them. The strange shivering sensation in the ground came again, but only for a second.

Jack and Jimmy set to digging with their hands, clearing the earth away from Fermy. It did not take them long; Fermy seemed so small and pitiful as he flopped about during their efforts. When they finally pulled him from the hole, they saw his whole body was wrapped in silvery netting, wire-like and sturdy, his arms secured. Elsie tugged at it in desperation, but it held fast.

"Try the hole," said Jack. Elsie pulled the little box from her bag and pulled the hole loose. She pulled it backwards and forwards and then handed an end to Jack.

"Jimmy, keep that torch steady. Jack, pull it as long as it will go," she said.

She and Jack held an impromptu mini tug-of-war until the hole was long and thin.

"Lay it on the netting, top to bottom," Elsie said, putting her end near the top of the wrapping near Fermy's neck. Jack nodded and laid it onto the netting, being careful to keep it straight. With an audible ping, the netting parted, and the two peeled it off Fermy and threw it to one side, Elsie plucking the hole off it as she did so. Fermy continued to breathe slowly, his chest rising and falling, but he did not wake up.

"We need to get him back to yours, Jack; Dorcas will be back by now with the medical stuff," said Elsie. She stood up, her knees creaking. Jack cradled Fermy in his arms and lifted him off the ground. The Feeorin lay limp in his arms, his breathing unaltered.

The three moved back towards the drive as fast as possible, avoiding the other mounds as they hurried. Once on the drive, Alvina flew to them.

"What about my children? You said you would help me!" she pleaded with the three.

Elsie looked at Jack and Jimmy. "We need to get Fermy back to Dorcas as soon as possible."

Jack took a deep breath. He had no desire to go back into Twillington House with all the bad memories it contained. Truth be told, he was relieved that they had found Fermy so quickly and could get out of here. But he shook his head to Elsie.

"We promised Alvina. We have to help her."

"I refuse to leave Fermy here while we go romping around that house," said Elsie, crossly. "Look at him."

"We won't have to. You take him back to Dorcas, and Jimmy and I will go with Alvina."

"Is that wise?" asked Elsie

"We promised. That okay with you, mate?"

"Sure," said Jimmy. "What's a little breaking and entering between friends?"

"Can you call me a taxi, Jack? Ask for it as soon as possible," said Elsie. "I'm not happy about leaving you, but we don't have much choice. We can't leave Fermy like this."

The five of them made their way back to the open gate and stood, Jack cradling Fermy in his arms. The Feeorin was light as a feather but felt cold to Jack's touch. His chest rose and fell with deep breaths, showing that he was still with them. As car headlights approached, he handed Fermy gently to Elsie.

"We'll be as quick as we can, don't worry," he said, rubbing the old lady's arm.

"Please be careful, Jack. Find the children and get out of there," she said.

The taxi glided to a stop, and Jimmy pulled open the door.

"See you soon," he said to Elsie, and Jack planted a kiss on her cheek as she got carefully into the back with Fermy cradled. "Get Fermy to safety."

Turning to Jimmy and Alvina, he said, "Okay, then. Let's go be burglars."

SAMMY'S EYES widened as the figure of Dorcas formed from the glittering lights, appearing like something out of those Star Trek programmes that David used to like. She clapped her hand to her mouth, not that the scream that was threatening to spill out had any volume. The plump figure that had appeared seemed to be like something from the show as well, short and tubby with skewwhiff corkscrew hair sticking out everywhere. Then she noticed the bright red cheek where the little figure had been slapped by this maniac woman, the blood on the shoulder of her shabby flowery print dress, and the tears on her cheeks. Sammy forgot about being scared and instead started to get angry at the plight of the pitiful little creature.

"Let's be formal about this, shall we?" said Anastasia. "Beast, introduce yourself to Sammy here."

Dorcas looked at Sammy directly and said, "I's Dorcas." Looking into Dorcas's pitiful face, Sammy noticed something else in Dorcas's eyes. Steely determination. Out of eyeshot of the others, Dorcas gave Sammy a quick wink.

"Thank you, Dorcas," said Anastasia pleasantly. "And now to business. I want to know where your son is, please, Sammy. My great aunt has the desire to meet the nasty little swine, although the good Lord only knows what she wants with one of the runts of the family. Still, mine is not to question the whims of my dear Great Aunt Agatha. No, mine is to bring her what she wants. Oh, and to fulfil a little old wish of my own!"

Sammy stared at Anastasia, mentally willing the woman to drop dead, as she continued.

"You see, Sammy, dear, I have a little bit of a problem with your oh so lovely David. He and his ilk just love these…these… damn devils," she spat, gesturing at Dorcas, "And has no time for honest god-fearing folk such as ourselves. Sad, isn't it?"

Anastasia mimed wiping away a tear.

"But the real problem is that your dearest David, in his love for these things, takes their side all the time, even against good people like his own family. And…"

She suddenly lunged over the sofa, and before Sammy could react, the mad woman was screaming into her face, eyes bulging. *"Don't you think that's wrong?"*

Benedict, standing over Dorcas, chuckled at his mother's antics.

263

Anastasia continued, this time in a low voice but still right in Sammy's face.

"Your David is so wrapped up in these things that he let my beloved Rudolph die. He stood and watched as he was taken from us. He left that poor boy..." she gestured at Benedict, "Without a father and me without the love of my life. Which is why...."

Anastasia stood up and moved back

"...I'm going to take the love of David's life and his brat away from him. Yes, a taste of his own medicine, I think."

"David did nots let Rudolph die, that's a..." began Dorcas but was silenced by a casual backhanded slap from Benedict, who did not even look at her.

"If it speaks again without my permission, Benedict, you can feed it its own tongue," said Anastasia, her eyes fixed on Sammy. Benedict stepped forward and rested a hand on the top of Dorcas's head, gentle but full of menace.

"Now then. Sammy. I will ask you again. However, before I do, know this. If you lie, or I think you are lying, Benedict here will hurt your friend. Moreover, if I so wish, he will destroy your friend and remove it from existence. Then he is going to start hurting you. Whether he removes you from existence, well..." she spread her arms wide, "...Who knows? Or cares? Certainly not your gracious hostess here, that's for certain." She gestured to herself.

Sitting down on the sofa next to Sammy, Anastasia demurely arranged her skirts. She then fixed Sammy with an expressionless look and said, "Where is Jack, and where is David?"

Sammy tried to speak but, of course, couldn't; her mouth opened to form the words, but no sounds came out.

"Oh, of course, of course. One moment," said Anastasia, performing a complex series of hand gestures before pointing at Sammy. "I've removed the silence glamour from you but have extended it around this pitiful little hovel of yours. We don't want to be disturbed by any good neighbours, do we? There's bound to be a lot of screams!" she finished, a huge smile on her face as she winked at Dorcas.

Sammy tried to speak and managed to croak out, "I already told you. David's dead."

"Ooooooh, a lie," said Anastasia. "Benedict, if you would, please?"

Benedict grabbed Dorcas by the hair again and yanked her backwards, kicking her legs out from under her as he did so. He then sat astride the brownie, pinning her on her back on the floor, and pulled out a pair of dark grey pliers. Dorcas shot Sammy a helpless glance.

"Okay, okay, I'm sorry," said Sammy, thinking quickly to buy some time. At the end of the sofa was the little coffee table that she used for her mugs of tea. On it, someone, presumably Elsie, had placed a vase of flowers – purple, white, and splendid to look at. Even more beautiful was the vase, which had been a wedding present to her and David many years ago. It was made of cut-glass crystal and was extremely heavy. And, with a bit of a shuffle, it would be within reach.

Sammy licked her lips and said, "David and Jack have just gone to get us some supper from the chippie in town. I'm expecting them back at any time now. You only just missed them when you arrived."

"There, that wasn't so hard now, was it?" said Anastasia, reaching out to stroke Sammy's face. Sammy recoiled backwards a little. Closer to the vase.

"And where is Elsie right now?" Anastasia continued.

"Great Aunt Elsie? She came to visit earlier, but she's gone home now."

"Oh, that is such a shame," said Anastasia. "I would have loved to have seen the old bag. I have a little thing to talk to her about too. Still, I expect that you have her address, don't you?"

Sammy sat up on the sofa and shifted slightly to get comfortable. Closer to the vase.

"What do you want with Auntie Elsie?" she said.

There was a slap and a whimper as Benedict hit Dorcas firmly across the face. "Mama is asking the questions. Please don't interrupt her."

"That…" said Anastasia, poking Sammy suddenly hard in the chest, "…is my business."

Sammy recoiled back again and then, with a sudden lunge, grabbed the vase off the table with a scream. She whipped round in a massive swing towards Anastasia's head, the momentum of the heavy vase causing her to twist awkwardly as she swung with all her strength. The vase whistled towards Anastasia and then just stopped in mid-air. Sammy screamed again and tried to force her arms forward, to strike the blow, and silence this evil woman. However, her arms were locked up, paralysed, as was the rest of her.

"Really, Sammy?" said Anastasia in an amused voice. "That's not very nice, is it? You'll break that lovely vase." She reached over and plucked the vase from Sammy's hands and placed it gently onto the coffee table in front of them.

"Go to hell," said Sammy through clenched teeth.

"I don't think that I will," said Anastasia pleasantly. "But I will be happy to send your little friend there in my stead. Benedict, please extinguish the devil; it will be better off if it's not here when the gentlemen of the house arrive home."

"It will be my pleasure, Mama," said Benedict, snipping the pliers backwards and forwards in front of Dorcas's face. He leaned forward, a horrible leer on his face as Dorcas tried to wriggle away from him. Benedict placed a hand on her chest to hold her still and moved the pliers' forwards towards her nose. Then he froze as a shadow fell over him.

"I don't think so, you evil, bloody swine," said Elsie from the open doorway.

~

JACK AND JIMMY met Alvina at the gate, where she was hovering anxiously, waiting for them. As they appeared, she flittered around them.

"Thank goodness; I thought that you were going to leave me here."

"We promised," said Jack simply. Turning to Jimmy, he said, "Any ideas on how to get in there?"

"Well, it's a big house," said Jimmy thoughtfully. "There's bound to be some other way in than just the front door. Maybe a window or something? You've been here before; did you see anything?"

"No. I went through the front door, shifted the table thing, then went into the kitchen. Shortly after that, I was pretty much trying to save my own skin, so nothing comes to mind. Although..."

Jack went quiet as he thought.

"In that kitchen, there's a door in the corner. I think it must lead to the cellars or something; that is where those blue-eyed creatures came from with a cart, anyway, and I heard it bumping as if it was coming upstairs. There are flats in this building, but I reckon if Alvina's kids have been grabbed, the cellar would be a good place to start looking for them?"

"Agreed. However, it doesn't solve how to get in there, does it? We can't use the 'broken-down car' routine now that Elsie's gone."

Jack frowned. "Then I guess we're going to have to wing it. I don't know about the security lights you mentioned earlier, but none came on while looking for Fermy in that horror show. Perhaps if we give the front porch a wide berth, we might be lucky; find another door or a window open or something."

"Only one way to find out. Let's keep an eye out for CCTV

as well. The last thing we want is any of the old fogies who live here calling the police on us."

The three went down the drive and stopped just before the hedges ended. They crouched in the darkness, looking at the house. There were no cameras visible at this distance; the winking red lights usually giving these away, but they could be hidden. They were just about to make a move when Jimmy slapped his head.

"Oh, stupid!" Raising the Hagstone to his eye, he looked at Alvina.

"Alvina. Do you think you could do a fly-by for us of the house? A quick circuit? We need to know if there is anything there that can spot us."

"I can, yes, but I don't know what I'm looking for," said Alvina anxiously.

"They don't have things like that in Faery, Jim; I walked quite a way and didn't notice anything like that, or burglar alarms boxes or anything."

"Right... Well, Alvina, look for anything that sticks out of the wall that has either a flashing light on it or big light bulbs. You know what a light bulb is?"

"I'm not completely ignorant of you lifers and your ways," said Alvina primly. "I will go and have a quick look around; see if there is anything unusual stuck to the walls."

"And see if there are any open windows or doors around the house," said Jack. "But before you go, can you reveal to Jimmy? It will make things easier if he doesn't have to keep waving that stone around." The fairy nodded her agreement, and in a muted shower of sparkles, appeared in the air in front of them.

"It is unusual to have to do this for lifers," she said. "But this is a matter of life or death, for my children at least. I have no regrets. Now, please wait here."

The fairy fluttered off at speed. The two boys stood in the shadows, waiting for her return.

"I really don't like this, Jimmy; that garden is completely wrong. Mr Binks is a right nutter," said Jack.

"You're not kidding," said Jimmy. "I've only known about this stuff for a day, and to be honest, I wish I didn't. It's no fairy tale, is it?"

Jack chuckled. "You're not wrong, mate. Although if I can get you to Faery, I think you'd love it. I've only seen a tiny part, and it's amazing."

"Well, I'd like to see that rodent machine, I...."

They were interrupted by the return of Alvina.

"Quick, quick," she said. "I've found an open window around the side. We must get in there."

"Did you see any lights or anything?" said Jimmy.

"No, no, nothing like that. We must get in there; I need to find my children."

The two boys followed Alvina in the shadows around the side of the house, where a sash window stood slightly open and no lights on in the room behind it. The window was obscured from the rest of the garden by a large bush.

"Perfect," said Jimmy. "Give me your phone a sec."

He activated the torch app and shone it into the room.

"It looks like a study or something," he said. "There's a great big desk and loads of books on shelves."

"That'll do us," said Jack, pushing at the bottom of the window and sliding it up to make room for them to climb in. Cocking one leg over the sill, he looked at Jimmy.

"If there's any trouble, anything at all, we need to make a pact. The other one runs and gets the police. I'd rather be in trouble with them than be captured by that Binks character."

"Agreed," said Jimmy. "Now, let's find these missing children."

CHAPTER 13

*T*he taxi that picked up Elsie had moved swiftly through the town's light traffic. Elsie had sat in the back, Fermy in her lap, stroking his head gently and willing him to wake up. She was extremely worried about her friend; she had never seen him in such a state. The taxi driver had tried the usual conversational gambits – the weather, the state of the roads, other drivers – but had been rebutted each time by Elsie's one-word answers. He had fallen into silence as the car swept into the part of town where Jack lived.

Pulling into Jack's road, he spoke. "Number thirty-seven was it, love?"

"Yes, please," said Elsie, still cradling Fermy on her lap.

As the car approached the address, the taxi driver spoke again. "Whoa, love, someone's got some cash around here, eh? Look at that Bentley! Is it yours?"

Elsie looked up to see the expensive car parked outside of Jack's house; a shadowy figure sat in the driver's seat. The hairs on the back of Elsie's neck prickled; something wasn't right.

"Sir, can you drive on, please? Take me round the block and stop at the top of the street?" she asked.

"No problem, love; unexpected visitors, is it?"

"I don't know," said Elsie.

"I'm the same with my relatives," the driver chuckled. "Turn up like a bad smell when you least expect them, then can't get rid of them."

"I think that you're probably right," said Elsie in a low voice.

The taxi circled the block, and as it drew level with the substation, Elsie said, "Just here, please." She had a plan now, and she rummaged in her bag for her purse to pay the driver, tucking her pen into her blouse pocket as she did so.

"Keep the change," she said, climbing carefully out of the car and, with the pretence of picking up her bag, lifted the little Feeorin. She crossed the road to the substation and then stood and watched as the taxi driver pulled away. Pulling out the pen, she quickly drew the travel glyph on the door to the substation, slapped it, and then yanked the door open.

"We need to see what is happening in that house, Fermy. Please wake up." The Feeorin continued to breathe with slow, steady breaths.

"Guess it's up to me then." Elsie drew the unlock glyph on the other side of the door, slapped it again, and pulled the door open quietly. This time, the substation worked, and she stepped out of the wardrobe into Sammy's bedroom, almost falling over a bulging bag that had been left on the floor. Elsie stood motionless for a few seconds, listening, and was rewarded with the sound of a strange female voice downstairs, raised in anger. Elsie couldn't make out what was being said; her hearing wasn't what it used to be, but the tone was enough.

"I'm going to have to hide you," she said to the unconscious Fermy. "I have a feeling that I am going to need both my hands free; I think that Sammy is in trouble. And I really hope that it isn't who I think it could be."

Elsie laid Fermy down on the bed and cast about for somewhere to hide him. The underneath of the bed was a no-go; the baseboard was solid, and there was no gap. She pulled open the wardrobe and pushed the few things littering the bottom to one side. Grabbing a pillow off the bed, she placed it in the gap she had just made and then gently placed Fermy onto it. Satisfied that he would be okay for now, she pushed the wardrobe door shut.

Turning to the bag, she knelt down and quietly rummaged through it. The contents were obviously from her cottage, and it looked like Dorcas had bought everything that could be remotely helpful, medicine-wise. 'Good girl,' she thought and then froze. Lying next to the bag, partially covered by the open flap, were two long metal pins with small handles attached to them. Bright red blood stained the tips of them. Elsie picked one up and turned it over; it looked to be made of iron.

"Oh, my goodness. Dorcas!" she exclaimed aloud and then clapped her hands over her mouth. She knelt, listening, but it would appear from the raised voices downstairs that she hadn't been heard. There came the sound of a loud slap, and the voices stopped momentarily before starting again in a more muted tone.

Elsie had heard enough. Sammy was obviously in trouble, and the absence of Dorcas made her particularly worried; she had known the brownie for long enough to know that she was no pushover. Steeling herself, she walked down the stairs as quietly as she could, pausing on the final step to listen again to what was going on. She heard the female voice say in a cold but amused tone, "Really, Sammy. That's not very nice, is it? You'll break that lovely vase." Followed by Sammy saying in a strained voice, "Go to hell."

The female voice again: "I don't think that I will. However, I will be happy to send your little friend there in my stead. Benedict, please extinguish the devil; it will be better off if it's not here when the gentlemen of the house arrive home."

Elsie's heart skipped a beat. Benedict. That could only mean that the other female voice was Anastasia. Elsie knew now that they were in serious trouble; she knew Anastasia of old. She and her husband, Rudolph, had been the scourge of the Fae for many years, and from what little she had heard, Benedict had been raised to be far worse. She had no idea what they were doing here, but whatever it was, it was terrible. If they had found Jack already, just days after the glamour had come off, then they had some profound reach. David has been adamant that Jack needed to be kept away from all of the Cracklocks. Elsie wasn't scared of Anastasia; she had years of Fae experience and was pretty adept at glamours. Nevertheless, she knew that that side of the family was particularly nasty, and hence that this was not going to be pleasant.

Elsie heard a snicking noise like pliers and then a gasp. Time to do something; otherwise, it would be too late.

Elsie stepped into the open doorway and took in the scene before her. A young man, presumably Benedict, had Dorcas pinned to the floor, and a familiar blonde woman sat next to Sammy on the sofa. The young man was attempting to lodge the pliers onto Dorcas' face.

"I don't think so, you evil bloody swine," said Elsie to Benedict as she started weaving a glamour gesture.

ANASTASIA RECOILED at the sight of the old woman standing in the doorway.

"Elsie," she snarled and then dove to the floor as a binding glamour whisked overhead, narrowly missing Sammy, who was dealing with her own glamour problem. Anastasia rolled over and jumped to her feet, her hands weaving backwards and forwards as she threw rapid stunning glamours at Elsie, who blocked these with similar gestures of her own.

While Benedict had held her down, Dorcas had not been

idle. Although her arms were pinned to her sides by Benedict's knees, she had sought out the pot of turmeric in her dress pocket, prising the lid from it and emptying a good amount into her palm. As Benedict shifted slightly to avoid a glamour his mother threw, Dorcas struck.

She yanked the hand out and slapped it across Benedict's face, none too gently, wiping the powder across his eyes and nose. The young man screamed, dropped the pliers, and frantically rubbed at his eyes, yellow tears starting to stream down his face.

Dorcas yanked the other hand free and pushed herself up into a sitting position, conscious of the glamours that the two women were throwing at each other as they whistled over her head in clouds of multiple sparks. Benedict was blinking rapidly now, his eyes clearing from the powder, and he looked at Dorcas with hatred in his eyes. He groped into his sleeve for something.

Dorcas didn't care. She grabbed Benedict by his tie and, rearing backwards, yanked the tie towards her as she shot her head forward. The result was a near-perfect head butt, Dorcas's forehead meeting Benedict's nose with a mighty crunching sound. The young man screamed again and grabbed for his face, blood streaming down over his mouth from between his cupped hands as he fell slowly to one side. Dorcas got to her feet and shoved the screeching Benedict away from her.

Looking down at the young man rolling around in agony, Dorcas said, "I's thinking that three is definitely nots a crowd today." She held out her hand, and her rolling pin appeared in it, skimming through from the kitchen. *"And now I's is really mad!"* she shouted as her cheeks flushed with colour. She caught Benedict across the chin with a vicious swipe, and he went out like a light and hit the floor. She then turned her attention towards Anastasia.

Sammy watched with disbelief as the blonde woman and

her aunt were apparently throwing sparks at each other, and the little Dorcas had dropped the boy/man Benedict with a well-placed head butt. The lounge was wrecked now; the pictures broken on the floor and the television screen cracked. Amazingly, the crystal vase stood untouched on the coffee table.

'*I have to help them,*' she thought, struggling against the paralysis that gripped her with everything she had. She felt her arms starting to move again, slowly, but she was gaining some control over them.

Elsie was starting to panic as she felt her strength starting to go; she was expending too many grockles defending herself and counterattacking. Anastasia, on the other hand, looked to be thoroughly enjoying herself, an insane grin plastered onto her face as she sent glamour after sparking glamour at Elsie in a relentless fashion.

"Oh, dear," she sneered. "Is the old battle-axe feeling tired? Not got the stamina for it nowadays, eh, Elsie? Still, I wouldn't worry; it'll all be over soon." She redoubled her efforts.

Elsie clutched the doorjamb as glamour after glamour struck her shield. She could feel it starting to wane now as she tried to reinforce it, stopping her retaliation as she tried desperately to defend herself.

Anastasia pressed home her advantage, taking a few steps towards Elsie as she did so. Glittering sparks flew as she directed her relentless glamours at Elsie, and she was finally rewarded as Elsie's shield collapsed in a flash of yellow sparks. Elsie slumped to her knees, panting, her hand on her chest.

"Ready for some pain, Elsie?" asked Anastasia as she weaved an immense sparking black glamour in the air. She pulled her hands back to throw it, and that was when a rolling pin, hurled with some force, hit her squarely in the face with a resounding *thunk.*

Anastasia staggered backwards, blinking, and raised her

hand to her face. Blood laced the palm, and she recoiled in anger.

Dorcas stood in front of Elsie, her hand outstretched as the rolling pin whirled through the air to return to it.

"*You's is done hurting my friends. Get out,*" she spat.

"You foul thing; you spill the blood of your betters and expect to get away with it?" snarled Anastasia. She then caught sight of Benedict, lying unconscious on the floor, and gave a scream.

"*I will kill you for this,*" she shrieked and started hurling glamours at Dorcas.

"I's not think so," said Dorcas, whose glamour shield had shot into place the minute Anastasia had moved her hands. Dorcas was not the best with combat glamours, preferring a more 'hands-on' approach, but Anastasia was weakened from her battle with Elsie. Her glamours dissipated against Dorcas's shield with coloured hisses.

"No," screamed Anastasia. "*Beast. I will do this the hard way.*"

Almost faster than the eye could see, Anastasia whipped her arm around, and a spinning object flew through the air at Dorcas. It passed through the shield charm without stopping, and Dorcas lashed frantically at it with the rolling pin. She felt the wood shudder as the object stuck in it and felt the familiar wave of nausea that iron bought. Looking at the rolling pin, a five-pointed metal star with sharp points was stuck firmly in the wooden shaft. Keeping her eyes on Anastasia, Dorcas rubbed the rolling pin on the door and the star dropped out. She felt instantly better.

Anastasia's eyes narrowed. "You're quick. I wonder just how quick you really are?" With a flash, two more objects streaked through the air. Dorcas was ready this time; the first object deflected with a swipe, the backswing catching the second object. However, this object was not solid and disintegrated as the rolling pin made contact with it. The air immediately filled with a cloud of fine reddish dust, and Dorcas started coughing. A feeling of weakness washed over her.

"You like that, my little devil?" crowed Anastasia. "Breathe it in, pant it in. Finely powdered iron. It doesn't taste great, does it? Although the smell..." she inhaled deeply, "Is like the finest ambrosia."

Dorcas went down onto one knee, wracked now with coughing as the dust swirled around in the air. She looked over at Elsie, who was also on her knees, clutching her chest and panting. Elsie's lips were a light shade of purple.

"Let's see how quick you are now then, you little brute!" smiled Anastasia, pulling a long silvery knife from her sleeve. Pushing her long hair back out of her face, she stepped over to Dorcas and seized a handful of the corkscrew hair. Dorcas raised the rolling pin in one trembling hand, and Anastasia kicked it away.

"Anastasia," whispered Elsie. "Please don't."

"Oh, but I must, Elsie, my dear, I must. To quote Matthew twenty-five, verse forty-one, *'Then he will say to those on his left, 'Depart from me, you cursed, into the eternal fire prepared for the devil and his angels.'* It is quite clear to us godly ones that these things are not permitted to live. But for your sake, I will at least make it quick. After all, we have things to discuss, and I'm not sure how much longer you will be able to talk, you sanctimonious old bag."

Anastasia pulled Dorcas's head back and gently moved the top of her dress away from her neck.

"Say goodbye then, Elsie." She pulled her hand back with the knife, ready to strike.

Then Anastasia slumped to the floor, her eyes rolling back into her head.

Sammy stood behind her, panting as she lowered the heavy crystal vase, now sporting a zigzag crack through it, which she had just brained Anastasia with.

"I don't know about what Matthew said, as I used to skive off of Sunday school. But I do remember that bit that says, *'Thou shalt not allow a witch to live.'*"

She dropped the vase with a sob and stooped down to Elsie, lifting her face gently. Elsie gestured her away.

"Get Dorcas outside into the fresh air; that dust will kill her," she whispered.

Sammy dragged Dorcas into the kitchen and pulled open the back door. She pulled off her jumper and put it under the brownie's head as it lay over the threshold of the open door.

Dorcas coughed a few times and said, "I's be alright. Look after Elsie."

Sammy dashed back to the now ruined lounge and bent down over Elsie. The old lady was breathing in short, hitching gasps, still clutching her chest.

"My heart. I think it's my heart," she whispered.

Sammy felt the fear rise in her. She moved into the lounge and started to throw things about, looking for her mobile phone. She glimpsed the edge of it sticking out from under the sofa, grabbed it, and dialled 999.

"Emergency, which service please?" came the operator's voice.

"Ambulance, please, and quickly. Police as well. We have intruders, and my aunt is having a heart attack."

JACK AND JIMMY stood in the dark study room with Alvina fluttering about them. Jack had covered the torchlight from his phone with his fingers to dim it and was tentatively shining it around the room.

"Looks like you were right, Jim; this is definitely a study or something."

Jimmy pulled a book off the shelf and thumbed through it.

"Zombie book. I read it; pretty cool," he said and threw it on the floor.

"We need to go," chirped Alvina.

"Okay, Jack, you've been here before. How do we get to this cellar place then?" said Jimmy, kicking the book out of sight underneath the desk.

"I'm no expert on this place; I've only been here once!" said Jack.

"Yeah, but that's once more than either of us. Where's the door to it?"

"It's in the kitchen, which is just off the main bit where you come through the front door. I reckon we need to get to the foyer without being spotted and make sure no one is in the kitchen. Then we hit that cellar and hope that is where they are. If they aren't, then we will have to search the house, which I really don't want to do. That Mr Binks could be anywhere in here."

Jimmy pulled open the study door a crack and stuck his eye to it. After a few seconds, he pulled the door open.

"All clear, just a corridor. Which way?"

Jack paused a moment to get his bearings. "Left, I think; that's the direction of the front door."

The two boys and Alvina crept slowly down the dimly lit corridor, its brown wooden panelling adding to the gloomy feeling. They kept their ears open for noises or people but heard nothing. Reaching the end, they approached the closed door with trepidation. Jack pushed it open a crack and sighed with relief. The main foyer was there, all dark apart from the lights on the landing overhead. Opening the door wider, Jack stepped through and then froze as he heard a click of a door handle. It came from the other end of the corridor behind him.

"Quick," he whispered, yanking Jimmy through the door. Alvina dashed over his head as he pushed the door almost shut, trying not to make any sound. He pressed his eye to the crack and gasped in horror. Mr Binks was walking down the corridor towards them, sprightly so, with no sign of his cane. It looked like he had not seen Jimmy disappearing through the door due to the dim light, but he was heading this way.

"What is it?" whispered Jimmy, and Jack gestured frantically at him to shush. He watched as Mr Binks paused outside the study door, and looked at it, a puzzled look on his face. He pushed the door and went in.

"Did you shut the study door?" he asked Jimmy.

"I don't think so."

Jack pushed the door shut, keeping the handle down to minimise any click of the latch.

"He's just gone into the study; must have seen the door open. I hope that he will not be too worried about it, but we need to get going. The kitchen's this way."

The three scuttled across the foyer, keeping to the shadows, and paused by the kitchen door. Jimmy nudged Jack and pointed to the gap beneath the door.

"No light on. I reckon it's empty but go steady."

Jack pushed the door open again and found Jimmy was right; nobody was in the dark kitchen. The stainless steel and chrome fittings gleamed dully from the light filtering through the door, but the spotlessly clean kitchen was empty. Jack pointed to the corner.

"There; that's the door I was talking about."

The three moved quickly through the kitchen to the door and stood, listening. Alvina started suddenly.

"That's my boy down there."

"I didn't hear anything?" said Jimmy. "Are you sure?"

"The faintest of whimpers. Please, please, open this door; we need to get down there."

Looking at Jack, Jimmy pulled open the door. The pair peered into the darkness and saw a short flight of steps leading down. Like a photographer's darkroom, a dim red light lit the room at the bottom of the steps.

"Should one of us stay up here, keep an eye out?" asked Jimmy nervously.

"I don't think we should split up," Jack replied. "May be easier to deal with things if we're both there, less chance to get caught or, if we do, for one of us to get away."

"Okay, let's go."

Alvina had already flown ahead of them, and the boys were halfway down the stairs when they heard an anguished wail from her. Dashing down the last few steps, they entered the dimly lit room and came to a quick stop, Jack's breath catching in his chest in horror at the scene before him. Beside him, Alvina let out a little scream, her shock stopping it short. "What the hell?" Jimmy gasped.

THE CREATURE KNOWN as Mr Binks was in a foul mood, even fouler than it usually was. It hated being contained within this lifer form, but it had no choice, bound to this location as it was. It was trapped until 'Dr Cracklock', as the idiot lifer called himself, saw fit to release him from this bond, and that would only happen once the debt was repaid. Nevertheless, it planned to pay back Dr Cracklock and all the others a little extra as soon as it was free, oh yes! Enslavement had never been sold as part of the agreement, but that was what it was, kowtowing to the Cracklocks with a "Yes, Sir," and "Sorry, Sir," whenever they deemed fit to come here and find fault with what it was doing. That would stop and no mistake. True, the old ones had not yielded the grackles required, but the slow drawing from them was providing a steady stream, like a battery slowly draining and recharging. If it was allowed to keep more Fae here, it could quickly boost the takings, but the

Cracklocks carted them off in bulk as they were caught; indeed, Dr Cracklock or one of his minions was due any time now for the latest batch. The house and gardens caught many Fae; it was like a magnet to them with the various glamour's cast over the place. Therefore, it was not as if they couldn't spare more for his use. The creature shook its head in anger.

It stood staring at the study door that was ajar; this was odd as it always closed the doors behind it to stop anything from escaping, and it was an ingrained habit. One of those damned Cracklock spies it had to put up with had probably left it open. Cursing whichever idiot was guilty with a snarl, it pushed the door and limped into the room to find the book that it wanted. One of the few pleasures it had was the time to read; it had never done so before and found it refreshing. It liked the zombie apocalypse books best; Fleet and Artinian; those guys had the style of writing it enjoyed the most. It trailed a hand along the books as it moved along the bookshelves, the wind from the open window fluttering the curtains as it moved around the room. The creature froze; why was the window open in the study? It bustled over to the open window and moved to pull it shut when it stopped. There was a footprint on the windowsill, moist earth outlining clear treads. Leaning out, the creature saw several prints in the flowerbed below the window.

It jerked backwards, a snarl on its face. Intruders, burglars, thieves. In its domain. Well, no matter; some fun could be had with them. Moreover, some grackles extracted perhaps, assuming that there was some left; the creature could get carried away sometimes in its rages. It stormed towards the study door and then stopped as it saw a book lying casually under the study table. The creature scooped it up and sniffed it. A lifer. A young male lifer; the faint odour of chocolate and sweat. The creature that wore Mr Binks's skin let out a growl and dashed to the door, sniffing the air. The hunt was on.

~

JACK AND JIMMY looked around the room, their hearts sinking at the sight before them. The room was full of cages haphazardly stacked on top of each. In the cages were Fae. Lots of them, all different shapes and sizes. Some were lying slumped in abject defeat; others were at the bars, hands outstretched, calling for help. Alvina was batting against one of the smaller cages at the top of a pile where two sets of tiny hands were sticking out, trying to pull the lock off.

"Help me; they're here," she said as she noticed the boys' entrance into the room. Jimmy took a quick glance through the Hagstone and dashed over, where he started pulling at the side where the lock was.

"It's locked firm," he called over to Jack in a low voice. "See if there's any keys or anything we can use to pry this door open."

Jack dashed further into the room and noticed a table set back in the shadows in the far corner. Moving over to this, he immediately saw that it was scattered with a variety of objects, tools mainly, but other things; small items of clothing and what appeared to be small ivory objects. Picking one up, he recoiled; it seemed to be a small bone. *'What is happening here?'* he thought to himself as he cast items aside, looking for something he could use. Pulling aside a pile of cloth, he found an ornate wooden chest, patterns carved on it, not much bigger than a money box. It was firmly closed with a clasp.

"Hurry, Jack," Jimmy whispered as loud as he dared.

Jack flipped the clasp, and there, sitting on a bed of dark material, was the tube. The item that Fermy had come here to get. Jack plucked it out of the box, and a sensation of pins and needles shot up his arm, quickly disappearing. He stuffed it into his pocket and resumed the search. Buried under a pile of old newspapers, he found a thick screwdriver and a hammer. He grabbed them and hurried over to Jimmy.

"These do?"

Jimmy pushed the screwdriver into the cage where the lock was and gave it a hard push. The cage was flimsy; it was intended to hold more diminutive Fae by the looks of it, and the lock popped straight open. Out flew two tiny Fae, male and female, straight into Alvina's arms.

"Yep, those will do it!" said Jimmy, with a strained smile.

"Thank you, oh thank you," she shrilled, clutching her children in a fierce hug. "Let's get out of here."

The din rose in the other cages. *"Help us, help us!"* the occupants were screaming and shaking the bars in their terror. *"We're done for if you leave us here. Please help us!"*

Jack glanced at Jimmy, who nodded.

"We can't leave them here, not having seen what is happening outside in that garden. We have to help them. Go and keep an eye out upstairs while I get these cages open. Use the Hagstone; you'll be able to see anyone that could be prowling about."

"Right. Be quick, though, mate; that Binks could be anywhere."

"I intend to be," said Jack, gesturing the occupant of the next cage to go to the back of the cage so that he could get the screwdriver into place.

Jimmy sprinted up the stairs, followed closely by Alvina and her children. He pushed the cellar door open quietly and peered into the still, dark kitchen. It was empty as before. Jimmy tiptoed over to the door to the main foyer and pulled it open a crack, pressing the Hagstone and his eye to it as the anxious faeries buzzed around him. The foyer was still empty as well, the lights from the landing casting shadows off the various ornaments that adorned the place.

Jack was having good luck in popping the cages open; for a lifer, they were not too sturdy at all. As the Fae were released, they milled about behind him, the abler of them supporting those that couldn't walk. Some of them appeared to be incredibly old, parchment-like skin covered in wrinkles and wispy white hair. As he popped the last cage open, the released Fae gathered around him.

"How are we going to get out?" sobbed one creature, its big eyes dripping tears. "This whole place is Fae locked outside."

"We managed to get in through the gates, so I am guessing that we can get out the same way. We just need to get out of this house," said Jack. There was an immediate outburst of questions from the Fae that Jack had trouble listening to as he turned this way and that at the questions fired at him. He gave up and raised both arms in the air.

"Listen, we just need to go. Up those stairs, through the kitchen, and out into the gardens. But you need to be quiet while we're doing it."

"Is that big lifer still here and those Redcaps?" asked one Fae, a quiver in its voice.

"Yes, he's upstairs, but we haven't seen the goblin things. I guess they are around somewhere. So, again, you need to be quiet."

Jack led the party up the stairs and stuck his head out of the door. Seeing Jimmy by the kitchen door, he called over in a loud whisper, "All clear?"

Jimmy was turning to acknowledge him when he heard a bang. He put his eye back to the gap and saw the figure of Mr Binks stride into the foyer. The man looked deranged; he was sniffing the air and darting his head backwards and forwards. Jimmy flapped his hand at Jack in a 'quiet' gesture and continued to watch.

Mr Binks pulled something from his pocket and blew into it. Jimmy couldn't hear anything, but Jack noticed many of the Fae he was with cover their ears, screwing up their faces as they did so. One of the childer Fae enquired quietly, "What was that noise, grandmama?"

Jimmy continued to watch as a trapdoor, previously hidden, flipped open in the foyer floor, and several of the creatures Jack had described from his last visit climbed out. Jimmy's stomach turned over slightly as he saw the evil faces and sharp teeth. He pushed the door shut quietly and looked at the lock. There was no key, but there was a small bolt. Jimmy snicked it home.

He crept across the kitchen to Jack, Hagstone to his eye and finger on his lips to the agitated Fae that was with him.

"He's in the foyer," he whispered. "And he's got those things with him. How are we supposed to get out then? That's the only way from the kitchen."

"I guess I could try the travel glyph, but Elsie was pretty sure it wouldn't work. If it doesn't, then we wait for a little, hope that they go..."

Jack was cut short as the handle on the kitchen door moved up and down, and a guttural voice called, "Why is this locked, Binks?"

Jack froze, gesturing for Jimmy to be quiet as he listened. A distant voice returned, "It shouldn't be. There's no one in the extraction room is there, you idiot; we're all here."

"But the door won't open, Binks." The handle jiggled again.

"Come with me," whispered Jack urgently to Jimmy. The two boys went over to the door and looked around. Behind them, the Fae were becoming agitated. "We need to block it," Jack said to Jimmy, his eyes wide with fear.

"Here, help me with this thing," said Jimmy, gesturing to the large stainless-steel cabinet that ran along the wall at waist height. It was a catering type one, with wheels in each corner. Jack grabbed one end of it and pushed, but it wouldn't move.

"Wait, wait," said Jimmy, looking at the wheels. He quickly moved to each one and then said, "Wheel locks. Try now."

The cabinet was heavy but moved quickly on its four wheels. The boys positioned it in front of the door and were snapping the wheel locks back on when the door handle gave a frantic wriggle, followed quickly by a loud bang. One of the Fae behind them gave a little scream.

"I know you're in there, boy," came a snarling old man's voice from behind the door. "And you better come out this instant. There's nothing of value unless you want old potatoes and tins of beans. Come out now, and I won't call the police." The door banged again, this time shaking on its hinges.

Jack and Jimmy stared at each other in shock; this was a right mess they were in. Behind them, the Fae clung to each other in terror.

"*Boy, open this door!*" demanded the voice again. Another bang and, this time, a tinkle as one of the screws from the bolt landed onto the steelwork surface. A crack laced its way up the centre pane of wood.

Jack whispered to Jimmy, "Say something; keep him distracted. I am going to try one of the windows."

He moved over to the nearest window, which was set high above the cooker and oven combination. He clambered onto the cooker and reached for the latch, but it wouldn't move. Locked. Behind him, he heard Jimmy say in a voice quite unlike his own, "Listen, geezer, I ain't coming out of here while you've got that tone going; you sound mental. Call the feds if you like. They won't stripe me up, innit."

Jimmy's statement was met with a flurry of bangs, causing the cabinet to judder slightly away from the door. Jimmy looked on in disbelief; how strong was this old codger? He shoved the cabinet back, the wheels protesting, and then leaned on it.

"*If you don't come out now, there will be no need for the police. I will put you in the garden with the others,*" came the snarling voice.

"Now, that ain't nice, is it, blud?" repeated Jimmy, gesturing at Jack to 'Do Something.' The banging on the door started now with routine blows.

"*I'm done asking nicely,*" screeched the old man's voice. '*Take it down.*'

There came a flurry of blows at the door and then a single dull thud. Then another. A few splinters fell away, and a gleam of metal reflected in the small gap.

"They're chopping it down," Jimmy mouthed at Jack in horror.

Jack hopped down from the cooker and started pulling open cabinet drawers. The first held tea towels and carefully folded aprons. Jack threw them onto the worktop and continued his search. In the third drawer, he found what he was looking for. He pulled out a heavy-looking metal meat tenderiser.

He dashed over at the huddled Fae, crouched down, and whispered to them.

"I need to break the window, but if he hears, he'll be outside waiting for us when we go. I need you to make a lot of noise when I give the signal; as much noise as you can – grab some pans or something. If we can hide the noise of the window breaking, and we can keep that door closed, we have a chance. Will you help us?"

The variety of heads all nodded in agreement, and they scattered, quietly gathering up pans and plates from the various shelves. Jack looked at Jimmy, who gave him the thumbs up. The banging on the door intensified.

Jack grabbed a handful of cloths and the tenderiser and climbed back onto the cooker. Behind him, Jimmy was jolted as the lock on the door broke, the head of the axe shearing it from its mount. The door was forced open to stop against the cabinet. Jimmy pressed back, his back against the cabinet and legs straining.

Jack placed a tea towel against the window and signalled to the Fae 'Now.'

There was a glorious cacophony of noise as the Fae set about wrecking the kitchen, throwing crockery and bashing pans against the floor and steel work surfaces. Jack struck the window through the cloth with the tenderiser and was rewarded with the sound of shattering glass, which was muted by the rest of the noise. He quickly used the tea towel to remove as many glass shards as possible and then swept the bottom and sides of the frame to remove the last few shards. He placed a few tea towels and aprons onto the bottom frame as a pad against any fragments and then gestured to the Fae. Those with wings streamed through the open window and then hovered there, Alvina and her children amongst them.

"*What are you doing in there?*" came the screeching voice. "*Just wait till I get my hands on you, you little thug.*"

"Looking for summat to defend myself with, innit," said Jimmy. "You's proper mental, mate."

Jack started to pull those Fae without wings up onto the cooker and boosted them up onto the windowsill. He pointed in the direction of the drive each time. "That way, go that way, follow Alvina. The gate is open, and you will be clear of the Fae lock. Once you are there, scatter! Don't wait for us; we'll be coming pretty quickly I think."

"Our thanks," said one old gnome as he clambered up onto the windowsill. "You are a fearless boy. What is your name?"

"Jack. Jack Cracklock," Jack replied.

The gnome gave a little double-take. "Son of David?" he asked.

"Yes. Look, please go."

The gnome hopped through the window and streaked off towards the drive in pursuit of the others. Jack helped the last two Fae through and then turned to Jimmy, who was fighting a losing battle against the door as it bashed the cabinet slowly forwards, inch by inch. Whoever was wielding the axe was chopping at the lower pane now, and the old man's fingers curled around the upper part door as he redoubled his efforts to shove it open.

Jack hopped down and grabbed the metal preparation table in the centre of the room. He dragged it over to the cabinet blocking the door, and wedged it firmly against it. Holding out his hand, he pulled Jimmy up from the floor, and the pair leaned against the cabinet, the door beating against it with dull thuds as their assailants tried to force entry.

"Why aren't they using glamours?" Jimmy croaked.

"Don't know. Time to go before they do," Jack panted. "You first."

Jimmy nodded and hopped onto the cooker, cocked one leg over the sill, and disappeared from view. Jack counted down mentally from three and then flew at the cooker, repeating Jimmy's move. As he got his leg over the sill, he heard a grating sound as the cabinet and worktable were shoved further out of the way, and the head of Mr Binks pushed its way through the gap. It focused straight away onto Jack, and he snarled, *"You!"*

Jack could see the old man's crazy face but superimposed over it, like a holographic image, was the grim, goblin-like face he had seen before. This time though, it wasn't flickering; it was like he could see two faces at once as Mr Binks's head bobbed up and down in his efforts to get in. The effect gave him a headache, but it was hypnotic to look at as the two sets of features swam together. The creature shoved its way into the room, the Redcaps streaming between its legs, and dashed towards him, grasping hands raised.

Jack shook his head, and without thinking, his fingers grasped the tenderiser on the windowsill. He threw it at the old man/monster thing, and it gave a screech of pain as the heavy item clipped its shoulder. It didn't stop it, though.

"I'm going to eat you alive," it screeched in rage, wholly lost in its madness.

Jack pushed himself out in a panic and dropped down from the window, stumbling as he landed. He was going over when a pair of hands grabbed him, and he looked up to see Jimmy.

From through the open window, he heard the shrill nasal voice scream, *"Outside. They're outside. They're escaping. Catch them!*" They heard a bang as the front door flew open from around the corner.

The two boys, eyes wide in horror, took to their heels, down the driveway and the gate to freedom, the screams of the monstrous old man echoing in their ears.

CHAPTER 14

*S*ammy watched the paramedics work on Elsie as Anastasia, and a now subdued Benedict were led from the other ambulance to a police car in handcuffs. Anastasia, a cotton pad pressed against her head, was snarling at the arresting officer, something about not knowing who she was, but Sammy ignored her, slamming the door shut as the officers left. They would be back to take formal statements but, given Elsie's situation, had simply taken Sammy's brief description of events and given a promise to call her. Dorcas stood in the background, being careful not to get in the way, chewing on turmeric that had turned the corners of her mouth a yellow colour. Sammy was still amazed that the paramedics completely disregarded the brownie; they hadn't even given her a second glance.

The paramedics had checked Elsie's heart rhythm with an ECG and had fixed an oxygen mask over her face. They had explained to Sammy that it looked to be a slight murmur rather than a full-blown attack, but given Elsie's age and the situation, they were taking no chances. They were getting her comfortable on a stretcher for the trip to the hospital.

"Had quite a shock, haven't you, Missus, er, Cracklock?" said the female paramedic. "Still, the police have got them now. Made a right mess, those intruders, eh?" Elsie nodded and gave a tired smile.

Sammy had told the police that the two had forced entry into the house, demanded money, and then wrecked the place trying to find it; it was simpler to lie than try and explain the craziness that had transpired. She was not convinced that the detective who had taken her brief statement believed her, but she had some time to embellish the story now. Besides, aside from Elsie's condition, she was anxious about Jack.

Elsie beckoned her over and moved her mask to the side so she could whisper to Sammy. "Tell...Dorcas, Fermy... Wardrobe upstairs. Needs help."

"Elsie, love, that ferret is that last thing that should be on your mind. What happened to Jack? Where is he?"

Elsie closed her eyes and then opened them. "He's...okay. With Jimmy. Back soon. Tell Dorcas...Fermy. They will...Jack."

"Excuse me, Mrs Crackley, but we need to take your aunt out to the ambulance now. Could you stand to one side, please?" said the paramedic politely. Sammy nodded and moved as the paramedics lifted the stretcher.

"Are you coming with your aunt?" the paramedic enquired. "There's room for you if you want to."

Sammy was torn. She wanted to go with Elsie but was still worried about Jack. Where was he? She felt a gentle tug on her jeans and looked down to see Dorcas.

"You's go with Elsie. I's wait here for Jack."

"Does he know you, and can he see you?" Sammy said in a low whisper so that the paramedics who were carrying Elsie out through the door didn't hear.

"Yes, of course. You knows's me as well; we will explain everything once Elsie's goods again. And when's we get's Fermy back." The brownie gave a sad little smile.

"I don't know what all the fuss is about over that bloody ferret, but Elsie told me to tell you it's in the wardrobe upstairs. I'll go with Elsie, but you tell Jack to ring me the second he's back. Do you understand what that is?"

Dorcas's eyes widened at this. "Of course. Dorcas has lived with lifers for a long's time. Silly tellybones's, peoples always lookings at them rather than each others. I will tell's Jack. Now, go with Elsie; I must see to Fermy." With that, she bounded up the stairs.

Sammy looked back at the house as she climbed into the ambulance. She had the strangest feeling of dread still. Patting Elsie's hand, she said, "We really need to have a talk, Auntie."

"Oh, this is nonsense," said Anastasia to the officers in the front of the police car. "We haven't done anything other than visit our relatives."

"That isn't what Mrs Crackley said. Now be quiet. You'll have your say when we get to the station."

"I'd strongly recommend that you let us go. Now."

"We don't let people go who attack old ladies, madam. Now, please sit back in the seat and calm down. We will be five minutes to the station, and then you can talk as much as you want. You are under oath."

"Oh, for the Lord's sake." Anastasia made a few gestures with her fingers, and the handcuffs fell off. Performing a complex series of gestures in the air with her freed hands, she then commanded, "Pull over."

"Yes, madam," said the driver, robotically.

"What the hell, Steve? What are you doing?" said the police officer in the passenger seat. "Keep driving."

The car pulled over to the side of the road. Anastasia

gestured again and said, "Go to sleep." The second officer slumped forward in the seat and started snoring.

"Erm, Mama?" said Benedict, holding up his handcuffed wrists.

"Benedict, you are old enough to work that glamour yourself. If you can't, then you can just continue to wear them," snapped Anastasia crossly. To the driver, she said, "Now, you, let us out."

"Yes, Madam," said the officer and turned off the car. He pushed the button that unlocked the rear doors, and Anastasia climbed out. Benedict followed her, now free of the handcuffs. Anastasia knocked on the driver's window.

"Our effects please?"

"Yes, Madam. In the boot." He pressed another button, and the boot door raised itself. Anastasia retrieved her bag and an evidence bag that contained various iron weapons that the arresting officers had confiscated. Benedict's eyes lit up when he saw a taser in its holster. He raised an eyebrow at Anastasia, who gave a resigned shrug.

"If you must," she said. Heading back to the driver's window, she said, "Many thanks for your hospitality. Now, what would you consider to be the furthest point from where we are?"

"Land's End, Madam."

"And do you have a family, officer?"

"Yes, Madam. Two boys."

"Good. Call your boys and tell them they will never see you again. Then drive to Land's End, and do not stop when you get there. Take the car for a swim."

Turning away from the police car, she rummaged in her bag and pulled out her phone. She spoke briefly into it, "Nigel, come and collect us, please," and hung up. She punched another number in and took a deep breath.

"Uncle, it's Anastasia. Yes, the imp was correct; I found them. No... No... There were complications, but the boy is there, and

Sammy told me David was too. Elsie? Yes, but she has had a little accident. Yes. Hospital. No... No... I'll send you the address but don't come now. There are several law officers there. No, tomorrow would be fine."

"Ask Great Uncle if we can burn it down?" said Benedict eagerly.

Anastasia listened and then shook her head to Benedict, who pulled a sulky face.

"Okay. We will see you tomorrow then," said Anastasia and hung up the phone. Turning to Benedict, she said, "Your Great Uncle is coming tomorrow to retrieve the boy. We will be here to assist him. I will see if you can set your fire after we are ready to leave."

"With the Fae in it?" said Benedict, his eyes gleaming.

"Whatever you want. I'd suggest that Dorcas beast could be part of your little barbecue if you wish; I will try to clear it with Uncle. But you know how he likes to enlist the bigger ones to his cause."

Benedict practically jumped for joy.

Dorcas lifted Fermy gently out of the wardrobe, wincing a little as she did so from the wounds in her shoulder. The Feeorin was still unconscious, breathing rhythmically in and out, but showed no signs of stirring. A slight rash dappled his cheek and chin from where the root had been. Dorcas placed him on the bed, a cushion under his head.

"Fermy, wakes up," said Dorcas, stroking his cheek. Nothing.

"Fermy wakes up, please." Still nothing.

"*Fermy, Wakes Up!*" Dorcas yelled, her mouth about an inch from his face. Nothing.

"This is very usual, me is thinking," Dorcas said aloud and scratched her chin. "So, what's could it be? Poisons? Glamours?

He does not seem's to have been beaten out; no bruises. Most unusual."

She turned to the bag that was still on the floor and started rummaging through it. She chucked out various bandages and things until she found her little satchel of antidotes. These were tiny little bottles of things but highly potent. Fishing out the hawthorn and ash tincture, she rubbed a little onto Fermy's lips. The Feeorin went on breathing but showed no other signs.

"Mmmmm, this not works? This always works for poisonings. Me try's another."

Dorcas went through the entire satchel of bottles with the same results.

"So's, not poisonings. Must be glamours then."

Dorcas was not adept at removing glamours, but she didn't have to be. She had a large bottle of something that Granny had made that the old woman simply called "Gone-Gone." Dorcas's family swore by it, particularly the younger ones who were always getting into scrapes and having glamours backfire on them. Just add a good measure to a bath, submerge, and it did its magic. The problem was that here in Jack's house, the bathtub was lifer size. Dorcas had spent the previous afternoon scrubbing it and had had real difficulties climbing out of the high sides when they were slippery with the soap she had used. Getting Fermy in and out of it would be an issue.

Dorcas looked at the Feeorin and realised that he would fit nicely into a bucket due to his small nature. She glamoured one into existence and then glamoured hot soapy water to fill it. She rooted the bottle out and poured a good dollop of the thick Gone-Gone into it, gave it a quick swirl which turned the water purple and then turned to Fermy.

"Should I take offs his clothes?" she asked herself and then blushed. Dorcas was surprisingly coy when it came to nudity and usually avoided it at all costs. "No, I's not think so."

She lifted Fermy off the bed with her hands tucked into his

armpits and gently lowered him up to the neck into the bucket of warm water. Nothing. She swished him about a few times, and still nothing. Hauling him out of the bucket, she realised that she had no towel, and with her hands full, couldn't glamour one into existence. She laid the now soaking wet Fermy onto the bedside rug and frowned.

"Not poisoning, not glamours. What's could it be? Thinks, Dorcas."

She absentmindedly starting picking things out of the bag, not really looking at them, and putting them in a row as she thought the problem through. The bag emptied rapidly as she pulled items out, and she was fishing about for the last few items when her hand closed over a glass bottle. Pulling it out, she realised that she was holding a bottle of 'Dantes Inferno' extra hot chilli sauce. She must have put it in by accident when she put the herbs and spices into the bag from the kitchen cupboard; the bottle lived next to them along with the ketchup and brown sauce. Elsie had a bit of a soft spot for this sauce and used it to pep up things when she was 'feeling spicy', as she put it. It was too hot for Dorcas, whose tastes stretched to a blander type of fare. Looking at the bottle with its big red chilli pepper label though, she had an idea. "I wonder's…" she said to herself.

Glamouring a spoon into existence, she pulled Fermy up into a sitting position and poured a generous measure of the sauce into the spoon. She pulled Fermy's jaw open, inserted the spoon, and tipped it back.

The effect was instantaneous. The Feeorin shot to his feet, eyes wide, both hands clutching his throat as he gave a garbled scream. He then bent over double, coughing and spitting out the dark red sauce as he wretched. As he was doing so, he made a choking noise, far back in his throat, and then spat out what looked like a bright blue slug. The thing writhed on the floor, its sucker-like mouth opening and closing. Fermy, his eyes red and streaming, looked at Dorcas, looked at the slug thing, and then stamped on it with all his might. It squished in a purple-blue pool of goo and then disappeared, soaking away into the bedroom carpet to leave a bluish stain.

Fermy was panting now, and Dorcas glamoured a glass of water, which she handed over. Fermy swallowed it in two gulps and gestured for another.

Taking his time with the second one, he looked at Dorcas.

"What was that stuff?" he hitched.

"Magic potion," said Dorcas, tucking the bottle behind her back. It was going in the medicine kit when she had some peace.

Fermy glanced around the bedroom. "How the grack did I get here? And why, by my grockles, am I soaking wet?"

JACK AND JIMMY sprinted down the drive towards the open gate, the Fae in the distance simply vanishing as they crossed the threshold. Jack could hear running footsteps behind them, and he risked a glance over his shoulder. He put on a burst of speed as he spotted four redcaps dashing some fifteen metres behind them, Mr Binks himself following up the rear with a weird loping run as he gave chase.

"Keep going," Jack panted to Jimmy. "They're right behind us."

Jimmy risked a glance himself but could only see the old man bouncing along. He sped up anyway on Jack's advice. As they approached the open gate and freedom, Jack suddenly veered off to the left and grabbed something from the bushes. It was a little dark for Jimmy to see, but the item appeared to be a long thin stick. Bursting through the gate and into the road, Jack spun around, raising the stick like a sword. He swung it at something, and Jimmy saw it stop in mid-air. Fumbling the Hagstone from his pocket, he raised it to his eye to see Jack take a swing at a second of the goblin creatures, the first rolling around on the ground and squealing.

"Get away, Binks, I'm warning you," Jack shouted into the dark drive. *"Call them off."* He swung at another of the creatures, the stick whistling through the air with a whipping noise.

Seeing the creatures through the Hagstone, Jimmy planted a kick on the one that was already on the ground as it struggled to its feet, causing it to howl.

"Get back here," came the nasal voice as Mr Binks loped into view in the light shed by the streetlights. The creatures immediately limped back towards him, the one from the floor clutching its arm and gazing daggers at Jack. Mr Binks walked to the open gate and then stopped. He placed his hands on his hips and smiled at the boys. It was not a pleasant look.

"Well, well, well. Master Crackley, all recovered from his accident and looking to steal from an old man. Also, a little friend too. Very intimidating. I should call the police."

"We haven't stolen anything from you, you psycho. What were you doing to those Fae? The ones in the cellar?" called Jack.

"So, you can see the Fae folk, can you? How very interesting. I knew that you were special from our last encounter. A little more special than your friend there, squinting through his piece of rock."

"Just making sure that those things of yours stay put," said Jimmy.

"Oh, but they will, they will. We cannot leave here, you see. Us inside, you outside. Sad, really, as I would very much like to suck the grackles from you. However, my terms are quite clear. Anyhow, enough of my woes. Let's talk about your punishment."

"You aren't going to be sucking the grackles out of anyone for a while," said Jack.

"Shush boy, you know nothing."

"I know about this," bluffed Jack, pulling the tube from his pocket. The effect on Mr Binks was instantaneous.

"How did you get that, you filthy little thief? Give it back this instant!" he screamed, clutching for Jack with his gnarled hands but stopping short of the gate threshold. The second face shifted, contorting into a screaming grimace, red eyes glowing.

Both the boys had jumped at the shout, but Jack was becoming more confident with the old man not coming out of the property.

"I would, but I know what you'd do with it. And I can't allow that to happen anymore."

"Oh, you little idiot," spat Mr Binks. "You have no idea of the forces you are messing with. Give it to me before you wake it up."

"Wake it up?" said Jack.

"Yes. It is dangerous. Give it here, boy, before you start something you will regret."

"I think I'll hold on to it," said Jack, nervously tucking the tube back into his pocket.

"Then you leave me no choice, boy!" thundered Mr Binks.

The old man took a step back from the gate and raised both his arms into the air. He started to mutter under his breath.

"He's going to Mexican wave us to death," said Jimmy to Jack, all fear forgotten now that he had seen the old man up close. Jack wasn't so sure. The second face had a sly, triumphant look on it, the red eyes rolling around. The arms shot down, the forefinger of both hands pointing at the ground.

"I think we'd better go," said Jack. "I don't know what he's...."

He didn't finish his sentence as a mighty shudder almost knocked the pair of them off their feet. The shuddering continued, fading slightly until it seemed to be just vibrations. It was followed by a massive crash from somewhere in the dark gardens behind where Mr Binks stood. The old man stood there, his arms folded and a broad grin on his face as he juddered slightly from the vibrations rippling through the ground.

"Oh, boys," he jeered in a cheerful tone. "I've got something for you!"

There was a dull thud from the darkness. It was followed by another. Then another, the frequency of them speeding up. At the end of the drive, the trees started rocking as if disturbed by a brisk breeze, rustling furiously as they shook. More thuds, and then the source became apparent. Jimmy raised the Hagstone with a trembling hand; all pretence of bravado now gone. A single substantial dark mass came into view, and then a second one; they appeared to be pillars, quite thick, dark, and very long. Another thud, and Jack and Jimmy both recoiled in horror when they saw the big picture.

The pillars were legs. Huge thick legs, thudding as they walked towards them up the dark drive. The legs were attached to an equally dark torso, strangely misshapen and lumpy. It was difficult to see in the dark, but two long thin arms swung by its side, and glowing yellow eyes peered from the top of the mass. The thing was huge, as tall as a house at least, as it pushed its way through the trees that hung over the drive, stomping towards Mr Binks and the open gate. Scarily, the thing cast no shadow; the shadows from the streetlights of Mr Binks and the Redcaps were evident, but not this thing.

As it got closer, more details were visible in the gloom of the drive. It appeared to be made from the garden itself; the boys could see the partially concealed heads of the trapped Fae, roots climbing into their orifices, sticking out of the torso like bizarre boils. The body was made of mud and grass, its legs and feet solid earth, with wriggling thick roots where its toes should be. The arms were thick and vine-like, intertwined together, grasping appendages at the ends that served as its fingers, claw-like. The creature stank of wet earth and mud, and Jack could see wriggling worms dropping from it as it got closer. Its vast, misshapen head had no features apparently, apart from its yellow eyes that flickered like dual candle flames in the middle of the lump of a face. The creature stumped to a halt just behind Mr Binks.

The glee on the old man's face was apparent. "Boys, I would normally like to make formal introductions to our resident Lisovyk, but there is no point. You are going to be spending a lot of time with it, I guarantee it. An eternity and they will never find you. Moreover, any clever travelling tricks won't help you; he doesn't allow long jumps. *Take them and bring me what's mine!*" he screamed suddenly and gestured at Jimmy and Jack.

The Lisovyk's head split open sideways to reveal a dark mouth, wriggling roots again present where the teeth should be. It gave a gargling, wet screech, ear piecing, and lumbered past Mr Binks and the Redcaps, its arms outstretched. Jack and Jimmy took a quick look at each other and ran for it, terror driving them on as they dashed down the hill. Behind them, they could hear the mushy resounding thud, thud, thud, thud of footsteps. Jack glanced over his shoulder and almost fell over; the creature was clear of the gates and in hot pursuit of them down the hill. Moreover, it looked like it could move, its arms swinging as it gathered speed, eager to do its master's bidding.

"FOR GOODNESS SAKE, DORCAS, STOP FUSSING," said Fermy, trying to fend off the towel-wielding brownie who was scrubbing at him furiously. "I'm fine, seriously." The Feeorin then bent over, coughing, wracking spasms coming out of him.

"You's is not fine; you's had some strange thing on you, and you's coughed up a slug," said Dorcas, cornering him and raising the towel menacingly.

"Oh my, the slug; I forgot about that," recoiled Fermy. "When I got there, it was easy enough to get in; the gates were wide open. I assumed ferret form and went up the drive via the bushes; there was nobody there. The front door was firmly shut, so I thought I would try around the side of the building. However, the minute I set foot on the lawn, I was snared; roots sprang from nowhere and grabbed me. I've seen those root things before; terrible, just terrible… And then that old man…." He shuddered at the memory.

"That foul old man came and looked at me; he said he knew who I was, but he didn't ask me anything. I activated the alert ring then; I felt it best while I still could. Then, the roots that bound me forced my mouth open, and he popped that wriggling blue thing in; I could feel it worming its way down my throat. Huuhhh." Fermy started to gag a little. "And then I woke up here in agony, my throat and mouth on fire from that wretched potion of yours and soaking wet into the bargain."

"I's sorry, Fermy, but I's had no choice. I's couldn't wake you."

"No matter, no matter. Now, get the others; we need to rethink our strategy for that house, as it has some awful protections on it. In fact, no, I'll come down to them; I don't feel too bad." Fermy started coughing.

"They's not here, Fermy."

"What? Where have they got to, then? They were supposed to wait here for me."

Dorcas sighed and explained about the alert and going off to the house to rescue him. Of Anastasia and Benedict and Elsie's reappearance. The battle and the outcome. Fermy being in the wardrobe. Sammy going off to the hospital with Elsie.

"What about Jack, and his friend, that Jimmy?" said Fermy, alert now.

"They's not come back yet. I's am waiting for him here to come back safe. But nothings yet."

"Oh my grockles, they went into that place alone?"

"I's don't know; Elsie couldn't tell us. But they went with her and didn't come back here when she did."

Fermy stared at Dorcas with a look of panic.

"We have to go after them. That garden, oh my grockles and grackles, it is not what they think it is. It's a Fae Forest Daemon, and it's taken land-form. I've seen one before, a long time ago; a Lickovick or something it's called. That time, the thing took my friends, all of them! I could do nothing. Nothing! They prefer Fae, but they will take lifers if the opportunity presents itself and it's hungry enough. And if it snares Jack...."

He doubled over again, coughing, but he sounded less throaty and wet than before. Looking up at Dorcas with teary eyes, he whispered. "We need to go after them, and we are going to need help."

"Is it still after us?" panted Jimmy as they powered down the hill. "I can't see it without the stone thingy."

Jack risked a glance over his shoulder, set his head back, and sped up. "Yes. About ten car lengths behind us."

The Lisovyk yomped on behind the boys, the steady thump of its feet clear to Jack as it kept pace with them. It didn't seem to be able to go any faster, but likewise, it didn't seem to be tiring like the boys were.

"What can we do?" gasped Jimmy as they reached the bottom of the hill. "How can we get rid of it?"

"I don't know," panted Jack. "I'm pretty new to this. Fermy or Elsie might know, but...."

The boys sprinted across the road at the bottom of the hill without stopping. Angry car horns sounded as motorists slammed on their brakes; the road bathed in red lights as the cars halted. The boys weaved through the slow-moving cars and sprinted into the small park and its comforting shadows. They were heading for the gate on the opposite side when they heard an enormous crash followed by the blare of a car horn. They turned in unison for Jack to see the Lisovyk in the middle of the road with a car folded around one of its trunk-like legs. Jimmy could see the car, its front formed into a 'V' shape around the considerable dent, and he raised the Hagstone to his eye with one trembling hand. The Lisovyk sprang into view, and boy, was it mad!

The Lisovyk roared its wet, throaty screech and beat at the car in a rage with its thrashing vine-like arms. The horn continued to blare as the creature continued its assault on the vehicle, the car rocking as the windscreen shattered. The driver scrambled out of the door and ran for it as the apparent supernatural attack on his vehicle continued. The Lisovyk bashed it a few more times and then wrapped its vines around the smashed windscreen and side windows. With a screeching gargle, it picked the car up before throwing it onto the row of parked cars at the side of the road. People had their phones out, filming the car rising, propelled by some hidden force, before spinning through the air onto the row of stationary vehicles. Car alarms started squawking at once, and the Lisovyk screamed again in its fury, adding to the near-deafening sound. It glanced around, looking for its quarry.

"Do you think it can see us? It's pretty dark," whispered Jimmy, his chest heaving.

The Lisovyk's yellow eyes suddenly glanced towards where the boys stood in the park, shrouded in shadows, and it screeched in its recognition. It raised its arms like appendages towards the sky and screamed again. Jimmy saw it appear to him in a shower of black sparks, and the creature pointed precisely to where they were, shrouded by the darkness. It began its loping stride towards them again.

"*That'd be a yes. Come on!*" shouted Jack, starting his sprint towards the gates again. Jimmy put his head down and ran with him.

"I'm...not...sure...how much...longer...I can go," wheezed Jimmy to Jack as they cleared the gate and turned right along the road. The thump-thump was getting closer again as the Lisovyk loped across the park towards them.

"We have to find a way to stop it," Jack gasped. "I just can't think while I'm running; I have no ideas."

The boys sprinted across another road at the traffic lights that were handily on red. Behind them, the screech of the Lisovyk filled Jack's ears as it leapt over the small fence of the park and continued its pursuit.

Down the road, the boys ran, out of breath and blowing, faces red with the exertion. At the end of this road was the main road, and they could see the headlights of cars zipping back and forth rapidly. Another crunching sound came as the Lisovyk jumped onto the row of parked cars as it came round the corner, the roof of one squashed flat as it pushed itself off.

The boys met the main road and turned left, starting to slow now as exhaustion set in. Further down the road was Bloxton Academy, now mostly in darkness as the school was finished for the day, the caretakers having finished with their cleaning. As the boys slowed to a jog, the roar of the Lisovyk came again as it temporarily lost sight of them as they went around the corner.

"We're done for," said Jimmy hoarsely. "We can't outrun it."

"I know," Jack replied. "There's nothing that we can do; it's going to..." He stopped, staring at a van across the road that was stationary in the traffic. The driver was bobbing his head to some unheard music. Emblazoned across the side of the van were the legend 'Bits and Creases Ironing Service' with the catchphrase in italics, 'Pressed for Time? Call us!'

"Of course," said Jack, staring at Jimmy. "I'm an idiot; I'd completely forgotten. Iron. The Fae hate iron. If that thing is a Fae, then we need to find some iron!"

Jimmy looked at Jack, gone out. "Iron? Where the hell are we going to find some iron? We're not ironmongers, and nothing is made of just iron nowadays. Plus, we don't know if that thing is even a Faery!"

Another roar prompted them to speed up, forcing tired legs onwards.

"You got any better ideas, then I'm all ears. As for iron, I have no idea. How about the scrapyard?"

"Too far," croaked Jimmy. "Plus, it's all old cars and stuff. Trying to find old iron railings or something in the dark will be nigh on impossible. And there's a guard dog; it had Andy Watkins when he climbed in there for a bet."

"Think, Jim. Where are we going to find iron?"

Jimmy was silent for a moment as they kept the pace and then said, "It's a long shot, but I've got an idea. We need to go to school."

"Jim, there's no iron there; the fence is all that wire stuff now."

"Trust me, Jack; I think this could work, assuming that iron will stop that thing. If nothing else, we can lose it there if we can get in; it's too big to fit into the corridors and stuff."

Jack looked over his shoulder to see the Lisovyk closing in on them. It whipped down its arm-vines, and a small rain of wet mud pattered down near them. With horror, Jack saw a small, blue slug-like thing land on Jimmy's shoulder. He brushed it away quickly. The two took to their heels again.

"Okay, but how are we going to get in? Gate's will be shut now, and they're too tall to climb over."

"Got us covered there as well," gasped Jimmy. "Come on!"

FERMY AND DORCAS appeared in the garden of the home across the road from Twillington House and anxiously parted the hedge branches to get a view of what was happening. Across the road, the gates were firmly closed, and the driveway looked to be dark. Every light was on, though; they could see the top of the house peeping over the surrounding wall.

"We will have to go and see, much as I don't want to," said Fermy faintly. "If they're in there, we need to try and get them out. However, stay off that garden, whatever you do. If we have to go in through the front door, then so be it." He steeled himself and set across the road at a trot. Dorcas patted the rolling pin in the flat of her hand. *'I's be getting my Jack back; make's no mistakes,'* she thought as she followed Fermy out of the shade of the bushes towards the sinister house and its gardens.

Getting to the gates, Fermy touched them and recoiled a little. "Fae locked," he said. "As will be the rest of the damn place. How are we going to get in it?"

Dorcas was studying the pavement outside the gate; there was a big smear of mud, the size of a dustbin lid, outside the gate. There was another one about two meters away, heading down the hill and away from the house. In that one lay a clod of earth with a worm wriggling in it. As Fermy tapped around the wall next to the gate, Dorcas moved a little further down the hill and saw a third mark. A little further on, a fourth.

"Fermy," she called. "Looks at these. Theys looks like footprints to me, and they go down that way. How odds!"

Fermy came over to look and went pale.

"Oh, my grockles; you're right! It has assumed a mobile form. If it's gone that way, away from its hunting ground, it must be chasing something. And I'll give you one guess who it's after."

Dorcas gave a shocked gasp. "Not my Jacks. I's not allow it to hurts my Jack. Come on." She started to trot down the hill, but Fermy called her back.

"There's nothing we can do, just the two of us. We will need help. One of those things took out my whole group the last time

I tackled one. Glamours don't work too well on it, and the one that was after us was immense. I doubt even you could take it down, Dorcas."

"I's willing to try," said Dorcas bravely but with a little shudder.

"I know, I know. However, I doubt that we will succeed. We need a Forest Fae, something that can appeal to its physical makeup. That thing will be made of mud and plants and all sorts of earth creatures. We need help from someone who can command those things, someone like a Pan or…."

He tailed off, thinking and then sang softly to himself

Though Solitary he would choose to stay,
He may help those who lose their way,
But don't misjudge this dark-haired fae,
Or you'll be the one he doth betray.

He looked at Dorcas. "I know where to find a Fae who can help us without too much searching. The dark-haired lad! As there are children involved, I am hopeful that he would not refuse, despite the shyness. He certainly has no love for those dark Faeries. Come on."

Fermy held up his hand, and Dorcas took it. With a fleeting whisper, they appeared in the wilds, a vast lake ahead of them, barely visible through the trees that hung overhead.

"We need to find a birch tree," Fermy said, glancing at the bristling trees, the wind whistling about them. With a snap of his fingers, he glamoured a floating ball of light and set it to float above their heads. Dorcas set off with a purpose, looking at each tree in the glimmering light as she moved around their area. The ground underneath was wet and marshy, and she tutted as she lifted her muddy shoes to examine them.

Calling over to Fermy, she said, "When we's arriving back to Jacks, you's is taking off your shoes before you's is going in that house. I spent too longs today cleaning the floors, and I have to set that lounge straight now."

"Shush," said Fermy, as he stopped under a large tree, the silvery bark glistening in the light of the glamour. He placed both hands against the tree and then leaned his forehead against it. He chanted under his breath a strange whispering tune, like leaves rustling in the wind. Finishing, he stood back and clapped both hands against the tree. He closed his eyes.

After a few minutes, Dorcas said, "Where is this dark-haired boy's then? Because we needs to get back and helps Jack and Jimmy. We can't stay's here."

"Help who?" came a tinkling voice, light and airy. From behind the silver birch trunk stepped a petite Fae, about a foot high and clad in moss and leaves. He had an aura of youth about him, and his hair was dark in the flickering light of Fermy's glamour.

"Ghillie Dhu," exclaimed Fermy. "It's been too long!"

"Well, hello, Fermerillion! You are right; it had been an aeon. How do you fare?"

"Well, thank you. As do you, I hope? May I introduce my good friend Dorcas to you?" Fermy gestured over at the brownie, who made an awkward curtsey, holding the bottom of her dress.

Ghillie Dhu acknowledged Dorcas with a nod of his head. Turning to Fermy, he said, "I would assume that you coming here, to the northern wilds in the dark, means that you are seeking something from me?"

"To the point as always, Ghillie. And yes, as always, I would ask for your help in a matter concerning two young friends of ours and a particularly nasty Lossovic...lickyvich....forest daemon Fae."

Ghillie Dhu looked at the two friends with a curious look on his face.

"A Lisovyk? Here on the island that the lifers call the Kingdom? That is most odd; those creatures do not belong in this land."

"Yes, I know. The last time I encountered one, it bested our whole group. But it was not here; it was in a land far away."

"They are of extraordinary power. And what does it want with the children?"

"That I don't know, but we know it is in pursuit of them. I was held enthralled by it until only a short time ago; only the administrations of my friends broke my entrapment. We need your help to stop it; I am no forest Fae and have no glamours that could do what we need."

Ghillie Dhu looked from one to the other. "Alas, I cannot help you directly on this matter; I have responsibilities of my own here to attend to."

"Can you recommend anyone who can help us?" said Fermy, a note of desperation in his voice. "We need to move against this creature now."

"I am afraid not. I know not of the location of the Lords of the Green or their retinue at this time; I believe that they may well be in Faery itself. And I know of no one else who would have the power to stop a Lisovyk if it is intent on its prey."

Dorcas stepped forward and fixed the Fae with an icy stare. "Looks, Master Dhu, my Jack is in's trouble with a monster Fae. We come's here to gets help, and we is not leaving without's it. If you wish, I can conks your noggin and takes you with us against your will. But you must help's us with this monster if you's can. And now."

Ghillie Dhu rubbed his chin and stared at the brownie. "Dorcas, Dorcas... You aren't the Dorcas that bested Jenny Greenteeth, are you? That story is a legend in the Fae taverns. Jenny Noteeth, they call her now, and she is really not happy."

Dorcas looked at her feet in embarrassment, scuffing her shoes in the mud. "She was trying to takes my Maisie with's her. She would nots take no for an answer."

Ghillie Dhu threw back his head and laughed a tinkling laugh that was far louder than his diminutive stature allowed. He patted Dorcas on the leg.

"Oh dear, oh, dear. I do not want to become the talk of Faery myself, at the hands of the fearsome Dorcas! I will help you in what little way I can. I will teach you the song of winter's sleep; that will help you, but it will not best the creature on its own. If it has taken form from the land it was within, it will be full of natural plants and animals; these will sleep away the winter. You can slow it down."

Dorcas curtsied again. "Thank yous, Master Dhu. However, please, teaches the song to Fermy here; he is much better at rememberings such things than me. My talents is different."

"Of that, I have little doubt, my legendary friend. Now, Fermerillion. Please take heed."

CHAPTER 15

"This way, quick," panted Jimmy, turning into an alleyway that ran adjacent to the school, the high fence bordering it. The thumping of the Lisovyk's pursuit rang heavily in their ears.

"Are you mad? This goes into Morningside," said Jack gasping again. "Saying that, if that thing wants to smash the place up, it'd be doing us all a favour."

"There's a way into the school through the hedge, just down here," gasped Jimmy. "Never...fenced...it."

Dashing down the alleyway, the boys took a right at the end and ran along the road that bordered the school. At the end of the road was a large, threadbare hedge and a couple of trees, and Jimmy led them towards this. Behind them, they could hear the wet roars of the Lisovyk as it took a more direct route through the fences that bordered the alleyway, leaving a trail of smashed panels in its wake.

The gap in the hedge loomed, the school playing fields on the other side. A few wayward branches grew across it, but Jimmy burst through, quickly followed by Jack. Both boys were breathing heavily now and rubbing at the stitches in their sides.

"What...is...the...plan?" Jack whispered through a dry mouth as they limped across the field to the dark school. Glancing behind him, he saw the Lisovyk clear the hedge with one of its long legs and come racing across the field towards them. It roared in triumph as its quarry was slowing down.

"Science...lab," panted Jimmy. Jack looked at Jimmy, puzzled, but was trying to save his breath.

The boys reached the main school building at a jog, tiring rapidly, and dashed around the corner.

"This...way," said Jimmy in a hoarse voice. "Try...the...side...door."

Jack grabbed the door handle and pulled it. Locked.

"Next one," he said, sprinting on.

The next door was locked, as was the main entrance. The boys heard a metallic crash from the side of the school, followed by more roars that echoed in Jack's ears.

"I think that was the bike sheds. It's close now. Come on!" he yelled to Jimmy, who was pushing at a window.

They'd almost finished a circuit of the main building, and all the doors were locked. A couple of lights shone on the upper floors, but there was no sign of any caretakers or anyone else through the mostly shuttered windows. Jimmy was starting to despair.

"There's no way in," he said, catching his breath in huge, hitching gasps.

"Why the science lab?" asked Jack

"Iron-containing chemicals. I'm sure there was some in there."

"But steel and stuff has iron in it, and it doesn't affect the Fae much," said Jack, his heart falling now that he realised what Jimmy's plan was. Jimmy looked at him.

"I know. But those chemicals in there are iron salts and stuff, counter ions. They'll have some free iron floating about in them. Worth a try."

"I've got nothing else," said Jack. "And if that thing is going to get us, I'm not going down without a fight. Let's do it."

"How are we going to get in, though?" said Jimmy.

"Like this," said Jack. He marched over to one of the many litter bins scattered around the school, pulled off the fibreglass top, and hauled the metal bucket out of it. He tipped it over, a cascade of empty crisp and sweet wrappers tumbling from it.

"Get back, Jim," he yelled and swung the metal bucket at the window. It bounced off with a metallic clang, but the window cracked. Jack swung it again and was rewarded with a huge piece of glass falling into the room with a smash. He swung again, dislodging even more glass and making a hole big enough for them to both climb through. He quickly rubbed the side of the bin against the bottom frame to clear the spikes of leftover glass and then threw the bin behind him.

"Quickly, get in."

"Don't have to tell me twice," said Jimmy, cocking a leg over the sill and hauling himself in. Jack followed him in as quickly as he could, avoiding the broken glass, and dropped onto the floor of the classroom.

"Language lab," said Jimmy, panting less now as he got his breath back. "Science department is on the other side of the school."

"Why is nothing ever easy?" replied Jack. "I guess we'd better get...."

He was cut off by a loud crunching noise outside as the Lisovyk stepped onto the metal bin they had left under the window. Vine-like hands appeared on either side of the broken window as the creature bent its misshapen face down to the gap and peered in at the boys with its candle-flame eyes. Its mouth opened, and it gave a colossal, gargling roar, its stinking breath smelling of old, wet earth as it glared at the boys.

Jack and Jimmy had backed up to the far side of the classroom against the whiteboard, staring at the creature in horror.

The Lisovyk pressed its face into the gap in the broken window, a root-like tongue tasting the air as it did. The sides of its face caught against the remaining shards of glass, and the creature stopped.

"Hah!" called Jimmy. "Too big and ugly to get in here, eh? Stay out there, you walking landfill!"

The creature seemed to draw in a breath, and then with a phlegmy cough, showered the boys with a splash of muddy, wet slime. Within the gunge was a multitude of blue squirming slugs that writhed on the boy's clothes and faces, trying to get a purchase.

Jack started to brush them off and realised that he was having difficulties moving his arms; it was as if some strange paralysis was setting over him. Jimmy was standing locked in place, his terrified eyes staring at Jack as he tried to speak, but he could not move his jaw muscles. Around him, the slugs moved slowly about on his forehead and cheeks, seemingly disorientated. The Lisovyk started to make guttural honking noises at the back of its throat, rhythmic, its head shaking. Its plant-like arms started to snake in through the window, slowly twisting towards them, taking its time as it relished the last few moments before the capture.

That thing is laughing at us, thought Jack. *Unbelievable! That thing is actually laughing at us! It nearly kills my friend, chases us across half the town, freezes us, and now it's laughing at us! I am going...* The following words came aloud in anger. "...To kill you, you lousy stinking pile of...."

Jack shrugged off the paralysis like he was tearing off cobwebs, and he turned to Jimmy and started wiping the slugs off his friend's skin, stamping on them as they hit the ground. Jimmy blinked a few times and then said in a small voice, "Thanks, Jack. I think I can move again, but..."

Behind them came a roar, its tone disbelief. The Lisovyk was staring at them, and the rage in its eyes was unmistakable.

Instead of reaching for the boys, the arms thrashed about, looking for purchase. Grasping onto a couple of desks, it pulled and pushed its head forward into the room through the broken window. The head and part of its torso hit the ground with a mushy splatting sound as it started to pull the rest of its body into the room. Its body was elongating, like a snake, as it fitted itself through the window. Jack was reminded of a video he had seen online of an octopus squeezing itself through a tiny opening.

Jack looked at Jimmy. "Time to go again!" he croaked in terror as Jimmy stared in disbelief at the creature forcing itself into the room. Jimmy twitched his legs; they seemed okay and moved again now that the slug's effects were fading.

"Good to go!" he cried. "Other end of the school to the chemistry department; then we'll see. Come on."

They shoved open the door to the corridor and dashed through it. The wailing of an alarm suddenly drowned out the screeching howl of the Lisovyk; the boys' movement triggered the school's motion sensor burglar alarm system.

"Oh, great," panted Jack. "Police will be here shortly."

"Don't worry about it; with the government cuts, they won't be here for hours," Jimmy gasped back. "This way."

The door crashed open behind them, and the Lisovyk pulled itself into the corridor. It appeared to be elongated, its legs no longer there, melded into its snake-like length. The heads of the trapped Fae could be seen along its back, like some sort of fin sticking out amongst the lumps of earth and tangled roots. It had retained its arm-vines, and its head was unaffected, lumpy with the slash of a mouth and candle-like eyes. It fixed the boys with a look of complete evil and screeched again before pulling itself rapidly towards them, swimming with its arms and writhing its body like a snake to get forward momentum

"Is that thing never going to give up?" screamed Jimmy over the noise. The boys sprinted around the corner of the corridor, the wailing of the alarm and the smashing and breaking noises loud as the Lisovyk continued its pursuit.

FERMY AND DORCAS reappeared next to the gates of Twillington House and immediately set off after the muddy footprints that led down the hill. Fermy started panting after a few minutes, his legs being a lot shorter than Dorcas's, so he held up one hand and called a stop.

"Why are we running? We'll just hop the distances, pick up the footprints each time?" Dorcas nodded, the concern for Jack and Jimmy etched on her face. She had a bad feeling about this monster. The two held hands and transported themselves to the bottom of the hill. Here they were met with the blue flashing lights of several police cars as they surveyed the damaged cars. Lifers were mingling everywhere, talking to the police and each other in high, agitated voices. Of course, none of them could see Fermy and Dorcas as they weaved their way between the legs of the lifers, Fermy on Dorcas's shoulder to stop him from being trampled on.

"Try the park," said Fermy, pointing, and the two jumped to the middle of the park. The footprints, clearly visible, went across the grassed area and over the fence. They jumped again and picked up the muddy splodges as they went around the corner and towards the main road. Here was another police officer talking to a man who was gesturing at his car, the roof caved in with a lump of mud-encrusted in the dent.

"We're on the right track," said Fermy.

"I hope's that it hasn't gots anywhere nears Jack yet," said Dorcas anxiously. "Next hop."

The two appeared near the main road and glanced around for footprints. They saw the muddy splotches leading off down the pavement towards a big dark building. The sound of an alarm could be heard faintly in the distance. They hopped to outside the gates and saw the sign 'Bloxton Academy' looming above them. There was no sign of any footprints, but the school alarm was blaring.

"Not here," said Fermy. "Go back to where we saw the last ones and...."

A dim roar stopped him mid-sentence. He glanced at Dorcas, who nodded. "In's there," she said, pointing at the school. "They must have gone in's there; it's their school. They must be trying to hides. Quick, Fermy."

The two hopped over to the main entrance, which stood in darkness. The alarm blared on and on as the two friends strained their ears to get a clue as to where the monster had gone. The sound of a distance crash followed by another roar confirmed where the creature was.

The two looked at each other, held hands, and appeared on the other side of the locked door.

"*Let's go get Jack away from that thing*," shouted Fermy with resolve over the wailing noise of the alarm.

"Rights. And if its hurts my Jack, then I will kills it," said Dorcas, her jaw set firmly. She pulled the rolling pin out of her pocket.

The two set off down the corridor in the direction of the last roar.

THE TWO BOYS ran through the science block doors, which bore the legend '*Department of Science. If you're not part of the solution, you're part of the precipitate.*' Jimmy made a rude gesture at the sign as he ran under it.

"Just not funny," he said. "That thing could do a lot worse than smash that sign down; do us all a favour!"

They rounded the corner, and Jimmy skidded to a halt on

the polished wooden floor and called to Jack, "Here. This door. This is it; the chemistry department and the stores are down there. If there's anything to be had, it'll be in there, locked up."

Jack tried the handle and cursed. "For the love of… Just once, I'd like one of these doors to be unlocked."

"I guess they lock it because of all the chemicals and stuff; I've been in the stores down here a few times, and the store's not exactly secure."

Behind them came a roar and a crashing sound.

"That'll be the sixth form lockers. Boy, are they going to be mad," said Jimmy. "How are we going to get through? There's nothing to smash this door down with, and it looks pretty sturdy."

"Time to try something. Chuck us the pen off that white-board," said Jack, cracking his knuckles. "Be quick."

Jack drew an 'open' travel glyph carefully onto the door and slapped it. It fell away in golden sparkles.

"Yes! First time!" he said, yanking the door open to see a corridor dancing with blue flames.

"I didn't know you could do that trick!" said Jimmy, dashing through the door.

"I've been practising," said Jack, drawing the 'unlock' glyph on the back of the door; he slapped it again and then yanked the door open. The corridor to the Chemistry department stood before them. Stepping through the door, they now stood on the other side of the locked door.

"That is so cool," said Jimmy. "You could be a criminal mastermind with that!"

"I don't think Auntie Elsie would let me, let alone Mum," said Jack.

"Can we use it to get away?" said Jimmy.

"Binks shouted that we couldn't. I'll try, though."

Jack quickly resketched the open glyph on the door and

slapped it. The golden dust fell away, but the door wouldn't open, despite them both tugging on it.

"I had home fixed in my mind. I guess that that thing must have some sort of power that stops people from getting a long way away from it."

Jimmy nodded. "Okay, Plan A, it still is. Let's get in there and see what we can find."

The boys walked down the corridor, and Jimmy stopped halfway down.

"This one," he said, and, pulling open the door, the boys stepped into the stores.

"Whoa...okay," said Jack. The room itself wasn't large and contained a stained desk underneath the window as its only furniture; papers stacked haphazardly on it. The room smelt strongly of chemicals, not offensive, but not particularly pleasant either. However, the cause of Jack's dismay was the shelves. They filled every part of the room up to ceiling level, and on them were all kinds of bottles of liquids, jars of powders, and plastic tubs of all colours and sizes.

Jack gulped and looked at Jimmy. "Okay then, brainbox, this was your idea. What are we looking for?"

"Anything that has 'Iron' on it, or the chemical symbol, 'Fe.' Stick it all on that desk there, and we've got ourselves some fightback materials."

The boys started skimming over the bottles but jumped at the sound of a resounding bang, clearly echoing over the sound of the continuously wailing alarm.

"What was that?" said Jimmy

"I think it's found us," said Jack. He stuck his head into the corridor and glanced up it. The locked door was still closed, but a large dark shape was blocking out the overhead lights through the privacy glass. There was a gurgling roar and another bang, the door shaking in its hinges.

"We need to find that iron. Now," said Jack, his eyes not leaving the door.

Another bang and the door creaked alarmingly, the window shattering. A vine-like arm slithered through, groping for purchase.

"Find some way to slow it down, Jack; I'll sort the chemicals," said Jimmy frantically, running back into the stores.

"How the heck am I supposed to do that?" he shouted to Jimmy's retreating back.

The Lisovyk's second arm trailed through the broken window, and it seized either side of the door. It pulled, and Jack could hear the wood cracking even through the noise of the wailing alarm. A large split appeared in the centre of the door, running the whole length.

'It's going to be through any second, what to do, what to do?' His panicked mind screamed at him as he glanced around. His eye caught the fire alarm button, bold and red, on the wall. Not that that would help over the security alarm, but…

Jack glanced up the corridor and saw what he was looking for. Bloxton Academy, for its fancy name, was still a school built in the early 1980s. An era of the sand bucket and the fire hose. And there it was, snug against the wall; a wheel painted a cream colour over the former red now to match the wall, the old hose wrapped around it. A couple of more modern fire extinguishers were next to it, mounted on the wall.

'Let's see if that still works,' thought Jack, dashing over to it and pulling at the hose. The hose unravelled a bit before sticking. Jack gave it a yank, and with a cloud of dust, it came free.

"*Yes!*" he shouted, pointed the end at the broken window, and turned the bar-like handle on the end of the hose. Nothing happened. The door gave another crack and suddenly folded in on itself. The Lisovyk gave a screech of triumph and pulled its slug-like body through the broken entrance, its flame-like eyes fixed on Jack.

Jack wiggled the handle a couple more times and nothing. He was starting to panic now as he looked at the hose. Why wasn't it working? Then, a small, still voice spoke in his head, the voice of his granddad.

"When you've got a problem, why not start at the beginning and see how to fix it?"

Jack looked at the hose and then over at the wall. Up the corridor, the Lisovyk hauled even more of its body through the gap, its movement becoming faster as it cleared the narrow doorway, the mud and earth oozing back into place along its bulky, slug-like body.

Jack spotted the problem straight away and gasped. There was a tap on the hose at the base, under the wheel. It was a lever tap, painted cream like the rest of the wheel, but he could see the original red through the paint.

'*Please don't be painted shut,*' he prayed as he grabbed it and yanked it up. It gave with the pressure, and immediately he could hear the hiss of water as the hose filled.

"*Yes!*" he shouted again and pointed the hose at the oncoming Lisovyk, twisting the handle on the nozzle. This time water shot out of the end in a powerful jet, the hose bucking in his hand with the power of the stream. The water was a murky red colour, dirty, and he wrestled the stream over and pointed it at the face of the Lisovyk as it slithered towards him. The result was instantaneous.

Great lumps of mud and earth were swept from the creature's misshapen head as the powerful jet streaked across the breadth of the creature, knocking off lumps and tangles of grass and leaves from its body. The creature stopped and swiped at the spray, its waving arms ineffective against the powerful jet as it blasted bits off it. The floor immediately became a filthy, muddy swamp as the water streamed off the monster. The Lisovyk roared again, and Jack quickly silenced it with a well-aimed jet into its wide, open mouth, the cry becoming even more of a gargle as the water streaked into it.

Jack backed up as the creature moved slowly down the corridor under the blast of water, aiming it at the head and bits of the torso he could see. However, earth and mud from further down its body seemed to ooze back up to replace those parts that were knocked off, and the slickness on the floor eased the creature's passage further; it pulled itself forward faster, the arm vines grasping at things to increase its momentum as it came.

"Jimmy, whatever you're doing in there, make it fast," Jack hollered, the hose now frantically spraying in all directions at the Lisovyk as it glided towards him. The creature shot out one of its twisted arms, stretching to an almost impossible length, fingers grasping, and Jack ducked underneath it. The creature then grabbed with its other arm, and Jack dodged again, slipping in the muck and water on the corridor floor. As he tried to regain his balance, the Lisovyk grabbed a loop of the hose. It stared at Jack, and he swore he saw gloating in its eyes as it tore the hose from his grasp, the shock of it causing Jack to slip over and land on his backside. The Lisovyk roared again, and it sounded like laughter, its head bobbing with each guttural utterance.

Jack frantically pedalled backwards, his shoes slipping on the slimy floor as he sought purchase. The Lisovyk dropped the hose and dragged itself towards him as he desperately tried to escape it. It quickly caught up with him and drew itself up; its head touched the ceiling, leaving muddy smears on the white foam tiles there. Jack watched in terror as the Lisovyk grabbed him by the leg and lifted him slowly off the floor.

"Jimmy, help!" screamed Jack. *"It's got me, help me, help me!"*

The Lisovyk lifted Jack towards its face, its head splitting horizontally as its mouth yawned open wide, and its throat widened. Jack could see its root-like teeth wriggling in its jaws as it lowered him slowly towards the gaping hole. Its throat was dark, muddy, but Jack could see a deep dark yellow at the bottom of the hole, like a fire but seemingly liquid that ebbed and flowed. He started to squeeze his eyes shut in despair of being swallowed when he saw through the narrow slits something spin past him and glance off the side of the Lisovyk's head. He opened his eyes again to see Jimmy, his arms clutching some chemical bottles as he launched another one at the massive open mouth.

"*Let him go!*" Jimmy screamed as he flicked the top off another bottle and flung it up, this time scoring a direct hit as it landed in the creature's open mouth. The blue liquid in the bottle glugged out, and the effects were startling. The Lisovyk gave a strangled shriek and dropped Jack, who landed awkwardly, his knee catching himself in the face and stunning him slightly. The Lisovyk's arms snaked into its mouth and pulled out the bottle, casting it aside to smash against the wall. What looked like steam issued from its mouth as its hands dug out vast globs of mud and earth and dropped them to the floor.

"Yes," shouted Jimmy triumphantly and threw another bottle, the liquid spilling from it as it arced through the air. It hit the side of the Lisovyk's head but lodged in the sticky mud there, the liquid running down its face. The Lisovyk gave another tremendous shriek and pulled at the side of its face to dislodge the bottle, yanking another considerable chunk of earth out and casting it aside. It lowered its head down from the ceiling, clamping its mouth shut, and its misshapen head, now more so with a large piece missing, fixed on Jimmy. Its yellow flame eyes looked murderous, and Jimmy stepped back a couple of steps, the last of his bottles held in one hand and a large plastic tub in the other. The Lisovyk screeched and started to flail its arms at Jimmy, who hopped back again, dropping his prizes as he raised his hands to protect his face. The Lisovyk whacked Jimmy several times, whip-cracking sounds which drove the boy to his knees, his arms wrapped around his head, screaming in pain and terror.

Jack shook his head to clear it from the stunning effect of his fall and saw drops of blood flick away as he did so. He raised his hand to his face and pulled it away bloody; his nose was gushing from taking a knee to it, but it didn't feel too painful, and he could touch it. The Lisovyk's attention was on his friend now as it flailed at him, so he got shakily to his feet and looked around for the hose. It was trapped under the oozing body of the Lisovyk now, and there was no way he'd be able to pull it free. He glanced around in despair for another weapon he could use, but there was nothing; he couldn't get to Jimmy and the chemicals he'd found as the arms snaked backwards and forwards, stopping him. The creature suddenly stopped its torment of Jimmy and reared up again, grasping the boy as it did so. Its mouth yawned open again as it started to raise the boy to swallow him. Jimmy didn't struggle at all; his eyes were closed, and his face was pale.

Jack didn't know what to do; he was frozen at the sight of his unconscious friend dangling in the air, helpless as the creature's maw yawned wider. Tears formed at the corners of his eyes when he heard a booming shout, far louder than the wailing alarm as if it was magically amplified.

"Hang on Jack. We're coming."

He whirled around, and at the other end of the corridor, Jack saw Dorcas dash into view, with Fermy riding on her shoulder.

"Help us!" he screamed at them. *"It's got Jimmy!"*

He watched as Fermy jumped down off Dorcas behind the Lisovyk and spread his arms wide. His lips seemed to be moving as if he was chanting. The Lisovyk stopped attempting to swallow Jimmy and turned its head towards the little Feeorin, a puzzled look upon its face. Jack saw that roots and branches that composed the creature's body were popping out of the muddy, slug-like body and twitching in the air. The vine-like arms had also stopped their movement and stood twitching in the air, Jimmy still suspended.

Dorcas, in the meantime, had leapt onto the rear of the creature and was running the length of it, her feet using the heads of the trapped Fae like stepping-stones to avoid the muck that made up the Lisovyk's back as she bounced towards Jack. Jack watched aghast as the brownie mounted the Lisovyk's head and, drawing up to her full height, raised her rolling pin up, both hands on one handle, the other handle sticking out of the main shaft like a blunt spike. With a roaring battle scream that drowned out the noise of the alarms, using all of her strength, Dorcas drove the blunt spike down and into one of the creature's yellow eyes. The rolling pin disappeared almost up to Dorcas's wrists, and the Lisovyk screamed in agony, thrashing its head as the yellow light snuffed out. It rocketed its head forwards, and Dorcas was thrown clear, the pin remaining stuck, skidding along the floor in the mud almost to Jack's feet.

The brownie didn't hang about and vaulted straight to her feet. The Lisovyk was clawing at its face again for the rolling pin, its arms still strangely slow, but it seemed unable to grasp the rolling pin that skewered its face. It dropped Jimmy to enable it to use both hands, and Dorcas was there to break his fall, catching the boy in her strong arms. She glanced over at Jack, taking him in now for the first time.

"Oh, Jack, your poor noses! I can fix thats, but you need's to help me now. Fermy can only slow that thing for so's long; it will get controls over its natural parts any time soon, and then we is in real troubles."

The two pulled Jimmy along the corridor out of the way of the thrashing Lisovyk, Jack looking at Dorcas with newfound respect.

"*How did you hurt it?*" he yelled over the creature's baying screeches and the alarm. "We've been trying to stop it in all kinds of ways, and look at us! You just took out its eye without even thinking about it."

"*Don'ts know*," Dorcas yelled back. "Just used Great Grannie's pin. It is glamoured; it always comes back. Monster there doesn't like glamoured weapons I is thinking,"

She held out her hand, and the rolling pin dislodged from the Lisovyk's eye, spinning through the air as it returned to her hand. The creature roared again and thrashed about, one single yellow eye rolling in its head maliciously. The two dragged Jimmy further down the corridor away from the creature. Jack could see Fermy still at the end of the corridor, eyes closed and arms wide, his lips moving.

"Jack!" Dorcas waved to get his attention. "Draws a travel glyph on that doors there. We needs to get out of here, and we's can't take you two alongs with us without travel glamours. You need to gets Jimmy out of here."

"It won't make any difference," Jack called back. "That thing has something that stops travelling a long distance so that it can follow us; it has been all night. It will just keep coming. Binks said our 'clever travelling tricks' won't help us."

"Then how's are we going to escape it?"

"Do you know where there are any other glamoured weapons we can use?" asked Jack.

"I's don't knows. I's not an expert on Faery glamours. Fermy may knows, but he's busy!"

"Jack," came a whisper, quiet and unheard.

All of a sudden, the Lisovyk stopped its screeching and turned its head towards Fermy. It hitched a couple of times and then coughed up a huge ball of muddy slime that it spat towards Fermy. The little Feeorin, with his eyes shut as he chanted, had no chance as the slime ball caught him and bowled him over. He coughed and spluttered and started frantically brushing at the blue slug-like creatures that were crawling all over him, shouting his disgust, his glamour song broken.

"Jack," came the whisper again.

The Lisovyk turned towards the other three, its movements faster now that Fermy's and Ghillie Dhu's song was no longer restricting it. The roots and branches retracted back into its body, and it sped up, oozing its way towards the three again. Its face and single flickering eye stared at the Jack and Dorcas, a look of sly cunning evident as it wormed its way towards them.

"Jack," came the whisper a third time, more urgently, and this time Jack heard. Glancing around, he saw Jimmy's bruised and pale face, eyes wide open, staring up at him.

"Jack," he said again and pointed at the plastic tub he had dropped. "I bought the big guns." Jimmy's head then dropped forward again as consciousness left him.

Jack looked at the oncoming Lisovyk and the plastic tub, judging the distance. He then launched himself forwards and grabbed the tub, slipping over again in the sludgy mud as he did so. The Lisovyk roared and grabbed for him, only to be distracted by the rolling pin that spun through the air, catching it just below its remaining eye. The momentary distraction gave Jack enough time to scramble back out of its reach, clutching his prize.

Back at Dorcas's side, he glanced at the label on the tub, and the label, which partially read "Property of Department of Physics." He shook the container and heard the rustle inside, remembering the lesson they had used this stuff. He glanced down at Jimmy and patted his friend.

"Big guns indeed!"

He turned to Dorcas and held up the tub. "I think that I can kill it, but I will need your help. I have to let it get me near its mouth. After that, I need whatever you can do to help me get away from it. If you can get its mouth closed as well, then do it; it has been pulling bits out of itself to avoid the chemicals. But DO NOT stay near it longer than necessary. Do you understand, Dorcas?"

"No, Jack. It is too dangerouses for you. Let me do this. What is that things?"

"A little something from the Physics department," he said with a dark grin. He showed her the tub more closely, and she recoiled a little.

"See, I can't let you, Dorcas. It has to be me."

Dorcas looked at Jack, and a huge smile split her face.

"I likes this. Yes, Jack. I is ready. I will do what is needed."

Jake smiled back and tucked the container into his coat in the big pocket, the little pocket already containing the hard-fought-for tube. He then stepped forward to the Lisovyk, his arms up. The creature stopped and regarded him in a puzzled manner.

"You win," shouted Jack, staring the creature in the face as it towered over him. "Take me but leave my friends alone."

The Lisovyk started to give its hitching gurgling laugh again and grabbed Jack by the legs with one of its vine-like arms, coiling itself around him like a constrictor. It hoisted him into the air, flipping him upside down, and held him, swaying, in front of its face, panting its foul breath.

"*Nooooo*," screamed Fermy from further down the corridor and hurled a glamour at the back of the creature's head. It didn't flinch as the red sparking ball hit it and dissipated.

"Fermy, it's okay," called Jack. "If it takes me, then it will leave you alone."

"Iiiiyyyy ttaakkkkesss yyoo aawwwwllll," gurgled the Lisovyk in a throaty, wet voice, laughing its wet chuckle as it did so. Its head started to split open again as it opened its huge mouth and hoisted Jack over it. Its panting breath stank of wet and rot, and it hovered Jack over its extended mouth. Jack could see the gouged-out parts of its throat where it had pulled out the earth and chemicals that Jimmy had thrown in there. And at the bottom of the throat, the liquid yellow fire swirled and ebbed. It started to lower Jack into its maw again, laughing its wet laugh as it did so.

Jack felt his earlier anger filling him again, a cold rage. He waited until he was well over its mouth and said quietly, "Stop."

The Lisovyk did stop, puzzled at the lack of fear in its victim.

"Last chance," said Jack, still quietly. "Let us go and go back to wherever you came from before you met Binks."

The creature spoke again, gargling as it did. "Nooohhh. Yooouu will allllll cooommmme wwithh meee, ffooooools," the words drawn out by its throaty warble.

"*You are not taking anyone else, you stinking pile of soil. Eat this!*" Jack suddenly screamed and pulled the tub from his jacket as he swung suspended over its mouth. He yanked the cap loose and hurled the tub as hard as he could down into the creature's throat. The tub twisted in mid-air, the contents spilling out in an arc, sprinkling the inside of the creature's throat as it fell, before plopping into the yellow liquid at the base of the throat, where it promptly sank.

The Lisovyk's single eye went wild, rolling around crazily as its body started to contort, bucking and twisting as it cast Jack aside for him to hit the wall, the impact driving the air from his lungs. It swirled and writhed in agony; its slug-like body tried to roll up into a coil as it thrashed about. Down the corridor, Fermy cast glamour after sparkling glamour at it in rapid succession, trying to bind it but only slowing it down marginally. The creature's arms snaked towards its mouth again.

Jack shook his head to clear it and screamed, "*Now, Dorcas! Do it if you can!*"

The brownie bounded over the giant thrashing body as it bucked towards where its head was rocking backwards and forwards in its throes, the rolling pin gripped firmly in hand. Dorcas stood ready, braced with feet apart, moving slightly to avoid the flailing creature as she bided her time. Then her moment came as the creature's head rocketed down towards the ground at speed, its open mouth screaming and screeching, almost as if it was going to crush her. As it came towards her on its downward arc, Dorcas held up the rolling pin like a spear and, using the creature's own weight, jammed the rolling pin through the bottom of its jaw, up through the open mouth and into the top of its palate. The weight of the creature bearing down jammed the pin into place, its mouth snapping shut as Dorcas rolled clear.

The Lisovyk started to give muted hollers, getting slowly quieter as it clutched over and over again at the rolling pin sealing its mouth shut, unable to get a grasp to pull it free as its root-like claws slipped off its surface. Its movements became slower and slower as it fell onto its side, the vine arms grasping and clawing at the floor as it twitched and thrashed. The creature fixed its one eye onto Jack, and the look of malicious hatred made Jack's skin crawl as it stared at him. The yellow flame eye stared at him as the creature's death throes stopped. With a final evil blink, the yellow flame suddenly snuffed out, and the creature became still.

Jack stood panting, his nose streaming blood as he stared at the vanquished creature. From down the corridor came a cry of, "Yes!", as Fermy made his way towards them through the slippery mud covering the hall floor. He ran to Jack and hugged him around his knees.

"You clever boy! You genius! What did you do?"

Jack wiped his streaming nose and gave the lid off the tub to Fermy, who gave a slight shudder as he held it. Printed neatly on the lid was the text 'Iron filings. Magnetism, KS3 Works'.

"It wasn't me; it was Jimmy," said Jack, gesturing at his friend who lay still and quiet on the floor.

"Jack, lets me look at that noses, please," said Dorcas anxiously. Jack knelt and tipped his head back. The brownie mopped at the blood with the hem of her dress and peered at it from side to side.

"It's not brokens, I think. My's medicine is back at the house; we should goes there now while we can, and I can fix this."

"What about these other Fae?" Jack said, gesturing to the heads sticking out of the still muddy body of the Lisovyk. "We can't leave them here."

"I will call in a favour from the Courts; I am sure that they will be very interested in what has happened here, and they can help these poor folk as well," said Fermy. "I will make contact as soon as we are away from this place and that damnable noise."

"I can get a travel glyph drawn now if we can find something to write with," said Jack, glancing around and patting his pockets. He felt the bulge inside the coat and smiled.

"Fermy, I got the tube thing as well when we went into the house. I've got it here."

"Jack, you are starting to amaze me, my friend! Pass it to me; I will keep it safe for now. We have no idea what it does."

Jack pulled out the dark oily tube from his pocket with his grimy hand. But as he grasped it, he felt it give a little shudder and start to vibrate. It gave a strange thrumming noise, and Jack stared as the vibrations started to increase.

"What is it?" asked Fermy

"It's vibrating, and... Oh, look!!"

The tube was visibly vibrating Jack's arm now, and its colour was changing from a black oily sheen to the dull brown of rich mahogany wood. Jack dropped it as the thrumming worked its way into his bones, and the tube hit the ground, rolling a few times before coming to a stop next to the wall. It continued to vibrate, the water on the floor giving off little ripples.

"*Fermy?*" shouted Jack, backing away from it.

"*I have no idea!*" Fermy shouted back, unable to take his eyes off the tube.

The vibrations started to shake the floor now as they worked their way up the three friend's legs. Jimmy opened his eyes as the vibrations worked through his prone form, waking him from unconsciousness quite effectively.

"I think that we'd better get out of here, right..." began Jack, when all of a sudden, the vibrations just stopped. There was a huge pop, like a firework or gunshot, which caused the friends to duck and shuffle backwards.

The wooden tube, now a vibrant light brown colour, suddenly rolled over of its own accord. On its surface, two bright blue shining eyes suddenly opened up from nothing and stared up at the four friends who were stunned to silence.

The tube rolled over again, and two thin sticks popped out of it about halfway up the tube. It pushed itself upright, and two further sticks popped out of the bottom, like two tiny legs. The tube clambered shakily to its feet and looked around at the slack-jawed friends as they stood there staring at it.

A quiet voice, firm and a little nervous but still challenging, chimed in all their heads as the tube thing looked up at them with its bright blue eyes, its body shaking a little.

Who...who are you? Where...where am I? I warn you now; you better leave me alone.

The friends stared at each other, their mouths agape.

"What the hell?" came Jimmy's voice over the braying of the alarm.

Standing in the muddy puddle, the tube raised its tiny fists at them, blue eyes seemingly narrowed.

'I mean it,' the voice chimed again in their heads. *'Get back, or else I'll remove you from existence.'*

TO BE CONTINUED IN THE CRACKLOCK SAGA BOOK 2 –
THE LOST AND THE DEPARTED.

ACKNOWLEDGMENTS

To my family first and foremost. For their encouragement and criticisms and everything else. And a special thank you to Sam, who helped me with all the electronic stuff that I am so awful at, but she dances around like it's her own glamours in action. Thanks, Sammy!

To my beta team. You guys showed me that one pair of eyes is never enough. Thanks for all that you caught. And special thanks to Angela, who has kicked me along when I needed it.

To the professional folk, the team at SR Press LLC. A brilliant editing team, and you couldn't hope to meet nicer, more helpful folks—my thanks.

And to you. The reader. Thank you for taking a punt on this book. Time is so precious, so the fact that you have chosen to spend some of yours with the Cracklocks makes me feel very humble. I hope that you think it is time well spent.

ABOUT THE AUTHOR

I live in the East Midlands, right in the centre of the UK, and when I'm not writing or working, I'm with the family or walking the dog in the local woodlands seeking those ever-elusive Fae. Or sitting, pint in hand with the good friends I grew up with. Some of them are hidden in the books themselves; quite a few characters are based on the people I know and love.

Publishing wise, I am a mere fledgling writer, having had a few short stories published to date but always trying for more. Check out other published works at:

• Spooky Tales From The Pub: Volume Two (https://www.a-mazon.co.uk/Spooky-Tales-Pub-M-Smith-ebook/dp/B08LV4JZ2W)

• Written Tales Magazine Volume 2: Night Terrors (https://www.amazon.co.uk/Written-Tales-Magazine-Night-Terrors-ebook)

And so, to the Cracklocks... "The Cracklock Saga" series of books came about from reading some pretty awful fairy books to my daughter over the years – she's 13 now and has now (with more than a little relief, I have to say) left those behind. But I always wondered what would happen if someone didn't like fairies, what they would do about it, and could anybody stop them? This idea grew, and the Cracklocks were born. I liked the idea of people who hated the Fae and everything they stood for. And who knew just how wicked those people were? I certainly didn't until Anastasia and Agatha got their claws into me!

The Cracklock Saga is my first series, and I have huge plans for it. The shadowy Tobias is begging for his tale to be told, and this will be forthcoming. Plus, I want to know more about Fermerillion, Dorcas and the rest of the good guys – where did they come from? And what really happened between Elsie and Malchiah all those years ago? I think I know, but they all have a habit of surprising me when I'm scribbling. More than you will ever know.

You can keep up to date with the happenings in the Cracklock world by visiting www.thecracklocksaga.com and signing up. I won't bombard you with spam as I'm not too fond of that sort of thing myself.

So, I do hope that you'll want to come along for the ride. You would be most welcome…

Printed in Great Britain
by Amazon